ACCLAIM FOR LISA UNGER'S

BLACK out

"Unger's latest keeps the adrenaline pumping with a roller-coaster plot and harrowing psychological suspense." —*People*

"Psychotic scary, all the way. . . . Unger leaves us twisting as to which is which, and what is actually happening." —*New York Daily News*

"A white hot page-turner. . . . Lisa Unger is not— or not yet—the American Dostoevsky, but she may be on her way." —*Naples Sun Times*

"*Black Out* is riveting psychological suspense of the first order. If you haven't yet experienced Lisa Unger, what are you waiting for?"
—Harlan Coben

"A sure hit. . . . A thriller with more twists than a cage full of snakes. Right about the time that you think you know what's going on, the story takes another angle. Hold on tight. . . . It's a scary ride!" —*Bookreporter*

LISA UNGER

BLACK out

Lisa Unger is the *New York Times* bestselling author of *Beautiful Lies* and *Sliver of Truth*. Her novels have been published in more than twenty-five countries. She lives in Florida with her husband and daughter and is working on her next novel.

www.lisaunger.com

BLACK out

BLACK out

A Novel

LISA UNGER

VINTAGE CRIME/BLACK LIZARD
Vintage Books
A Division of Random House, Inc.
New York

FIRST VINTAGE CRIME/BLACK LIZARD EDITION, APRIL 2009

Copyright © 2008 by Lisa Unger
Excerpt from Die for You *copyright © 2009 by Lisa Unger*

All rights reserved. Published in the United States by Vintage Books, a
division of Random House, Inc., New York, and in Canada by Random
House of Canada Limited, Toronto. Originally published in hardcover
in the United States by Shaye Areheart Books, an imprint of the Crown
Publishing Group, a division of Random House, Inc., New York, in 2008.

Vintage is a registered trademark and Vintage Crime/Black Lizard and
colophon are trademarks of Random House, Inc.

This book contains an excerpt from the forthcoming book *Die for You* by
Lisa Unger. This excerpt has been set for this edition only and may not
reflect the final content of the forthcoming edition.

This is a work of fiction. Names, characters, places, and incidents are
either the product of the author's imagination or are used fictitiously.
Any resemblance to actual persons, living or dead, events, or locales
is entirely coincidental.

The Library of Congress has cataloged the Shaye Areheart edition
as follows:
Unger, Lisa, 1970–
Black out : a novel / Lisa Unger.—1st ed.
p. cm.
1. Florida—Fiction.   2. Psychological Fiction.   I. Title.
PS3621.N486B56 2008
813'.6—dc22   2007033301

Vintage ISBN: 978-0-307-47229-8

Book design by Lynne Amft

www.vintagebooks.com

Printed in the United States of America
10   9   8   7   6   5   4   3   2   1

For
Ocean Rae, Sophie, Lucy, Matilda, Zoé, and Josie,
my daughter and the daughters of women
I love and admire . . .

Let's love our girls well and protect their spirits,
Introduce them to their own strength and power, and
Keep them as bright and beautiful as the day
they were born.

Prologue

Today something interesting happened. I died. *How awful,* they'll say. *How tragic. And she was so young, with everything ahead of her.* There will be an article in the paper about how I burned too bright and died too young. My funeral will be small . . . a few weeping friends, some sniffling neighbors and acquaintances. How they'll clamor to comfort my poor husband, Gray. They'll promise to be there for our daughter as she grows up without me. *So sad,* they'll say to each other. *What was she thinking?*

But after a time this sadness will fade, their lives will resume a normal rhythm, and I'll become a memory, a memory that makes them just a little sad, that reminds them how quickly it can all come to an end, but one at which they can also smile. Because there were good times. So many good times where we drank too much, where we shared belly laughs and big steaks off the grill.

I'll miss them, too, and remember them well. But not the same way. Because my life with them was a smoke screen, a carefully constructed lie. And although I got to know some of them and to love them, not one of them ever knew me, not really. They knew only the parts of myself I chose to share, and even some of those things were invention. I'll remember them as one remembers a favorite film; beautiful moments and phrases will come back to me, move me again. But ultimately I'll know that my time with them was fiction, as fragile and insubstantial as pages in a book.

Now I'm standing at the bow of a cargo ship. It cuts through the night with surprising speed for its size, throwing up great whispering plumes of foam as it eats the high waves. The water around me is black. My face is wet with sea spray and so windburned it's starting to go numb. A week ago I was so terrified of the water that I wouldn't have dreamed of sitting close enough to feel it on my skin. Because there is such a myriad of things to fear now, I have been forced to conquer this one.

The man at the helm has already gestured at me twice, made a large gathering motion with his arm to indicate that I should come inside. I lift a hand to show I'm all right. It hurts out here; it's painful, and that's what I want. But more than that, the bow of this boat represents the farthest point away from the life I've left behind. I'll need more distance before I can climb back inside, maybe get some sleep.

I can feel the heat of my predator's breath on my neck. For him I will never be just a memory. I'll always be a goal, always the thing that lies ahead just out of reach. If I have anything to do with it, that's where I'll remain. But I know his hunger, his patience, his relentlessness. His heart beats once for every ten times mine does. And I'm so tired now. I wonder here in the frigid cold if the chase will end tonight and which of us will be dead, really dead, when it's done.

I stand in the bow and support myself on the rail. I remind myself that death is my easy escape; I can go there anytime. All I have to do is to bend, drop my weight over the railing, and I will fall into black. But I won't do that, not tonight. We cling to life, don't we? Even the most pathetic among us, those of us with the fewest reasons to keep drawing breath, we hold on. Still, it gives me some small comfort to know that death is an option, handy and at the ready.

Finally the cold and the wind are too much for me. I turn to make my way back to my tiny cabin, and that's when I see it: the round, white eye of a spotlight coming up behind us, the small red and green navigation lights beneath it. The craft is still too far for me to hear its engine. I can just see the white point bouncing in the black. I turn to signal to the captain, but he's no longer at the helm. I think about climbing up to warn him, but I'm not sure it will do any good. I hesitate a moment and then decide I'd be better off finding a place to hide myself. If he's found me, there's nothing anyone will be able to do. I realize I am not surprised; I am not at all surprised that he has found me. I have been waiting.

There is a familiar thud-thud in my chest as I look over into the big waters and think again about that dark temptation. It would be the ultimate defiance, to rob him of the only thing he's ever wanted, the ultimate way to show him that my life belonged to me and no one else. But a small round face, with deep brown eyes framed by a chaos of golden curls, a tiny valentine of a mouth, keeps me on deck. She doesn't know that her mommy died today. I hope she won't have to grieve me, to grow up broken and damaged by my early demise. That's why I have to stay alive. So that someday, hopefully sooner rather than later, I can go back to her and tell her why I named her what I did, so that I can take her in my arms and be the mother to her that I always wanted to be.

But first I have to fight and win. I'm not sure how much fight I have left in me, but I *will* fight. Not so much for the shattered, cored-out woman I have become but for my daughter, Victory.

PART ONE
cracked

The fair Ophelia!—Nymph, in thy orisons
Be all my sins remember'd.

HAMLET, III.1

1

When my mother named me Ophelia, she thought she was being literary. She didn't realize she was being tragic. But then, I'm not sure she understood the concept of tragedy, the same way that people who are born into money don't realize they're rich, don't even know there's another way to live. She thought the name was beautiful, thought it sounded like a flower, knew it was from a famous story (play or novel, she wouldn't have been able to tell you). I guess I should consider myself lucky, since her other choices were Lolita and Gypsy Rose. At least Ophelia had some dignity.

I'm thinking this as I push a cart through the produce aisle of my local supermarket, past rows of gleaming green apples and crisp blooms of lettuce, of fat, shiny oranges and taut, waxy red peppers. The overly familiar man in meats waves at me and gives me what I'm sure he thinks is a winning smile but which only serves to make my skin crawl. "Hi, honey," he'll say. Or "Hi, sweetie." And I'll wonder

what it is about me that invites him to be so solici-
tous. I am certainly not an open or welcoming person; I can't afford to be too friendly. Of course, I can't
afford to be too *unfriendly*, either. I look at my reflection in the metal siding of the meat case to confirm
that I am aloof and unapproachable, but not
strangely so. My reflection is warped and distorted
by the various dings and scars in the metal.

"Hi there, darlin'," he says with an elaborate
sweep of his hand and a slight bow.

I give him a cool smile, more just an upturning
of the corner of my mouth. He steps aside with a
flourish to let me pass.

I have become the type of woman who would
have intimidated my mother. Most days I pull my
freshly washed, still-wet blond hair back severely into
a ponytail at the base of my neck. The simplicity of
this appeals to me. I wear plain, easy clothes—a pair
of cropped chinos and an oversize white cotton
blouse beneath a navy barn jacket. Nothing special,
except that my bag and my shoes cost more than my
mother might have made in two months. She would
have noticed something like that. It would have
made her act badly, turned her catty and mean. I
don't feel anything about this. It's a fact, plain and
simple, as facts tend to be. Well, some of them, anyway. But I still see her in my reflection, her peaches-

and-cream skin, her high cheekbones, her deep brown eyes. I see her in my daughter, too.

"Annie? *Hel-lo-oh?*"

I'm back in produce, though, honestly, I don't remember what caused me to drift back here. I am holding a shiny, ripe nectarine in my hand. I must have been gazing at it as if it were a crystal ball, trying to divine the future. I look up to see my neighbor Ella Singer watching me with equal parts amusement and concern. I'm not sure how long she has been trying to get my attention or how long I've been staring at the nectarine. We're more than neighbors; we're friends, too. Everyone here calls me Annie, even Gray, who knows better.

"Where were *you?*" she asks.

"Sorry," I say, with a smile and a quick shake of my head. "Just out of it."

"You okay?"

"Yeah. Good. Great."

She nods, grabs a few nectarines of her own. "Where's Vicky?"

All the women in our neighborhood, her teachers, her friends' mothers, call my daughter Vicky. I don't correct them, but it always makes me cringe internally. It's not her name. I named her Victory because it meant something to me, and I hope in time it will mean something to her. True, I named her in a fit of overconfidence. But Gray understood my choice and agreed. We were both feeling over-confident that day. I'm still clinging to that feeling. Though recently, for reasons I can't explain, it has begun to fade.

"She's with Gray's stepmom. Swimming lessons with Grandma," I say, dropping the fruit into a clear plastic bag. The nectarines give off a fresh, sweet aroma. They are almost to the point of being over-ripe, fairly bursting with themselves. An old woman inches past, leaning heavily on an aluminum walker. Some mangled, Muzak version of "Don't Stand So Close to Me" by the Police plays tinny and staticky from unseen speakers.

"That's nice," Ella says with a nod. "Time for a cappuccino?"

I look at my watch, as if calculating whether or not I can fit it into my busy schedule, even though we both know I have nothing else to do and Victory will be hours yet—between the swimming lessons and her favorite lunch and time with the neighborhood kids. They're all bigger, older boys, but she commands them like a queen. And they love her for it.

"Sure," I say. And Ella smiles.

"Great, meet you over there when you're done." She means the little spot by the beach where we always go.

"See you in a few."

She pushes off. I like Ella a lot. She is so easy, so warm and open, so trusting and unfailingly kind; she makes me feel bad about myself, as though I'm some icy bitch. I smile and give her a small wave. My heart is doing a little dance. I think it's just that I've had too much caffeine already and my heart is protesting the thought of more. Maybe I'll just have some chamomile.

On my way to check out, I see a sullen teenage girl, standing beside her mother at the deli counter. She is so thin her hip bones jut out against her jeans. Her lips are moist and sparkling with pink gloss. She holds a cell phone to her ear and chews on the nail of her right thumb.

"Taylor, cut that out," her mother says, pulling her daughter's hand away from her mouth. They look at each other like rival gang members. I wonder if Victory and I will ever come to that place, that bloody rumble of adolescence. Somehow I doubt it. I am always afraid I won't have the luxury of warring with my teenage daughter.

I step out to load the groceries into my car. I see Ella pulling out of the parking lot; she holds up her fingers indicating five minutes. She's headed home to put away her groceries before we meet for coffee, and I'll do the same since we both live just minutes from here. Then we don't have to worry about the chicken going bad, the ice cream melting, those suburban concerns I appreciate so much for their simplicity and relative safety. But it's as I slam my trunk that I feel it.

It's as if the sun has dipped behind a thick cloud cover and the sky has gone charcoal. Only they haven't. It is a bright, unseasonably cool, spring day in Florida. The parking lot is packed, populated by moms and nannies with their kids of all ages on spring break before Easter. I hear laughter, a gull calling; I smell the salt from the Gulf of Mexico. But inside I am quaking. There's cool black ink in my veins.

I slip into my SUV and lock the door, grip the wheel, and try to calm myself. I've had these panics before. Usually they are isolated incidents, intense but brief like the summer storms here. In the last few days, though, they've come one after another, surprising me with their ferocity. False alarms, Gray calls them. I've always thought of them more as an early-warning system.

This one is deeper, blacker than I'm used to. I am truly afraid, sweating and going pale. My breathing starts to come ragged, and I glance in my rear- and sideview mirrors but see nothing out of the ordinary. The contrast makes me dizzy, almost angry at the day for being so clear, at the people in the parking lot living their lives so benignly.

After a while I pull out from the lot, still shaky, and drive carefully the short distance to our home. I pass through the residents' side of the security gate with a wave to the watchman, cruise past ridiculously opulent homes nestled beneath clusters of tall palms with their barrel-tile roofs and colorful mailboxes shaped like manatees, dolphins, flamingos, or miniature versions of the larger house. Late-model luxury cars rest on stone-paved driveways.

As I pull up my drive, a neighbor is watering her flowers and lifts a friendly hand to me. I return the greeting and try to smile as I open the garage door with the remote on my rearview mirror. Afraid there's an inane conversation in my immediate future, I close the garage door while I'm still in the car. I turn off the engine and sit for a minute; my heart slows its dance. *I'm safe,* I tell myself. *This house is safe.* The shaking starts to subside. My breathing steadies. I press a button on my dash and hear a dial tone.

"Call Grandma," I say.

"Calling Grandma," the car phone answers stiffly. Victory *loves* this, giggles uncontrollably every time she hears it.

After only one ring, a smooth male voice answers, "Hello."

"It's Annie," I say, and I know my voice sounds wobbly. There's a pause; he hears it, too. He is a man who misses nothing.

"Hi, Annie." The ever-calm tones of my father-in-law, Drew. I imagine him sitting behind the oak desk of his home office, surrounded by all his degrees and military decorations, photos of his Navy SEAL buddies—eerie, grainy images of men too young, too happy to be holding guns. "They're in the pool."

"Everything's all right?" I ask, hating the words as they tumble from my lips.

"Everything's fine here," he answers, solid and sure. I am soothed by the certainty and reassurance in his voice, as much as I hate to reveal any weakness in front of him.

"Is everything all right there?" he asks after a beat has passed. I try not to hear the note of contempt.

"Yes," I say too quickly. Then I have to say it again, lighter, more slowly to balance it out. "Yes. Everything's fine. Don't bother them. I'll be by around two for Victory."

I end the call before he can ask any more questions, and I start unloading the groceries. As I'm putting things away, I turn on the television in the kitchen and am greeted by the image of a sad-looking, emaciated blonde. The caption beneath her photo reads, *Woman's body found in Central Florida; the sixth in a five-year period.* In the background a slurry male voice with a thick Florida accent goes on about the lack of evidence, the similarities between cases. I turn it off quickly; this is the last thing I need to hear right now.

I try to shake off the uneasy feeling that seems to have settled in me and go about my day—meet Ella for coffee, run a few errands, then pick Victory up from Drew and Vivian's. By the time I walk though the door at Vivian's and greet my little girl, the black patch is mostly past. But it's not forgotten. It follows me like a specter.

"Everything all right, dear?" Vivian asks as I lift my daughter onto my hip. (*She's too big to carry, Annie. You baby her,* says Gray.) Victory leans her full weight against me in her fatigue, smelling of some magic mix of sunscreen, chlorine, and baby shampoo.

I turn around and try for a smile. "False alarm," I say. We all know the lingo.

"You're sure," she says. I notice that she looks tired, puffy gray half-moons under her eyes. She wears a certain expression, a mingling of worry and love, that makes me want to weep in her arms. It wouldn't be the first time.

Behind her I can see the Gulf lapping unenthusiastically against the shore. The whole back of her house is glass. An infinity pool outside seems to flow into the ocean beyond, but that's a carefully constructed illusion. In this family we're quite good at that.

"Mommy's worried," Victory says softly into my neck. "Don't be worried." She tightens her tiny arms around me, and I squeeze.

"Not worried, darling," I say, feeling a tingle of guilt. "Just tired."

I'm sure she doesn't believe me. You can't fool children, you know. You shouldn't even bother trying; they just grow up doubting themselves.

"Did you call Gray?" says Vivian, her brow creased. She smells like lemon verbena. She puts a hand on my arm and rubs gently.

I offer her what I hope is a dismissive, self-deprecating smile. "No need."

She looks at me skeptically but says nothing more, just places a kiss on my cheek, one on Victory's, then squeezes us both with her expansive arms. As I pull away down the drive, I see Drew watching me from the upstairs window.

That afternoon while Victory is down for her nap, I sit on the lanai, looking out onto our own view of the ocean, and start to think about all the ways that I can die.

Gray is late coming home, and Victory is already sound asleep upstairs in her room. I am sitting on a leather sofa I didn't choose and don't actually like, watching the high, dancing flames in our fireplace as he walks through the front door. For a second he is just a long shadow in the foyer; he could be anyone. But then he steps into the light and he is my husband, looking strained and tired. He doesn't know I'm watching him. When he sees me, though, he smiles and looks a little less world-weary.

"Hey," I say, getting up and going to him.

"Hey." His embrace is powerful and I sink into it, hold on to him tightly. There is no softness to him; the muscles on his body are hard and defined. In this place I am moored. The churning of my day comes to calm.

"Want a drink?" I ask as I shift away from him. He holds me for a second longer, tries to catch my eyes, then lets me go.

"What are you having?" he wants to know.

"Vodka on the rocks."

"Sounds about right."

I walk over to the bar that in the daylight looks out onto our back deck. At night all I can see is my reflection in the glass doors as I fill a square lowball with ice and pour cold vodka from the freezer. This is another feature I didn't choose about our house, a wet bar stocked with liquor we rarely touch. There is so much about this place, a ridiculously extravagant wedding gift from my father-in-law, furnished and decorated by Vivian, that has nothing to do with me—or Gray. It is hard to ever be grateful enough for such a gift and impossible to complain about the various features that don't appeal. Sometimes I feel like we live in a model home, everything shiny and perfect but just slightly off from what we would have chosen ourselves.

I walk back over to him, hand him his drink, and we sit together. I put my legs up on his lap, take my waiting glass from the table. The ice has melted, the vodka gone watery and tepid. I drink it anyway, too lazy to make myself another.

I have one of the glass doors open, and the unseasonably cold salt air drifts in, warmed by the fire. I see him glance over at it. I know he's thinking that the door should be closed and locked, but he doesn't say anything. I notice the deep crescent of a scar between his right eye and his temple. I realize that I barely see his scars anymore. In the beginning they made me wary of him, made him seem hard and distant. I wondered what kind of violence could leave so many marks on a man. But I know the answer now. And I know his heart.

"It's happening again," I say after a minute of us just sitting there staring at the flames. Somehow the words seem melodramatic even before I add, "Worse than it's ever been."

He barely reacts, but I see a muscle clench in his jaw beneath the shadow of black stubble. He stares at the fire, closes and opens his eyes slowly, and takes a breath. We've been here before.

He puts a hand on my arm, turns his eyes to mine. I can't see their color in the dim light, but they're steel gray, have been since the day he was born, hence his name.

"He's dead," he says. "Long dead."

He's always gentle with me, no matter how many times we've been through this. I curl my legs beneath me and move into the hollow of his arm.

"How do you know for sure?" I say. I've asked this question a thousand times, just to hear the answer.

"Because I killed him, Annie." He turns my face up to his to show me how unflinchingly certain he is. "I watched him die."

I start to cry then, because I know that he

believes what he says to be true. And I want so badly to believe it, too.

"Do you need to start up the meds again?"

I don't want that. He leans forward to put his drink on the table. I move back into him, and he wraps me up in his arms and lets me cry and cry until I feel all right again. There's no telling how long this can take. But he's always so patient.

2

I descend a narrow, rusting stairway and walk quickly down the long hall, steadying myself against the walls. The lighting is dim and flickering. I struggle to remember what my cabin number is—203, I think. There are five men on board other than the captain, and I don't see any of them.

I reach my cabin and fumble with the lock for a second, then push into my room. A small berth nestles in the far corner. Beneath it is a drawer where I have stowed my things. I kneel and pull out my bag, unzip it, and fish inside until I find what I'm looking for—my gun. A sleek Glock nine-millimeter, flat black and cold. I check the magazine and take another from the bag, slip it into the pocket of my coat. The Glock goes into the waist of my jeans. I've drilled the reach-and-draw from that place about a million times; my arm will know what to do even if my brain freezes. Muscle memory.

I consider my options. Once again suicide tops

the list for its ease and finality. Aggression comes a close second, which would just be a roundabout way toward the first option. Hide and wait comes in third. Make him work for it. Make him fight his way through the people charged with protecting me and then find me on this ship. Then be waiting for him with my gun when he does.

The thrumming in my chest has stilled, and I listen for the sounds that will signify that the fight has begun, but there's only silence and the distant hum of engines. I'm not afraid at all—or else fear has become so much a part of me that it has come to feel like peace.

3

My father is a tattoo artist and a pathological liar. The latter is nearly the only thing I can count on, that, likely as not, every word out of his mouth is a lie. He truly can't help it.

"How are you, Dad?" I'll ask.

"Great," he'll say enthusiastically. "I'm packing."

"Packing for what?" I'll say, skeptical.

"I'm taking a Mediterranean cruise, heading out tomorrow."

Or:

"Did I ever tell you I was a Navy SEAL?"

"Really, Dad?" I'll go along, half listening. "When?"

"Served in Vietnam."

"Wow. Tell me about it."

"I can't; too painful. I'd rather forget."

That's how it goes. It doesn't even bother me anymore, partly because he usually doesn't lie about anything important. Just weird stuff. Almost like hiccups, they seem to bubble up from within, unbidden, unstoppable. I generally play along, because in spite of all the lies there's something true about him. Even though he was a lousy father, he loves me and I know it, always have.

When he comes to the phone, I can hear chatter in the background, the hummingbird buzz of the tattoo needle. His shop, Body Art, is located on Great Jones Street in NoHo. And though it's a hole in the wall, barely five hundred square feet, people from all over the world travel there for my father's skill. Rock stars, supermodels, even (it is rumored) rebelling young Saudi royals have been beneath my father's needle. He'd told me this for years, but naturally I didn't believe him. Finally he sent me a *Village Voice* article about him, and I realized he'd been telling the truth. How about that?

"Everything all right?" he asks, lowering his voice when he realizes it's me.

"Great," I say. "We're doing great."

He's quiet for a moment, and I know he heard the lie in my voice. Takes one to know one. I listen to him breathing as he ponders what to say. I remember a lot of heavy silences over long-distance lines with my father, me desperate, him inadequate or unwilling to help. At last I say, "Tell me again, Dad."

"Oh, honey," he says after a slow exhale. "Come on. I thought you were past this."

I sigh and listen to Victory chatting to her doll in the other room. "You're so pretty," she tells it. "On the outside *and* the inside. And you're smart and strong." She's mimicking the things I've told her about herself, and it makes me smile.

"Opie, are you there?"

My father always thought my name was silly. He calls me "O" or "Opie" or sometimes just "Ope." As if *those* aren't silly things to call someone. I think he used them to annoy my mother. And they did, to no end. But those silly nicknames stuck, at least between us.

"Just tell me," I say, trying to keep the edge out of my voice.

I close my eyes, and I can see my father's face, brown and wrinkled from too much time in the sun on his Harley. When he was a younger man, he wore his hair in a long black mane down to the middle of his back. I've never seen the entirety of my father's face, hidden as it has always been behind a thick black beard. The last time I saw him, years ago now, his hair and beard were well on their way to ash gray. He is forever dressed in a T-shirt and jeans, motorcycle boots. His voice sounds like cigarettes and whiskey.

"You were kids when you came here, you and him," he says, because he knows that's where I want him to start. "Right away I didn't like him. Something not right about his eyes." He issues an angry grunt. "I *really* didn't like how you were mooning over him. It made me jealous. Even though you said otherwise, I knew you were in big trouble. But I let you down, kid. I'm still sorry about that."

I just listen and remember.

"I should have taken care of the guy right then and there. Or called the police or something, but I didn't. That was always one of my biggest flaws as a parent: I was always trying to be your friend."

My father had multiple "flaws as a parent," lying and abandonment chief among them. Trying to be my friend was not high on my list of things for which he should be sorry, but I don't say this.

"I let you hide out at my place for a while. I didn't know how bad things had gotten. I really didn't."

I hear the stuttering wail of a siren in the background. Someone comes into the room and coughs. I hear my father put his hand over the receiver and say something that sounds like, "Give me a minute, for fuck's sake."

"You'd never done a tattoo like that. Never before and never since," I prompt impatiently.

"That's right," he says quickly. "I gave the bastard a tattoo. It was unique in all the world. His drawing, my bodywork."

"It couldn't be duplicated," I say.

He releases a disdainful breath. "Not by anyone I know in the industry. And I know *everyone*. It was the kind of art I wanted to do for you. But you never wanted that."

I never have. Life is hard enough, leaves enough scars—why voluntarily put your flesh under a needle? Piercing is another thing I've managed to avoid. I don't get people who take pleasure in pain.

"Tell me about the tattoo."

He sighs before going on, as if he regrets starting down this road with me. "I've never seen anything like it. That was part of the reason I wanted to do it. It was a nice piece. Stormy seas, breaking waves on these crags that jutted out of the water like shark teeth—lots of lines and shadows, lots of small hidden images within, even the shadow of a girl's face. Your face, Opie. That's how I know."

He doesn't have to describe it; I can see it so clearly in my mind's eye. It's an image that comes back to me again and again in my dreams, and sometimes when I'm awake.

"And when they showed you the picture, there was no mistaking it."

There's silence. "No, girl. There was no mistaking it." Then, "He's dead, Opie."

"Call me Annie."

I know he hates the name Annie even more than he does Ophelia. He thinks it's common. But it's no more common than his name, Teddy March. Everyone calls him "Bear." Anyway, I'd give my right arm to be common.

"He's dead, Annie. He'll never hurt you again. Not you or anyone else. He didn't kill you back then. You fought and won." I like his words; I try to let them in and become my truth. Pathological liar or not, he has a kind of horse sense that always calms me.

"Don't turn your life over to him now," he goes on. "You're hurting yourself and Victory—and that husband of yours. Move on, kid."

These are my little rituals, the things I do and need to hear to comfort myself. In the past couple of years, knowing what I know, it has taken only one or two of these things to calm me, to assure myself that it is safe to live my life. But this time nothing's working; I don't know why. I feel like I'm seeing these signs that no one else is seeing: the dog running in circles because some vibration in the ground has told him that an earthquake is coming, a hundred crows landing on the lawn. I tell myself it's not real, that it's all in my head. Of course, there's no worse place for it to be. Maybe I *do* need to talk to the doctor.

Esperanza, our maid and nanny, is unloading the dishwasher, putting the plates and bowls and silverware away with her usual quick and quiet efficiency. She's got the television on, and again there's that image of the now-dead woman on the screen. It's as though nothing else is ever on the news. I find myself staring at the victim, her limp hair, her straining collarbone and tired eyes. Something about her expression in that image, maybe an old school portrait, makes her look as though she *knew* she was going to die badly, that her mutilated body would be found submerged in water. There's a look of grim hopelessness about her.

"Terrible, no?" said Esperanza, when she sees me watching. She taps her temple. "People are sick."

I nod. "Terrible," I agree. I pull my eyes away from the screen with effort and leave the kitchen; as I climb the stairs, I hear Esperanza humming to herself.

Upstairs, Victory's happily playing in her room. She'll go on like this for a while before she needs some company or attention from me. For now she's rapt in the world she's created with her dolls, Claude and Isabel. Her babies, as she calls them.

In my bedroom I can hear her whispering to

them on the baby monitor I still keep in her bedroom. The sound of her breathing at night is my
sweet lullaby. I wonder when she'll make me take it
out of her room. How old will she be when she doesn't
want me to hear her every breath any longer? *Mom,*
she'll say, *get a life.*

When I was sixteen, my mother moved us from government housing on the Lower East Side of Manhat-
tan to a trailer park in Florida so that she could be
closer to a man with whom she'd become involved.
They'd been having a white-hot correspondence for
a number of months, involving thick letters written
in red ink and the occasional collect telephone call
where my mother cooed into the phone, holding the
receiver to her mouth so intimately that I'd half
expected her to start sucking on it. After some tearful
proclamations and heartfelt promises between them,
my mother and I packed our few belongings into the
back of a brown Chevy Citation we bought for seven
hundred dollars and headed south to begin our new
life.

    "We can live much better in Florida," my
mother told me with certainty. "Our money will go a
lot farther. And it's *so pretty* there."

    I watched the Lower East Side pass outside the

car window and wondered how anything could be more beautiful than New York City. Sure, it can be cold and dangerous—a frightening place, a lonely one for all its crowds. But the grand architecture, the street noise, the energy of millions of people living their lives—you can never mistake yourself as being anywhere else when you're there; there's no mistaking that heartbeat. It's unique in all the world. If one considers the great beauties in history— Cleopatra, the *Mona Lisa,* Ava Gardner—none of them were pretty in that cheap, cookie-cutter way that seems to pass for gorgeous these days. They were beautiful for what was *unique* about them from the inside out, for features that might have been ugly on anyone else. If you don't know how to look at her, her hidden alleys and minuscule precious side streets, her aura of mischief, her throbbing nightlife, you might find yourself intimidated by New York City, even repulsed by her odors and sounds, you might even turn away from her because she's too brash, too haughty. But it would be your loss.

I thought my father would put up more of a fight when my mother wanted to leave with me. But he seemed to agree that the move would do me good. I'd been getting into some trouble in school for insolence, tardiness, and absence. The city offered too much temptation to a young girl with too little parental supervision. In any case, my needs always came last in any decision-making process my parents employed. My mom was motivated only by male attention. My father could never love anything as much as he loved his art. I fit in there somewhere, I think. I'm not saying they didn't love me.

"Don't worry about it, kid. Florida's a hop and a jump. We'll be back and forth all the time," my father told me as I sobbed into his chest.

He never once came to Florida to see me, though. And I didn't see him again until I ran away almost two years later. But I'm getting ahead of myself.

So we moved into a trailer park, and my mother got a job as a waitress in a diner that was just a few blocks away, which was good because that Chevy overheated about three times on the drive to Florida and died altogether on our arrival.

"Well, everything happens for a reason," my mother said with her usual depraved optimism as the car sputtered and went on to a better place. "At least whatever we need is walking distance. If there's an emergency, we can take a cab. And I can take the bus to see Frank. Meanwhile, we'll save on gas and insurance." If there was ever anyone with less reason to look on the bright side, I wouldn't want to meet her. Nothing *ever* worked out for my mother. And if there was any reason for the things that happened to her, it has never been made clear to me.

Take the man for whom we moved down to Florida. He was an all right guy, sort of soft-spoken and not unkind to me during visits. But there was one problem: He was a convicted rapist and murderer on death row in the Florida State Prison. My mother had "met" him during a letter-writing campaign initiated by her church. The goal was to spread the word of the Lord to the lost souls on death row, to "save" them before they faced their earthly punishment for the wrongs they'd done. My mother, obviously, took the whole saving thing a little bit too far.

I'll never forget our first August in Florida. I didn't even know it could get that hot; the humidity felt like wet gauze on my skin; it crawled into my lungs and expanded. Violent lightning storms lit the sky for hours, and the rain made rivers out of the street in front of our trailer park. And the palmetto bugs— they made New York City roaches look like ladybugs. The only thing that redeemed Florida for me was how the full moon hung over the swaying palm trees and how the air sometimes smelled of orange blossoms. But generally speaking, it was a hellhole. I hated it, and I hated my mother for moving us there.

The Florida I live in now with Gray and Victory is different. This is the wealthy person's Florida, of shiny convertibles and palatial homes, ocean views and white-sand beaches, margaritas and Jimmy Buffett. This is the Florida of central air and crisp cotton golf shirts over khakis, country-club days and fifty-foot yachts. To be honest, I hate it just as much. It's so fake, so tacky and nouveau riche, so proud of its silicone-filled and bleached-blond Barbie women.

Give me concrete and street noise any day. Give me Yellow Cabs and hot-dog stands. Give me legless, homeless guys pushing themselves on dollies through the subway cars, shaking their change jars with self-righteous aplomb.

I am thinking about this as I sit on the floor by the bed and reach up under the box spring. I've cut out a large hole there. Inside, I keep things that Gray and my doctor would be very unhappy about. They just wouldn't understand. I reach around and don't feel anything at first. Maybe Gray found them, I think, panic threatening. Maybe he took them away to see how long it would be before I looked for them again. But then, with a wash of relief, I feel the smooth, cool surface of one of these things.

"Mommy." It's Victory, whispering into her baby monitor. I can hear her, but she can't hear me, and she gets that. "Mommy," she says, louder. "Come to my room. There's a *strange* man on our beach."

She hasn't even finished the sentence and I'm

already running. In my panic, the hall seems to lengthen and stretch as I make my way to her. But when I finally burst through the door, breathless and afraid, there's no one on our stretch of sand. Out her window, there's just the moody black-gray sky, and the green, whitecapped ocean.

We live near the tip of a long beach, right before a state nature preserve. There are about five other houses within walking distance of ours, and three of those are empty for much of the year. They are weekend homes and winter homes. So essentially we're alone here among the great blue herons and snowy egrets, the wild parrots and nesting sea turtles. It's silent except for the Gulf and the gulls. People walk along the beach during tourist season, but very few linger here, as all the restaurants, bars, and hotels are a mile south.

"Where, Victory?" I say too loudly. She's gone back to playing with her dolls. They're having a tea party. She looks up from her game, examines my expression because she doesn't understand my tone. I try to keep the fear off my face, and I might have succeeded. She comes over to the window and offers a shrug.

"Gone," she says casually, and returns to her babies, sits herself back down on the floor.

"What was he doing?" I ask her, my eyes scanning the tall grass and sea oats that separate our property from the beach. I don't see any movement, but I imagine someone slithering toward our house. We wouldn't see him until he reached the pool deck. We've been lax about security lately, lulled into a false sense of safety. I should have known better.

"He was watching," she says. My heart goes cold.

"Watching the house, Victory?"

She looks at me, cocks her head. "No. The birds. He was watching the birds."

Victory begins pouring little imaginary cups of tea. Esperanza is still humming in the kitchen. There is no one on the beach. The sun moves from behind the clouds and paints everything gold. I decide it's time to call my shrink.

4

A couple of months after my mother and I moved to Florida and I had settled reluctantly into my new school, she started to act strangely. Her usual manic highs and despondent lows were replaced with a kind of even keel that felt odd, even a little spooky.

The early changes were subtle. The first thing I noticed was that she'd stopped wearing makeup. She was a pretty woman, with good bone structure and long hair, silky and fine. Like her hair, her lashes and brows were blond, invisible without mascara and a brow pencil. When she didn't wear makeup, she looked tired, washed out. She'd always been meticulous about her appearance. "Beauty is power," she would tell me, though I'd never seen any evidence of this.

We were in the kitchen on a Saturday morning. I was eating cereal and watching cartoons on the small black-and-white set we had sitting on the counter; she was getting ready for the lunch shift at the diner. The ancient air conditioner in the window was struggling against the August heat, and I could feel beads of sweat on my brow and lip in spite of its best efforts.

I looked over at my mother, leaning against the counter, sipping coffee from a red mug, her bag over her shoulder. She stared blankly, zoning out, somewhere else.

"Mom, aren't you going to 'put your face on'?" I said, nastily mimicking the chipper way she always said it.

"No," she said absently. "I'm not wearing makeup anymore."

"Why not?"

"Because it's cheap. Frank thinks it makes me look like a whore."

I felt a knot in my stomach at her words, though at the time I couldn't have explained why.

"He said that?"

She nodded. "He said he couldn't sleep at night knowing that I was walking around looking like that, that other men were leering at me, thinking they could have me at any price. He said I should display my face as God made it. And he's right."

I didn't know *what* to say. But even at sixteen— almost seventeen by then—I knew that it was so screwed up in so many ways that there was no way to address it.

"Mom," I said finally, "that's bullshit."

"Watch your mouth, Ophelia," she snapped, turning angry eyes on me. "I didn't raise you to talk that way. When Frank comes home, there won't be any talking like that."

She looked away from me after a moment and stared out the window as if she were expecting someone.

"Mom, Frank's on death row," I said calmly. "He's not coming *home*."

She turned and looked at me sharply. "Don't say that."

"It's true, Mom. You know it's true."

"Ophelia, you don't know what you're talking about," she said, raising her voice. "There's new evidence. Evidence that will prove there is no way Frank did the things they say he did. He's innocent. God won't let an innocent man die for crimes he didn't commit."

Her tone had gone shrill, and there were tears in her eyes. She slammed her empty coffee cup on the counter and left without another word.

We've talked about this a hundred times at least, my shrink and I. This first moment between my mother and me when I knew that something was wrong, really wrong.

"And how were you feeling after she left that morning?"

"Sick," I say. "Scared."

"Why?"

"Because she seemed . . . different. And I didn't want Frank to 'come home.' I figured he was just a phase she was going through, that it would go bad like all her relationships, and we'd move back to New York."

"You were afraid of him?"

It seems like a stupid question. "He was a convicted rapist and murderer," I say slowly. My doctor gives a deferential nod but doesn't say anything, waits for me to go on. When I don't, he says, "Your mother thought he was innocent. Wasn't it possible? Plenty of people have been convicted of crimes they didn't commit." He does this, plays devil's advocate to encourage me to defend my position. I find it annoying rather than helpful.

"My mother thought he was innocent, yes," I say. I remember those awkward visits where they would put their hands against the glass that separated them until one of the guards barked at them to stop. I remember how he'd look at me, ask me about school. I remember his cool gaze and soft voice. Something about him made me want to run screaming. "There was something dead in his eyes," I say.

"Even when he smiled, there was something . . . *missing*. And then all these changes in my mother. If he had such an effect on her from behind bars, what could he do to her if he was living with us?"

My doctor is silent for a moment.

"What do you think you could have done at this point that might have changed the events that followed?" he asks finally.

This is my thing. There was something about that morning in the trailer with my mother. I feel strongly that it was the last moment where things might have turned out differently. If I had chased after my mother and forced her to tell me what she was talking about. If I had told her that I felt sick and scared and that Frank *was* guilty and that he could not, should *never,* come live with us, she might have listened. I tell this to my shrink.

"But do you really think she would have heard you, Annie?"

"I guess I'll never know."

He lets the words hang in the air. We've both heard them a hundred times. And somehow they never rest easier with me.

"What did you do instead?" he asks.

"I finished my cereal, watched some more television. Told myself that she was nuts, an idiot. I pushed it out of my head."

"You're good at that."

"Pushing things out of my head? Oh, yes."

His office is uncomfortable. The chenille sofa is soft but cheap, seems to push me out rather than welcome me in. It's far too cold in the refrigerated way that indoor spaces get too cold in Florida. The tip of my nose feels cold even though it's blazing outside, and I can see the sunlight glinting off the warm green waters of the Intracoastal.

I don't lie on the couch but sit cross-legged in the corner; on my first visit he told me I could recline if it made me feel comfortable. I told him it wouldn't. He sits across from me in a huge chair that he easily fills, a low cocktail table covered with art books—Picasso, Rembrandt, Georgia O'Keeffe—between us. The space is trying very hard to be a living room and not a doctor's office. Everything is faux here—the table, the bookshelves, his desk all made of cheap wood veneer, the kind of stuff that comes in a box, just a pile of wood, a bag of screws, and a booklet of indecipherable instructions. It seems transient and not very comforting. I feel as if his furniture should be made of oak, something heavy and substantial. Outside his window should be a blustery, autumn New England day with leaves turning, maybe just the hint of snow. He should be wearing a sweater. Brown.

He doesn't take notes; he has never taped our sessions. I've been adamant about this. I don't want a record of my thoughts anywhere. He's okay with that, said we'd do whatever made me comfortable. But I've always wondered if he scribbles down his thoughts right after I leave. He always seems to have perfect recall of the things we've discussed.

As much as I've revealed to him, I have kept a lot of secrets. I have been coming to him on and off for over a year, ever since Vivian first recommended him. (*He's Martha's friend,* she said. *Martha? Oh, you remember Martha. The fund-raiser last August? Never mind. I hear he's* wonderful.) During our sessions I reveal the truth of my feelings but have altered the names of the players in my tale. There is much about me he can never know.

"Annie," he says now, "why are we back here?"

I rub my eyes, hard, as though I can wipe all the tension away. "Because I feel him."

I look up at him and he has kind, warm eyes on me. I like how he looks, even without the brown sweater, an older man with white-gray hair and a face so tan and wrinkled it looks like an old catcher's mitt . . . but not in a bad way. He wears chinos and a chambray shirt, canvas sandals. Not very shrinklike, more like your favorite uncle or a nice neighbor you enjoy chatting with at the mailbox.

"You *don't* feel him, Annie," he says softly but firmly. "You think you do, but you don't. You have to be careful of the language you use with yourself. Call this what it is. An episode, a panic attack, whatever. Don't imagine you have some psychic feeling that a dead man has returned for you."

I nod my head. I know he's right.

"Why is it so hard?" I say. "It feels so real. So much worse than ever before."

"What's the date today?" he asks. I think about it and tell him. I realize then what he's getting at, and I shake my head.

"That's not it."

"Are you sure?"

I don't say anything then, because of course I'm not *sure* of that or really anything. Maybe he's right. "But I don't remember."

"Part of you remembers. Though your conscious mind refuses to recall certain events, the memory lives in you. It wants to be recognized, embraced, and released. It will use any opportunity to surface. When you're strong enough to face them, I think all the memories will return. You're stronger than you've been since I've known you, Annie. Maybe it's time to face down some of these demons. Maybe that's why these feelings are so intense this time."

Looking at him, I almost believe I can do it, peer

into those murky spaces within myself, face and defeat whatever lives there.

"He's dead, Annie. But as long as you haven't dealt with the memories of the things he has done to you, he'll live on. We'll always have to face these times when you think he's returned for you. You'll never be free."

It is a vague echo of my father's words, and Gray's words. And intellectually I know they're all right. But my heart and my blood know something different, like the gazelle on the Serengeti, the mouse on the forest floor. I am the prey. I know my place in the food chain and must be ever vigilant to scent and shadow.

5

I am crouched in my cabin; I will be hidden in the corner by the door when it swings open. My breathing has slowed, and my legs are starting to ache from the position I've been holding for I don't know how long. I can hear the thrum of the engine and nothing else. I start to wonder if maybe everything is all right. It's conceivable that there might not even be another boat out there, I tell myself. Could just be a trick of the night, my own paranoid imagination, or some combination of those things. As I start to accept this possibility, there's a knock at the door. Scares me so badly that my head jerks and I hit it on the wall behind me.

"Annie." A muffled male voice. "Are you in there?"

I recognize the Australian accent; it's the voice of one of the men who have been hired to help me. I open the door for him. His eyes fall immediately to the gun at my waist. He gives a quick nod of approval.

"There's a boat trailing us," he tells me. He has sharp, bright eyes and is thick with muscle. I search my memory for his name. They all have these hard, tight names that sound like punches to the jaw. Dax, I think he told me. That's right, Dax. "Might be a fishing vessel, poachers—or even pirates. We hailed them, and they didn't respond."

His eyes scan the room. He walks over and checks the lock on the porthole, seems to satisfy himself that the room is as secure as it can be. He's like that. They all are, these men, always checking the perimeter, scanning for vulnerability. I like that about them.

"Just turn out the lights in here and lock the door. I'll come get you when I know it's safe."

"Okay," I say, trying to sound as solid and in control as he seems.

He leaves, casting a sympathetic look behind him as he goes, and I lock the door after him. It seems as flimsy as cardboard. I turn off the lights and resume my crouch.

6

The day after I see my shrink, I'm feeling better. It might just be the residual effects of the pill Gray encouraged me to take last night so that I could sleep. Either way, as I sit with him in the sun-washed kitchen drinking coffee, the sense of foreboding is gone.

"It helped you to see Dr. Brown?" Gray asks. It's oddly off-putting to hear Gray use his name. I try so hard to keep these parts of myself separate. Here I'm Annie, Gray's wife and Victory's mom. There I'm a mental patient haunted by my traumatic past. I don't want those two selves to touch.

"Yeah, I'm fine," I say with a dismissive, oh-it's-nothing wave. "It's just that time of year, he thinks."

Gray puts a hand on my shoulder. He is headed out of town for a few days. I don't know where he is going or when he will be back. This is part of our life together.

"Vivian can come stay with you. Or you guys

could go there?" he says. He is careful to keep concern out of his voice and worry out of his eyes.

"No, no," I say lightly. "Really. It's not necessary. I'll call her if I need her."

I love Vivian, Gray's stepmother. But I hate the way she looks at me sometimes, as if I'm a precious bauble in the grasp of a toddler, always just headed for the floor, always promising to shatter into a thousand pieces. I wonder if she thinks I'm a bad mother, if she worries for Victory. I know better than to ask questions for which I don't want the answers.

Gray and I chat awhile about a few mundane things, how the gardener is really awful and the lawn looks terrible but he's too nice to fire, how the pipes are making a funny sound when the hot water runs and should I call a plumber, how Victory's new preschool teacher seems kind. Then Gray gets up to leave. He takes me in his arms and holds me tight. I squeeze him hard and kiss his mouth. I don't say, *Be careful.* I don't say, *Call when you can.* I just say, "I love you. See you soon." And then he's gone.

"I really *don't* need to go to school today, Mommy," says Victory from her car seat behind me. We're driving along the road that edges the water. Her school is just ten minutes from the house. An old plantation home converted into a progressive preschool where lucky little girls and boys paint and sing and sculpt with clay, learn the alphabet and the numbers.

"Oh, no?" I say.

"No," she says simply. She gives me a look in the rearview mirror; it's her innocent, helpful look. "You might need me today."

My heart sinks a bit. I *am* a bad mother. My four-year-old daughter has sensed my agitation and is worried about whether she can leave me or not.

"Why do you say that, Victory?"

In the rearview mirror, I see her shrug. She's fingering the piping on her pink backpack now. "I don't know," she says, drawing out the words in that sweet way she has. "Esperanza said she was going to make cookies today. She might need help."

"Oh," I say, with relief. "And you don't think I can help."

"Well, sometimes when *you* help, the bottoms get black. They taste *bad*."

I am a terrible cook. Everyone knows this about me.

"Well, I guess we'll just have to wait until you get home so that you can help Esperanza," I say.

She looks up at the mirror and offers a smile and a vigorous nod. "Okay," she says. "Good."

It is settled. I drop her off, chitchat with the other moms on the front porch. Before I walk back to the car, I look in the window to see Victory donning a red smock and settling in for finger painting. I feel a familiar twist in my heart; I feel this whenever I leave her someplace, even a place as safe and happy as this little school.

When I return home, Esperanza is gone. Probably off to run errands or to pick up whatever I forgot to get at the store the other day—I always forget something, even when I take a list. I can smell her famous chili simmering in the slow cooker; she probably went to get fresh tortillas from the Mexican grocery downtown. I nuke some leftover coffee from earlier and walk up to the second level. At the door to Gray's office, I enter a code on the keypad over the knob and slip inside.

It's dim; the plantation shutters are closed. This is a very manly room, all leather and oak, towering shelves of books, a huge globe on a stand in the corner, a samurai sword in a case on the wall. I stare at the sword a minute and think how *not* like Gray it is to have a weapon hanging on his wall like some kind of trophy. This is another affectation of Drew's. The only things in this room that Gray chose for himself are the photos of Victory and me on his desk.

I sink into the roomy leather chair behind his desk and boot up his computer. I stare at the enormous screen as it goes through its various electronic songs and images. When it's ready, I enter my code and open the Internet browser.

My doctor asked me to spend time trying to remember the things that I have locked away somewhere inside me, to explore those gaping blank spaces that constitute my past. I've decided that I am going to do that, just as soon as I've done this one last thing, my last tic to assure myself that everything is okay.

I enter his name in the powerful search engine to which we subscribe and spend the next two hours reading about his crimes, the pursuit of him, and his ultimate death. Then I open Gray's case file, read the notes he took during an investigation that spanned two years and five states. I stare at crime-scene photos, drinking in the gore, the horror of it all. When I'm done, I feel an almost total sense of relief. I move over to the leather couch and lie down, close my eyes, and try to relax myself with deep breathing. But the harder I grasp for my memories, the more they slip away. I get frustrated and angry with myself quickly and decide instead to go for a run.

* * *

I run along the beach, passing the empty winter houses that look more like well-appointed bed-and-breakfast hotels than private homes. The sky is turning from an airy blue to gray, and far off I can hear the rumble of the storm that's headed in this direction. The towering cumulous clouds are soft mountains of white and black against a silver sky, threatening and beautiful. I run hard and fast. I want pain and exhaustion. I want to collapse when I'm done, have a headache from the exertion.

After I pass the last house, I am on the nature preserve. The beach ahead of me is empty; to the east there are sea oats, tall grass swaying, all varieties of tall palms. Every few feet, small signs warn walkers to stay to the water's edge and not venture into the sea grass, because birds and turtles nest in the protected patch of land. It's hard to believe that there can be a place this empty, this private, in Florida the way it is today, so overdeveloped, condo buildings rising fast on the horizon as if they sprang fully formed from the earth. The locals joke that the building crane is the state bird. I cherish this quiet and emptiness about where we live, wondering how long it can last. At the tip of the island, exhausted and breathless, I turn back. I slow a bit, thinking I should pace myself to make the distance back to the house.

The Gulf is a relatively calm body of water, the warm, anemic waves a disappointment to anyone accustomed to the roaring of the Atlantic coastline. But today the waves come in high and strong, the water an eerie, churning gunmetal. The sky is ever darker, and I realize that I might not beat the storm home. It's not wise to be the only thing on the beach when lightning threatens here. It's far too early and too cool for this type of weather, I think. I pick up my pace again, though my body protests.

As the wind begins to assert itself, I see something lying on the beach that I don't think was there on my way up. It's far ahead of me still, a kind of large, form-less black lump lying half in and half out of the water. A garbage bag, maybe. A mass of seaweed. A dead tar-pon or grouper, both large gray fish. Something tells me to slow down, to stay away from it. But there's no other route home, and I can hear the thunder louder now, see the clouds flashing. I press on.

The grass and sea oats have started to dance and whisper in the wind. The form ahead of me—I've just seen it shift. Could be the wind, but I don't know. In spite of the encroaching storm, I slow my pace.

I move over to the side to give the thing a wide

berth as I pass. I won't stop to investigate as Victory would. She insists on throwing every stranded thing back into the sea or weeps inconsolably in my arms for those she cannot save. I don't have that kind of heart anymore. We're *all* washed ashore, thrashing, looking for our way home. "Every man for himself" is more my motto these days.

My heart lurches as I draw close enough to see that the form is a man, his back to me. His black clothes are soaked; he is draped in sea grass from shoulders to knees. I can see one of his hands, mottled with sand, dead white. I stop, look up and down the beach. Not a soul. The sky is nearly black now, the thunder closer. I should keep running; I know this. Move fast, get to a phone, call for help. But I slow to a walk, approach the man. I remember that I thought I saw him move in the distance. But that could have been the wind billowing his clothes. Still, I find myself thinking, *Maybe he's alive. Maybe I can save him.*

"Hello," I say loudly to the man who is most likely a corpse, washed in from sea. I don't feel the fear that I should, just this ferocious curiosity. "Are you all right?"

That's when I hear him groan, low and terrible. A slender, white bolt of lightning slices the sky some miles away. I move in quickly without thinking and put my hand on his cold, wet shoulder, turn him on his back. I see his face then, the face I always see, white and terrible, a deep gouge in his cheek, his mouth gaping, his eyes fixed and staring.

From deep inside his chest, he growls, "You belong to me."

I wake up then on the couch, an afternoon storm raging outside, the rain coming down in slicing sheets. My chest is heaving, and I'm sweating.

"Mrs. Annie!" Esperanza's knocking on the door. I get up and open it for her. She steps back and looks down at her feet when I do, as though she's embarrassed. She's a youngish-looking fortysomething with a wide, pretty face, café au lait skin, and the kind of deep brown eyes that men drown in. She looks up at me with concern; she's been witness to my waking from these types of dreams before. I'm the one who should be embarrassed. I must have cried out; that must be what brought her to the door. I don't know, and I don't ask. We both just pretend it didn't happen.

"One half hour until you have to pick up Miss Victory," she says quietly.

I nod and look at my watch. I resist the urge

to snap at her, to say, *You don't think I know I have to pick up my daughter?* She loves my daughter and takes care of us, while I nap on the couch in the afternoon. I can never muster anything but gratitude for her.

"Thank you, Esperanza."

7

Impossibly, I have drifted off in my crouch behind the door. That's the level and nature of my fatigue. I am not sure how long it has been since Dax came to tell me about the other boat. Might be minutes, might be hours. Through my porthole I can see that the sun has not risen, that there's not even a hint of morning light in the sky.

My feet and legs are aching with that horrible tingle of having too much weight on them awkwardly for too long. I stand painfully and stretch, try to walk it off. As I make tight circles in my small cabin, trying to get blood flowing to my limbs, I have a growing sense of unease. Something's wrong. It takes another minute of anxious pacing, but I realize eventually what's bothering me: I can't hear the engines anymore. The boat has come to a stop.

I'm not sure what this means, but suddenly I'm a fox in a trap; I'm stuck in the box of my cabin. When he finds me, I'll have no place to hide. It's almost as though he choreographed it that way, like some elaborate dance that we do, that we have always done. But for the first time since we've met, I won't allow myself to be led, to be circled around and dipped at the finale. Tonight I'll take the lead.

I open the door just a crack and peek out into the empty hallway. As I do this, I hear the boat power down, and everything falls into pitch black. There's not even a pinprick of light, and I'm rendered blind. I draw my gun, step into the corridor, and put my back to the wall, then start edging my way toward the staircase that leads to the deck.

8

After an early and incredibly healthy dinner of fish sticks, macaroni and cheese, and a side of broccoli spears that no one eats, Esperanza, Victory, and I make chocolate chip cookies. Or Esperanza and Victory make cookies and I watch with rapt attention, sitting on a stool at the bar that separates the kitchen from the family room. It still thrills me to watch Victory walk and do things like hold the hand mixer from her stepstool. She's such a little person that it's already impossible to imagine she came from my body.

"I don't think you put enough vanilla in there," I say, trying to be helpful.

"Oh, Mommy," says Victory with a sigh. I smile into my cup of chamomile tea. After the last couple of days, I've decided no more caffeine for me. I clearly don't need any extra stimulation.

The sun is setting, painting the horizon purple and pink. I have pushed my dream as far away as it will go and focus on being present for this time with my daughter. When the cookies are ready, the three of us eat them together on the deck. I've built a fire in the chimenea, and we help Esperanza practice her English as the sun makes its final bow. When the air gets too cold, we all go inside.

"When does Daddy come home?" Victory asks as we head upstairs for her bath.

"Soon," I tell her.

"Soon when?" she asks, dissatisfied with my answer.

"Soon," I say, resting a hand on her hair.

She nods and looks a little sad. I feel bad that I can't tell her more. But the truth is, I don't know the answer to her question, and even if I did, I still wouldn't be able to tell her where her daddy goes.

By the time she's lathered up and playing with her bath toys, I'm off the hook; Victory has forgotten all about poor Gray. She's far too wrapped up in the drama unfolding between Mr. Duck and Mr. Frog, who are in a heated debate about who is faster. I'm cheering for Mr. Frog when Esperanza comes in.

"Telephone for you, Mrs. Annie," she says, coming to take my place beside the tub.

"Who is it?"

She shrugs and looks uncomfortable. She searches for the words in English, then finally gives up. *"No sé. Pero pienso que es importante."*

"She says she doesn't know but she thinks it's important," translates Victory, my little bilingual.

I nod and go to the phone. My heart is thudding as I walk down the hall to our bedroom. I am always afraid when the phone rings while Gray is away. I'm always waiting for *the call.* I remind myself that if anything were really wrong, they'd come in person.

"Hello."

"Annie." It's my father. He sounds tense, urgent. He's not supposed to call me. In fact, I'm not really supposed to call him, either. But every once in a while, like the other day, I can't help it. In recent years we've become a little careless. Part of the over-confident phase I've been going through.

"Where are you calling from?"

"From a friend's place."

"What's wrong?"

"There was someone looking for Ophelia today. He came by the shop, said he was a cop. But he wasn't. A bald, beefy guy making a show of himself with a big gun in a holster."

"Okay." This is the hard part. I don't know if he's lying or not.

"Seriously," he says into the silence. "No bull-shit."

"What did you tell him?"

"I told him that my daughter has been dead for over five years."

"Okay." This seems to be the only word I can manage. I realize that my whole body is tense, that I'm gripping the phone too hard.

"He didn't believe me. He wasn't just casting for information; he *knew* something. He got all friendly with me, said there was a reward, a big one, for any information about you. I went crazy on him, started to cry and shit about how you were dead and how dare he play these kinds of games with an old man. Then he left in a hurry."

"But he wasn't a cop."

"No way. You can always tell a cop, even the bad ones. They think they got the law on their side. This guy was too dirty even to be a dirty cop."

"Okay," I repeat again, not wanting to say too much.

"Be careful," he says, and hangs up.

I sit for a second with the phone in my hand. I'm not sure what to think about what he's told me. Ophelia has been dead for so long. After so much time I'd come to believe that everyone had forgotten her except me. I hang up the phone and then pick it back up, punch in a number I know very well.

"Hello?" says Drew.

"Can you come by later? It's Annie."

"Sure," he says after a second's hesitation. "Something wrong?"

"I don't know."

Drew always looks at me as though I'm an unwelcome solicitor at his door asking for a donation to a charity in which he doesn't believe. I don't like the woman I see reflected in his gaze. She's someone unworthy, not to be trusted. But maybe I'm just projecting, as my doctor might say.

He sits at our dining-room table, a bottle of Corona nearly disappearing in his big, thick hand. His brow furrows with deep lines as I tell him what my father told me. He is a heavier, harder version of Gray. He has the same storm-cloud eyes without any of the wisdom or kindness I see in his son's.

"Could just be someone fishing," he says with a shrug. He takes a long swallow of his beer, puts the bottle down heavily on the table. "Unfortunately, the circumstances of Ophelia's death wouldn't hold up to any real scrutiny. We never expected anyone to come looking."

I feel a little jolt at hearing that name from him. I hate the way it sounds coming from his mouth, the way it bounces on the walls of this house.

"But there might be a few people who haven't forgotten her," he says when I don't say anything. He rests his eyes on me, and I fight the urge to shift beneath his gaze. I hear the television playing in Esperanza's room; she's watching one of her *novelas*. I can tell by the staccato of Spanish and the strains of melodramatic music. (*¡Ay, Dios!* Esperanza will exclaim about one of the characters. *She is so bad!*) Outside, a strong wind bends our palms, whispering through the fronds. I wish I hadn't called Drew.

"I'll have someone look into it," he says finally.

I realize I haven't really participated in the conversation, though he doesn't seem to have noticed. "Thanks," I say.

"In the meantime," he says after draining the rest of the beer, "tighten up around here. Keep the system armed, no doors or windows left open. No more phone calls to Ophelia's father or anyone from her past. You've gotten careless by talking to him. That phone call you made last week might be the reason someone's looking for her."

"Okay," I say, feeling contrite. I know he's right.

He gets up to leave.

"Any word on Gray?" I ask.

"No news is good news," he says, patting me on the shoulder in an uncommonly friendly gesture. I wonder if our relationship might be improving.

* * *

It stormed the day Frank's son came. Of course it did. One of those storms that roll in from the coast and make a blue day turn black suddenly, as though someone drew a curtain. Wind kicks in and turns the leaves white side up. The barometric pressure plummets, and the sky starts to rumble. We were alone, me and Mom. She'd worked the morning shift, I'd had a half day at school because of some teachers' conference. We sat on her bed and watched *As the World Turns* on the tiny black-and-white television that we'd moved in from the kitchen, eating fried-bologna sandwiches. This was a ritual we'd practiced as long as I could remember; I'd been watching the soaps with her for probably longer than that. Even now I'll sometimes turn one on guiltily in the middle of the day and disappear for a little while, remembering what it was like to be close to my mother, to smell her perfume and hold her delicate white hand.

I heard the knock on the door before my mother did.

"Was that the door?" I asked.

"Uh-uh," she said absently, eyes glued to the screen. "I don't think so."

I heard the knocking again. "I think it is."

"Well, go check," she said, patting me on the ass. "I've been on my feet all morning."

I walked to the door and looked through the small window. He stood there, leaves and rain blowing around him, his hair tousled. He carried a large bag over one shoulder and had on a worn blue sweat jacket over T-shirt and jeans. Something about his face, his whole bearing, made my heart lurch. I'd never seen anyone so beautiful, the features of his face smooth and flawless as if he'd been blown from glass. I thought he'd turn and I'd see a pair of wings grow from his back. He lifted his hand to knock again but saw my face in the window.

"Frank said I should come!" he yelled over the wind. His eyes were so dark they seemed almost black from where he stood; his long hair was the same inky black, in deep contrast to the white of his skin.

"Why?" I asked him. Something about him was frightening, too. True beauty is like that, as terrifying as it is mesmerizing. I didn't want him to come in. I wanted to lean my weight against the door and brace it against him.

"He says I should see Carla." He adjusted the heavy bag on his shoulder. His hand was like a boulder, big and round with large, long fingers.

I looked at him, examined the thin line of his

mouth, the square of his jaw. I couldn't tell how old he was. "My mother," I said.

He looked down at his feet, back at me. I felt the full weight of his gaze. "I don't have anywhere else to go."

My mother came up behind me. "Let him in," she said to me, but didn't reach for the door herself.

"Who is he?"

"He's Frank's boy," she said, looking at me sheepishly, then at him.

"You knew he was coming?"

"I knew he *might* come," she said, turning her face back to me but keeping her eyes on him, as though she couldn't pull her gaze away.

"And?" I said, feeling my stomach clench.

"And now he might stay on here awhile."

"Where?" I said. "There's no room for him."

She nodded over toward the couch. It was small and dirty, uncomfortable even to sit on, never mind sleep. "There. Just for a few nights. Don't worry; I'm not going to give him your room."

"Hello?" he called from outside. "It's raining pretty hard."

"Well?" my mother said.

I turned and looked at him through the window. Even then something deep inside me knew not to open the door, but I did. He brought the storm in with him, dripping on the floor and smelling like rain. He was tall, taller than he'd seemed standing outside. He didn't have to slouch to come in through the door, but almost. He dropped his bag on the floor and it landed with a heavy thump.

My mother made him a fried-bologna sandwich, then another. I watched while he inhaled them as if he hadn't eaten in days. He had a thick neck and broad, heavily muscled shoulders. He wrapped his free arm around the plate, gazing up every so often, as if he were afraid someone would come and take the food away from him.

"I've only got six months to emancipation," he told us, making his childhood sound like a kind of slavery. But he didn't look like a boy, as my mother had called him. At seventeen going on eighteen, he was more man than child, I suppose. There was something feral about him, something hungry and knowing.

I stood in the corner sullen, angry, but watching him with secret interest. The look on my mother's face, vacant and eager to please, made me sick. This is how she acted around men.

"Then I'm going to join the Corps," he said. "No one's going to fuck with me after that."

"Wow, the marines!" my mother gushed, twirling a strand of her hair. "Frank didn't tell me."

"How long are you planning on staying here?" I asked with naked annoyance.

He shrugged and gave my mom a hangdog look. It was so fake. Couldn't she see that?

She patted his shoulder and gave me a warning glare over his head. "You can stay as long as you need to, Martin."

"My name's Marlowe," he said quickly, angrily. I saw the ugly in him for a second, a dog baring his teeth. Then he softened, turned a sweet smile on my mother. "Please call me Marlowe."

"Sure, honey," she said, petting him again. "Marlowe. Do you want something else to eat?"

"Yes, please," he said to her, and then he moved his eyes over to me.

My recall of Marlowe's arrival has a funny, sepia-toned quality. I remember weird, hyperfocused details, like my mother's cuticles, jagged from her endless gnawing at them, and that the tag on her shirt was turned out. I remember hearing the dramatic voices from the soap opera blaring from the other room. But it's as though I'm remembering something I saw on a television screen, all of it happening behind a thick piece of glass. I don't feel like I was a participant, but rather an impotent observer watching mute and helpless as things unfolded. It was another of those moments that I had dissected again and again with my shrink. Another place where I might have made a difference.

"Try to remember," Dr. Brown says, "you were a child; your mother was the adult. You didn't have any power. Your mother was responsible for inviting these men, her boyfriend and his son, into your lives."

"I opened the door."

"If you hadn't, she would have."

He was right. My mother was not a smart woman, not intelligent, not instinctual. She lived in her own little world. She never saw him coming.

9

The next night I force myself to go to Ella's cocktail party. In spite of my efforts to isolate myself from the crowd and appear generally antisocial, an older woman clad entirely in white drifts over to me and asks me what I do. She looks as though someone sprayed her with shellac, so unmoving and stiff are the various parts of her—her flesh, her bobbed hair, the muscles in her face. She's so thin I can see the tiny bones in her wrist.

"I'm a housewife and a mother," I say without the sheepish tone in which I've heard so many women deliver this information. What I don't say is that I'm a housewife who doesn't do much cooking or cleaning. And that my daughter is in preschool most days. My life consists of these big blocks of free time while I wait for Victory to be done with the various activities in her busy little life. It's dangerous for someone like me; I should really think about getting a job. The devil would find work for idle hands, my mother used to say when she was in one of her Jesus moods. Or, in my case, work for idle minds.

"That's wonderful," the woman in white says with a smile, real or fake, who can tell? "It's the most important job in the world." Everything about her is perfectly manicured: her fingernails are square and pink, her lips lined and glossed, her eyebrows plucked into high arches. A huge diamond glints on her hand. She is painstakingly casual in a flowing linen skirt and top, leather thongs on her feet.

The conversation falters, mainly because I don't participate, and she moves away, raising her glass and muttering an excuse. I've come alone to this party because I promised Gray I would attend just to "get out of the house and be with people other than Victory," but I'd rather be home with her and Esperanza watching *The Incredibles* on DVD for the hundredth time.

I lean on the fence that edges the pool deck and look out onto the black stretch that ends in the Gulf. I can't see the water because of the elaborate lighting and landscaping on the property, but I can hear it and smell the salt in the humid air. My mind is full of thoughts I'm trying not to have—my black patch, my dream, Gray, the man looking for Ophelia. I shouldn't be here. I'm not cocktail-party material even on my best days. I endure things that other people find entertaining.

My eyes fall on a girl standing alone a few feet away. She's leaning on the fence like I am and lost in thought looking out into the night. She must have felt my eyes on her, because she turns to look at me. I recognize her then, but I can't place her. I suddenly feel a terrible need to remember who she is; my heart starts to beat a little faster with the urgency I feel. She's pretty and far too thin, wearing just a pair of jeans and a T-shirt, a ratty old pair of sneakers. She's not the type to be at one of Ella's cocktail parties—too young, not enough money. I wonder if she's the new maid Ella's been complaining about. We're staring at each other, neither one of us looking away. Finally she smiles. But it's not a friendly smile; in it I see some combination of malice and pity. My gut lurches a bit. I look away quickly.

"Has anyone ever told you that you're not a very social person?" Ella says, coming up behind me. I jump slightly, and she laughs, surprised. "You need another drink," she says, patting my back. "You're too tense."

"Who's that girl?" I say, looking back over in the stranger's direction. But she's gone.

"Who?" Ella asks, following my eyes.

I scan the crowd. I don't see her among Ella's well-dressed guests.

"She was wearing jeans and a T-shirt. Pretty, young, too thin?" I'm still looking for her. In fact, I feel almost desperate to see her again.

"If she's here, we should kick her out," says Ella, mock jealous.

"Your new maid?" I say, hopeful.

"No, she's off tonight."

I can feel Ella's attention shift from curious to concerned.

"You okay?" she asks after another moment.

"Yeah," I say, smiling a bright fake smile. "I just thought she looked familiar."

She gives me another rub on the shoulder, then returns my smile. "When's Gray coming back? You're lost without him at these things."

"At the end of next week," I say vaguely. I'm still looking over her shoulder.

"I never realized insurance executives had to travel so much," she says. I snap back to the conversation and listen for signs of skepticism in her voice. But there's just her usual light and musing tone, the wide-open expression on her face.

"Client risk assessment, large claim investigations," I say with a shrug, as if this should explain it. She nods.

"Still," she says, "he leaves you alone too much."

She's not looking at me. She's looking out into the night. I can't tell if she's just making conversation.

"You're one to talk," I say with a smile. "You're gone as often as he is."

"True. But my trips are *important*," she says. "Shopping in New York City, detoxing at Canyon Ranch, sunning in Fiji."

"Hmm," I say. She laughs.

"Where is he this time?"

"Cleveland," I answer.

"See? What could possibly be important in Cleveland?" she says.

We both laugh. I wonder whether she'd be laughing if she knew how easily lies come to me.

"Can I get you a refill?" she asks, pointing to my empty glass after a minute of us both staring into the night. "Seems like you could really use one, girl."

"No thanks," I say. "I'm going to sneak out of here and walk home down the beach."

She knows better than to argue that I should stay, have another drink. She's right; I'm lost without Gray at these things. I don't know how to do Friday-evening cocktail parties, make small talk with neighbors and strangers, network, mingle, whatever it is one is supposed to do. There's too much going on in my head for that sort of thing.

Even though I know I shouldn't, even though this is not the type of behavior Drew would see as "tightening up," after we say good night, I slip out the back gate, walk down a paved path lined with palms and recessed lighting that leads to the beach. I give one last look back at Ella's gathering, but there's no sign of the girl I saw.

Marlowe slept on the couch, his feet hanging over the edge, the sound of his deep breathing filling the whole place. Not for days, as my mother promised, but for weeks, with no sign of any intention to leave. I hated him and was fascinated by him in equal measure. He didn't go to school, had dropped out and gotten his GED, he claimed. He spent his days writing and sketching in a collection of battered, mottled notebooks. But somehow he always had money, bought groceries, little gifts for my mother. He'd cooked dinner for us a couple of times, which basically sent my mother into convulsions over him. She raved about his pork chops and Rice-a-Roni like he was Julia Child; she was overcome by his consideration and sweetness. Meanwhile, the fact that I'd cooked dinner five days out of seven (the other two days we had pizza or fried-bologna sandwiches) for I don't know how long had never even been acknowledged. It made me furious, and I raged about it.

"You're just jealous," my mother said, patting my shoulder. "He's sweet. And we're all he has right now. Try to be nice."

God, she was pathetic. She'd do anything for a man—even a teenage boy—who showed her the smallest amount of attention. And there was nothing sweet about him, as far as I could see. The act he put on for my mother, he didn't bother to use on me. For me Marlowe saved furtive looks—menace or desire, I couldn't tell. But those eyes, those looks kept me up nights thinking about him, listening to him breathe out on the couch.

I was in a constant state of anxiety—worry about my mother, fear about this killer who might be coming to live with us, hatred for his son who was crashing on our couch, and yes, some secret fascination with Marlowe, too.

He awakened something within my body that was thrilling and unfamiliar. I was spastic around him, clumsy and prone to emotional outbursts or awkward laughter. I hated myself, couldn't seem to get a grip when he was in the room. The half smile he wore when we were together told me he knew it.

At night our trailer park came alive with sound: singing frogs competing with television sets and rock music, our neighbors yelling and fighting, later stumbling in drunk and noisy, slamming doors. I would lie awake some nights just listening, wondering why I had been exiled to this life. I knew enough to know that I didn't belong among these poor and angry people, living such ugly lives. But that knowledge wasn't enough to lift me out.

"Get me out of here, Dad," I pleaded during one of our weekly telephone conversations. It was a Sunday night; my mother was working late. I cradled the phone to my ear and kept my back to Marlowe, whose presence in our trailer seemed as eternal and unpleasant as the roach problem. He was *always* there. Watching. Listening.

"Just hang in there, Opie," my father said calmly on the other line. "It's all going to work out. You'll see."

"Okay," I said miserably, believing he was alluding to some master plan he was concocting to rescue me, something he couldn't discuss over the phone.

I was still young enough to hope that he was going to show up one day and demand custody of me. I didn't understand back then that though my father loved me, he wasn't really father material. He didn't have the strength, the selflessness it takes to be a real parent. Neither one of them did. But my mom at least wanted me with her—some of the time, anyway.

The conversation ended, and I went into my room to cry into my pillow.

"He's not coming for you, you know."

I turned, startled and embarrassed to see Marlowe standing there in the narrow doorway. He leaned against the frame, hands in the pockets of his faded, dirty jeans. He wasn't smiling; his expression was grim.

"I mean, I'm sorry," he said, looking down at his feet and then back up at me. "I can see you're clinging to that. But he's not coming." His voice was bass and throaty. There was an odd accent to his words, not quite a southern twang. Florida cracker, my mother told me, all their family born and raised in this hot, miserable swamp of a state.

"Shut up," I said. "What do you know about *anything?*"

My voice shook; his words were a blow to the solar plexus, the pain spreading, taking my breath. In my deepest heart, I was afraid that he was right—and I hated him for it.

"If he was going to come, he'd have come by now. He has money, right? And time? As long as I've been here, he's never even once called you. It's always you calling him. How long have you been waiting for him to come?"

"Shut up!" The words just burst from me in an

angry scream, a belch of rage. I got up and pushed past him, ran out of the trailer into the night.

I ran clumsily, crying, until I got a pain in my side and came to a stop at the ancient strangler fig that stood at the end of the park. I put my hand against its textured bark and rested, trying to catch my breath. The wide canopy of the tree sheltered me. The carpet of fallen and rotting leaves at its base was wet and stinking. Behind it was a teeming forest of palms and ferns, pond cypress and loblolly pine, surrounding a stream. I knew that the wooded area was rife with snakes and citrus rats, a terrible sampling of insects and spiders. Part of me wanted to enter its cover and be consumed by it. It seemed wild and barely contained, like most of Florida, as if it were only waiting for us to stop moving and clearing and digging, manicuring and trimming, for even just a minute, so that the lush greenness of this place could swallow all our silly structures, take back its rightful place on the earth. I sank between the thick roots of the tree and wept against its bark, ignoring the damp that seeped through my jeans, the mosquitoes making a meal out of my blood.

"Crying is not going to lift you out of this shithole."

He'd followed me.

"If you want to get out of this place, this life," he

said as he swept his arm toward the trailer park behind him, "you're going to have to do it yourself."

I looked up at him, wiped my eyes on the sleeve of my shirt. He moved closer until he was standing right in front of me, our feet nearly touching. He offered me his hand.

The strangler fig, native to Florida, begins its life as an epiphyte, a plant that grows on another living plant. Its seeds make a home in the cracks and crevices in the bark of a host tree. At first the strangler grows slowly, insinuating itself gradually into the systems of the other tree. Over time, the strangler begins to cover the trunk of the original tree, forcing it to compete with the strangler for light, air, and water. Eventually the host tree dies. But the strangler doesn't die with it. By that time the strangler has planted its own roots, grown its own branches, formed an intricate latticework of living tree around the host's withered and hollow shell.

I gave Marlowe my hand, let my fingers entwine with his, let him hoist me off the wet ground.

I walk up the beach from Ella's. I can see the lights from my own house just ahead, not more than two or three hundred feet away. I see that Victory's bedroom light is off, and I smile to myself, wondering how Esperanza always convinces her to go to sleep without any fuss. I generally wind up lying on the floor of her bedroom, chatting with her quietly as the colored fish from her rotating night-light swim on the walls and ceiling.

"Aren't you tired, Victory?" I'll ask her.

"No, Mommy. I'm not," she'll say, then fall asleep a few minutes later.

The problem is, I love that time. I don't mind staying with her until she falls asleep. And she knows it. I've rocked her and nursed her to sleep since she was a baby. They tell you not to do that, that then you'll have to do it for longer than you want, that they'll never learn to "self-comfort." But I always figure the day will come when I'll ache for those moments. And I figure if you don't have a half hour to be with your child as she goes to sleep, if you think she's better off crying alone in her bed so you can be sure of who's in charge, then maybe you shouldn't have kids. I'm thinking about this when I hear it.

"Ophelia."

I stop, startled, and spin around to see the empty beach. The word, my name, cuts through me. My eyes scan the beach. The grass and sea oats rustle slightly in the wind, just as they did in my dream. There is no one ahead of me or behind me. My heart is jackhammering in my throat. The voice was low and male, more like a growl. I take a deep breath and start a light jog.

"Ophelia." I stop and turn again. Except my father on the phone the other day, no one has called me by my real name in years. Even Drew used it with a kind of distance, referring to someone who was long gone. No one else in this life even knows about that name.

That's when I see it—the long, bulky shape of a man rising from the grass. I can't discern a thing about him, not his face, not the color of his jacket; he is a black shadow emerging from other black shadows like a plume of smoke. We stand there that way for a moment. The whole world is on an ugly, pitching tilt.

My mind grasps at the situation. Is this real? Another dream? The terrible twilight between the actual and the imagined?

I decide to figure it out later and break into a dead sprint for home. I don't even look back to see if he has given chase. I just think about getting home to Victory.

With my lungs aching in my chest, I race up the wooden walkway that leads to my house and crash through the rear gate. I pause there and see the black form moving slowly toward me still far behind, just a shade, silent and ephemeral. There is no urgency to his progress.

"Ophelia." I hear it on the wind. The word doesn't seem to come from anywhere at all. At the back door, I fumble with the keys, my hands clumsy with adrenaline. I look behind me, but I don't see him. When I finally get the door open, I slam and lock it after me, activate the house security system with shaking fingers. I think about bringing down the hurricane shutters, but Esperanza comes up behind me and I turn to look at her.

"Mrs. Annie! What's wrong?" Her face is a mask of alarm; she must have heard the door slam. She wraps her robe about her pajamas, glances first at me and then through the glass panes in the door.

"There was someone out there. On the beach," I say in a fierce whisper. I turn off the lights and look outside, scanning the darkness. Esperanza watches me with an expression somewhere between pity and fear.

"Mrs. Annie," she asks carefully, "are you sure?"

"I'm sure, Esperanza," I answer, though now, in the safety of the house, I'm not. Everything's already fading away as if it never happened. The truth is, I *can't* be sure. Too much bad history with myself.

She looks again out the window. Then her eyes

go wide. She backs away from the door and turns to me, incredulous. "There's someone."

I see the form at the end of our walkway to the beach. He is just standing there. A terrible tide of fear battles with an odd relief that it isn't just my mind playing tricks on me again.

"Is everything else locked?" I ask her. I feel suddenly solid and sure of what to do next. You can keep the earthly threats at bay with locks and security systems . . . at least for a while.

She nods vigorously, not looking away from the figure.

"You're sure?"

She nods again. Then, "I'll check." She scurries off and I hear her tugging on doors and checking windows. I move to the kitchen, keeping my eyes on the form through the window, reach for the phone, and dial Drew, my heart a running engine in my ears. I tell him what's happened.

"He's still there now?" Drew asks sharply.

"Yes. Esperanza sees him, too." I feel like I have to add this for credibility.

"*Don't* call the police. I'll be right there." The line goes dead.

I stand there still watching as I put the phone down.

Esperanza returns, holding her cell phone. "I

called the police," she says, looking out the window.
My heart sinks. I want to tell her that she shouldn't
have done that, but I don't. It would seem suspicious.
I'll just have to play it out.

I look back at our visitor. He is so still. He radiates an aura of calm, the predator so sure of his prey
that there's no need for frenzy. When I hear the distant whine of sirens, he seems to sink into the blackness from which he emerged. And he is gone.

Tonight is the five-year anniversary of his alleged
death. The doctor is right: Though I remember
nothing about the events of that night, something
that lies dormant in my memory resurrects itself as
regularly as seasons. Both a terrible dread and a terrible longing dwell side by side within me. I've been
here before, this is true. But not like this.

The clinically depressed and functionally mentally ill
do a little dance, a kind of two-step with their meds.
I need them; I don't really need them. I need them; I
don't really need them. Cha-cha-cha. After you've
been on them for a while and the chemicals in your
brain have normalized somewhat, you'll read an article about the dangers of long-term use of the particular medication you're taking, or you'll just start to feel
like maybe all those times when you couldn't get out

of bed for three weeks were simply a lack of self-discipline. You convince yourself that you're not as creative, productive, mentally sharp as you are when you're off them. So maybe you miss a dose, then two. The next thing you know, you're off them altogether. Again.

Of course, some people don't really need to be on medication long-term. Maybe they took something to get them through a bad patch—the death of a loved one, a divorce, even a nervous breakdown. Maybe some irresponsible doctor suggested an anti-depressant for a general malaise that could have been addressed by taking a hard look at their lives. When those types of people choose not to take the medication that has been prescribed, it's not such a big deal. But for some people it's quite the opposite. I guess I'm not sure which of those people I am. I do know this much: If Esperanza hadn't seen the man I'd seen, I'd have no way to be certain if he'd actually been there or not.

In my life I have suffered periods when, due to cumulative and acute trauma, I have dissociated from reality and essentially disappeared, figuratively and literally. I have seen a number of doctors and received as many diagnoses for these "episodes"—one called them fugues, another psychotic breaks. One doctor believed I was bipolar. None of the diagnoses have agreed with the others or quite fit the nature of *my* episodes, and I suppose I don't really know what's wrong with me, clinically speaking.

I have suffered dreams that seemed like reality and endured realities that might have been dreams. I have found myself on buses headed for parts unknown, on park benches in unfamiliar cities, with no idea how I arrived there. I have lost huge pieces of my life; there are black, gaping holes in my memory that have swallowed months, even years. I have not had these episodes since Victory's birth, but I know they are always waiting on the periphery of my life, like vultures circling a limping coyote in the desert.

I watch the cops on the beach using their flashlights to look for the man or some trace of the man who followed me home. I sit on the couch with Victory on my lap. She has curled herself up into a little ball and, half asleep now after being awakened by the sirens and the men at the door, is sucking on the ear of her stuffed puppy. I hold her tight; she is my anchor in the world. Ella sits on the other couch, looking anxious and gnawing on the cuticle of her thumb.

"I just can't believe this," she says absently. She looks over at me. "You seem so calm."

Esperanza's call had resulted in three screaming cruisers and a couple of plainclothes officers showing up, attracting the attention of all the neighbors. It's a quiet beach town, not much going on usually; this was making everyone's night. Most of the neighbors had called or come by to see if everything was all right. Ella had left her husband to tend to the stragglers at their party while she came down to be with us.

"It was probably nothing," I say lightly. "Some vagrant."

Drew throws me a look from the chair by the window. He's tense and not hiding it well, with a white-knuckled grip on the chair arm. Vivian stands behind him looking out into the night, frowning with worry.

"I told you not to call the fucking cops," he'd whispered harshly on his arrival. He took me into his arms so that everyone in the room thought he was embracing me. He smelled of cigars. "What were you thinking?"

"It was Esperanza."

He pushed a disdainful breath out of his nose. "And I told you two to hire an illegal. *They* don't call the police."

He'd released me and given me a disapproving scowl, reminding me how much I actually dislike him. Drew is a cold mountain of a man, as distant as the summit of Everest and about as easy to reach. Even if you got there, you'd want to leave right away.

"Annie," Ella says, looking at me gravely, "someone followed you home. It's something."

One of the plainclothes officers walks in through the open door leading from the pool deck. We've already been through how I couldn't identify the man, haven't noticed anyone following me at any other time, and have no history with a lover, old boyfriend, or stalker. Of course, I *do* have a history—just not one I can share.

"To be honest, Mrs. Powers, there's really not much we can do," he says, closing the door behind him. I find myself liking him for some reason. He has a quiet air and seems like a careful person, observant and slow to react.

"I do see tracks leading from the beach; a smaller set leads up to the door to your house. They're yours, I'm assuming. The larger set stops at the edge of your property. Technically, whoever followed you didn't set foot on your land. And even if he had, we wouldn't be making molds and tracking down boot manufacturers unless . . ."

"Unless he'd killed me," I say, feeling Drew's eyes on me. Wouldn't *that* have made his day?

The cop clears his throat, runs a tan hand through salt-and-pepper hair. "That's right. Honestly, I probably wouldn't be here at all except that there's been a rash of break-ins over the last few weeks. Usually the uniformed officers would have come to take a report."

"That's great," says Ella. "That's just great." She has the sense of entitlement that pampered, wealthy people have, but not in that awful way. Just naïve. "How is she supposed to sleep at night?"

I look at her. I want to tell her I haven't slept in years.

"This house has a good security system," he says. "Keep the doors locked, and you might think about getting a dog."

"A dog?" says Ella. "*That's* your advice?"

I give the cop an apologetic look.

Drew stays silent. Vivian walks over and sits beside me, rests a hand on my leg. I examine her face for signs of judgment and disapproval. But I just see compassion and worry. And the shade of something else I can't quite put my finger on.

"Mrs. Powers," says the cop. Everyone's looking at me. He has asked me something that, lost in thought, I didn't hear. "Are you sure?"

"I'm sorry," I say, rubbing the bridge of my nose with my free hand. "Sure of what?"

He lets a beat pass. "That you have no idea who might have reason to follow you."

"Yes, of course," I say.

His expression tells me he doesn't believe me. He has picked up on something; he glances over at Drew, then back at me. I feel my shoulders go stiff at the tension in the room.

"All right," says Ella, rising. "She said she's sure. If there's nothing else you can do, you might as well just go and let her get some rest."

I focus on Victory, who has somehow, in spite of all the talking, drifted fully asleep in my arms. I listen to her deep, restful breathing.

He places a card on the coffee table, throws another glance at Drew. "If you need anything tonight, Mrs. Powers, give me a call. I'm on all night."

"Thanks," I say. "You've been a big help. Really."

He looks at me uncertainly. If I sound sarcastic, I don't mean to.

After the police have left, I put my daughter in her bed and convince Ella to go home.

"Did you call Gray?" Ella asks as we stand on my front porch, waiting for her husband to pick her up.

"Yes," I lie.

"Is he coming home?"

"He says he'll try," I say with a shrug.

She doesn't seem to like my answer but reserves comment. She takes me in her arms and holds me tight. "Anything? You call. I mean it. Anything."

"I will," I promise.

I watch her glide down the stairs as her husband pulls up. He gives a wave from the street but doesn't get out of the car; he always holds himself aloof, gives me odd looks. He doesn't seem to like me very much, and I'm not sure why. Maybe he senses that I hold most of myself back, too. Maybe it makes me seem untrustworthy. As much as I try to blend in, I guess I don't.

I can't convince Drew to leave. Vivian is going home, and he intends to sleep on the couch until morning. He couldn't care less about me; it's Victory he's worried about. I'm sure they'd try to take her home with them if they thought I'd let them.

"It's not necessary, Drew." I might as well be talking to a gargoyle.

"It's his pleasure," says Vivian, pulling her bag over her shoulder. "Give the old watchdog something to do. Unless you, Victory, and Esperanza want to come home with us?"

"No. We're okay," I say. She pulls me into a hug.

"Don't let Drew get to you," she whispers. "He does care about you, in spite of how it seems. More than you know."

I nod and wonder what good that kind of caring is to anyone. She leaves, and I stand at the door with my hand on the knob for a second. I feel Drew's eyes on me.

"This could be a shitstorm."

I turn to face him. From where he's standing, I can just see the dark bulk of him, not the features of his face.

"Was it him, Drew?" I ask. The house sighs as the air-conditioning kicks on, and I feel its cold breath on my neck.

Drew crosses his arms across his chest. "He's dead. You know that."

"Then who? Who knows that name?"

"Someone's fucking with you, girl. We'll find out who. Don't worry." His words are benevolent, but his tone doesn't quite make it. He doesn't move closer or step into the light.

"Okay," I say.

"Get some sleep."

In the dim light of my bedroom, I get down on my knees and reach into the hole in my box spring. I search around until I find what I'm looking for, a small velvet box. I open it. Inside is a gold necklace, half of a heart.

There are some other, more useful items in my box spring as well: a Glock nine-millimeter and some ammunition, a Canadian passport with my picture and someone else's name, twenty thousand dollars in cash in four neat bundles of five thousand each. There's also a small black notebook containing vital pieces of information, among them the account number and PIN for a bank account where I've saved a bit of money, and the name and contact information for a man who promised me a long time ago that he'd help me disappear—for good, if necessary.

10

The morning hasn't yet dawned when I hear Gray come in downstairs. I've spent the night in a kind of vigil, watching the beach from my window, waiting for the form to rise again from the grass. But no, there has been nothing like that. A couple took a midnight dip in the ocean, made out on the shore, then slowly strolled up the beach, arms wrapped around each other. Someone—a young man or a boyishly shaped woman, I couldn't tell—took a jog at 4 A.M.; I watched the loping figure pass the house and then return twenty minutes later. I suppose I should be pleased, feel some sense of relief. But these mundane occurrences are something of a disappointment to me.

I listen to the low rumble of Gray's conversation with his father. I imagine Drew filling him in on the evening's events, imagine his superior tone and the lightly condescending roll of his eyes. Then I hear Gray taking stairs two at a time. He slows and opens the door quietly, expecting me to be asleep.

"What happened?" he asks when he sees me sitting in the chair. The sight of him makes me angry and relieved at the same time. Something about the way he looks right now—or maybe it's just the night and all that's taken place, or how this terrible anniversary is also, coincidentally the anniversary of the day we met—makes me remember the first time I saw him.

"He's back for me," I say. I'm not sure I really believe this; I'm testing out the words on the air. He steps into our room, closes the door behind him, and turns on the light. I hear the door open and shut downstairs; Drew's SUV rumbles to life in the driveway, then drifts off.

"Annie," he says quietly.

"It's different this time. I can't explain how. It's different."

He sits on the bed. I can see the purple shadow of a shiner under his right eye. His bottom lip is split and swollen. He doesn't need any more scars. His body is a minefield of injured and broken places, places that have been cut and ruptured and never healed quite right. We're compatible that way, except that my skin is flawless. It's my psyche that's a minefield.

I tell him what happened on the beach. He listens with his eyes on me; I can't read his expression. He taps his foot quickly on the floor as I talk, something he does when he's stressed or working a solution to a problem. When I'm done, he's quiet for a while, as though he's searching for the words he needs. He asks a few questions: Did I see his face? What was he wearing? Was it very windy?

"Did Drew tell you about the phone call from my father?" I ask when he gets up and walks over to the doors leading to our balcony. He's looking at the beach; the clouds have parted, and the beach is washed in gauzy silver moonlight.

He nods. "Maybe that's what has you so spooked, Annie. Maybe that's what's different about this time." He extends his hand to me, and I join him by the doors. He points out the window.

"Look how much light there is out there. Look at that couple walking on the beach."

There's a young girl in a sweater and jeans, holding the hand of a tall, thin young man. They walk slowly, arms swinging.

"With so much light, you would have been able to see *something* about him."

"There *was* someone there," I say quickly. "Esperanza saw him. The police saw his footprints."

"I don't doubt there was someone. But it wasn't Marlowe Geary." He turns to me, touches my face. "Isn't it possible that you saw someone, became frightened, and your mind did the rest?"

I don't answer immediately. Then, "He called me Ophelia."

He walks away from me, lies down on the bed with a sharp exhale of breath. I stay by the door watching him.

Gray is not a handsome man, not in the classical sense. Though there's something in the way he carries himself that makes a girl forget he's not easy on the eyes. He is older than I am by twelve years. There's a hard silence to him, a shell you're not sure you want to crack. There was no reason for me to fall in love with him. In fact, the circumstances of our meeting were not conducive to the start of a relationship. The first time I met Gray, he handcuffed me and threw me in the back of his car. He wasn't sure what to do with me, and he couldn't leave me as he found me, or so he would tell me later. I was a mess of a girl, nearly starved and half crazy with fear and grief. Anyone else in his position might have just left me to fend for myself. He could have turned me over to the police or dropped me at a hospital. But he didn't.

"I loved you before I even knew I loved you," he told me once.

"Then why the handcuffs?"

"I loved you, but I didn't trust you. You can't trust a beaten dog. Not until *it* learns to trust you."

"That's not a very flattering analogy." Though I suppose that's what I was then, a dog so badly beaten that I wouldn't have known the difference between a hand poised to strike and one poised to caress.

He touched me in that way he had, to soften his words, a gentle stroke on the back of my head that ends in him tracing my jaw and then resting his hand on my cheek. "Sorry."

There was no reason for us ever to be together and every reason for us never to see each other again after he got me the help I needed and then made Ophelia disappear completely. I fell in love with him because he was the only upright person I had ever known. He was the first safe place I found in my life. Because he came every day to be with me, even if I couldn't talk or didn't want to, even when I ranted and hated him and threw him out. He always came back.

I try to remember that now as I watch his chest rise and fall. I sit back down in the chair. After a minute I wonder if he's fallen asleep. Sometimes he is so exhausted after he's been away that he falls asleep during arguments or while making love. I try not to take it personally.

"Annie," he says finally with a sigh. He sits up

and comes over to me, kneels before me on the floor. He takes my hands in his and puts them to his mouth for a second. Then, "Whatever is going on, I swear to you, Marlowe Geary is dead."

Over the last few hours, sitting in my vigil, I had convinced myself that Marlowe didn't die that night, that Gray has lied to me all these years. I thought of at least five ways he might have survived. My twisted imagination spun a web around me, and I was sure of all of this, positive. But now, with Gray to ground me, I'm more inclined to believe that my mind is playing tricks on me—again. Maybe Drew's right; someone knows my secrets and is trying to get to me. Or maybe, as Gray seems to think, it was just a stranger on the beach and my mind did the rest.

"Okay?" he asks when I don't say anything. I put my hand to his face, trace the bruise under his eye, place my finger gently on his broken lip. There are deep wrinkles around his mouth, but somehow they don't make him look old, just rugged and wise. I love him, I truly do. And I know he loves me. I can see it in the stormy depths of his eyes. My first safe place.

"He said, 'Ophelia,' " I tell him again.

"Are you sure?"

I'm not certain now. I was deep in thought at the time. It *was* windy. Maybe I should go back on the medication, endure the dull fog that falls over my life, the mental lethargy. At least I know what's real. That's something, isn't it?

"I don't know," I say.

"We're going to find out what's happening," he says. "We'll find out who went to see your father, who was on the beach." He pats the mattress. "Don't do anything stupid in the meantime."

I look at him blankly.

"You don't think I know, Annie, what you have under the bed?"

I feel a wash of shame. I don't say anything.

"I know it makes you feel safe. I understand. Just stay cool."

I slide down onto the floor with him and let him enfold me. I want to remember what it feels like to be held by him. I don't want to forget when I'm gone.

"I know what you two are up to," my mother hissed. She'd cornered me in the bathroom, come up behind me and put her mouth up close to my ear. "I see the way you look at each other."

There was venom in her; it was her jealousy. I'd seen this face before.

"I don't know what you're talking about," I said, examining my teeth in the mirror over the sink, not looking at her. She grabbed my arm and pulled me in close to her.

"It's practically incest," she said. I could feel her hot breath in my ear. "He's going to be your step-brother."

My mother and Frank planned to have a jail-house wedding. Disgusting. The thought of it made me ill. She was squeezing my arm so hard it brought tears to my eyes. But I would rather she'd pulled my arm out of its socket than let her see me cry. I blinked my eyes hard and turned my face from her.

"I don't know what you're talking about," I repeated.

Her eyes were two angry, black points. When she was mad, her pretty face turned into an ugly grimace of bared yellowed teeth and furrowed brow. I could smell the coffee on her breath, the bleach on her waitress uniform.

"I won't have *my* daughter acting like a *whore*," she said to me.

Even then I knew she didn't care about my chastity or my morality. She wasn't afraid that her sixteen-year-old daughter was in too deep with someone who clearly had major problems. She just couldn't stand it when someone paid attention to me instead of her. It made her feel old.

I forced my face to go blank and my body to go limp in her grasp while she hurled a few Bible passages at me. She never got them quite right, usually wound up tongue-tied and sounding foolish. When she didn't get a reaction from me, she released me in disgust and stalked off.

"You'll reap what you sow, little girl," she said loudly as she left me. I heard her storm and bang through the trailer and then finally exit with a slam of the door that was too weak to make much of a noise.

We all reap what we sow, don't we?

I was so ripe for him. There were so many empty spaces within me that he could fill; it's nothing short of a miracle that I didn't disappear altogether.

"She's jealous, Ophelia," Marlowe said, coming up behind me. I always loved the way he said my name. I'd gone through phases with it, hating it, loving it, hating it again when I was introduced to *Hamlet* in my honors English class. When Marlowe said my name, it took on a new life. *O–feeel-ya.* The *O* was short and sharp. He drew out the *eee* like he was caressing it with his tongue. The final syllable was soft and breathy, like a sigh.

I saw his face in the mirror beside my own. He rubbed my shoulders and then wrapped his arms around me. I hid my eyes from him, too. I've never wanted anyone to see me cry; I can't bear the vulnerability of it.

"I hate her," I said. And I meant it, but only in the way that every teenage girl hates her mother.

When I raised my eyes from my hands again, he was still watching me in the mirror, a lopsided smile on his face. I could see that my anger at my mother pleased him and I was soothed by this.

"I wish she was dead," I said, the words feeling forced and uncomfortable. But when his smile widened, I basked in the warmth of his approval.

When the rage of adolescence is contained by

rules and boundaries, banked by the assurance of strong and present parents, it burns white hot but burns out fast. When it's allowed to run unchecked, it turns everything to ash.

A few days after her bathroom sermon, my mother made me accompany her to choose her wedding dress. We took the bus to a strip mall off the highway and picked through racks of used gowns in various states of disrepair—this one stained with red wine, that one with the hem ripped out. She was sweet and happy on this day, excited in this girlish way she had. If she remembered that just a few days earlier she'd bruised my arm and called me a whore, accused me of sleeping with my soon-to-be stepbrother, she didn't let on. She wanted to be happy that day; she didn't want to think about me.

What do you think of this one, Ophelia? Oh, look! Frank would love this one.

I sat in the shabby dressing room and watched as she twirled in front of the mirror, losing herself in a fantasy of the life before her. She had hard miles on her but she was still beautiful. Her hair had lost most of its estrogenic glow, and her skin looked papery, lined around the mouth and eyes. But she had true beauty, not just the prettiness that fades with age.

Looking at her that day, I thought she could have had *any* man once, she could have been *anyone,* but instead she was *this,* this desperate woman in a used bridal gown getting ready to marry a convicted murderer. It was as if before she was born, God hung a sign on her that read, KICK ME. And every single person and circumstance she'd run into had obliged.

"Do you have to look at me like that?" she asked.

I snapped out of the trance I was in and caught sight of myself in the mirror, slouched and sullen, staring at her blackly.

"Mom," I said, sitting up, "are you really going to do this?"

She walked over to me and sat in the chair beside me. She rubbed her forehead with one hand.

"Why can't you be happy for me, Ophelia?" she asked in a whisper. "I just want us to have a normal life, you know? We deserve that. Don't we?"

She reached down and pulled a tissue from her purse, dabbed at tears I hadn't seen.

"Mom," I said. She looked so tired and sad.

"Please, Ophelia," she said, dropping the tissue into her lap and grabbing my hands. "Please. I love him."

She loved him. How sad. Frank Edward Geary, my mother's death-row sweetheart, had been convicted of raping and murdering three women in

Central Florida between March 1979 and August 1981. He was suspected for the murders of several others as well. There was just no evidence to link him conclusively to those crimes. The women he killed were all pretty and blond, petite and fine-featured. They all had a brittleness to their bearing, as though if you looked at them closely, you'd see them quivering like Chihuahuas. They each bore a striking resemblance to my mother.

"What did you say to her?" my shrink prodded, though we've been through this before. It was another of those moments that were caught on a loop in my mind. These various markers on the way to the point of no return.

"I told her that I *was* happy for her. That I'd try to be more optimistic."

"But that's not how you felt."

"No," I said flatly. "That's not how I felt."

"So why did you tell her that?"

"I don't know," I said.

He looked down at his hands. This was not an acceptable answer in his office. *I'm not ready to discuss it* or *I need to think about that*—those were okay. *I don't know* was a cop-out.

After a minute, "I really *did* want her to be

happy. And I didn't want her to start shrieking about the new evidence that was going to set him free. That God wouldn't let an innocent man die for crimes he didn't commit. I didn't want to hear about her prayers and about the private investigator she'd paid for while we ate fried-bologna sandwiches and left-over food she snuck home from the restaurant. I guess for an afternoon I just wanted to visit that fantasy she seemed to be living in. Christ. Maybe *I* wanted to be happy."

He let a beat pass, let the words float around the room and come back to my ears.

"That's good, Annie," he said. "That's really good."

I wake up hearing my shrink's voice in my ears. I am dreaming of my sessions lately, this bizarre mingling of the past events of my life and composites of conversations I've had with the doctor. I'm not sure why. I suppose he would say that it's my subconscious mind working overtime.

Gray is sleeping deeply beside me. He'll sleep like this until the middle of the day, his exhaustion is so total. There's no telling the last time he slept in a bed, or slept at all. I slip on a pair of jeans and a sweatshirt and quietly head down the hall. She hasn't made a sound, but I know that my daughter is awake. She's always waiting for me in the morning; it's our time.

We usually walk down to the beach. We started doing this as soon as she was able to walk, and I would let her toddle as far and as fast as she could. I'd let her run from me to give her a taste of freedom. On the beach she was safe. She could never leave my sight, any fall was a soft one, and what she found here she could keep. The windowsills and shelves of her room were lined with her treasures: dried pieces of coral, all sizes and shapes of shells, sea glass, and ice-cream-colored rocks.

Today there is heavy rain, and after last night the beach doesn't seem very safe. I pad down the hallway and slip into her room. I can see the crown of her head and the subtle rise and fall of the blankets. I try for stealth, just in case she is still asleep after all. I won't wake her if she is. But as I draw close, she pulls the covers away and jumps up.

"Boo!" she yells, smiling and pleased with herself.

I feign surprise, then scoop her up and smother her with kisses.

"Shhhh," I say as she laughs the helpless giggle of the tickled. "Daddy's sleeping."

"Daddy's home?" She is wiggling out of my arms and then off like a bolt down the hall. I'm always thrown over for Gray. He's the celebrity parent. I'm just the everyday slog who wipes up puke, burns the cookies, and combs tangles out of hair. He's the rough-and-tumble, hide-and-seek, carry-me, read-it-again barrel of fun. I can't get to her before she's leaping onto our bed and Gray is issuing a groan as she lands full weight on his chest. Then she disappears beneath the covers, shrieking with delight.

After a few minutes of Victory love-torturing poor, exhausted Gray, I convince her to let him sleep and come downstairs for breakfast. Only toaster waffles will do this morning. We sit together at the table and eat our waffles with peanut butter and jelly. Outside, the rain has stopped and the thick gray cloud cover has parted to reveal a fresh blue sky. The wind is wild. My eyes rest on the place where my visitor stood last night, and I'm only half listening as Victory tells me about the girl who wouldn't share red during finger painting and the little boy who won't come to school without his blankie. The events of last night seem not to have affected her in the least.

We bundle up and head outside. The golden sun has emerged, making the beach seem like our place again. At the edge of our path, Victory breaks into a run toward the ocean and expects me to give chase. But something in the sand by the gate has caught my eye, a glint of gold. I bend down and pick it up. It's a gold necklace, half of a heart.

I'd seen girls at school—*those* girls with their silky hair and adult bodies, the girls whose boyfriends drove shiny sports cars and walked them to class, brought them roses on Valentine's Day—wearing necklaces like that. Now I can see how cheap they were, how tacky and common. But back then I always felt a twinge whenever I noticed one hanging around some girl's slender neck, something akin to jealousy without being quite that. Really, it was more of a sad wondering what it was like to feel a part of something, to be the cherished half of a whole, not to have to beg and act out for attention. It was more of an ache, an awareness of this empty place inside me.

After that night under the strangler fig, I fell hard in love with Marlowe in a way that's possible only once in your life. I was on fire and burned beyond recognition. I am ashamed of it now, the way I loved him. More than that, I am ashamed of how vividly I remember that love. Even now, when the barometric pressure drops before a thunderstorm and the sky turns that deadly black, I think of the summer he arrived in my life when there were violent, torrential downpours every afternoon. I remember what it was like to love without boundaries, without reason. As adults we learn not to love like that. But when we're young, we don't know better than to give ourselves over to it. The falling is so sweet that we never even wonder where we'll land.

Sometimes I can't recall what I had to eat yesterday, but that time with Marlowe lives in the cells of my body, even though I've tried to forget, even with every horror that followed. I have forgotten so much, but not that. And I remember understanding on some level, even in the throes of it, that it could never last—just like those storms that turn the streets into rushing rivers and whip up dangerous tornadoes but can only sustain themselves for a brief time.

I absorbed each moment like a person going blind, trying to soak up all the color, all the little details: the way he smelled of Ivory soap and charcoal, the way the stubble on his face was sharp against my mouth. The way the wind howled against the thin walls of our trailer, how the rain pounded on the roof, but how we were safe inside, my mother at work or off to visit Frank.

It was my birthday; I'd turned seventeen. My mother made pancakes before she went to work that morning and placed a candle on my stack. Together, she and Marlowe sang to me. My mother gave me a shirt I'd admired during a trip we'd taken to Macy's, a tiny pink sparkling makeup bag containing a bottle of nail polish, a tube of lipstick, and fifteen dollars, and a card that read, *To my beautiful daughter.* I think it had a picture of a fairy princess on it. She was sweet that day, a loving mother. I remember that, remember feeling giddy with her attention.

She left after breakfast, giving me a quick hug and a kiss, promising pizza for dinner and a real birthday cake.

"What's your birthday wish, Ophelia?" he asked me when we were alone, as I cleared the table of our dishes. The question, his grave tone in asking it, put me on guard. He had bizarre, ugly mood swings; I'd grown to fear them already. Not because he'd ever hurt me, but because they took him someplace I couldn't follow. His gaze would go empty, his body slack. He might disappear like that for hours, then return to me as though he were waking from a nap. I was too naïve to understand that this was not normal. That's what I tell myself, anyway.

"To be with you," I said, because I knew that was the answer he wanted. I remember that the sunlight had a way of coming in golden at that time of day. It made the place seem less dingy than normal.

"Forever?" he asked, reaching out his hand. I took it, and he pulled me onto his lap. He held on to me hard, buried his face in my neck. I wrapped my arms around him.

"Forever," I whispered in his ear, drawing in the scent of him. And I meant it as only a teenage girl could mean it, with a fairy tale in my heart.

He released me and took a small black box from his pocket. I snatched it from him quickly with a squeal of delight that made him laugh. I opened it and saw the gold half heart glinting back at me. He pulled back the collar of his shirt and showed me the other half around his neck.

"You belong to me," he said as he hung the pendant around my neck. It sounded so strange for a moment, it moved through me like a chill. But when I turned to look at him, he was smiling. No one had ever said anything like that to me. It was a drug—I couldn't get enough.

I told my shrink about this. I hadn't told anyone else; I have been ashamed of the way I loved him, of the things I allowed myself to do to keep that love. Just like my mother. Worse.

The doctor said, in that soothing manner of his, "It's not how we feel about someone that makes us love them, Annie, it's how they make us feel about *ourselves*. For the first time in your life, you were the center of someone's attention, the primary object of someone's love. Not waiting for a sliver of truth to shine through all your father's lies or for your mother to put *your* needs before *her* need to be with a man. You were the one. At least that's how he made you feel."

I heard the truth in that but thought it was a kind of clinical way to look at love. Isn't it more than that? Isn't it more than just two people holding up mirrors to each other? I asked him this much.

"In a healthy relationship, yes, there's much more to it. There's support, respect, attraction, passion. There's admiration for the other person, his character and qualities." Then the doctor asked, "What did you love about him? Tell me about him."

But when I thought of him, he was a phantom slipping away into the shady corners of my memory. The adult, the woman who had survived him, couldn't remember what the girl in her had loved.

The cheap necklace glints in my hand. I remember how a tacky piece of jewelry, for a while and for the very first time, made me feel loved. And I hear the echo of a voice, the voice I heard last night on the beach:

When the time is right, I'll find you and you'll be waiting. That's our karma, our bond, Ophelia. I'll leave my necklace somewhere for you to find. That's how you'll know I've come for you.

When and under what circumstances Marlowe spoke these words to me, I can't recall, but they are ringing in my ears now, drowning out the sound of the surf.

"What's wrong, Mommy?" Victory has come back and is looking at me with an uncertain, worried expression. I'm in space; I've already stuffed the necklace in my pocket.

"Nothing, sweetie," I say, resting my hand on her head.

"You look scared," she says. She is small, her hair a golden flurry about her in the strong wind.

"No," I answer, forcing a smile. "Race?"

She takes off in a run, shrieking. I chase her to the water, let her beat me there. When I catch her, I pick her up and spin her in a wide circle, then pull her body to mine and squeeze her tight before releasing her. She takes off again. All the while I pretend I don't know that my time is up.

12

I am thinking about my daughter as I edge my way along the hall. She is my shield and my weapon. Everything I have done and will do is to keep her safe, so that I can return to her. I force myself to breathe against the adrenaline thumping. Fear has always been my disadvantage. It makes me clumsy and sloppy. I have made so many mistakes acting out of fear.

Now that the engine is off, the ship has started to pitch in the high seas, and my stomach churns. I pause at the bottom of the staircase that leads up to the deck. I can hear the wind and the waves slapping the side of the ship. I strain to hear the sound of voices, but there's nothing, just my own breathing, ragged and too fast in my ears.

I make my way up the stairs, my back pressed against the wall. My palm is so sweaty that I'm afraid I'll drop my gun. I grab on to it tightly as I step onto the deck. I am struck by the cold and the smell of salt. The sea is a black roil. The deck is empty to the bow and to the stern; the light on the bridge has gone dark, like all the other lights.

Suddenly I am paralyzed. I can't go back to the cabin, but I don't want to move outside. I don't know what to do. I close my eyes for a second and will myself to calm, to steady my breath. The water calls to me; I feel its terrible pull.

13

There wasn't much to Detective Ray Harrison. At least there didn't seem to be at first blush. He was a man you'd pass in the grocery store and wouldn't glance at twice—medium height, medium build, passable looks. He'd hold the door for you, you'd thank him and never think of him again. But watching from an upstairs window as Detective Harrison approaches the house, my heart is an engine in my chest. The gold necklace in my pocket is burning my thigh. I go downstairs to greet him before Esperanza can get to the door and let him in.

I remember his face from last night; he'd seemed nice. Kind and without artifice. I'd liked him. But there's something else I see in him as I open the door that I don't like: suspicion. Today he's a wolf at my door.

"Detective Harrison," I say, offering my best fake smile. "Are you checking in on us?" I keep my body in the door frame, careful not to welcome him in with my words or gestures.

He smiles back at me, squints his eyes. I notice a few things about him: His watch is an old Timex on a flexible metal band, his breath smells faintly of onion, his nails are chewed to the quick. "Everything all right here last night after we left?"

"Fine," I say with a light laugh and a wave of my hand. "I think Esperanza overreacted a little by calling the police."

He keeps that slow, careful nod going, his eyes looking past me into the house. "You seemed pretty freaked out yourself," he says.

Freaked out. It strikes me as an odd turn of phrase, unprofessional and ever so slightly disrespectful.

"It was just the moment," I say. "Today in the sun, it all seems a little silly, to tell you the truth. I'm kind of embarrassed about the whole thing—you all showing up like that. I almost wish there had been a real reason for the cavalry to come riding in." I'm talking too much.

"That's what we're here for," says the detective.

An uncomfortable beat passes. "I was wondering, though," he says, "if I could ask you a few more questions."

"Regarding?"

"Can I come in?"

I have a hard grip on the door; I can hear the blood rushing in my ears. "I don't know what else we have to discuss," I say. "I told you everything that happened last night."

"It'll just take a minute, Mrs. Powers." His tone has shifted from friendly and chatty to slightly more serious. He has stopped nodding and smiling and has fixed me with his gaze.

I find myself moving aside to let him in, in spite of knowing that this is a mistake. But I don't want to seem like I have anything to hide. So I force another smile and offer him a glass of water, which he declines. He seems to look around and take inventory as I escort him into the living room.

"If you don't mind my asking, what kind of work do you and your husband do?" he says as he makes himself comfortable on the couch. Everything I liked about him last night is gone. I don't see the kindness and the empathy I imagined in him. His eyes seem narrow and watchful now. There's an unpleasant smugness emerging.

I have the feeling it's a mistake to lie, but I do it anyway. Force of habit. "I'm a stay-at-home mom, and Gray is an insurance investigator."

He turns up the corners of his mouth. "But that's not really the truth, is it, Annie? Can I call you Annie?"

I don't answer, just keep my eyes on him.

"Your husband and his father own a company, Powers and Powers, Inc. Isn't that right?"

I give him a shrug. "It's in the interest of our safety that no one around here is aware of that."

"I understand. Can't be too careful in his business."

"Detective, what does this have to do with anything?" I ask. I have stayed standing by the archway that leads into our living room. I lean against the wall and keep my arms wrapped around my middle.

"It could be relevant. Your intruder last night might have something to do with your husband's work." He takes out a small notebook, flips through its pages. "They call themselves security consultants, but it's a little more than that, right?"

"It's a privatized military company," says Gray, entering the room. He has been sleeping, but he doesn't look it. He's alert and on guard. The detective is clearly startled, like he expected me to be alone here. He rises quickly and offers Gray his hand.

"Detective Ray Harrison," he says. "I answered the 911 call last night."

Gray leans in and gives his hand a brief, powerful shake. "Thanks for taking care of things," says Gray, his voice flat and cool.

My husband pins the detective with a hard,

unyielding gaze, and Harrison seems to shrink back a bit. I notice that he looks past Gray, as if interested in something on the wall. We all stand in an awkward silence for a second, in which Gray crosses his arms and offers neither question nor statement, just a scowl of assessment directed at Harrison.

Finally the detective clears his throat and says, "When I learned the nature of your business, I wondered if it had something to do with the man who followed your wife."

The detective is looking toward the door now. He hasn't seated himself again, stands with his hands in his pockets. He does a little rocking thing, heel to toe, toe to heel. That Cheshire-cat look he had is long gone. *He's a coward,* I think. The kind of bully who would corner the skinny kid on a playground, then lift his palms and widen his eyes in mock innocence when the teacher comes.

"I really doubt that has anything to do with it," says Gray with a patient smile. "Most of the work I do is overseas. And in the unlikely event that someone developed a personal vendetta against me, I promise you we'd have more to worry about than someone lurking on the edge of our property."

The two men engage in a brief staring contest until the detective averts his eyes and brings them to rest on me.

"Well, it was just a thought," he says. He has a lot more to say, but he won't say it now. "Sorry to have bothered you."

Harrison walks toward the door, and Gray follows.

"There was just one other thing," he says as Gray opens the door for him. "I noticed that Mrs. Powers was born in Kentucky. But I swear I hear New York in your accent, ma'am."

Noticed where? I wonder. Did he check me out after he left here last night, look at my driving record or something?

"I was born in Kentucky but moved to New York with my family when I was a child."

Kentucky, land of lenient birth-records release policies. Just a little easily obtained information—birth date, mother's maiden name—and you're on your way to a brand-new life. If he keeps asking questions and checks on my answers, these lies won't hold. But he just gives me a half smile and a long look.

"We'll keep you posted on the area break-ins and if we learn anything more about who might have followed you on the beach last night," he says as he moves down the stairs. "Have a good one."

We wave as he drives off. Gray has taken my

hand and is holding it tight. I look at him, and he's watching the detective's SUV.

Detective Ray Harrison, on the day he began to suspect that I wasn't who I was pretending to be, was in a bit of a mess. He wasn't a corrupt man, not totally. Nor was he an especially honorable one. He was a man who'd made some bad choices, taken a few back alleys, and found himself dangerously close to rock bottom. One wouldn't have known it to look at him. He drove a late-model Ford Explorer, had never missed a payment on his mortgage, had never in his career taken a sick day. But there was debt. A lot of it. In fact, he was drowning in it. He went to bed and woke up thinking about it, could barely look his wife in the eye lately. It was making him sick; he was vomiting up blood from his ulcer. But it wasn't the kind of debt you could get help with; he didn't owe money to Citibank or Discover. The detective had a gambling problem. The problem was that he lost, often and extravagantly. The day before Esperanza's 911 call, a man to whom he owed money sent the detective a picture of his wife at the mall as she buckled their nine-month-old daughter into her car seat. On the back his creditor had scrawled, *Where's my fucking money?*

That's the hole he was in when he had a hunch about me, a vague idea that I might be hiding something. So he started doing a little poking around, not really going out of his way. A totally blank credit report was the first red flag. A driver's license granted just five years ago was the second. Finally a birth certificate issued in Kentucky when he was certain he'd heard just the hint of New York in my accent.

Detective Harrison was the kind of man who noticed how much things were worth: our house on the beach, the ring on my finger, the secret I had to keep. He did a little calculating and decided to take a gamble, as he was wont to do.

I don't know any of this as Gray and I watch him cruise away from the house. His visit is just another bad omen.

14

When I try to visualize Marlowe as he was when we were young, I can't quite pin him down. The memory writhes and fades away; I can see the white of his skin, the jet of his eyes, the square of his hand, but the whole picture is nebulous and changing, as though I'm watching him underwater.

He is lost to me. Part of that has to do with my blotchy memories. There's so much that exists in a black box inside me. But part of it has to do with him. Because, like all manipulators, Marlowe was a shape-shifter. He was always exactly what he needed to be to control me—loving or distant, kind or cruel. Maybe I never even saw the real Marlowe. Maybe the doctor was right about love after all, at least this particular brand.

At first Marlowe wouldn't talk much about his father. If I brought Frank up, he'd change the subject. Or he'd talk about him vaguely in the past tense, the way a person mentions a distant relative he remembers from his childhood. He'd make random comments such as, *My father liked the smell of orange blossoms. My father had a red hat like that.* Or, *My father gave me a baseball bat for my fifth birthday.* His memories seemed to visit him in vivid snapshots, bright and two-dimensional. The first time I pressed for more, he went to that dark place. We were talking on my bed, sharing a cigarette I'd lifted from my mother's purse.

"Didn't you know what he was doing?" I asked. I took a shallow drag, tried not to cough, and then handed it to him.

"Of course not," he said. "I was just a kid."

"How could you not have known?" I asked, staring at my cuticles, which were gnawed and dry just like my mother's. "You weren't *that* young."

He didn't answer me, and finally I turned my eyes back to him. It was the strangest thing. He was leaning against the wall, the smoke forgotten in his hand, arms akimbo. He stared at nothing, eyes glazed as though he were daydreaming.

"Marlowe."

I took the cigarette from him and put it out in the soda can we'd been using as an ashtray, where it extinguished with a sharp hiss. I grabbed him by the shoulders and gave him a gentle shake, thinking he might be horsing around. But he fell softly to his side on the bed, head coming to rest against an old stuffed bear that I'd had since I was a little girl. He stayed like that nearly an hour, as I whispered and yelled, soothed and cajoled, stroked and shook, pleaded and wept. I was about to dial 911 when he returned to himself, drained and dazed.

"What happened?" he asked me, I suppose taking in my tear-streaked cheeks and frightened expression. He was a person waking from a deep sleep, rubbing his eyes and issuing a yawn.

"You, like, *checked out*," I said, weary with relief to hear him talking again.

"Oh," he said with a shrug. "It happens sometimes. Like a seizure or something."

"It was scary," I said. "Really scary."

"It's nothing," he said sharply. I didn't press.

Slowly the grim picture of his life with Frank started to emerge. They went to parks, to churches, and to grocery stores, he told me, in a black beater Eldorado that was always breaking down. Frank Geary was the sad and oh-so-handsome widower, lonely and hardworking, with a good job and a nice house. Marlowe was the beautiful teenage boy without a mother. Together, Marlowe told me, they were the perfect lure for a certain type of woman.

"It was more than just how they looked," he said. "It wasn't just the color of their hair or eyes; it wasn't just their physical bearing. They were like dogs aching for a beating. My father sought the ones that wanted to be punished on some level. In a way he was looking for the ones who were looking for *him*. He saw it in them. And after a while I saw it, too. I knew the ones that would wind up coming home with us before he did."

And the women were all the same: on the wrong side of forty, pretty once but fading fast, too thin, never married, aching for the things their friends and sisters had acquired with relative ease. Somehow it just never worked out: This one beat her, that one ran out with her next-door neighbor, the other went to prison for check forgery. They all had a laundry list of failed relationships, histories of abuse and addiction. They were waitresses and topless dancers, convenience-store clerks and motel maids. Frank Geary listened to their sad histories, let them cry on his shoulder, maybe cried a little himself about how much he missed his wife, how hard it was to raise a boy on his own.

According to Marlowe, the seduction usually took only an afternoon. If they didn't leave the house before dinnertime, they left in the trunk of the Eldorado the next morning. More than three for certain, Marlowe remembered. He wasn't sure how many more. At the time, of course, he had no idea what was going on, he claimed. He never saw or heard anything that frightened him, right up until the day the police came and took Frank away. I still wondered how he couldn't have known. What did he think happened to those women who stayed the night and whom he never saw again? But I knew better than to force the issue.

During the years between Frank's arrest and Marlowe's appearance on our doorstep, he was shuttled from relative to relative and then finally into foster care. It never occurred to me to wonder why he'd never found a home, why he'd never been in one place more than a few months. I just figured that's how it was when your father was in prison and your mother was dead. In the housing projects where we'd lived in New York, I'd known enough foster kids to understand that it was difficult to find a place where you were safe and wanted, nearly impossible to find a real home where you could stay, where you were loved.

"Nobody wants the son of a convicted rapist and murderer around their children," he told me one night. "Not even if he's part of your own family."

But I imagine it was more than just that. There was an unsettling quiet to Marlowe, an eerie watchfulness, even back then. At the time this strangeness, as much as it frightened me, also intrigued me.

* * *

In the early weeks after Frank's arrest, Marlowe claimed he didn't believe the things they said about his father. But over time, away from Frank's influence, he started to remember things from years back. Once he found a collection of women's purses in his father's closet, once a woman's shoe—a cheap black sandal with a broken heel—under the porch. One morning before dawn, he saw his father put a bundle wrapped in a white sheet into the trunk of his car. Old clothes for Goodwill, he told his son.

"These things would come back on me like nightmares," he told me. "I'd be lying in some strange bed, scared and alone, and I'd remember things I'd seen when I was young. Maybe I was too young to understand them at the time; maybe I needed to be away from him to understand what he was. I don't know."

Marlowe started to wonder about the mother that supposedly ran off on them, left them all alone. Though Frank called himself a widower, he'd told Marlowe that his mother had rejected both of them, ran off in the night with some mechanic. Still, Marlowe kept a photo of her in his wallet; it was creased and soft with age. She was a delicate-featured blonde in a flowered sundress, standing under a tree as leaves wafted down around her. She looked at something off frame, her pinkie in the corner of her mouth. He carried this picture with him all the time, even though his father had beaten him once for doing so.

It only occurred to me later that he spoke about these things with very little emotion, that he seemed to have a center forged from ice. I found his tragedy romantic. He was a wounded bird I'd found. I nursed an adolescent fantasy that I could heal him and comfort him.

Meanwhile, of course, my mother nursed her own fantasy. Every six weeks she took a bus to the Florida State Prison, where she got to spend time with her fiancé separated by a sheet of bulletproof glass. She had never held, kissed, or even touched the hand of the man she planned to marry—and possibly never would. She wore this fact like a badge of courage. "But bars and armed guards can't keep people from loving each other. They can't stop the Lord's will," she'd say.

She spent her free time lobbying for a new trial for Frank. She wrote letters, contacted law firms that specialized in pro bono death-row appeals. The private investigator she hired had told her that Frank Geary's arresting officer had a career fraught with allegations of excessive force and coerced confessions, that one of his recent arrests and convictions had been overturned. This seemed to give her hope, even though Frank had never confessed to any of the murders; he maintained his innocence all along— even in the face of damning eyewitness testimony.

Apparently when the Eldorado died on him for the last time, Frank was forced to take the contents of his trunk and carry them down the length of a deserted Florida back road. It was dark, and he wouldn't have seen the woman watching from the window of her house, set back from the road. He might not even have seen the old house at all as he passed by with the load over his shoulders, heading to a sinkhole known to local cave divers as "Little Blue."

"She was an old woman," my mother said. "It was dark. She didn't know *what* she saw. Frank wasn't the only man driving an Eldorado in Florida that night."

The witness had died of a stroke since Frank's trial. My mother took this as proof that she'd wronged Frank.

"The Lord struck her down for ruining a man's life," she said with quiet conviction.

Even the hard physical evidence didn't discourage my mother: the blood and the blond hair in his trunk, the dead woman's wallet containing her driver's license, partially burned in a rusted metal drum in his backyard, fingerprints in his house matching two of the women he was suspected of murdering.

"Cops plant evidence all the time," she'd say. "And that cop who arrested him? He was dirty. The pressure was on. They needed an arrest, and Frank was the perfect scapegoat."

I'd stopped arguing with her, but when she sent me to the post office with letters going to the governor, death-row lawyers, and death-penalty activist groups, I threw them in the trash. Even though I didn't really believe in God, I prayed every night that Frank Geary would die in the electric chair before he had a chance to slip a ring on my mother's finger beneath the gaze of armed corrections officers in a prison chapel, or see me in the hideous pink dress my mother had bought me to wear as her bridesmaid.

1 5

While my eyes are closed and I'm paralyzed with fear, I feel the gun snatched from my hand. My lids spring open and I'm face-to-face with Dax.

"*What* about my instructions eluded you?" he asks in a harsh whisper. He grabs me by the arm and moves me toward the stern.

"Where are we going?" I ask him.

"We have to get off this ship," he says.

It's then I notice that his clothes are covered with blood. When he turns around to look at me, I see that his face is smeared with it.

"Off the ship? And go where?" I look out into the angry waters. There's nothing but black.

"There are islands. There," he says, and points off into the darkness. I don't see what he sees. I look around for the other boat I saw in the distance, but now it's gone, or at least its lights are off and it's disappeared in the black. I don't understand what's happening, but I am emptied out by fear, as if that's all there is to me. I stop moving, force him to stop with me.

"Where are the other men?"

He doesn't answer me. He climbs down a ladder at the stern to a platform where a Boston Whaler sits waiting, tied off on one of the cleats. It bucks and pitches like a mechanical bull. It's so tiny I feel sick just looking at it.

"You must be joking," I say from the top of the ladder. "Are you trying to get us both killed?"

He looks up at me, reaches up his hand. "Everyone else on this boat is dead," he says. "We have vastly underestimated our opponent. Leave with me or die here tonight."

"I don't understand," I say stubbornly. A fog seems to have settled in my brain; the whole situation has taken on the cast of dream, of nonreality.

"Dead," he says loudly, startling me into the moment. "As in not breathing. Ever. Again."

His words are a punch in the jaw; I'm reeling from the impact. Four other men, all trained paramilitary professionals like Gray, dead. I look back at the boat, where everything is still dark, where there is no movement or sound. It's a ghost ship. Panic starts to undermine my sanity.

"Who did this?" I ask.

Dax starts moving back up the ladder. "I don't

know," he answers, not looking at me. "There was a team. Well trained. They thought I was dead, so they left me where I lay." The wind is kicking up, and he has raised his voice so I can hear him. The water is slapping angrily against the boat, the Whaler knocking against the stern. "I figured they'd come after you next; I thought I'd find you missing or dead. The boat they arrived on? It's gone."

"Then let's get this one moving again." These waters must be full of sharks. That little boat looks like an hors d'oeuvre tray. Suddenly dying out there seems less attractive than it did before.

He climbs back onto the deck, runs his hands through his hair in a gesture of frustration. "The engine's *dead*," he says flatly. "Whoever has done this disabled the boat. They left you on it. Leads me to believe they'll be back or that they've rigged the boat to explode when they're far enough away. We need to *go. Now.*"

"No," I say.

Dax is looking at me hard. He might have been a handsome guy once, but his eyes tell me something about the things he's done and seen. His skin is creased and weather-worn; his mouth is a thin, tight line, a mouth that looks as though it has never smiled. He puts his hand on my arm again. I wonder if he's going to try to muscle me onto the Whaler.

"I want my gun back," I say, bracing myself.

He squints at me. Then after a second's hesitation, he takes the gun from his waist and hands it over. "Let's go," he says, pulling me back toward the ladder.

"You go," I say. "I can't. I need this to end tonight. One way or another. I can't just keep going and going. I get in this Whaler and then what? We hang out on some island until the sun comes up? Or we drive until the boat runs out of gas? We're sitting ducks then, too."

"We've been out of contact for over an hour. Another team will come for us before either of those things happens," he says. He's yelling now out of frustration, not just so I can hear him. His eyes are scanning the horizon as if he's already looking for the lights of another ship.

"When they do, bring them back," I say. I sound calm and sure, not at all how I feel.

"Don't be an idiot," he says, tightening his grip. He looks at me with some combination of concern and disdain. "You're so far out of your league you don't even know what you're playing at."

"You work for me, right?" I ask. He nods. "Then you're fired."

He shakes his head in disbelief but releases my arm and doesn't move to stop me as I run back toward the stairway that leads to the helm. Before I step inside, I hear the engine of the Whaler and turn to see the white of the boat get swallowed by the night. My heart sinks as it disappears. I wonder how big a mistake I've just made and what it's going to cost me.

16

When Victory was first born, I was terrified of her. She was this tiny, swaddled bundle, her small head nearly disappearing in her newborn cap. She wasn't one of those screaming babies who want the whole world to know they're here to stay. She was still and quiet, almost observant. When I looked into the deep brown of her eyes, I wasn't sure what I saw there; she seemed tired and a bit shocked, maybe even disappointed. It didn't seem as though she'd made her decision whether to stick around or not. Her breathing seemed too shallow, her limbs impossibly delicate. I felt as if she could disappear at any moment. Several times a night, I would startle from sleep and slip over to her bassinet, not to see if she was still breathing but to see if she was still there.

Victory always appeared relieved in Gray's care, though she seemed even tinier against the wide expanse of his chest. I imagined her issuing a faint sigh and turning up the corners of her mouth just slightly. Sometimes when I was nursing her and she had her wide, watchful eyes on my face, I could swear she was thinking, *Are you sure you know what you're doing here? Are you really qualified for this?* With Gray she seemed utterly peaceful, as if she knew that in his thick, capable arms she was totally safe. With me she wasn't so sure.

I used to dream that she'd be taken from me. In those first heady weeks, the sleep I got was riven with nightmares. I dreamed that the nurses came to the delivery room and shuttled her off, with me screaming after her. I dreamed I brought her to the pediatrician for her first visit and they refused to let me leave with her, citing my obvious lack of competence. I would wake up breathless, shame and rage racing through me like a white-water current.

When I first started going out of the house with her, I was afraid that I would accidentally leave her somewhere, that I would absentmindedly walk off and forget her in the grocery store or at the bank. I imagined in vivid detail tripping and losing my grip on the stroller and watching helplessly as it careened into oncoming traffic, or botching the fastening on the front carrier and being unable to catch her as she fell from it. In other words, I was a basket case most of the time.

"Every new mother has these kinds of feelings,"

my shrink would tell me. "It's a normal response to the massive and unfamiliar responsibilities in your life. Victory relies on you totally for her survival. That's an awesome realization. Then, of course, there's your lack of a good role model. Though obviously your mother didn't do everything wrong. *You* survived, after all."

"Just barely," I said. I always felt this childish wash of anger with anything less than his total indictment of my mother. Especially in conversations that centered on Victory.

"Well," he said, with a deferential nod, "yes. But consider this: Just because your mother didn't love you enough doesn't mean you start with a deficit of love for Victory."

I didn't follow, and my expression must have communicated that.

"I'm saying that you don't need to make up for what your mother didn't give her little girl—you— by overcompensating with Victory. That doesn't make you a better mother. A child needs a whole and healthy mother, someone separated from her to a certain degree. Otherwise, when she naturally starts to move away, she will feel as though she's taking something from you. She'll feel that you need her too much. It will cause her pain, guilt, impede her emotional development. Does that make sense to you?"

I made the appropriate affirming noises, but I didn't see how a mother could love her child too much. Seemed like only a man could imply such a thing.

That afternoon, after the detective's visit, while Victory is still in school and Gray has gone off to do whatever it is he does in a crisis situation, I move my stash to a locker at the bus station in the downtown area.

It's a small and seedy place about a block away from the police department. A homeless man drinks from something wrapped in brown paper and watches me from the bench where he reclines. I feel his eyes on the back of my neck as I shove my bag into the locker and take the small, orange-capped key. Feeling conspicuous and a bit silly, I wonder what well-intentioned or aboveboard reason someone might have for stowing belongings in a bus-station locker. As I walk back to my car, the homeless guy's still looking at me. He's wiry, dirty in a red-and-white checked shirt and jeans, beat-up old sneakers.

I don't judge him. Once, I woke up to find myself lying on a public bench, unwashed, disoriented; I wonder if this man, like me, is mentally ill. But he doesn't seem afraid or unstable. If anything, he seems comfortable, resigned. I wonder what he's thinking about me and my obviously guilty errand as I drive off. But I don't suppose he's in any position to judge me, either.

I stop at the gas station on the way back to the house. The only thing more depressing or suspect than a public locker is a gas-station pay phone. Maybe because they remind me of all the miserable calls I made to my father from just such a phone. They make me think of teenage runaways huddled against the rain, succumbing finally to desperation and fear, calling their parents and begging to come home. Or adulterers sneaking off to call their lovers. Only under such bad conditions would one find it necessary or desirable to huddle in the little metal shell, press her mouth and ear against the filthy receiver.

Paying with cash, I buy a calling card from the clerk and then walk over to the phone. I call the number I have memorized.

"Leave a message," answers a low male voice. "No names. No numbers. If I don't know who you are, you shouldn't be calling me."

His voice brings back memories of a sunny common room, the smell of institutionally prepared food in the air, the jangling and cheering of a television game show, the volume down low. We played Go Fish in our pajamas every day for a month, drawn to each other I suppose because we were the only patients connected to reality at all. Everyone around us drooled and stared, issued the occasional scream, or called out a name.

His name was Oscar, or so he told me. He was depressed, he claimed, suicidal. He'd thought about taking a leap off the Verrazano, but he thought about it too long and the cops came and pulled him back over the railing. "You make enough people disappear and the world doesn't even seem real anymore. Nothing *matters*."

"What do you mean, disappear?" I asked, not sure I really wanted to know.

He cleared his throat, glanced around. He reminded me oddly of that stock image of Albert Einstein, though much younger, with crazy hair everywhere, thick and spiky like pipe cleaners, and bright, clear eyes.

"You'd be amazed how many people want or need to walk away from their lives."

Like me, I thought, looking at the cards in my hand. "Really?" I said.

"I'm the one they call," he whispered, leaning in close. He tapped his chest. "I arrange the details."

"I see," I said politely.

"Oh," he said, suddenly indignant. He let his cards tip, and I saw his hand. "You don't believe me.

Because we're in here." He swept his arm around the room, at the zombies in repose.

"Well, let me tell you something," he went on when I didn't answer. "You got to be someone or know someone to be in this place. They don't let just *anyone* in here."

I stayed silent, remembering how Gray had told me his father knew the doctor who ran this posh and privately funded hospital, that favors were called in. *This is a place mainly for former military personnel, lots of Special Forces guys,* Gray had said. *Guys suffering posttraumatic stress disorder and the like.*

"Which leads me to ask, little miss," said Oscar. "Just who the fuck are you?"

"I'm no one," I answered.

He gave a soft grunt. "Aren't we all?"

"Queen of hearts," I challenged.

"Go fish." I'd seen the card when he inadvertently revealed his hand earlier. But I drew from the pile between us, anyway. I figured the fact that we were both cheating made us even.

I just say the one-word code Oscar gave me, years ago now, on the night he checked out of the hospital. "Maybe you never need it," he said. "Maybe you and me never see each other again. But hey, just in case."

"Vanish," I say, and hang up.

It seems improbable that he'll remember me, but I don't have any choice other than to follow the instructions he gave me back then. Or maybe he was crazy, as crazy as I am, and this call will come to nothing. In any case, as I drive away, I feel light-headed, sick to my stomach that I've even taken things this far. I have a kind of vertigo as I lean over the edge of my life and look down. I will just tip over and be gone.

17

Everything that happened next happened so fast that I remember it like a landscape passing outside the window of a moving train. Believe it or not, my mother succeeded in getting Frank a new trial. The young death-row appeals lawyer she found was hot to make a name for himself; a high-profile case like Frank's was exactly what he needed. After a few phone calls back and forth, and my mother scurrying off to the post office with newspaper clippings and the research compiled by the private investigator, he agreed to bring Frank's case before a judge.

Between the dirty arresting officer and new testimony from the deceased eyewitness's ophthalmologist, who claimed that the old woman's vision was so poor she wouldn't have been able to see much of anything at night, this lawyer was able to convince a judge that Frank deserved a new trial.

I came home one day to find my mother on the steps of our trailer surrounded by reporters. They flitted around her like moths to light, asking their questions. She looked beautiful and regal; no one would have guessed she was a waitress with a ninth-grade education. She spoke with the authority of someone who'd done her research on the legal system, mimicking all the right phrases, certain of her convictions. I stood in the back of the crowd and listened to my mother crow about her crusade, her faith, her belief in Frank Geary's innocence. I felt dizzy as I determined from their questions that a new trial would begin in a month.

I pushed my way through the crowd and past my mother, shaking her off as she tried to introduce me to reporters, not hearing the questions they shouted.

"What's the matter with you?" she complained when she entered the trailer. "Everyone will be looking at us now. We have to show our support for Frank."

I was speechless. I felt like my chest and my head were going to explode with the sheer force of my anger and disbelief. How could this be happening?

"I told you, Ophelia," she said triumphantly. "I told you the Lord wouldn't let an innocent man die." She was behaving as if he'd already been acquitted and was moving home.

In a desperate rush, I told her all the things that

Marlowe had told me, about the purses and the shoe under the porch. She scoffed, pulling her shoulders back and sticking out her chin.

"Marlowe's testimony was thrown out of court, Ophelia. Do you know why? Because he's a compulsive liar, just like your father. A child psychologist testified that Marlowe's statements were unreliable. No one ever found those purses or that shoe."

"Mom!" I yelled. "He's a rapist and a murderer. He is going to *kill* you."

She slapped me so hard I saw stars in front of my eyes. I stood there for a second, my face burning, my eyes filling with tears. My mother took a step back, closed her eyes, and rubbed her forehead with both hands.

"Ophelia, I swear," she said in a gasp through her fingers. "You bring out the worst in me."

I left with her yelling after me and went straight to the pay phone outside the gas station across the street from our trailer park. I was sure this would be the thing that convinced my father to come get me.

"I need to speak to my dad," I told the woman at the tattoo parlor who accepted my collect call. I think her name was Tawny.

"Ophelia, honey," she said, sounding strained. "He's gone." Something about the way she said it made my throat go dry.

"Gone where?" I asked, trying to keep the shake out of my voice. "When will he be back?"

"Honey, I thought he would have told you."

"Told me what?" My voice broke then, and I couldn't hold back my tears or the sob that lodged in my throat. There was a long silence on the line as I wept, cradling the phone in my hand.

"He got himself a new Harley," she said gently. "He's taken off on a road trip to California. We don't know when he'll be back. It might be a month or more."

Marlowe's words hit home then. *He's not coming for you,* he'd said.

"I don't have any way to reach him," she said. "But if he calls to check in, I'll tell him you need him."

I hung up then without another word. I remember holding on to the phone booth for support, feeling as though someone had punched a hole through my center, where a cold wind blew through. I don't know how long I stood there, crying hot, angry tears.

Drew and Vivian are at the house when I get back, sitting in the kitchen with Gray, drinking coffee and looking grim. They all turn to look at me when I walk through the door from the garage. The small television on the kitchen counter is on, with the volume down. I see the face of the murdered woman again; she looks so sad in the photograph they chose. Couldn't they have found a picture where she looked happier? I don't know why it should bother me, but it does.

"What is this?" I say with a fake laugh. "An intervention?" They must know what I've done. I check the coffeepot to see if it's still warm, and I pour myself a cup. I keep my eyes on the black liquid in my mug as I turn around.

"We're just worried about you, Annie," says Vivian. "You seem . . . *frayed.*"

"I'm fine," I say, looking up at them.

"Where were you just now?" Gray asks, standing and walking over to me.

"Out. Driving. Thinking," I answer. I am washed over by annoyance and anger; I'm sick of being treated like a mental patient. It has been more than four years since my last episode. I know why they're concerned—they're alarmed by my recent black patch because I haven't had one of those in Victory's lifetime. But I don't answer to any of these people.

When Gray takes me into his arms, my anger fades and is replaced with guilt for lying, for doing what I did. I'm suddenly unsure of myself, of this flight response I'm having to the threats I perceive in my world. The worry on their faces reminds me that it could be real or all of it could be imagined.

"We were wondering if we could have Victory for the weekend, Annie," says Vivian from the table. She is a big, strong woman, but beautiful and feminine, with a neat steel gray bob, flawlessly smooth skin, and square pink fingernails. She's always in silk and denim. "It will give you and Gray some time to yourselves."

I don't say anything but my anger and annoyance creep back. There's always this implication that I need time away from Victory. Or is it that they think she needs time away from me, her crazy mother? If I protest, it makes me seem selfish or unstable or both.

"Just tonight and tomorrow night," says Vivian soothingly. "We'll take her to school on Monday morning, and you can pick her up Monday afternoon."

Drew says nothing, just sips his coffee and looks out the window. He never says anything unless absolutely necessary. He lets Vivian do all the talking for him. Gray says his real mother wasn't strong like Vivian, that the life Drew led was hard on her, that she suffered. She spent some time in hospitals, I think, though Gray's memories are a touch vague.

What he does remember pains him—more than he says, I suspect.

He remembers bringing her glasses of water and small blue pills while she lay in bed, the shades drawn. He remembers listening to her cry at night after she thought he was asleep. There were long absences, when it was just Gray and his father. *Your mother needs some rest, son. She's not well.*

I've seen pictures of his mother looking thin and unhappy, dwarfed beneath Drew's possessive arm. In some of the old photographs, there's a little girl, blond and cherubic like Victory, a sister who died before Gray was born. It was an accident Drew has never been able to discuss, Gray tells me. She drowned somehow . . . in a pool, in the bathtub or the ocean, Gray doesn't know. It is an absolutely taboo subject, never once discussed between father and son as long as I've known them. The thought of this drowned child, the forgotten girl whose name I don't even know, makes me shudder. I hate the water.

"I need some time with you," Gray whispers in my ear. I look over at Drew, who still stares out the window as if he has nothing to do with this. But I know that this is coming from him; Vivian and Gray are his foot soldiers. There have been other conversations like this—about the beautiful house that I never wanted to live in, about the wonderful preschool I thought Victory was too young to attend, about the luxurious family vacations that I didn't want to take.

I feel trapped, like I have no choice but to agree. There's no space for me to say no, no way. I don't want to be away from my child right now, not even for two nights. It will make me seem clinging and desperate in this context.

"It would mean a lot to us, Annie," Vivian says.

That's the other thing they do: make it seem like I'm doing them a favor, that if I refuse, then I'd be denying them something after everything they've done for me. I move away from Gray under the guise of getting some cream from the refrigerator.

"Sure, Vivian," I say. "Of course."

I know they treasure my daughter and that Victory loves every minute she spends with them. She'll be thrilled, won't even throw a second glance back at me and Gray. I take my coffee and go up to her room to pack a bag without another word. I can feel all their eyes on me as I leave the room.

After a minute Gray follows me up the stairs.

"Why are you doing this?" I ask when he has entered Victory's room and closed the door. We are surrounded by smiling dolls and plush animals. The walls are painted blue with clouds, stars on the ceiling. The space is a happy clutter of all manner of toys, a tiny white table with four chairs, stacks of books and games. This is my favorite room in the house, the place I made for my daughter.

"Honestly?" he says, sitting down on Victory's bed, atop the comforter that is a riot of orange, yellow, and pink flowers.

"I'm concerned. I want her gone for a couple of days while I figure out what's going on. Don't you agree?"

I give him a grudging nod and sit beside him.

"And I meant what I said." He puts a hand on my leg and rubs gently. "We haven't had a day to ourselves in months. I need some time with you."

"We have live-in help," I say. "We have all the time alone we want."

I let him pull me into an embrace and I rest slack against his chest. I don't like it when he aligns with Drew and Vivian against me. They all seem so strong, so certain. I am flotsam in their current.

"You do whatever he wants," I say. I feel him tighten up. It's an old argument, a sore spot for both of us. Bringing it up is an invitation to rumble.

"That's not true," he says stiffly. "And you know it."

"It *is* true," I say as he releases me.

"This is not about my father." His tone holds a familiar controlled anger, the tone he always has when we fight about Drew, as if there's a well of rage he would never dare acknowledge.

"Whose idea was it?" I ask. "To get Victory out of the way for a few days so you could figure out what's going on?"

He walks over to the bookshelf and lifts a snow globe up to the light. He stares into the orb at the pre-9/11 skyline of New York City. He is all hard angles, a dark tower against the sherbet-colored plush of toys and downy blankets. His silence is my answer.

Gray's working with his father represents a kind of cease-fire. After a troubled adolescence and many years of estrangement in adulthood, Gray and his father have finally come to a demilitarized zone in their relationship. I think Gray likes it there; he doesn't want to go back to war. I understand this, but I resent it, too. We fight again and again about it, with no resolution.

"You know, I'm not crazy," I say, apropos of nothing, after a few minutes of silence, each of us isolated by our private, angry thoughts. I just feel I have to assert this.

"I know that," he says, returning to sit beside me again. He has a look on his face that reminds me he's seen me at my worst. Sometimes I think those memories prevent him from seeing how far I've come. I worry that I'll always be the crazy girl he found and rescued. Maybe part of him wants me to be that.

"The doctor says I'm stronger than I've been since he's known me."

"It's true," says Gray. "This is not about your mental health. There are real threats we have to assess. Victory is safer with my father than she is with Esperanza, right?"

He's right, I know he is. Why do I feel bound and gagged by his logic? Why does every nerve in my body tingle at the thought of being separated from Victory right now? But I go along. Of course I do.

Gray and I finish packing Victory's little pink suitcase, and we go with Vivian and Drew to pick her up at school. She is predictably delighted. Disney is in her future. She kisses us each carelessly and hops into the car seat in the back of Drew and Vivian's SUV. I see her tiny hand lift above the car seat in a wave good-bye. And they're gone. I fight the urge to run after the car.

"Why didn't you just say no?" asks my shrink later that afternoon.

"Because they were right. I *am* frayed."

The problem here is that I can't really tell him about the intruder on my property, the visit paid to my father, the cop and his questions. There's too much about me that he doesn't know, that I used to be someone else. That the person I used to be is guilty of some grave mistakes. He thinks I'm Annie Powers, formerly Annie Fowler. He thinks my husband is an insurance investigator. He knows about my dreams, the black patch, my history of fugue and disassociation, my choice to stop taking medication. He knows that I've been well and stable since Victory's birth. He knows a version of my past wherein names have been changed to protect the guilty, myself included. But he's ignorant of some crucial details and the very real recent threats. I think he must be aware of this, that he knows he's helping me only as much as I'll allow.

"Well, even so. You have a right to say what you want, Annie. Even if other people have legitimate and well-meaning reasons for asking something of you, it doesn't mean you have to comply."

I know he's right, and I tell him so. "Anyway, they're gone."

"It's something to keep in mind for next time. You have a right to say no, even if your reasons don't seem logical to anyone else. Due to traumatic circumstances in your life, you have had breaks from reality when you were unfit to make judgments. But it has been nearly five years since one of these episodes has occurred. You have been dealing with the root cause of your illness, and you are well, even without your medication. You aren't defined by those moments in your life; don't allow your husband and in-laws to make that mistake, either."

He's right, of course, even with all he doesn't know. The essential truths of our lives sometimes exist above day-to-day events. He thinks Gray found me in a bus station, that in a fit of altruism he took me to a hospital and, in an unlikely turn of events, fell in love with me during visits he made while I recovered. This is not very far from the truth, without being the whole truth.

"Gray fell in love with you while you were help-less and mentally unstable," the doctor reminds me.

"So maybe he doesn't want me to be strong?"

"Is that what you think, Annie?"

"I don't know."

Someone like Gray is at his finest when there's a crisis to be handled. He is the man you want when the sky is falling. But when the sky is not falling, does he feel a little lost? I think about our family and all the things we are forced to conceal, all the secrets we keep.

Florida rests on a network of limestone mazes, a labyrinth of wet and dry caves and crevices referred to as a karst topography. A layer of quartz sand thinly mantles the underground landscape formed by the movement of water through rock over millions of years. It's another world, filled with dark passages, populated by creatures that couldn't exist on the earth's surface. Sometimes I think of Florida's secret places, its wet darkness, its silent corridors, and I feel right at home.

18

Most of us don't live in the present tense. We dwell in a mental place where our regrets and grudges from our past compete with our fears about the future. Sometimes we barely notice what's going on around us, we're so busy time traveling. Before Victory was born, I could spend whole days trying to sort out the things that have happened to me, the terrible mistakes I've made. I marinated in my anger and self-loathing, cataloged all the different ways my parents failed me, cast myself as the victim and played the role like I was gunning for a gold statuette.

Motherhood changed that for me. Victory forced me into the moment. She demanded that I focus on her needs, that I live by her schedule. When I was with her—feeding her, changing her—just looking at her or playing with her, everything in the past and the future fell away. I was aware that we would be together like this for only a short time, that in a heartbeat she'd be walking away from me, living her own life. I didn't want to waste a second thinking about what might have been, what might be. Love makes you present. So does mortal fear.

I am fully present as I race up the stairs to the bridge. I burst through the door and am confronted by the body of the captain who waved to me earlier. He has a bullet hole between his eyes and an expression of profound peace on his face. I step over him to get to the control panel and nearly lose my footing. The floor is slick with blood. Another body lies in a pile of itself by the door. I register all this but don't have time to feel the full rush of horror the situation demands.

I stare at the knobs and switches before me. I have never been on the bridge of a ship like this one; I have no idea how to start the engine or even what to do next if I succeed. Outside, there is nothing but pitch black. It's bitterly cold, my ragged breath visible on the air, but I'm sweating from stress. I start randomly pressing buttons and turning knobs, but after a few fruitless minutes I give up. I sit in the captain's chair and take in the scene—the dead night, the dead ship, the dead men around me, the only person who could have helped me gone because I sent him away. My mind is racing through my limited options. Did I really send Dax away because I wanted to face down my enemy? Or did I do it because I wanted to surrender? I don't know. But I do know I have to take responsibility for this desperate moment, at least partially. I am as guilty as anyone for how my life has turned out.

My fingers reach for the gold pendant at my neck. I feel the jagged edges of the half heart. When I left my family behind, I put it back on for the first time in five years. I did this to remind myself that he was right: I did belong to him. And until I claimed myself, I always would.

I am swallowed by the silence. I have never heard such quiet. I close my eyes and pray to a God I'm not sure exists. Then I hear a distant hum, a speedboat engine. Hope and dread compete for control over my chest. Either reinforcements have arrived or I am about to make my last stand. Only time will tell.

19

About a week after it hit the news that my mother had succeeded in her lobbying to getting Frank a new trial, a woman came by the trailer to see her. She knocked loudly on the door, and I opened it, expecting to see our landlord come to collect late rent—an all-too-familiar scenario. But standing there instead was a tiny woman with watery eyes and a quivering line for a mouth.

"I'm here to see Carla March," she said. Her voice was timid, little more than a raspy murmur. But there was an odd resolve there, too, an unmistakable mettle to her bearing.

"She's working," I said. "She'll be back in a few hours."

"I'll wait," she said. Before I could say anything else, she moved over to one of the white plastic chairs we kept outside by the door. My mother had imagined us sitting out there in the evenings. But the humidity and the mosquitoes kept us inside beneath the A/C. The stranger sat herself firmly down, clasped her pocketbook in her lap, pulled her shoulders back, and stared off in the direction from which she'd arrived.

"I mean, like, *four* hours," I said, wondering if she'd misunderstood. "Maybe more."

"That's fine, young lady," she said without looking at me again, and pulled a Bible from her purse. Her hands were covered with dry and split patches of skin. Her skin was deeply lined, and there were the dark smudges of fatigue under her eyes. Still, she had a palpable aura of pride and righteousness in spite of the shabby condition of her apparel—a cotton floral-print skirt with the hem hanging, a white button-down blouse, yellowed at the neck and cuffs, white shoes covered in polish to hide the cracked and graying leather. She made me nervous; I didn't want her waiting there.

"What do you want?" I asked her.

She turned her head toward me, said clearly, "I want to speak to your mother, and I'm not leaving until I do." Her tone brooked no further questioning.

I went inside and watched television, did my homework, and got dinner started. All this time the woman waited outside, reading, her head nodding as if in agreement with some unseen person. I tried to call my mother, but the grouchy German

man she worked for wouldn't let her come to the phone.

"It's not possible," he barked at me, and hung up.

As the afternoon turned to evening, the woman waited. Finally I saw her rise from her seat as my mother approached the trailer slowly, smoking a cigarette. She was lost in thought, her eyes on the ground. She didn't see the woman until she was nearly at the door, where she let the cigarette drop and stamped it out with her foot.

"Are you Carla March?" I heard the woman ask.

I opened the door and watched as the woman blocked my mother's path and held something out to her.

"Who are you?" my mother asked sharply. "What do you want?" She looked tired; I could tell she'd had a hard day.

"My name is Janet Parker," the woman said, squaring her shoulders. "This is a photograph of my daughter, Melissa."

My mother's face paled. "You need to get out of here right now," she said softly. I saw her eyes dart around, checking to see if anyone was watching them. "You have no right to be here."

Janet Parker didn't give way and didn't lower her hand. Finally my mother released an angry breath and snatched the photo. I could see that her fingers were shaking as she held it up, squinted at it in the dimming light of evening.

"My daughter was a good person who died a horrible death," Janet Parker said as if she'd practiced the words a thousand times. "She didn't deserve to die like that."

My mother tried to push past her, but Janet wouldn't let her, grabbed hold of her wrist.

"Frank Geary killed her," she said, her voice climbing to a quaking yell. "He *beat* her, *strangled* her, and *raped* her as she died." She paused a second, tried to compose herself. Her voice was hoarse as she went on. "Then he dumped her body in a sinkhole."

She stopped again, her whole body starting to shake visibly. My mother seemed hypnotized by the woman, stared at her wide-eyed. Janet Parker took a deep, ragged breath. This time it was like a levy had burst; her voice came out in a wail. "And she was *there,* floating in the cold, dark water for *three months.* My *baby.* Alone in the dark, cold water."

My mother let the photo drop to the ground and kept her eyes down as she wrested her arm away from Janet Parker and moved toward the door.

"You have a daughter!" the woman howled, throwing a pointed finger in my direction. "Look at her. Young and beautiful, with everything before her."

I gaped at her as my mother pulled me from the doorway and took my place there.

"The only thing that gave me any peace at all was the knowledge that he'd die for what he did," Janet Parker said, more quietly. "That he'll burn in hell." She wasn't yelling anymore, but the pain in her voice was embarrassing. I felt like I should avert my eyes, but I couldn't turn away from her.

"Frank Geary is an innocent man, wrongly convicted," said my mother. She sounded weak and foolish, her righteousness shallow before the depths of Janet Parker's abyss of grief and rage. "I'm sorry for your loss. But Frank didn't kill your daughter."

The woman lowered her head and took in a deep breath. "They found her purse in his house," she said, her face flushed and wet with tears she didn't bother to wipe away.

"That evidence was planted," my mother said. "I'm sorry."

My mother shut the door on Janet Parker then. The other woman ran to the door and began pounding on it with both fists.

"He killed her! He killed my little girl! My baby! My little girl!" Her voice took on the pitch and qual-

ity of a roar. She kept pounding and yelling, even as a crowd of people gathered around the trailer.

My mother locked herself in her room, and I sat paralyzed in the kitchen listening to Janet Parker's terrible baying, which continued even as the police arrived and hauled her away. I never forgot the sound of her voice; years later it remains in my mind the very sound of grief and outrage. It chilled me then; I knew it was an omen.

After she was gone, my mother came out of her room.

"God," she said with a harsh laugh. "What a crazy bitch."

She left the trailer and returned a few minutes later with a six-pack from the convenience store across the street. She popped the lid on one and sat down in front of the television but didn't turn it on. She sat staring, silent. I wondered if Janet Parker's words were ringing in her ears, as they were in mine. The beer was gone in under ten minutes. She rose, got herself another, and sat back down. There was no such thing as one beer where my mother was concerned.

I left her to it, went to my room, and closed the door. As I lay in bed a while later, I heard her stumble from the trailer and knew she was on her way to the convenience store for more. My mother liked to drink. It was a mad dog she kept on a chain. When it got loose, it chewed through our lives.

I knew how it would go. She'd drink until she passed out tonight. Tomorrow she'd be hungover and mean. She'd fight it for a few more days, then start sneaking booze when she could. Soon we'd be back to where we were before she found Jesus and got sober the last time—with her stumbling in from wherever, enraged or maudlin, sickly sweet or violent, causing some kind of scene until she passed out on the floor or over the toilet. Eventually she'd lose her job. I could see we were in the wide, early circles of a downward spiral.

A few weeks later, my mother and Frank were married on either side of a sheet of bulletproof glass. As if things couldn't be more ugly and uncomfortable, Frank forced Marlowe to stand in for him beside my mother, put the ring on her finger, and offer her a chaste kiss on the cheek. My boyfriend became my stepbrother before my eyes. I watched in horror as my mother and her new husband leaned their bodies against the glass that separated them until guards dragged Frank back to his cell.

On the bus my mother cried all the way home in

the tatty, short wedding dress she wore under a rain-coat. Marlowe had some kind of look on his face that I couldn't read. I tried to take his hand so my mother wouldn't see. He pushed me away cruelly. I went to the back of the bus to sit alone, hollowed out and numb. After a while my mother fell asleep and Marlowe moved back beside me. He took my hand and rested his head on my shoulder.

"I'm sorry," he said. "Everything's going to be okay."

I thought about my father and his false assurances and then how he'd left without a word. I thought about what my mother had told me about Marlowe, that he was a liar just like my dad. The bus smelled like cigarettes and vomit. I leaned my head against the windows and watched the orange groves roll by.

With the death-row wedding and Frank's new trial starting just a week later, I became a pariah at school. I was no one before all that; I was quiet and flying under the radar, doing well but not well enough to attract attention. I wasn't especially ugly or notice-ably sexy, so no one even saw me. As the trial dragged on, though, people had somehow become confused by the media coverage and thought I was Frank's daughter. Someone left a dead bird in my locker; someone tripped me in the hallway; someone flung spaghetti at me in the cafeteria. I wept in the bathroom, trying to wash the sauce out of my hair.

And then, just when I thought things couldn't get worse, Frank was acquitted. My mother's prayers had been answered. Her husband was coming home.

20

When I return from my appointment, the house has an aura of emptiness. There will be no mealtime negotiations *(Eat three pieces of broccoli, Victory, and then we can have dessert),* no bathtime adventures (the race between Mr. Duck and Mr. Frog continues), no quiet time in Victory's room before she drifts off to sleep. All the comforting rituals of the day have been suspended.

As I pour myself a cup of coffee—not that I need any more caffeine—I hear Esperanza in the laundry room. I call her name, but she doesn't answer. I decide to wait awhile before I tell her she can have the rest of the evening off. I don't want to be alone, knocking around this house that never feels quite like home unless Victory is in it, too.

Gray has gone to the offices of Powers and Powers, Inc., in the city just forty minutes away—for what, I don't know. I have been there myself only a couple of times. It's a small space with an open floor of cubicles and a couple of conference rooms with long wooden tables and ergonomic swivel chairs, big flat-screen monitors, and state-of-the-art video-conferencing equipment. It's like any other office where any other business is conducted—antiseptic, impersonal, the smell of bad coffee or burned micro-wave popcorn wafting from the break room. The printer jams, someone has to change the enormous bottle on top of the watercooler, people stick pictures of their kids on the sides of their computer monitors.

Gray's work is not as Mission Impossible as it sounds. After the end of the Cold War, firms like this have begun to play a role in world warfare in a way that had always been reserved for the military. Powers and Powers, Inc., refer to themselves as private security consultants, as Detective Harrison mentioned, and that's accurate. But they have also sent their operatives to help suppress the Revolutionary United Front in Sierra Leone, end the crisis in the former Yugoslavia, and support the rebuilding effort in Kosovo. At their best, privatized military companies provide targeted and specialized services formerly associated with government military forces. When working in conjunction with established and recognized states, they can be very effective. If, however, they operate without conscience—and there has been enough of this to make people worry—these companies, employing the most highly trained paramilitary personnel throughout the world, can have a destabilizing effect on established states.

Powers and Powers employs a staff of just under a thousand former Special Forces and elite law-enforcement personnel. Their services range from hostage negotiation to emergency response, from arms training to small tactical operations to private security. They hire out their services to governments, corporations, and individuals. There has been a lot of controversy about the industry, so Drew and Gray prefer to keep a low profile. Few who know us, in fact, know what they do. Even other tenants in their building don't know the true nature of their work. And even I don't have any knowledge of their specific operations at any given time. I find I don't mind this. I guess I'm more comfortable than most with secrets and lies.

I take advantage of Gray's trip to the office and go down to an Internet café on the beach, order a latte, and log in to an account I created a long time ago. Amid the slew of spam, there's a message from Oscar. It reads, "What's the problem, Annie?"

I'm surprised that he remembers me, though he assured me he would. I'm also a little frightened. Part of me was hoping that he'd no longer be operating.

I sit for a second, not sure how to answer his question. I look around me and spot a young girl in a wetsuit hanging open to reveal a bikini top. She's tan and bleached blond, sipping an energy drink and surfing the Web. There's an old man in a tank top, shorts, and flip-flops eyeing her over his coffee. You can tell he thinks he's still got it. But he doesn't.

"I have reason to believe the past is about to catch up with me," I write. "I need an escape hatch."

I send the message and wait, sip on my latte. It's weak and foamy; I wish for New York City coffee, coffee that's like a punch in the face. There's a television mounted in the corner of the café tuned to CNN. On the screen: a gallery of murdered women and a caption that reads, COPYCAT? The sound is down, and white closed captions scroll across the screen. ". . . *similar to the murders that took place nearly ten years ago, less than fifty miles from here. But the man accused and convicted of those crimes was killed when . . .*" I look away, my heart racing for some reason, a deafening rushing sound in my ears. I don't want to see any more.

I check the e-mail in-box. There's already a message waiting.

"I'll consider myself on standby," it reads. "In the meantime start telling people you're taking up a new hobby. Tell people you want your scuba certification.

When you're sure you're ready, you know what to do. Don't be hasty. This is for keeps."

I finish my coffee and reflect on his words. Sitting in the café watching the old man try his game with the surfer chick, everything takes on a nebulous unreality, as though I'm waking from one of my dreams. I remind myself that nothing is done yet. I'm still okay. I'm still Annie Powers.

After a while I leave the café and walk toward my car. I have a terrible headache behind my right eye. As I put the key in the lock, I see the girl I noticed at Ella's party. She's standing over by the entrance to the café; I didn't see her when I first came out. She's leaning against the masonry wall, staring at me with that same expression, looking more unkempt than I remembered but still waifishly pretty. As I move toward her, she turns and starts to walk away quickly. I follow.

"Hey," I call after her, though why I am following her or what I'll say when I catch up to her, I have no idea. I just feel this desperation to know her name. She takes a left, is out of sight, and I pick up my pace almost to a run. But when I make the turn, she's gone. I look up and down the street. She's nowhere to be seen. My heart is pounding as though I've just run a marathon; a familiar panic is blooming in my chest. I get back to my car, shut and lock the door. My airways are constricting, and there's a dance of white spots before my eyes. It's a full-blown panic attack. I try to breathe my way through it, like my shrink has taught me. I turn on the car and blast the A/C; the air is hot at first, then chill. I start to calm down. I catch sight of myself in the rearview mirror. My face is a mask of terror.

"What is wrong with you?" I say aloud. "Pull yourself together."

After a while, when I can breathe again and the inner quake has subsided, I drive home. My headache has reached operatic proportions.

Gray is waiting for me at the kitchen table when I return home.

"Where'd you go?" he asks with false lightness.

I'm sure he knows I moved the things under our bed. I sense he's worried about me and what I might do. What I love about him is that he always gives me my space, gives me the benefit of the doubt.

"To the store," I say, putting a plastic grocery bag filled with things I didn't need on the counter—moisturizer, shampoo, nail polish. He gets up and comes over to me. He sifts through the bag, and I know he's not fooled by my pointless purchases. He takes my hand.

"Sit down a second," he says, indicating a chair.

As I take a seat, he slides a poor-quality photograph printed from a color printer onto the table in front of me. The man in it has a pocked, fleshy face, with a bent nose and dead, mean eyes.

"Do you know who this is?" he asks.

My headache is so bad now it's making me sick to my stomach. Something black starts to spread across the inside of my brain.

I rub my head. "No," I say.

"Are you sure?"

I look again, but I feel like I can't focus on the face. "I don't think so."

He sits down next to me and rests his eyes on the photograph, taps it with his finger.

"I went to the office and called your father from a secure line. I got a description of the guy who came to see him. Turns out he also left a name and phone number. The name is a fake, of course. The number is just a pager. But the name, Buddy Starr, is on a list of aliases for a guy called Simon Briggs. He's a bounty hunter. Not as in bail bondsman, more like a private contractor. He's the guy you hire when you want to find someone and aren't necessarily worried in what condition. His list of criminal associations is long and colorful."

"Why would he be looking for Ophelia?" I ask.

The sun streaming in through the windows is way too bright. I cover my eyes.

"That's what we need to find out," he says. "The point is, though, that he's likely working for someone."

I stare at the picture, then close and rub my eyes again.

"Hey, you okay?" Gray says after a minute. "You look pale." He puts his hand on my arm.

"I just have a headache." I feel his gaze, but I don't meet his eyes.

"Maybe you've seen this guy before and you don't remember?"

"No," I say, not wanting to admit that it's not only possible but even likely, given my reaction to the photo. I put my head down in my arms. They come on hard and fast like this for me. If it gets any worse, I could be lying in a cocoon of pain for hours.

"I don't know," I admit.

I let Gray lead me upstairs. He puts me into bed and closes the shades. I hear him take my migraine medication from the medicine cabinet in the bathroom, run water into the glass by the sink. When he returns to me, I sit up and swallow the pills. He's very good at taking care of me.

* * *

That afternoon Detective Harrison finally got lucky. A few telephone calls to the records office in the Kentucky town where Annie Fowler was born yielded a faxed copy of her death certificate. She and her infant son had been killed in a road accident when she was just twenty-one years old.

"A real tragedy," the records clerk told him, over the phone. "She went to school with my son."

"That's terrible. How sad," he said, trying to keep the excitement out of his voice. "Do you mind telling me what she looked like?"

"Red hair and freckles, sweet-faced, petite— maybe not even five foot two, and a little on the plump side. A lovely girl, though. Just really . . . *pretty.*" Nothing like the Annie Fowler he knew.

"I come from a small town myself," the detective told her, though that wasn't quite the case. It was just a way he had to lube people up, get them talking. "I know how hard a tragedy like this can be for everyone."

"It's true. It's true," the clerk said, sounding wistful and as though she were tearing up. "Her parents have never been the same." Then, "I *am* curious, sir. What's your interest?"

"I can't say much, ma'am," mimicking her polite tone. "But I have reason to believe that someone might have used her information to create a false identity." He paused when he heard the clerk gasp. "Since her death have you had any queries at your office for her birth certificate?"

In fact, there had been. A young man came to the records office just a few months after Annie Fowler's death, claimed that he'd been adopted, was searching for his birth family. He thought Annie might be his sister.

"He was distraught when I told him about her death. But I was acquainted with her parents. If there had been a baby given up for adoption, *I'd* have known it. Anyway, he asked for copies of her birth and death certificates. I wasn't sure why he wanted them, but he had the required information and money to pay the fee."

"Do you remember his name?"

"No, I surely don't. But I might have it somewhere. Can I call you back?"

"I'd appreciate it."

That afternoon Detective Harrison didn't know that the real Annie Fowler had died just a few months before Ophelia March was killed in a car accident in New Mexico. He didn't know who I was or what I was hiding, but he knew who I *wasn't*. And he felt, as all gamblers do just before they lose it all, that he was about to have the biggest win of his life.

21

During the awkward dinner the four of us shared on Frank's first night home, my mother doted, Marlowe stared at the table, and I watched Frank with a kind of numb horror as he piled food onto his plate and ate with gusto.

"We're a real family now," my mother said as she sat beside Frank around the cramped Formica table in our trailer.

"That's right," Frank said, patting my mother on the arm. She nuzzled up to him like a house cat.

I was too depressed even to be a smart-ass about it. All I could do was stare at Frank's hands and think about Janet Parker's mournful wailing, about the way her daughter had died. I'd never once believed that Frank was innocent. His trial had hinged on the charges against the investigating officer, the suppression of evidence that officer claimed to have found at Frank's house, and the testimony of the ophthalmologist who the prosecutor claimed had been paid off. Basically, Frank got lucky. And the hands he'd used to murder an unknown number of women were now placing mashed potatoes on my plate.

Frank was a tall, quiet man with narrow blue eyes and long, slender fingers. His blond hair was going white, and his thin lips disappeared into the flesh of his face. He spoke softly, almost in a raspy whisper. I felt him watch me as I ate.

"I see a lot of your mother in you, girl," he said, finally breaking the silence that hung over the table. His words sounded like a warning, and I felt the hairs rise on my arms. My mother shot me a black look. I made a mental note to draw as little attention to myself as possible.

Outside our trailer there were a few protesters, family members of Frank's victims. In subdued but persistent voices, they chanted, "Murderer, murderer, murderer." We all pretended not to hear.

"We'll be leaving here by week's end," said Frank, getting up from his seat and walking over to the window. With those ghoulish fingers, he pushed the curtain back, releasing a heavy sigh as he looked out. The chanting grew louder.

I remember thinking, *If he were innocent, he'd be angry.* He'd be railing against the injustice of those people chanting outside his door. But he seemed simply annoyed, perhaps even disgusted, as though he looked down on their grief and their rage. They were emotions he didn't understand. He turned and saw me staring. His eyes were flat, empty, rimmed by dark circles. They made me think of the sinkhole where Melissa Parker's body had floated. There was nothing in his gaze that I recognized.

The state paid Frank some restitution money, about ten thousand dollars. And he'd used that and some other money he had to put a down payment on a horse ranch in the middle of Nowhere, Florida. True to his word, a week after he was released, we were living there. It happened so fast I didn't even have time to protest. All we brought from the trailer were our clothes. Everything else he declared as junk to be left behind.

Our new house sat back on twenty acres of property, fully a half mile from the road. We were completely isolated from our neighbors, flanked by orange groves to the east and a dairy to the west, a half-hour drive from the nearest town. As we rode up the long drive for the first time, my only thought was that I could scream until my head popped off and no one would hear me.

I awoke my first morning there in my new room; outside my window, sunlight glinted on the dewy grass. I could hear the soft, slow clopping of the horses' hooves as they milled about their pen, could hear them snuffling and neighing as if in quiet conversation. It would have been the nicest place I'd ever lived if I hadn't been so sad and so afraid of the man sleeping in my mother's bed.

Frank's presence in our lives was a blanket of snow—everything grew white and silent. Including my mother, who seemed brittle and frozen, following blankly in his thrall. She worked the ranch like a hired hand, cooked and cleaned as I'd never seen her do. She hardly looked at me, except to assign me chores. She touched me only when she took my hand as we said grace before meals.

As for me, I just was numb, on autopilot. I dressed myself carefully in baggy, formless clothes so as not to attract any attention from Frank. I went to my new school during the day and, when I got home, did the work I was assigned around the ranch. I tried futilely to reach my father every night. My desire to rage and fight with my mother was drained by my fear of Frank. It was as if he emitted a noxious energy that sucked the life from all of us.

I thought Marlowe and I would be gone before I was living under the same roof with Frank Geary. But Marlowe's promises of rescue seemed to have evaporated. Something about Frank's presence changed him, too; he became as unnatural as his father. There was no trace of the passion he'd claimed to have for me, except the dark looks he gave me when he thought no one was watching. I trailed him, trying to steal moments alone with him. But he avoided me until one night I awoke to find him standing in my room.

I sat up in my bed, my center flooding with hope. "Marlowe."

He didn't answer me.

"What's wrong with you?" I asked when he stayed in the corner of my room, unmoving. After a long minute, my hope evaporated; a dark flower of fear bloomed in its place. I wondered how long he'd stood there watching as I slept, and why.

"He can't know there was ever anything between us," he said finally, moving into the light where I could see him.

"I thought we were leaving," I said. I kept my voice flat and unemotional. I didn't want him to know my heart—how afraid I was, how much I needed him.

"We can't," he said quietly. "He'll find us. And when he does, he'll kill you. I'm not allowed to love anything."

I was too desperate to hear the sickness in his words. I heard only that he was letting me down, like everyone else. "You promised me," I said, my voice sounding childish even to my own ears.

"That was before," he said tightly. "I never thought he'd be released."

I'd seen the way Marlowe followed his father around, looking at him with begging eyes, waiting for scraps of attention. "You don't want to leave him," I said.

"You don't understand," he said. He came and sat on the edge of my bed. "No one leaves him."

Marlowe had seemed so strong, so much wiser than anyone I'd known. Now I could see he was just a scared kid, just like me.

"You'll be eighteen in seven months," he said weakly. "You can legally leave then. I'll be eighteen next month, and I'm going to join the marines. He won't be able to get to me there."

I was washed over by hopelessness, and I turned to weep into my pillow. He didn't move to comfort me, just sat there as I cried. I thought there was no end to the well of sadness within me. I thought I didn't have enough tears.

Then, "There might be a way, Ophelia. I just don't know if you're strong enough."

Something in his tone chilled me, even as I felt a little lift. "What are you talking about?" I said into my pillow.

"It's the *only* way," he said, moving into me. He rubbed my back with the flat of his hand. It was the first time he'd touched me in weeks. I sat up and moved into his arms, let him hold me. It felt so good to be close to him again, to be close to anyone.

"I don't know what you mean," I said. He bent down and kissed me. My body lit up for him. He slipped beneath the covers with me, his hands roaming my skin. My mother had been wrong about me: I'd never made love to Marlowe. I was still a virgin then. We only engaged in these heavy petting sessions. Now I see I was such a child, so starved for affection. I just wanted the physical closeness of another person; this felt like love to me. After a few minutes, when I was hot and aching and alive with my need for him, he pulled away.

"Forget it," he said. "You're not ready. You're too young."

He got out of the bed and went back to the window. "This time next month, I'll be gone," he said.

"I'm not too young," I said. I curled myself up into a ball and hugged my knees to my chest. "Don't leave me here."

He came back to the bed. I lifted a finger and traced the lines of his mouth.

"I'll do anything," I said.

"Say it," he said.

"I belong to you."

* * *

"Annie!"

I awake to find Gray holding me by the shoulders. "It's okay. Wake up."

I am drenched in sweat, my heart thudding. Mercifully, the pounding in my head has subsided. But I feel weak, as if I've just run a hundred miles.

"What happened?" I ask, disoriented. I can't tell if it's day or night.

"You were dreaming," he says. He pushes a few damp strands of hair away from my eyes. "What were you dreaming about?"

I try to shake the fog from my brain, to grasp at the faded images from my dream that are already slipping away. I move away from Gray and turn on the light.

"I think I'm remembering," I tell him. He looks at me with some odd mixture of hope and fear.

"What? What do you remember?"

"I don't know," I say after a minute. Suddenly I don't want to tell him what I saw in my dream. I don't want to say what I think I may have done.

"Tell me."

I close my eyes and rest against him. "Gray, do you ever wonder what it would be like to be married to someone normal?"

He laughs a little. "I'd die from boredom."

"Seriously."

"You're normal," he says, pulling back a little so that he can look into my face. "You're fine."

I wonder how he can say that, if he really believes it to be true. I find I can't hold his eyes; I lean against him again so that I don't have to look away.

"She can never know who I've been and the things I've done," I say into his shoulder. "I can never let Ophelia touch her. You know that, Gray."

"Ophelia was never the problem."

"You know what I mean."

"I know," he says. "I know."

22

When people think of Florida, they think of oranges and pink flamingos, palm trees and beaches, the blue-green ocean. They think of Disney and margaritas. Florida is light and fluffy, kitschy, a place for the family vacation. And it is all that, of course. But it has a feral heart, a teeming center that would rage out of control if not for the concrete and rebar that keeps it caged. There are vast untamed places: shadowy mangroves, deep sinkholes, miles of caverns and caves, acres of living swamps. There is a part of Florida that will recover itself when it gets its chance. Its wet, murky fingers will reach out and close us into its fist. This is how I feel about my life.

I walk through the mall with Ella. Anyone looking at us as we wander through the shops would see two women with time and money to burn. They might assume that the worst of our problems is a cheating husband or a kid with ADD. As I examine an obscenely expensive handbag at Gucci, I hear a shotgun blast ringing in my ears. I smell smoke. I see Frank Geary's chest exploding and watch as he falls backward down a flight of stairs. I hear my mother screaming. I don't know where these bloody images have come from, if they are memory or dream.

"You seem distracted," Ella says as we sit down to drink espresso in the food court. "Everything okay?"

"Yeah," I say lightly. I keep seeing Simon Briggs in my mind's eye. He's the headache I can't shake. His face, so rough and ugly, is familiar without being recognizable. There are so many things like this that I can't quite remember—people, events slipping through my fingers like sand. "I'm just . . . not sleeping much."

"Well," she says knowingly, "you're probably still freaked out by that incident on the beach. That would keep *me* up at night."

Freaked out. There's that phrase again.

"I guess so," I say vaguely. We both take a sip of coffee.

I let a beat pass. Then, "I'm going to get my scuba-diving certification."

Ella peers at me over her little cup. "I thought you hated the water."

"I do," I say, taking another sip of the black, bitter coffee. "But, you know, I have a daughter now. I want her to see me work to conquer my fears."

She gives a careful nod. She's very diplomatic, slow to judge. I like this about her.

"Maybe you should start with swimming lessons," she suggests delicately. "You know, in a pool?"

"Baptism by fire," I say with a smile.

She looks at me uncertainly. *"Oo-kaay,"* she says slowly, drawing out the word.

"Well," I say, putting down my cup with a delicate clink in its saucer. "The lessons start off in the pool."

"Good," she says brightly. "You know what? I'm proud of you. That's great."

Her cell phone rings, and she looks at me apologetically as she answers it. I can tell by the shift in her tone that it's her husband. Her voice gets softer. She turns her head away from me. I stare at the other shoppers, think of Gray off trying to figure out who might be looking for me. I think of Victory off with her grandparents. I'm counting the hours until I can pick her up at school tomorrow. I'm just here killing time. I should be home meditating, trying to remember who Simon Briggs might have been to me. But I suppose part of me doesn't want to remember. That's what my shrink believes, anyway.

"I have to go," Ella says, snapping her phone closed. She looks strained.

"Everything all right?" I ask gently.

"Yeah," she says with a fake laugh and a weak flutter of her hand. We're both such liars. I hope she's lying about less awful things, for her sake.

"What about your Prada loafers?" I ask.

"They'll wait," she says. "You coming?"

I shake my head quickly, down the rest of my espresso, and stand up. "I want to pick up a few things for Victory."

"Okay," she says, tucking her bag under her arm. "Sorry."

I wave her off. "Don't worry about it."

She looks pale, a little red around the eyes. She never talks about her husband or their relationship except in the broadest strokes. *He works so hard,* she'll say. *He travels so much. He's very protective.* She seems stiff and nervous in his presence. Occasionally our visits are cut short by calls like the one she just received. I know better than to pry. I like to let people keep their façades intact. That way they're less likely to come poking around at mine.

She rushes off, and I watch until I can't see her anymore. I wish I could be a better friend to Ella. But I can't.

When I turn back to grab my purse and shopping bags, I'm face-to-face with Detective Ray Harrison. My stomach bottoms out at the look in his eyes. He looks hungry.

"Let's talk, Annie."

"Are you following me?" I say. My voice raises an octave, though I didn't intend it, and a woman at the next table turns to stare at me.

"Don't make a scene," he says with a smile. "You can't afford to make a scene."

I smile at him and let him take my arm. I pick up my bags from the floor, and we walk toward the exit.

"That purse you bought. It cost more than my wife's food budget for an entire month."

There's some mixture of astonishment and reprimand in his voice. I don't say anything. "The mercenary business must be booming," he says.

He means Gray and Drew's company, though *mercenary* is not a word they use in the industry. And indeed, since September 11, business *is* booming.

"One of the hardest things about being a cop," he says when we're outside, "is watching the criminals live better than you do." We're walking through the rows of cars. I'm not sure where we're going, and finally I come to a stop. I'm not walking into the deserted part of the lot with this man, cop or no cop.

"What do you want?" I ask him.

He looks around us. The lot is crowded, plenty of activity. People walking, pushing kids in strollers, pulling in and out in their late-model cars. He lets go of my arm and puts his hand in his pocket, starts that rocking thing he does. I'm not even sure he's aware of it.

He keeps that fake smile on his face. People walking by might think we're neighbors who bumped into each other at the mall, that we're having a friendly chat. I know then that his interest in me is not professional, not legal. If it were, he would have put his handcuffs on me and we'd be in the cruiser heading into the station. This alternative is not necessarily good news.

"I mean, I spend my whole life working hard, providing for my family, paying taxes, saving for retirement. Every vacation, every new appliance we need, every repair on the house—we budget and save, you know? And then I walk into some perp's garage and I'm looking at a Hummer. Or I go into his crib and there's a flat-screen and audio system that could pay for a year of private school for my kid. I think, here's a person with no respect for the law, for human life, and he's living large. I tell you, it eats at me sometimes. It really does."

There's something whiny about his righteous indignation. I get where he's coming from, but it doesn't seem quite sincere.

"What do you want?" I repeat.

"Let me tell you a little bit about Annie Fowler. She was born in a small town in Kentucky, where she lived her entire life until she and her infant son were killed by a drunk driver just a few years back. She was a good girl, sweet and pretty. She played by the rules, but still she was mowed down by some asshole with no respect for anyone or anything. That's what I'm talking about. That's what kills me, you know?"

I notice something about him that I hadn't before. Over his right ear, there's a shock of white hair about an inch thick. It's so striking, the light of it against the rest of his brown locks, that I can't believe I didn't see it earlier. Somehow it makes him seem more menacing; I am oddly unnerved by it.

"And then," he continues, "she's violated again— by yet another person with no regard for the living or the dead. Someone steals her identity. Someone trying to escape the past takes her Social Security number and uses it to start over. What was this person trying to escape? I wonder. Or who? Must be pretty bad, whatever it was."

"You're making a mistake," I tell him. "I have no idea what you're talking about."

He takes a pair of sunglasses from the pocket of his shirt and puts them on.

"Mrs. Powers," he says with that same fake smile; it's starting to look as though it will split his face in half. "Can I call you Annie? Annie, you're looking a little pale. I won't keep you. I'm sure you want to get back to your family."

He turns and starts to walk away. Then he stops and comes back. I can tell he's played this scene out in his mind a hundred times, rehearsed it for maximum effect.

"You know, Annie, we all have our secret lives, the parts of ourselves we'd rather not share. I understand that. I truly do. The question is, how much are those secrets worth? How much are we willing to pay to keep them buried? I'll let you think about it."

He leaves me standing there, watching him walk off. He doesn't look back, just gets into his Explorer parked nearby and slowly drives away.

When a ship gets lost at sea, it might never be found. If its engine dies and it goes adrift, it could move through the vastness of the ocean and never come to shore, never be seen by another craft or from the air. Even if you hire the kind of people who are able to recover a runaway vessel, even if you have an idea of when it was lost, along with an understanding of the day's tides and currents—even then you might never find it. Most people can't wrap their heads around the idea that the oceans of the world are so vast and that something so solid could be so permanently lost yet still out there, still floating around, just never to be seen again by human eyes. But that's how large the world is. Things disappear and are never found simply because there's too much ground to cover. People, too.

The idea of shifting off your skin and walking away in a new one is foreign to most people, the stuff of fiction. But it can be done with relative ease. A driver's license, passport, even a Social Security card—all can be obtained with a birth certificate. Birth certificates can be had just by filling out a form and paying a fee at any local records office. You can use this document to get pretty much anything else you need to establish a new identity. Then it's just a matter of flying below the radar. It's better not to work or get pulled over for speeding. And if you're far enough away from people who have known you, you can drift about in the world and never be found again, just like a ship lost at sea. The world is that big.

Ophelia March died on a dry, cool New Mexico night. In a stolen black '67 Mustang, she and Marlowe Geary drove off the edge of the Taos High Road into the Rio Grande Valley below. She was presumed dead, though her body was not recovered. Or so the official reports go.

But Ophelia wasn't in that Mustang. She was handcuffed and drugged in the back of a black Suburban parked off the public square in Santa Fe, in the shadow of St. Francis Cathedral. About two hours after the Mustang burst into flames on impact, a man, beaten and dirty and smelling like smoke, got into the driver's seat of the Suburban and took her away. Ophelia March was dead. Annie Fowler had just been reborn.

I am thinking of that night as I stand in the parking lot of the mall, my shopping bags at my feet. I'm sick with fear. But is there also the glimmer of relief in my heart? Am I also a little glad that Ophelia still lives, and that one way or another she might have to pay for the things she has done? There are plenty of people who believe that Ophelia was Marlowe's victim, his captive toward the end. But I know it was more complicated than that. I feel those black fingers tugging at me. I am as afraid of Ophelia as I am of Marlowe.

The only thing I like about Gray's office is that it's filled with books. Big, thick books bound in leather, with gilt-edged pages, texts on war and military theory, encyclopedic tomes on world history, classic literature, poetry. But it's not a library collected after a lifetime of reading. It is a library that has been purchased for show—Drew's idea of which books should line the shelves of a military man's office. He has a similar collection in his own office. Most of the books have never even been opened, eyes have never rested on their words, fingers have never caressed their pages. They are as untouched and virginal as nuns.

I scan the covers: Sun-tzu, Machiavelli, Tolstoy, Shakespeare, Byron, Shelley. Anyone sitting in my husband's office would think him a great reader. He's not. My husband opens a book, he falls asleep.

Curled on the leather couch, I recount my meeting with Detective Harrison for Gray. His face is a knot of concern.

"He doesn't know anything," he says after I'm done. "If he did, he'd have used your name."

"He knows I'm not Annie Fowler."

Gray nods his assent. "But his interest is not legal. He didn't come to you as a cop. He didn't bring you in for questioning. He's corrupt. And that's a good thing. We pay him off, he goes away."

Gray's sitting behind his desk, capping and uncapping a pen, swiveling his chair slightly from side to side. I don't say anything. I don't think it's going to be that simple.

"Anyway," he says, "there's no connection whatsoever between Annie Fowler and Ophelia March. Nothing links them. He could dig into Annie Fowler until her bones shake in the ground and he's not going to find Ophelia."

I wonder whom he's trying to convince.

"So it's a coincidence, then, that there's someone looking for Ophelia in New York and this cop down in Florida is asking questions about Annie Fowler. That someone followed me on the beach."

I can't read his expression. He's the one who doesn't believe in coincidence.

"I don't see a connection," he says finally. I wonder if he's just in denial, stubbornly refusing to see what's right in front us. It's not like him. "I really don't see one."

But there's always a connection, isn't there? Sometimes it's just deep beneath the surface, like Florida's network of caves, dark and echoing, winding silent and treacherous under our feet.

I came home after school one afternoon and found my mother weeping in her bedroom. I stood in her doorway, watching. We were downwind from the stable that day, so the air held just the lightest scent of horse manure. She looked so tiny lying there, so frail on the white sheets beneath the large wooden cross hanging over the bed. The room was spare and plain, like all the rooms in the house. There was just the bed on a frame, two nightstands, and a dresser, all made from pine.

"We use what we need." That was Frank's mantra. He didn't like any flourish, any decoration. "That's the Lord's way."

I was glad to see she was living with as much despair as I was. It wasn't that I wanted her to be unhappy. I was just relieved to see she felt anything at all. She'd been acting like a zombie for the eight weeks we'd been there, steadily losing weight. Every day she seemed a little weaker, had less color in her cheeks. It was as if Frank were slowly draining the life from her and one day she'd collapse into a pile of ash before my eyes.

I could smell alcohol, mingling with the horse odor. I watched her until she sensed me standing there. She sat up with a start.

"Oh, Ophelia. You scared the life out of me."

Frank's truck hadn't been in the drive, so I knew he wasn't home. I went over and sat beside her on the bed. She pulled me to her. She wrapped her arms around me from behind, and we lay as we used to when I was a child, before I knew how many different ways a person could fail as a mother.

"What's wrong, Mom?" I asked. "Why are you crying?"

She didn't answer right away. Then, "Ophelia,

he's so . . . *so cold.* I think I've made an awful mistake bringing us here."

I sat up quickly and turned to face her. "Then let's go."

She rolled her eyes and pulled her mouth into an annoyed grimace. "Go *where,* Ophelia?"

"Anywhere."

She sat up and wrapped her arms around her knees. "He can't *be* with me, you know?"

"Mom," I said, feeling my face go hot with anger and embarrassment. I didn't want to hear about her sexual problems with Frank Geary. I just wanted her unhappiness to spur her into action. But she was like a cow in the road; no matter how undesirable or dangerous her location, she'd stay rooted until someone came at her with a stick. I knew this about her.

"He can't . . . you know, *perform,*" she went on, as if she were thinking aloud, as if I weren't even in the room. "There's something wrong with him. Something really, really wrong."

"Let's leave, Mom," I said again, grabbing her hands. "We can go back to New York."

She released a heavy sigh. "We don't have a car, any money. How are we going to leave?"

I just stared at her.

"*How* can we leave, Ophelia?" she asked again. I realized that it wasn't a rhetorical question; she was really asking *me* how to leave. She wanted *me* to save her. I hated her then, for her weakness, for her stupidity. I'd hated that she'd handed all her power over to Frank Geary and that we were trapped on a horse farm in the middle of nowhere, with no money and no means of leaving if we chose. I hated my father for disappearing and leaving me to this fate. I felt the rage rise up in my chest, and I made a silent promise to myself never to be powerless like my mother.

"Ophelia," she said, covering her eyes. "Don't look at me like that."

I left her without another word. She called after me, but then I heard Frank's truck pulling up the drive. A moment later the water was running in the bathroom, and I knew she was brushing her teeth so he wouldn't smell the booze on her. She'd probably taken the whiskey from Frank's secret stash I saw in the barn. There were always two or three bottles of Jack in a crate near the back under a pile of flannel blankets. Twice I'd found Frank passed out in the barn, a bottle nearly drained, cigarette butts in an ashtray beside him. Dangerous behavior in a barn filled with hay.

Later that night I found Marlowe sitting on the floor of the stable smoking a cigarette. We hadn't spoken since that night in my room when he'd suggested unthinkable things to me. Instead we'd been circling each other ever since. I was simultaneously drawn to him and repelled by what he'd whispered to me that night. His eighteenth birthday was just a week away, and then he'd be gone. I'd be all alone here.

I sat down beside him, and he offered me a drag, which I took.

"He met someone today," he said as I exhaled smoke. "A woman at the feed store. It won't be long."

I took in the lean lines of him, the hair in front of his eyes, his arm draped over one bent knee.

"He started chatting her up, flirting with her in that way he has," he said when I didn't respond.

I had a hard time imagining Frank "flirting" with anyone. He was as gray and stiff as an old piece of wood. The air was still and thick with humidity. I felt a sheen of perspiration rise on my forehead, a bead drip down my back.

"It's like an appetite. It rises up in him. He can't control it."

He had an odd half smile on his face as he stubbed out the cigarette, started fingering the butt, rolling it between his thumb and forefinger so that tiny brown pieces of tobacco left there drifted onto his leg. The smell of burned tar settled in my sinuses.

"He'll start out slow at first, but then it will escalate. Before long it'll be your mother."

An anxious dread moved through me, made my fingers and the back of my neck tingle. I stared out through the open doors of the barn. I could see the house from where I sat. A light glowed in my mother's window.

"No," I said, but it was more like a prayer than a denial. Even though I'd never seen a hint of violence in Frank, I thought I could feel the truth in what Marlowe said. It wouldn't be long before terrible things started happening; it seemed electric in the air.

"After her it will be you." He'd dropped his voice to a whisper, peered at me through the strands of hair that hung in front of his eyes.

I pulled my legs in tight to my chest and held them there.

"Why do you think he keeps your mother so isolated? He doesn't even let her go to the grocery store," Marlowe asked. "No one here even knows she exists."

If he noticed that I'd only said one word since I joined him, it didn't seem to bother him. I traced circles in the dirt on the ground.

"When you're missed at school, it'll be weeks before they send someone to look for you," he went on. "Then he'll tell them your mother left him, took you with her. He'll tell them he doesn't know where you've gone."

"My father will come looking for me," I said lamely.

"Eventually," he said with a shrug. "Maybe. But what good will it do you? You'll already be dead."

One of the things I liked about the horse ranch was the sky at night. I never knew there were so many stars. I gazed up at them through the open door and wished I were as high and far away as that.

"Do you see how he was manipulating you?" the doctor asks. "How he used your fear, your alienation from your parents to spin a web around you?"

I nodded, chewed on my fingernails, something I did in our sessions only when we talked about the past.

"You were seventeen years old. Literally abandoned by your father, emotionally abandoned by your mother, living with a man you believed to be a serial rapist and murderer who was about to start killing again—who might even kill you. You were afraid and very vulnerable."

I nodded grudgingly. Ophelia *was* afraid, but she was also desperate, starving for love and acceptance.

"What could you have done at that point that you didn't do?" he wants to know.

We do this, go round and round, rehashing the past. Thinking of alternatives for Ophelia and shooting them down like bottles on a shelf. The doctor thinks I'm too hard on her. He thinks she was just a kid. But he doesn't know the whole story—and neither do I, for that matter. I wonder if I'm not hard enough.

"I could have gone to the police."

He gives a slow, careful nod. "Your stepfather was an innocent man in the eyes of the law. You had no evidence that he'd done anything wrong or planned to. What do you think the police could have done for you?"

I look at anything else but him—the degrees hanging on his wall, the view outside his window, the glass paperweight on his desk, its facets taking in light and casting rainbow points on the wall. "I'm not sure."

He sighs and shifts in his seat. Behind him, outside his window, the sun is setting in a riot of color—purple, orange, pink—over the Intracoastal Waterway.

"So what did you do?"

"I don't remember."

He lifts his chin up, puts his hand to his face, and

starts rubbing at his jaw. The stubble there and the dry, hard skin on his hands makes an irritating scratching sound. He regards me carefully, seems to think twice before deciding to say, "You're not being honest with me, Annie."

"I don't remember," I say quickly. "You know that."

"I'm starting to get the feeling that there's a great deal you're not sharing with me. I'm afraid it's affecting how much good I can do."

I give a slow shake of my head and purse my lips. There's a moment—no, a millisecond—when I think maybe, just maybe, I'll come clean, tell him everything. But the moment passes in silence.

He looks at his watch and stands up. This means our session is over. "I can't help you if you won't face the truth. Okay?"

"Okay," I say, getting up and walking to the door. I think we're coming to the end of our relationship. He doesn't know Ophelia; he doesn't even know her name. I have kept that from him. I wonder if he thinks I'm making the whole thing up, if he's just humoring me and taking my money.

"See you next week?"

"Yes. Next week," I say with a nod. I stop at the door, turn to look at him. He's a nice man and a good doctor. I know he has tried his best to help me. "Did I tell you I'm considering scuba-diving lessons?"

"I thought you were afraid of the water," he says with a surprised smile.

"You're the one who's always on me about facing down my fears. I thought this might be a good first step."

"Is it helping?"

"It's too soon to tell."

"Take care of yourself, Annie," he says. This is what he says after every session, but I wonder if I detect an extra bit of concern, a final note of farewell.

The corridor outside the doctor's office is empty, and I wait in the silence for the elevator. I listen to the electronic beep as the elevator passes each floor on its way to me. I never see anyone in this corridor; no one ever comes and goes from the other office suites. It has never seemed odd before, but today it does. The quiet is total, as though there is no one else behind the other doors.

Maybe I never noticed before because I am always lost in thought when I leave the doctor, but this time I feel a strange unease as I wait for the eleva-tor that seems to take forever. It has paused two floors down and not continued its ascent. I wait for a minute longer, then decide to take the stairs, but when I try the door to the staircase, it's locked. I guess I don't have any choice but to wait for the sluggish elevator.

I hear something then, I'm not sure what. It might have been a shout or something falling to the floor. Then there are voices lifted in argument, just a few words, and then it is silent so suddenly again that I'm not sure that's what I heard at all. It's then that I find myself walking back down the hall toward the doctor's office.

Of course the elevator picks this moment to arrive. I listen to the doors open and close as I enter the waiting room and knock lightly on the door to the doctor's office. There's no answer, but I'm certain he's there—I don't think there's another exit. I wonder if he's in the bathroom. I put my ear to the door, wait a second, but I don't hear voices inside. I knock again. As I do, the door pushes open slightly, and I help it along.

"Doctor," I say, "is everything all right?"

It takes a beat for the scene to register in my head. The doctor is slumped over his desk, blood pooling on its surface and dripping over the side onto the floor beneath. On the window I can see a high ghastly arc of blood against the sunset.

"Doctor," I say as I move toward him. My voice sounds like it's coming from the end of a long tunnel. "Paul?"

I approach the body, battling the urge to run in the other direction. I put my hand on his neck. But there's no pulse. His skin is still warm, but he is dead.

I try to draw a breath into my lungs, but panic is constricting my airways. My flight response is in high gear; it's all I can do not to break into a sprint. Then I notice that the door to the bathroom is ajar; the light is on inside. I think I see a flicker of movement, but I'm not certain.

My brain has stopped working; adrenaline kicking, my body takes over. I move toward the exit, keeping my eyes on the thin rectangle of light shining through the opening in the bathroom door. I am not thinking about the poor doctor and the awful way he has died or about who might still be hiding in the bathroom. I am just thinking about getting out of here as fast as possible. I can't help the doctor, and I can't afford another run-in with the police.

I start moving backward, my eyes still on the bathroom door. As I do, it starts to open. I find myself paralyzed; I can't move. I stand and watch it swing wide. She is pale and grim, the young woman I have seen at Ella's party and standing outside the

Internet café. She is soaked in blood. There's a knife in her hand. Her chest is heaving with the deep, shuttering breaths she is drawing and releasing. We stare at each other for a moment. And then I recognize her. It's Ophelia.

23

It's nearly dark when I wake up in my car in the parking lot of my doctor's office. The sun has disappeared below the horizon line, and the sky is glowing a deep blue-black. My peripheral vision is almost gone from the migraine I have coming on. I am struggling to orient myself, to separate reality from fantasy. I see her face again, her blood-drenched clothes. I see my doctor slumped over his desk, blood draining from him onto the floor.

I don't feel the appropriate level of terror, I'm just stunned, numb. I look at my watch; it has been only forty minutes since my session with the doctor ended, which seems impossible given what's happened. There's a large bloodstain, still wet but drying quickly, on my jacket. I shrug out of it, crumble it into a ball. I don't want to look at the blood. Then my cell phone, balancing on the dash, starts ringing. I answer.

"Hi, Annie."

I already recognize the voice—it's Detective Harrison. I don't say anything.

"Just wondering if you've had any time to think things over."

"Why are you doing this to me?" I ask him. My voice sounds hysterical, even to my own ears. I am shaking as I put the key in the ignition and start the car. "Did you do this?"

There's a pause on the other end, as if he's registering the pitch and tone of my words.

"Annie, what's wrong?" he asks me. He sounds legitimately concerned. "Where are you?"

"Why are you doing this?" I say again. It must be Harrison. He has done this somehow. He knows about me and is trying to drive me insane. "For *money?* You can have whatever you want."

"Take it easy," he says. His tone is calm and soothing; he must be used to talking to hysterical people. "What's going on?"

There's something in his voice that reminds me why I liked him that first night. Even though he's trying to destroy my life, it's almost as though he would put that on hold to be a cop for me in this moment. I'm half considering telling him about the doctor, but since I'm not a hundred percent sure that he's dead and that it wasn't me who killed him, I decide against it. I'd be admitting that I'm either mentally ill or a murderer, probably both.

"What happened, Annie?" he says, more firmly this time.

But his voice sounds tinny and distant. I end the call and throw the phone on the seat beside me. I drive out of the parking lot, heading for home.

The small causeway that leads to our island is not heavily trafficked in the evening. I pull over and grab the jacket from the passenger seat, race to the railing, and toss it over. I watch for a moment as it drifts into the water, then quickly get back to the car and start driving again, too fast. The sight of a cruiser hiding in a speed trap encourages me to slow down, to take the rest of the drive at the speed limit.

I wave at the guard as I pull through the gateway to our neighborhood. Lights glow in windows, televisions flicker, and there are a couple of kids still playing in the street even though it's fully dark now. Everything is so quiet, so normal. I do not belong here. I realize more than ever that I never have.

I park the car in the drive and walk, though I want to run, into the house. As I shut the door, I hear Gray in the kitchen making dinner.

"You're late," he calls with a smile in his voice when he hears me enter.

There are candles lit on the table and lobsters in

a huge pot on the stove. When he turns to look at me, his smile fades, he goes a little pale. My legs buckle when he reaches me, and I sink into him.

"What happened?" he asks. His frightened expression tells me how bad I look. "What the hell happened?"

I awoke in the middle of the night with a start to the sound of the horses. They were restless in their stalls, agitated and making noise. I'd heard them act like that twice since we'd been there. Once a Florida panther had been spotted the next day on a neighbor's property. The second time we never figured why they'd been anxious. I slipped from beneath the covers of my bed and walked over to the window. The doors to the barn stood open. Frank's truck sat idling, the hatch wide, waiting like a mouth. A full yellow moon cast a strange glow.

I moved to the side of the window and peered through the curtains. I'm not sure how long I stood there, but finally Frank emerged from the dark interior of the barn. In his arms he carried a large bundle wrapped in horse blankets. He leaned back against the weight of it and then dropped it awkwardly into the truck. He closed the hatch quietly, glancing up at the windows of the house. He looked stricken, like a man grieving a terrible loss. Then he got into the driver's seat of the truck and rolled out of sight.

I stood rooted, my whole body shaking. I thought of all the things Marlowe had told me. Part of me hadn't really believed him . . . the collection of purses, the shoe under the porch, his recent dire predictions that Frank's "appetites" couldn't be kept at bay much longer.

I saw Marlowe leave the barn then, a garbage bag in his hand. He pulled the doors closed behind him and locked them with the key. As he did this, he turned and looked up at my window. Maybe he could sense my eyes on him. I was certain he couldn't see me where I stood. But something in his face told me that he knew I was there.

I got back into my bed quickly, wrapped myself up in the covers, and closed my eyes. I measured my breathing, made it deep and steady. After a minute I heard Marlowe creaking on the stairs. The floor-boards outside my door groaned beneath his weight, and I heard the knob on my door start to turn. I tried to control the quaking of my body, to fight the urge to scream as I heard the door open just a little. The seconds dragged on as I waited to hear him come in or to speak my name. But he didn't. After a moment I heard him walk away and go back down the stairs.

When I thought it was safe, I raced to my

mother's room. I was sure I'd see an empty bed. But when I burst through her door, she was sleeping soundly, undisturbed by the events that had just transpired. I thought of waking her, telling her what I'd seen, but I didn't. I just went back to my bed, lay there wide-eyed and listening to the night. Frank didn't return until just before dawn.

24

It is several hours later when Gray and I return to the doctor's office. I have told him everything that's happened. We've gone over and over every detail a thousand times. He has made me shower, and while I stood with the scalding water beating down on my skin, scrubbing myself so hard that my skin turned raw and red, Gray disposed of my clothes. I'm not even sure why; it makes me wonder if he thinks I may have actually killed my doctor. I haven't asked him if this is what he thinks.

We pull in to the lot, which is empty now. I expected to see a swarm of police vehicles and ambulances, some news vans. I expected to see Detective Harrison waiting for me. Instead there's only a sea of blacktop edged by the Intracoastal. The tall street-lamps cast an eerie amber glow as Gray stops the car. My stomach is churning. There are still some lights burning in the windows of the office building. A night guard sits at the reception desk reading a paperback.

"Wait here," Gray says, putting a hand on my leg.

"No," I say, unbuckling my seat belt. "I'm coming."

He doesn't argue, waits as I get out of the car and then drops his arm around me as I come to stand beside him. We walk toward the building. I'm keeping my migraine at bay with the medicine I've taken, but it's waiting for me like a predator in the brush.

"It's okay," he tells me.

The old bulldog of a guard looks at us with sullen boredom over the edge of his novel. He has dull eyes and a thin mouth that disappears into the flesh of his face.

"I had a doctor's appointment earlier," I tell him. "I left my cell phone."

"It'll have to wait till tomorrow," he says. "The building's closed."

"It's important," I tell him.

"Sorry."

A hundred-dollar bill from Gray changes his mind. From the looks of him, I think he would have done it for fifty. He gives us a disinterested nod and heaves his body out of the chair, which groans its relief. He slides an enormous ring of keys off the desktop, and we take the elevator up to the seventh floor.

"Was this elevator broken earlier?" I ask.

He shrugs. "Not that I'm aware."

I am sweating, becoming more and more tense as the elevator climbs. Gray is armed, his hand tucked beneath his jacket, resting on the butt of his gun. He is at his best, cool and in control. When we arrive, the hallway is dark, lit only by fire-exit lights.

I walk us toward the doctor's door, which is shut and locked. Something's off; I'm not certain yet what it is. The guard seems oblivious to our tension.

"Are you sure this is it?" he asks as he unlocks the door and swings it open. That's when I realize that the nameplate on the doctor's door is gone. The waiting room is empty. No chairs, no silk plants, no magazine racks. We walk through to the office. It's vacant. The desk, the bookshelves, the Murano glass vase on the table by the window, the cheap, uncomfortable furniture—all gone. Gray walks the perimeter of the room, runs his finger over the windowsill. His eyes scan the empty space. I see his brow wrinkle into a frown, then his eyes come to rest on me.

I walk to the bathroom door and push it open. I'm confronted by my own reflection in the mirror on the far wall. I look haggard, afraid.

"Are we on the seventh floor?" I ask. I look around—even the knobs and lighting fixtures are gone. There's nothing to connect this place to the

office I've been visiting for years. I check at the walls
for shadows where I know photographs and degrees
were hanging, but there are no telltale marks or stray
picture hangers. There is no blood on the window.

"Yes, ma'am," the guard says, casting a suspicious
glance. "I thought maybe you knew something I
didn't. It was my understanding that this floor has
been vacant for months, waiting on renovations.
Some real-estate agency moving in here."

I don't know what to say. I blink back tears of
frustration, put my hand to my forehead so neither
of them can see my face. I am afraid and ashamed in
equal measure.

"You sure you got the right building?" the guard
asks gently.

I nod, not trusting my voice.

"You have a building directory downstairs?" asks
Gray.

"Believe so," the guard says. He looks uncomfortable now, shifting from foot to foot and avoiding
eye contact. I've seen people act like this before. A
kind of mystified embarrassment comes over people
when they encounter someone who might be entirely
off her rocker.

He keeps his distance as we walk down the hallway and get into the elevator. My mind is racing
through options: wrong floor, wrong office, wrong

building. The doctor's dead; someone hid his body and cleaned out his office. Or someone, as Drew so eloquently put it, is fucking with me. I can see from the look on Gray's face that he's running the same catalog of possibilities in his mind. He's holding my hand tightly, as if he thinks I'm going to make a run for it.

At the desk the guard gives Gray the building directory. I notice that the pages on the clipboard are crisp and new. On the list, Dr. Paul Brown, Ph.D., is nowhere to be found.

"This looks like a brand-new directory. When was it printed?" asks Gray.

The guard shrugs. "Does look new," he admits, peering over Gray's shoulder. "Maybe he moved his office. I don't know."

"Do you know him?" I ask. "Dr. Brown?"

He shakes his head. "But I'm just the night guy. Come on after most people have gone home for the day. I don't really know anyone in the building."

The guard is looking at me with pity now. He takes a piece of scrap paper from the drawer, writes down a name and a number.

"Nobody moved anything out of here in the last few hours?" I ask, trying not to sound as desperate and hysterical as I feel. I force my face into a mask of calm. I have learned in moments like this to keep the surface still even though the depths are raging. Animals hide fear and illness; they cannot afford weakness in the wild.

"No, no. Nothing like that tonight," he says, handing me the paper. "This is the daytime building manager. He'd know better about all of this."

Gray thanks him, and we leave. We walk in silence to the car, neither of us knowing what to say. We get inside and just sit for a minute. I examine the dashboard, since there's nowhere else to rest my eyes. I can't bring myself to look at Gray.

"I didn't imagine the doctor—or what happened tonight," I say.

"I know," says Gray a little too quickly. I wonder if he's humoring me. He puts a hand on my leg. When I find the strength to meet his eyes, I see his love for me, his compassion. This causes the tension in my shoulders to relax, my breathing to come easier.

"I saw her," I say, remembering the moment and feeling a shudder move through my body. "I saw Ophelia."

Worry is etched now in all the lines on his face. "You saw *someone*," he says. "In the terror of the moment, your mind played a trick on you."

"I've seen her before, at a cocktail party and on the street. I just didn't recognize her."

He moves his hand from my leg to my arm and squeezes firmly. "What are you saying, Annie? You *are* Ophelia. She's not a separate person from you."

"I know that," I snap. What *am* I saying?

"Then what are you telling me?"

I take in a deep breath. "Nothing. I don't know."

"There was no dust on the windowsill," he says, changing the subject. He doesn't want to talk about Ophelia. He wants to deal with the facts, with the empirical evidence, not ghosts and hallucinations. "If it had been sitting empty for weeks, there would be dust."

"Really?" I say, feeling hope release some of the tightness in my chest. "What does that mean?"

"It could mean that something happened there tonight, and between then and now someone cleaned and took the furniture out." Gray releases a long breath. Does he believe this, or is he just saying it to make me feel better? I don't know, and I don't ask.

Anyway, I do know what he's thinking. He wishes I'd let him meet the doctor. But I never have. I've needed my present happy home life never to mingle with the nightmare of my past. But maybe that was part of my folly, to ever believe that I might separate the parts of myself like that, that I could keep the person I was from poisoning the person I am . . . especially when my present self is a fictional character I have created to escape my own heart, my own past, my own deeds.

You belong to me. But it's not Marlowe's voice I hear this time. It's Ophelia's.

25

They waited on the road rain or shine, blistering heat or lightning storms, with posters featuring pictures of their daughters, sisters, mothers, chanting, "Murderer. Murderer. Murderer." They were careful to stay on the public road. For the most part, they were orderly and nonviolent. Even so, the police could have caused the group, which called itself the Families of Frank Geary's Victims, to disperse—but they didn't. There wasn't much sympathy for Frank among the citizens or law enforcement in our new hometown.

I saw them when I left for school in the morning and usually when I came home. They seemed to work in shifts, the same ten or fifteen people taking turns on the road in front of our property. Twice I saw Janet Parker, appearing shrunken and even more haggard than she had when I first met her at our trailer. Her grief and pain were wasting her; she was slowly disappearing. Every time I saw her, I thought about her daughter floating in the water where Frank had left her.

There was one man, the father of one of Frank's victims, who was so sick with rage that he looked like he'd stuck his finger in a socket every time he laid eyes on Frank. He'd go from this slack, tired-looking man to someone whose whole body was rigid and red with fury. He'd scream and hurl obscenities.

The morning after I'd watched Frank place the unidentified bundle in the trunk of his car, the Angry Man (as I'd come to think of him) tried to throw a rock at us before the others in his group stopped him. He collapsed, wailing, into the arms of a woman.

"These people need to move on," my mother said that morning, annoyed by their grief and suffering. She was driving me to school, and Marlowe was along for the ride. "Frank's not even in the car. Why would he be throwing rocks at us?"

"He wants revenge," said Marlowe from the backseat. We locked eyes in the rearview mirror.

"He wants it from the wrong man," said my mother. If she remembered her confession to me about Frank, about his strangeness, she showed no sign. I hadn't even bothered to tell her what I saw the night before; she wouldn't have believed me, and I didn't want her to tell Frank. Fear was a stone I carried in my chest, so heavy I could barely stand upright. I thought of her in her used wedding dress, how she'd pranced about like Cinderella at the ball, thinking no one could see the frayed edges or the cigarette burn in the lace. The story of her life.

At school that day, I just sort of drifted from class to class, not participating, not hearing anything that was said to me. I had the feeling that I'd stepped out of normal life, that my circumstances so separated me from everyone around me that I could no longer communicate in this world. I wonder if this is when I started "dissociating," as they say. Nothing seemed real to me, everything took on a kind of foggy quality. The change in me must have been apparent. People who had harassed and taunted me because of Frank were suddenly giving me a wide berth. My social-studies teacher asked me to stay after class and inquired about my home life. *Is everything okay? I don't know you that well, Ophelia, I admit, but you don't seem like yourself.* He'd placed a call to my mother, he told me, to tell her my grades were in a precipitous drop from my prior school records, but she hadn't called back. *The honors English teacher from your former school wrote to say what a talented writer you were, how remarkably well read you were for someone your age. We've seen no evidence of any of that here, Ophelia. How can we help?* He seemed so sincerely worried that I didn't have the heart to tell him no one at all cared about me or my grades.

That is another of those moments I reflect upon. This teacher was throwing me a lifeline, and if I had grabbed at it, maybe things wouldn't have continued on their deadly trajectory. But I was too far gone by then, too alienated from the world around me to know a way out when I saw it.

As I stepped off the school bus that afternoon, I crossed the street to avoid the protesters. To their credit, they generally left me alone. They must have recognized me as the victim I was, as helplessly cast in this miserable production as they were. They threw alternately pitying and suspicious looks in my direction as I came and went each school day. That day I saw Janet Parker watching me. She held a cup of coffee, raised it slowly to her lips. I glanced away from her, and as I did, I noticed Marlowe standing beside her. It looked like he was whispering something in her ear. I turned away quickly, cast my eyes to the ground, and walked through the gate to make the long trek to our house.

Gray Powers is not a man who is often wrong. With a name like that, it seems almost impossible that he could ever be mistaken about anything. He should be jumping into telephone booths, slipping into super-hero garb, and saving the day—which is actually not that far from what he does. But he was wrong about Detective Ray Harrison. Gray had sized him up as a small-town cop, corrupt and not that bright, looking for a big payday. He's the one who always says that the worst mistake you can make in a fight is to underestimate your opponent. And it's true.

I go through the motions even though my head is reeling from the events of the night before. I put on a big show for Victory, who races toward me when she sees me waiting for her after school. I squeeze her hard and hold on until she squirms and giggles, and says, "Mommy, you're squishing me!"

In the car she regales me with stories of princesses and castles, giant cartoon characters, end-less junk food, and the big bed in her room at Drew and Vivian's suite. As I listen, I push back images of Simon Briggs, the dark shadow on the beach, my slain psychiatrist. I want to be present for my daughter's joy. But I can't. I'm sure she senses it, as her enthusiasm wanes and her tale peters out.

Probably about the same time I was driving Victory back home, Detective Harrison was making connections Gray didn't think he'd be able to make. There *was* something to link Annie Fowler and

Ophelia March. It should have been obvious, since it was Gray. The articles I searched online to ease myself out of the black patches were among the same ones that Detective Harrison found when he researched Gray Powers. Of course there was the slew of articles about Gray's military career as a decorated Navy SEAL, the articles about Powers and Powers and the rise of privatized military companies. After scrolling though page after page, Detective Harrison found an old item, an article from the *Albuquerque Journal.* The headline read: INVESTIGATOR HUNTS, KILLS CRIME-SPREE KILLER MARLOWE GEARY: *Ophelia March, believed to be Geary's captive or his accomplice, also killed.* He might otherwise have glanced over the article except for the picture of Ophelia, which he quickly recognized. It was all there for him to see, my ugly past.

Maybe it's the disappearance (death? murder?) of my (imaginary?) shrink or the fact that I can feel Harrison's breath on my neck. Or maybe it's as my doctor believed, that I'm stronger than I've ever been, that I'm ready to face the things I have packed away. Whatever the reason, the flashes of memory I've had, the dreamlike images, begin to coalesce. The blanks start to fill in.

It's not as dramatic as I believed it would be, this return of my past. I envisioned being bowled over by it, taking to my bed, feeling helpless to do anything as the memories trampled me like runaway horses. But it is more like watching the rerun of a black-and-white horror film I saw as a child. The images are familiar, but too grainy and drained of power to be truly frightening.

After I put Victory to bed her first night back home, I start to remember. I tuck her beneath her sky blue sheets and sit with her as she drifts off, watching the delicate rise and fall of her chest. As I get up quietly and slip from her room, she says sleepily, "I want my baby." I find Claude on the floor and put him beside her, but she is already sound asleep again. As I leave the room, I hear Janet Parker's voice and there's a terrible ringing in my ears. Once I'm back in my bedroom, I'm swept away, traveling back to a place I haven't visited in a lifetime.

I watched Marlowe leave the house that night. He had his headphones on, and he walked out the front door and disappeared into the trees. As usual, Frank was gone and my mother was in a stupor in front of the television. *Don't you wonder where Frank goes at night?* Marlowe had asked. *He's hunting.* I easily slipped out after him. In the dark, I saw his form move quickly through the woods, and I followed. I could smell the acrid scent of his cigarette smoke hanging in the air.

He walked for so long and he was so fast that I didn't think I'd be able to keep up. By the time he came to a stop, I was breathless and sweating. My legs had been lashed by the overgrowth. The mosquitoes were in a feeding frenzy at my ankles and my neck.

He came to a creek that ran through the property and waded across. Through the trees I could see a trailer, a rusted-out old thing up on concrete blocks, not much smaller than the one I'd lived in with my mother. He opened the door and went inside. I saw a light come on. I stood in the darkness, waiting, not sure whether to follow or to go back home. As I was about to walk over to the trailer, he emerged again. He came back to the creek and squatted there, looked into the water as though gazing at his own reflection. I approached him.

At first I thought he was laughing, laughing at me for following him. It was only as I drew closer that I realized he was crying. His whole body was shivering with it. I didn't know what to do. I stood and watched him for I don't know how long, listening to the sound of his weeping, an owl calling up above us, tree frogs singing all around.

"Marlowe," I said finally, softly.

He didn't jump at the sound of my voice, and I assumed he couldn't hear me, that he had the Cure or the Smiths blasting in his ears.

"We have to get out of here," he said, his voice a choked whisper. "It's started again. You saw. I know you did."

I had the strong urge to turn and run from him, even though I'd followed him out there. Or was I just a fish on a line, he the fisherman reeling me in—too foolish, too naïve to feel the hook in my cheek?

"You helped him," I said. His back was still to me. "Who was it?"

He stood and spun around then, came and grabbed me by the shoulders. "Does it fucking matter who it was?" he hissed. "Do you understand now?"

I saw him then, saw what he was. This is why I can't forgive Ophelia. She knew.

"I'm ready," I told him. And his face changed again. It was as white as the thin slice of moon.

"Are you sure?"

"Yes." And I was.

He brought me into the trailer. There was a kitchen and a small bedroom. A bathroom that didn't work, of course. No electricity or running water. The lights were all battery-operated. I recognized the bedding, the pots and dishes from our old trailer. The table was piled high with Marlowe's books and note-books.

"What is this place?"

"I found it walking one night when we first came. Abandoned, gone to shit. I've been fixing it up, staying out here sometimes. You could live out here, you know. If you have provisions, you could live out here forever. He doesn't know about it. No one does."

He took me by the hand and led me to the bed, turning out the little plastic lights as we went. In the darkness we lay close. I couldn't see his face anymore. I was grateful that the darkness was so total. I could only hear the sound of his voice, feel the warmth of his body next to mine. We talked about what we would do. It didn't seem real. It was all a dream.

When I come back to myself sitting on the edge of my bed, my daughter sleeping down the hall, an hour has passed. I feel shaken and weak. I'm not sure I want to remember the things I have forgotten. But I know that the memories will come now, unbidden, the dead rising.

26

In music a fugue is a movement in which different voices combine to state or develop a single theme. These voices mingle and weave together, each tone complementing the other, creating a multilayered but unified part of the composition. In psychology the term refers to a dissociative state characterized by a sudden departure from one's life, bouts of amnesia or confusion regarding one's identity, significant distress, generally the result of a major emotional or physical trauma. I have no musical ability whatsoever, but I'm painfully familiar with fugue. Or so I'm told.

Yet this is not a fugue, this most recent flight from my life. For the first time maybe, I am sure of who I am and what I must do. This has been a purposeful escape to protect my daughter from mistakes that I have made, to protect her from the woman I have been. If I can't do that, then she's better off without me.

The boat is pitching horribly now, and I cling to

the rail on the wall as I make my way back to my cabin. The wind is wailing, and I think of Dax on his little boat and wonder how he is faring in the big waters and if he'll survive, if he'll come back for me. My stomach is in full mutiny, and I hold back vomit as I move through the door, pull it closed behind me, and resume my crouch in the small triangle of space that will be created when the door swings open. I listen to the wind and the churning water.

It isn't long before I hear the thrum of a powerful boat engine, then footfalls on the deck above me. I take the gun from my waist and am comforted by its heft. I am aware of a tremendous sense of relief, something akin to the euphoria that sweeps over me when a migraine has passed, the wonderful lightness that follows the cessation of pain. It feels good to be Ophelia again, to face the things that Annie never could. My memories have come back to me; I remember it all. I am not proud, but I am whole, at last.

It was Gray who gave me the name Annie Fowler. It was someone from his company who created the documents I needed—driver's license, passport, Social Security card—to move about the world as someone else. But I made Annie what Ophelia always wanted to be—a wife and mother with a big house and a beautiful child, a husband who cherished her—someone totally different from who her mother had been. Annie had a past unmarred by shame and regret; she was not haunted by the things she had done or the things that had been done to her. I became Annie—rich and pampered, dependent on Gray for strength, dependent on Victory for a feeling of purpose. Like everyone else in her life, I abandoned Ophelia, left her to die in a fiery blaze.

As the heavy footfalls draw closer, I am grateful that Ophelia has returned. She is so many things that Annie was not. She is temperamental where Annie was cool. She is angry where Annie was numb. And unlike Annie, the loving wife and doting mother, princess of suburbia, Ophelia March is a stone-cold killer.

They're kicking open doors now; there's more than one man on this boat, and they're searching the cabins one by one. I don't know how many men or how many cabins they have to go before they get to mine. But I'm ready.

When they kick my door open and enter the room, I wait for the door to swing back before opening fire. There are two men, both wearing black paramilitary gear—mask, vests, boots. I get one of them in the shoulder, and he issues a terrible scream. The other one takes a round in the vest and is knocked back hard against the wall with a groan. I break from the room but am surprised in the hallway by two more men. They disarm me quickly and bind my arms, slip a heavy hood over my head. It happens so fast I'm in darkness before I even know what hit me. I hear a dull thud, then see a flash of white. Before I lose consciousness, I have enough time to wonder if there's more to what is happening here than I have imagined. I see my daughter's face, then nothing.

It's not terribly hard to take a life. Or anyway, not as hard as you'd imagine. There are those who would tell you I was not in my right mind, that I had dissociated from reality, from myself, on the night I made this discovery. But I'm not so sure. In my memories I am quite willing. Of course, all I did was leave the gate open. But that was enough, wasn't it?

I don't remember feeling anything, less than a week later after the night out in the woods, as I walked the drive on the horse farm to open that gate. I was basically sleepwalking.

Marlowe told me to wait until the house was quiet, to get to the gate before midnight. I wasn't afraid of the long road or the errand before me. And as I let the gate swing open before I walked back to the stable, where I was supposed to meet Marlowe, I didn't feel any anticipation or excitement or dread—I just felt empty. Even when a black sedan passed me with its lights off, slow and deadly like a shark through dark water, I observed it with detachment.

All the lights in and around the house were off, and a heavy quiet blanketed the night; even my soft footfalls seemed to echo. In the stable the horses were restless in their stalls again. I heard them shuffling, exhaling loud breaths from their nostrils. But Marlowe was nowhere in sight. The black sedan, a Lincoln I recognized as belonging to one of the protesters, was parked to the side of the barn, its engine clicking as it cooled.

Something about that sound brought me into the reality of what we were about to do. I felt as though I'd been startled awake. That's when I noticed a flickering orange glow in the windows that had been dark just moments before. The scent of burning wood began to fill the air. I started running toward the house, my legs feeling impossibly slow and heavy, the house seeming so far away. As I burst through the door, the air was already thick with smoke.

"Mom!" I yelled, grabbing the banister and racing up the stairs. I covered my mouth and nose with my arm, but the smoke was insidious, burning my eyes, clawing at the back of my throat. By the time I got to the top landing, I was coughing and light-headed.

I found my mother alone in her bed, passed out cold, oblivious to the fire raging through the house. I don't know what I thought would happen to her in all this, but I couldn't leave her to die. I shook her but couldn't rouse her. Finally I dragged her until she stumbled from the bed, leaning her full weight on me.

"What's happening?" she muttered.

"There's a fire!" I yelled, struggling to get to the door. "Where's Frank?"

But she didn't seem to hear. "Ophelia," she slurred, "let me sleep."

I dragged her into the hall, where through the smoke I saw two figures on the staircase, one long and lean, the other smaller by far but holding a gun. The taller was Frank, halfway up the stairs, probably headed up to get my mother. Where he'd been, I had no idea. But he'd stopped and turned to face the figure behind him. As I moved closer, I recognized. There was a wild look to Janet Parker, desperate and so, so sad. *She doesn't care what happens to her,* I thought. Her whole body was rigid, as though it took the strength of all her muscles to hold that gun steady.

"You're making a mistake, ma'am," Frank said

soothingly. He had one hand lifted as if to deflect the shot. His eyes fell on us.

The scene seemed to sober my mother a bit. "What's happening?" she said, groggy and confused. "Frank, what's going on?"

"You let my wife and her daughter leave the house," he said to Janet Parker. "They're innocent here."

I heard a crash come from behind us, and the shattering of glass. My mother let go a little scream.

"Let them leave," Frank said again. "They've got nothing to do with any of this."

Janet Parker nodded at us, barely seeing us, and I grabbed my mother's arm, dragged her toward the staircase.

"What are you doing?" my mother yelled as we moved past Frank down the stairs. My mother reached for Frank, and he clasped her to him, then pushed her away.

"Go," he told her.

I saw then that they truly loved each other, and it shocked me. I'd seen them as these sick, damaged people who had formed an insane union. It never occurred to me that they'd actually cared for each other.

"The only peace I had was knowing you'd burn in hell for what you done!" Janet Parker yelled when we reached the bottom of the stairs. These were almost exactly the words she'd said at the trailer park.

"I didn't kill your child, ma'am. I've never killed anyone. I swear it." He sounded so sincere I almost believed him.

"Frank!" my mother shouted as I dragged her out the door and away from the house. I could see the flames coming out of the roof now, and as we watched, my bedroom window blew out, raining glass onto the ground below. I stood staring, disbelieving my own eyes. The house was burning. Where was Marlowe?

My mother broke away from me then and ran. I chased after her, but she moved back through the front door before I could stop her. I heard her screaming, a terrible howl of protest, and I came up behind her just in time to see Frank's chest exploding as Janet Parker shot him dead center. He spun and seemed to pause in midstride, as though he'd decided to walk away from her but changed his mind. Then he fell flat and hard onto the stairs and slid down like a plank.

I looked up at Janet Parker, and for the first time I saw her smile. Then she turned the barrel and stuck the gun into her own mouth and pulled the trigger. I saw an awful spray of red.

My mother was wailing as I pulled her away

from Frank's body, and as we moved through the door, two more windows burst upstairs. She threw herself to the ground outside and wept as the fire raged. I stood beside her staring. The world seemed to lose all its sound, the ground was gone from beneath my feet and I was spinning. Regret and fear cut a valley through me. *What did we do? Oh, my God, what did we do?* The things I'd seen had changed something within me, like one bright red sock in a white wash. Everything in my world was a different color now.

I saw him then, standing beside the barn, just another shadow in the darkness, licked by the orange light of the flames. He might have been laughing, he might have been crying. I don't know—I couldn't see his face. That was the thing about Marlowe, you could *never* see his face. I walked to him as if he'd called me. He'd cast and directed us all; we'd each played our roles for him perfectly. That was his gift.

I got into the passenger side of the Lincoln and watched him climb behind the wheel. He looked at me as he started the ignition, didn't say a word as we started down the long, dark drive. My mother didn't even raise her head from the ground. She never noticed I'd gone.

*   *   *

"Are you okay?" It's Gray standing in our doorway.

I am sitting on the edge of our bed in the dark, staring at the wall as though my memories are playing on a screen there.

"I'm fine," I tell him. "Just tired."

I don't want to share my memories with him; I'm not sure why.

"Look," he says, "we're going to find out what's happening and put an end to it."

"What are you going to do?"

"I'm going to go see Harrison, find out what he wants, and give it to him."

He has come to sit beside me and is holding my hands in his. I'm surprised by what he's saying. It sounds like a desperate move. It's not like him. "Always operate from a position of strength"—that has been his motto as long as I've known him. It sounds to me now as if he's waving a white flag.

"Whoever came to see your father, whoever was on the beach, whatever happened to your psychiatrist—these are unknowns. Maybe you were right, maybe it's all part of the same problem. I don't know. But Harrison is a threat we can deal with. Buy him off, he goes away. Who knows? Maybe everything else goes away, too."

I feel a glimmer of hope, that maybe we just have to write a check and all of this disappears. I can go back to being Annie Powers and Ophelia can slip back into the darkness where she belongs. Maybe it's really that easy.

"Okay," I say.

"I'll be home soon," he says, kissing me softly on the mouth. I reach for him, pull him to me, and hold on tight. He leaves me, and I listen to him on the stairs and then watch as his car pulls from the drive. I get up quickly and grab my keys.

"I'm going to run out for a second," I tell Esperanza as I pass by the family room on my way to the garage. "Gray's gone, too."

"It's late," she says.

"I won't be long," I say. "Victory's sleeping."

I don't hear what she says as I leave. At the end of our street, I just catch a glimpse of Gray's taillights as he makes a left. I'm following him. I don't know why.

27

"He was gone most of the time," Gray said of his father. "And when he was home, he was this brooding presence. Sullen, staring at the television or angry at my mother for something she'd bought or had done to the house while he was gone. I hovered around him, wanting and fearing his attention. Occasionally I'd get these quick pats on the back or we'd try to play catch or build a tree house, something that fathers and sons might do together. But it was never quite right. We always walked away feeling like we'd failed at something indefinable. We just couldn't connect, not really. Not ever."

He used to spend time talking to me like this, even when he thought I might not be able to hear him or that I didn't care. He'd sit in my room at the psychiatric hospital in New Jersey where he'd admitted me as Annie Fowler and talk. I'd stare off into space, not responding. I wasn't exactly catatonic, but

I'd sort of lost my will to exist. I didn't speak, barely ate, just stared at the window in my room watching the leaves fall from the trees, the clouds drift past. I didn't know why he'd talk to me, a stranger, like this. *What does he want from me? Why doesn't he just leave me here?*

"My mother was just so damned sad, *all the time*. She was clinically depressed, I realize now. But then, she was unsupported, didn't even know she needed treatment. She never recovered from the loss of her daughter, my sister who I never knew. I suppose my father never recovered, either. Maybe that's what happens to you when you're born to parents who've lost a child. You just never fit somehow."

He'd talk, sometimes for hours, as though he'd been holding it in all his life, waiting for some silence where he could safely release the words. Maybe, in a way, I was *his* first safe place, someone in no position to judge him for his sins and loss of faith.

"After high school I joined the navy. Everyone was pleased, proud. But I just wanted to get away from them. It seemed like the right thing to do. It was what my father did. I had no idea what I was doing, not really. Maybe I'm more like my mother than my father. I wasn't cut out for the things that lay ahead."

I found myself listening even though, during that time, I hated him. He was six feet of muscles and hard places, scars and dark looks. I found him ugly, too harsh around the eyes and mouth. He smelled strongly of Ivory soap and sometimes alcohol. I couldn't decide whether he was the person who'd rescued me or destroyed me. He'd killed Marlowe, the first person I'd ever loved. He'd saved me from a killer, brought me to this hospital, and stayed with me, came every day with books and magazines, candy and little gifts that sat in an untouched pile in the closet by the bathroom.

He told me how a few years after the First Gulf War he was honorably discharged from the Navy SEALs. He left sick with rage and disillusionment with the military and the government. He was angry at his father for pushing him into a career he was never sure he wanted, angry at himself for not knowing any other way to live. He drifted from New York to Florida, drinking too much, doing some odd private-investigator work here and there.

"I'd done and seen some truly heinous things," he told me. "They didn't seem to have any meaning or purpose. Nothing good ever came from the bad, not that I could see. It was making me sick back then. I didn't know what I was going to do with the

rest of my life, how long I could carry all the baggage
I had."

I cooperated with my admittance to the hospital
and with my name change because I knew I didn't
have any choice. It was that or prison. The truth is,
I didn't have anywhere else to go; I knew that neither of my parents would help me. But more than
that, I was eager to be rid of Ophelia and the things
she'd done—what I could remember, anyway. Gray
and I were alike in that respect, coming to terms with
past deeds that seemed right at the time but under
the glare of reality revealed themselves as dead
wrong.

"When I found you, I thought maybe you were
the one who makes all the wrong things right," he
said one night about a month after I'd been in the
hospital. "I thought, if I can do right by her, maybe it
gives meaning to everything else."

"That's bullshit," I said, finally answering him. I
didn't want to be his penance. I didn't want to be the
one who made things right for him. "That's not the
way life works. There's no balance sheet."

"No?" he said, sitting up in the chair where he'd
been slouching. "Then how do we move on from our
mistakes?"

"We don't get to *move on*," I said, resting my eyes
on him for the first time.

He leaned his head back and gave a mirthless laugh. "So we just languish in regret until we die?"

"Maybe that's what we deserve," I said, turning away from him again.

He let a beat pass. Then, "I hope you're wrong."

Tonight I stay far enough away from Gray's car that he can't see me but close enough not to lose him. This isn't as easy as it sounds. Someone like Gray instinctively knows when he's being tailed. Maybe that's because he's usually doing the tailing. Takes one to know one. And, of course, if he sees my car in the rearview mirror, he'll know right away that it's me. I'm not sure how I'll explain myself, since I have no idea what I'm doing.

He's moving fast, crossing the causeway and pulling on to the highway. He's not stopping at the police station. He's headed into the city, which seems odd. I never thought to ask him how he knows where Harrison lives. He has his methods.

"I was in a bar in the East Village once, a place called Downtown Beirut. You know it?" Gray asked me one night at the hospital. Our relationship had improved by this time, but I didn't answer. I almost never did. I don't think he minded. He knew I was listening.

"A real dump, the biggest dive you ever saw— *what* a shithole. I used to drink there a lot. Just find a corner and pound them back until I could barely get myself home to my apartment on First Avenue. It wasn't every night that I'd get drunk like this, only when I couldn't sleep, when it was all too much with me. My mother passed after I was discharged, a stroke. I blamed my dad. I blamed him for almost everything. Sometimes my anger felt like a physical pain in my chest. You ever felt like that?"

Yes, I'd felt like that, for most of my life, in fact. But I didn't say so. That night he'd brought flowers— daisies, if I remember correctly—and some dough- nuts in a box. They both sat untouched on the table beside me.

"Anyway, I was sitting there one night, well on my way to oblivion, when an old wreck of a guy, an aging biker covered with tats and a mess of long gray hair, pulled up a chair."

I heard him shift in his chair, crack his neck.

"I told him I wasn't looking for company. He told me he wasn't looking for company, either. He was looking for his daughter. A friend we had in common told him I could help."

I turned to look at Gray. He was sitting in the

same chair he'd been sitting in most nights for a month. His feet were up on the windowsill, his head back as if he were talking to the ceiling. He wore jeans and a black sweater, army-issue boots. His jacket, a beat-up old denim thing, was on the foot of my bed. He had a big scar on his neck; his hands were square and looked as hard as boulders.

I think I saw him for the first time that night. Outside my window it was snowing, fat flakes glittering under the streetlamps, tapping at the window like cold fingers. I saw the strong line of his jaw, his full red lips, the snaking muscles of his shoulders and arms. He took his eyes from the ceiling and fixed me in their cool gray stare. I felt a little shock at their lightness; there was something spooky about his gaze.

He knew he had my attention and kept talking. "The old guy said, 'I've failed this girl in every way a father can fail his daughter. I left her for the wolves, you know. If I fail her now, nothing else in my life means much. I got some money if you got some time and need the work. My buddy said you have a talent for finding people who don't want to be found.'"

"My father," I said, incredulous. Gray nodded.

"I had the time and I needed the work," he went on. "He asked me to fix Marlowe Geary and take care of you, whatever that meant."

"He paid you?"

"At first, but after a while we became friends. It became more than a job to me."

"I know. You were looking to atone for your sins."

He shrugged. "That was part of it. Yes."

I see Gray pull off the highway before the downtown exits and into the slums that surround the city. I follow him through a neighborhood where the streetlamps are shot out and bulky forms hover in doorways and huddle on corners. Houses are dark, but the blue light of television screens flickers in windows. I stay back far, about one turn behind, following more on instinct sometimes than on being able to see his car. *Where is he going?* I know for sure Harrison doesn't live here.

The residential neighborhood yields to an industrial area, warehouses with gates drawn, the highway up above us now. I can see he's headed to the underpass. I stop my car and watch through the overgrowth of an empty lot as he, too, comes to a stop. We both sit and wait.

My cell phone rings then. I can see from the caller ID that it's Detective Harrison. I watch the display blinking on the screen and wonder why he'd be calling me if he were meeting Gray. I don't answer. After a minute I hear the beep that tells me he's left a message. Keeping my eyes on Gray's car, which is still idle, hidden partially in the dark, I access my messages.

"More food for thought," Harrison says. "How much do you really know about your husband?"

As I sit in the dark and watch a white unmarked van pull up beside Gray's car, I think, *Good question.*

I was in that hospital for over two months before it was decided, by some criteria to which I was not privy, that I could leave. If the doctors who helped me knew who I really was or had any idea that I was wanted in three states, no one ever let on. It wasn't until much later that I learned I was there by an arrangement Drew had made. A contact of his owned the private hospital.

On the afternoon that Gray took me out of there, I still couldn't remember much of what happened to me. The night Marlowe and I left the ranch was a dark blur, a series of disjointed images. I vaguely remembered going to my father for help. Everything else that came after was a black hole that pulled me apart, molecule by molecule, if I spent too long trying to think about it. The doctors diagnosed me as having experienced a fugue state, for lack of anything better to call it, brought on by the prolonged trauma of my terrible childhood and the event of my stepfather's murder. They told me that I left myself behind that night when I got into that black sedan with Marlowe, that Ophelia ceased to exist and a new girl took her place.

So who am I now? I remember wondering as Gray shouldered the bag filled with the things he bought for me and we walked through the automatic doors into the cold parking lot. *Am I Annie Fowler or Ophelia March or someone else entirely?* Two and a half years of my life were gone.

I got into the black Suburban and wrapped my arms around myself against the cold. I was shivering, from cold, from fear. On the day I left Frank Geary's horse ranch, I was seventeen, nearly eighteen. On the day I left the hospital with Gray, my twenty-first birthday was just three months away.

Gray turned on the heat, and we sat for a while in the car. I was scared. I didn't know who I was or what I was going to do with myself now. But I stayed quiet. I couldn't afford to show any weakness.

"I know a woman, a friend of my father's," he said after a few minutes. "I'm going to take you to her, and she's going to help you pull your life together, okay?"

"Where?"

"Florida."

He was staring straight ahead, not looking at me. I watched a muscle work in his jaw. My body stiffened. I thought he was done with me. He'd saved me, and now he didn't need me to feel better about himself. At some point during our visits, I'd stopped hating him, started seeing him for what he was, the first good man I'd ever known. And now I thought I was losing him.

A few weeks earlier, Gray gave me a letter my father had written. It was to be our last communication for a long time. Ophelia was dead; there would be no phone calls or visits—in other words, not very different from when Ophelia lived. My father wrote how Gray had tracked me and Marlowe for two years, gave over his whole life to looking for me.

"There's a lot of things about that time he'll need to tell you," my father wrote. "But I think along the way he fell in love with you, Opie. Don't hurt him too bad."

Sitting in the car with Gray, I hoped it was true. But I couldn't think of one good reason Gray would love me. I was a mess of a girl with nothing to offer.

"Where are *you* going?" I asked, examining my fingernails, bracing myself for his answer.

"I'm coming with you," he said quickly, looking ahead and gripping the wheel. Then he added softly, "If you want me to."

I felt relief flood through my body. I lifted my eyes to him, and he was looking at me.

"Was that a smile?" he asked with a little laugh.

"Maybe," I said, letting it spread wide across my face. It almost hurt, it had been so long.

"I've never seen you smile before," he said, putting a hand on my cheek. His touch was surprisingly gentle. I put my hand to his, and we sat there like that for a minute. In that moment he was the most beautiful man I'd ever seen.

"What are you going to do down there?" I asked.

"My father has a company that's doing some good in the world. There's a place for me there."

I couldn't hide my surprise. "But you don't really get along, do you?"

He gave a slow, careful nod. I could see he'd given it some thought. "We've had a lot of really hard times—we might always have problems—but we're working on it. He came through for me—for you."

On the radio David Bowie crooned sad and slow with Bing Crosby about the little drummer boy.

"It just seems important now to put all that

anger behind me," he said suddenly. He moved closer to me. "To make a place, a home for you—for us. I mean, look at me, forty's right around the corner, and I don't even own a futon."

He kissed me then, and the warmth, the love of it, moved over me like a salve. It *did* seem important, critical, to make a safe place in the world.

"There's something you need to know, Gray."

"What's that?" he said, pushing the hair away from my eyes.

"I think I'm pregnant."

It should have been a bombshell, but—oddly—the words landed softly on both of us. He held my eyes. I couldn't see what he was feeling. Those gray eyes have never revealed anything he hasn't wanted them to.

Out the window the parking lot was full of dirty cars, covered with salt and snow. I thought he'd hate me then, for loving Marlowe Geary as I had in spite of everything he'd been and everything he'd done to me, for carrying his child.

"I've never been with anyone but him," I said. I hated my voice for cracking then, and the tears that seemed to spring from a well in my middle. I closed my eyes in the silence that followed, shame burning my cheeks. Then I felt his hand on my shoulder. When I turned to him, he leaned in and kissed me again. I reached for him, clung to him. I would have drowned if not for him.

"Let me take care of you," he said. It sounded like a plea, a prayer he was making. I nodded into his shoulder. I didn't have any words. Then he pulled away and started the car. He seemed a little awkward for a second, as if he were uncomfortable with the charge of emotion between us.

"I won't give her up," I said, wrapping my arms around myself. I didn't know the sex of my child, but I hated saying "it."

I saw his body stiffen. "I'd never suggest that. Never," he almost whispered. He turned from the wheel and took my shoulders.

"Listen to me," he said, with so much passion that I released a little sob. "I'm going to take care of you." He'd been so even, so unflappable up to this point, I hardly recognized the man beside me. Maybe he was drowning, too.

"I'm going to make a home for you and for that baby." He looked down at my belly. "Whatever it takes. I'll do whatever it takes."

We drove for two days and finally wound up at Vivian's place on the beach. She and Drew were just dating at the time, so I lived alone with her. Gray took an apartment nearby. He wanted me to have some time to get to know myself, to get to know him.

"We'll date," he said. "Like normal people."

Vivian took me into her house and treated me like her daughter. She cooked for me and stayed up late listening to me talk. She offered me a sort of kindness that no one else ever had. As I got my GED and started taking classes at the local college, my belly grew bigger. Gray and I dated. It was the happiest time of my life.

I suppose some people would have considered ending the pregnancy. But it didn't even cross my mind. I've never once thought of Victory as Marlowe Geary's daughter. She has always been mine and mine alone.

I watch as Gray gets out of the car with a black duffel bag. He puts the bag on the ground and leans against the vehicle. I feel as though I have lost every ounce of moisture in my body. A heavy man emerges from the white van and walks slowly over to Gray. He wears a long black raincoat, which fans behind him in the wind. His head is enormous over wide shoulders. He looks the approximate size of a refrigerator.

They shake hands, briefly. Even in the dark and with the distance, I recognize him. It's Simon Briggs, the man who went to my father looking for Ophelia. They exchange a few words. I see Gray shake his head. I watch Briggs lift his palms. I can tell just from the way he's standing that Gray is not happy. Finally Gray turns the bag over to him. They exchange a few more words. Then Simon Briggs turns and walks back toward his van.

As Briggs reaches for the handle to open the door, I see Gray lift his hand from his pocket and raise a gun. I draw in a hard breath and grip the wheel. With a single, silent shot, Briggs's head explodes in a red cloud and he crumbles to the ground. Gray walks over to the body and fires again, retrieves the duffel bag, and walks calmly back to the car and gets inside. His vehicle rumbles to life, and he drives away with as little hurry as if he's just picked up a carton of milk at the convenience store and is heading home.

I sit there for a minute, allowing what I've just seen to sink into my mind. I run through the possible reasons Gray might have shot Simon Briggs beneath an overpass and can only come up with one that makes sense: Gray had arranged to meet Briggs for a payoff but decided he'd be better off dead than rich. He wouldn't have told me he planned to kill Briggs; he wouldn't have incriminated me that way. I feel something like relief, and yet it doesn't quite take. It's the handshake that keeps me wondering. *How much do you really know about your husband?*

Gray and I were married by the time Victory was born. I think I fell in love with him in the parking lot of the psychiatric hospital when it was clear that he accepted me for everything I was. He knew Ophelia March; he loved her. I knew he would take care of me, that with Gray I'd always be safe. Maybe that's not really love, but it passed for that. His name is on Victory's birth certificate; he's her father in every way that counts. No one—not Drew, not Vivian—knows that Victory is Marlowe Geary's child. We both agreed everyone would be better off never knowing, including Victory. But I'd be lying if I said it didn't feel like a kind of betrayal.

Maybe because of that, there were terrible black patches during the pregnancy where I was consumed by fear that Marlowe had returned for me and for his daughter. I wouldn't take the medication I was supposed to because of the baby, so I was buffeted by my hormones and the rogue chemicals in my brain. There were blackouts and terrible migraines. Once I woke up on a Greyhound bus headed for New York City, with no idea how I'd gotten there. One of my fugue states, as the doctors called them, a sudden flight from my life. *Where was Ophelia going?* I wondered, as I got off the bus in Valdosta, Georgia, and called Gray. *Did she know things Annie Fowler, soon to be Powers, had forgotten?*

After I disembarked from the Greyhound that night, I sat in a diner and waited for Gray to come get me. I was nothing but trouble. I don't know why he loved me. On the way back to Florida in the Suburban, I asked him, "Why do you do this? Why do you always come for me?"

"I do well in crisis mode," he told me. "Besides, I didn't chase you all over the country to let you go now."

It reminded me of all the things my father said I didn't know about the years Gray trailed me and Marlowe. I'd never asked, mainly because I wasn't sure how much I wanted to know. That night, less than a week before our wedding, when I was five months pregnant, suddenly I *needed* to know.

"My father said that he paid you at first, and then you wouldn't accept any more money."

He shrugged. "At a certain point, I wasn't working for him any longer. I was looking for you."

"Why?"

He just stared at the road ahead, and I wondered if he was going to answer me. I'd pieced some things together from newspapers, what I could bear to read.

"I caught up with you for the first time in Amarillo, Texas," he said finally. "There'd been a liquor-store robbery a few miles east of there a day before. The girl working the counter had been tortured and finally killed. I heard about it on the radio, thought it might be Marlowe Geary. That's what he did— tortured, killed, and robbed. He cut a bloody gash across the country, leaving at least nineteen young women dead."

I wanted to tell him that it couldn't be true, though I'd read this much. I don't think I could have witnessed these crimes and done nothing, but the truth was, I didn't know for sure.

"A few weeks earlier, a witness, a stock boy Geary left for dead in the back room, said he saw you. He was badly wounded, unable to help the girl Geary was torturing. All he could do was listen to her screams, thinking he was about to die himself. He said you were virtually catatonic, that you sat in a corner and rocked, gnawing on your cuticles. That Geary led you out when he was done. You went with him like a child."

I covered my face in shame. I hated to think of myself this way, weak and in a killer's thrall, just like my mother.

"Up till then I wasn't sure. Your mother said you went with Geary willingly. But your father said when you came to New York that you weren't right, you weren't the girl he knew. He said it was like you were under some kind of spell. It makes sense, knowing what we know now about your mental state."

"I knew enough to go to my father."

He shrugged. "Even your subconscious was hoping he would save you."

"I was always hoping for that," I said.

"Well, he took his time, but he came through in the end. More or less."

"Less."

"Anyway, in Amarillo, after stopping at every shit motel in the area, I saw a car matching the description of the vehicle Geary was last seen driving. I sat and waited. After a few hours, Geary got into the vehicle and drove off. I should have called the cops right then, or taken him myself, but at that point all I was thinking about was you. I suppose I was obsessed, maybe not thinking clearly anymore."

Gray told me how he found me in the corner of the hotel room, just sitting there rocking. The television was on, and I stared at the screen. My arms were covered with bruises, my lip was split. I was so thin he could see my collarbone straining against the skin, the knobs of my elbows. For a second he wasn't sure I was the girl in the photograph he carried in his pocket.

"I pulled you to your feet and was moving you to the door when Geary returned."

He told me how he and Marlowe fought, tore the room apart.

"Marlowe knocked me unconscious with a lamp by the bed. When I came to, you were long gone. I didn't catch up with you again until nearly a year later in New Mexico."

"You're leaving something out."

"No."

"I can handle it."

He sighed. Then, "You shot me. In the shoulder. Though you were probably aiming to kill me and weren't strong enough to handle the gun."

I thought of the star-shaped scar on his shoulder. I closed my eyes and tried hard to remember shooting him. But there was nothing there.

"I don't remember," I said, looking out the window. I should have felt worse about it, but I couldn't connect at all to the memory. I felt bad that he'd been shot, but I didn't feel guilty. "I'm sorry."

"I know," he said. "It wasn't you."

He put his hand on my leg. And I rested my

hand on his. Three days later we were married on the beach at Vivian's house. I remembered Drew standing on the edge of it all like a gargoyle. Who could blame him? I'd tried to kill his son.

I lose Gray because I sit stunned in my car for too long. I don't know what to do: try to catch up or just go home? I find myself driving back to the underpass where Simon Briggs is facedown on the concrete. In a moment of monumental stupidity, I exit my car and walk over to the body. There's a terrible ringing in my ears as I reach him.

A dark pool of blood is growing from beneath him. His van is still running. And in a flash that feels like a blow to the head, I remember where I've seen him before. I lean against the van. Another bad motel somewhere out west. I had just come out of the shower, was wrapped in one of the tiny, cheap towels. He was sitting on the bed, smoking a big cigar. He was a dirty guy, stains on his clothes, something black under his nails. I saw a bit of wax in his outer ear. I'm sure he smelled, but the stench of his cigar covered it up.

"I've got no problem with you," he said, as if continuing a conversation we'd already been having.

"It's him I need. Help me, I'll give you ten percent and turn my back while you run."

But that's all I remember. The memory fades into nothing. Did I help him? Did I get away from him somehow? I look down at his body now. The stillness of death is unmistakable. My rational mind is screaming for me to get out of there. But something stronger compels me to move toward the cab of the van. Traffic races above me, the tires on asphalt sounding like whispering voices. The driver's side door is wide open. On the passenger seat, a cardboard box of cheap cigars, a purple lighter in the shape of a naked woman's body, an empty can of diet soda, a half-eaten Philly cheese steak. The inside of the vehicle reeks of onions, stale smoke, and body odor. The world will be a cleaner place without Simon Briggs.

Beneath the detritus I see a large, worn manila envelope bulging with its contents. I want it, but I don't want to touch anything in the car. I snake my arm in carefully and grab the edge of the envelope with my fingertips without touching anything else. As I lift it carefully, the garbage littered on top of it falls to the floor of the van.

The envelope is thick and heavy, and I don't pause to peer inside, just move quickly back to my car. I slide the envelope under the passenger seat, start the engine, and get out of there. As I pull back on to the highway to start toward home, I wonder why Gray didn't search the van. He knew that Simon Briggs was looking for me, that Detective Harrison was all over me, but he left everything there for the police to find. It doesn't make any sense.

My cell phone rings. It's Detective Harrison again. This time I answer.

"What do you want, Detective? Is it money? Just tell me what you need to leave me alone and it's yours."

"Yesterday it was money. Today I'm not so sure."

I'm driving too fast. I change lanes carelessly, and the Toyota behind me honks in protest. I lift a hand.

"Cell phones kill," says the detective. "Did you know that you're just as impaired driving while talking on one as you would be if you got behind the wheel drunk?"

I've given up talking. He's one of *those* guys, the ones who won't get to the point until they're ready no matter what you say. He's running an agenda; my presence in the conversation isn't necessary.

"Let's get together," he says then.

"Really," I say, angry now. "You know what? Fuck off, Detective."

"No. *You* fuck off, Ophelia." He leans on the name hard.

My stomach bottoms out. "Have you lost your mind?" I say. "Do you even know who you're talking to? Or are you blackmailing so many people you've lost track?"

He doesn't even play the game, just tells me where to meet him, a rest stop about twenty miles south of where I am. I have no intention of meeting him. I'd have to be insane to do that.

"I have to get home," I tell him. "I'll be missed. I have a *family*, Detective."

He issues a nasty little laugh. "Let me tell you something: You don't have anything unless I say you do."

He ends the call. I hold the dead phone in my hand. Desperation and panic are eating an acid hole in my center. I try Gray on his cell phone and don't get an answer. I hang up without leaving a message. After driving a few more miles, my mind racing through my various options, I exit the highway and make a turn, get back on, and head south. *I'll meet him,* I tell myself. *I'll give him what he wants. Then he'll go away.* Just like Gray said. Why Gray didn't go to see him, why he wound up killing Simon Briggs instead, I don't know. There's no time to think about it. I just need to finish this and get home.

.   .   .

As far as I know, my mother still lives on Frank Geary's horse ranch in Central Florida. She believes I'm dead. I know from my father that she blames me for everything that happened to Frank, to her. She has turned the farm into a safe house for women in love with death-row inmates. She helps them lobby for new trials, conducts letter-writing campaigns for the examination of old evidence with new technology, comforts them when the worst happens. She even has a website, freetheinnocent.org.

A couple of years ago, I saw her on a talk show, defending herself against the families of murder victims. She looked old and worn, all her prettiness gone. I felt nothing when I saw her, except a slight nausea that she could have devoted so much time and feeling to this cause when she never showed a fraction of that love or concern for her own daughter. She wears a picture of Frank in a locket around her neck.

"He was an innocent man who died for crimes he didn't commit," she kept repeating. She made a weird rocking motion, seemed edgy and unstable. Even the other people onstage—a woman dating a death-row inmate, a death-row appeals lawyer, the wife of a man wrongly convicted and executed— stared at her, leaned their bodies away in an effort to distance themselves.

The show itself was sensational garbage, designed to create conflict among the participants. Families of victims were grouped on the other side of the stage— the mother of an abducted and murdered girl, the husband of a woman who was raped and murdered in their home, the sister of a young man who was the victim of a serial killer. Things started out well enough but naturally devolved into bitter tears and screaming matches. The audience jeered.

Eventually the questions turned to me and Marlowe. I watched with rapt attention, though I knew I shouldn't. I just couldn't turn it off.

"Do you think it's something genetic or something learned?" the host asked my mother, a barely concealed look of disgust on his face. "How do you explain your daughter's involvement with murderer Marlowe Geary?"

"I believe Marlowe Geary was innocent of the crimes he was accused of committing, just as his father was," she said, jutting her chin out and blinking her eyes oddly. "He never had a trial. He was tried and convicted in the media."

"The evidence is overwhelming," said the host, a gray-haired man with a chiseled, heavily made-up face.

"Evidence lies," she said, staring directly at the camera. "We all know that."

About a year after Frank died, new DNA technology proved beyond a shadow of a doubt that he had killed at least two of the women he went to jail for initially—a local waitress named Lauren Miter and Sadie Atkins, a motel maid. Their families never stopped lobbying to prove Frank's guilt and finally succeeded. I knew it must have been cold comfort, but maybe that's better than nothing. I wondered about Janet Parker. She didn't need technology to prove that Frank had killed her daughter. Her body knew, and the knowledge wasted her.

I have often wondered about the other women, a suspected thirteen in all. Women who went missing in a twenty-mile radius around the Geary home whose bodies were never found. What happened to them? Did they all die at the hands of Frank Geary?

"You didn't answer my question," the host said when the audience quieted down. "How do you explain your daughter's involvement with Marlowe Geary?"

"I won't speak ill of the dead. But my stepson was a good, good boy. I knew him to be gentle and kind. Ophelia was a very troubled young girl, headstrong and unhappy."

"So what are you saying?" asked the host, incredulous.

"If he did anything wrong, she might have been the corrupting influence," my mother said, widening her eyes and looking straight at the camera again.

I was stunned by the injustice of her words, the absolute delusional world she lived in. But still I couldn't turn off the television. In the oddest way, it was good to see my mother, a comfort to hear her voice. We love our parents so much, even when we hate them, even when they abuse and betray us. We want so badly to be loved in return. If they only knew their power.

The show ended with a solitary man onstage, a representative from an organization dedicated to counseling the victims of violent crime and their families. He was a small, frail-looking man with a silky drift of strawberry-blond hair and sparkling green jewels for eyes. His voice wobbled slightly as he spoke in vagaries about how victims have to face down their fears rather than wallow in them. The techniques of his organization, he said, were "experimental and controversial but highly effective."

"When we're victimized or when we lose someone to violence, it changes the way we see the world. It opens a hole in the perception of our lives, and it seems like every bad thing, every monster, can enter through that opening. Facing the fear that's left after you or someone you love has been victimized is the hardest thing you'll do. But if you don't do it, the fear will kill you slowly, like the most insidious cancer, cell by cell."

He wouldn't be specific about the organization's techniques but offered a website: nomorefear.biz. I jotted it down, but when I visited it later, there was only an error page.

For three days following, my mother's words ate a hole in my gut. I couldn't eat or sleep, unable to rid myself of the sight of her, used up and unstable, blaming me for Marlowe's crimes. I made a few more attempts to visit the website, but it was down every time.

For some reason I'm thinking about this as I pull off at the rest stop. The air is charged with bad possibilities as I drive down the access road and the highway disappears from my rearview mirror. I see Harrison's SUV parked beyond the restrooms, in the farthest corner of the lot. I wonder if there's anyplace more desolate and menacing than an empty rest stop in the middle of the night.

I come to a halt at a distance from his vehicle. I'm not going to pull up to him. I'm not going to approach his car. I'm going to stay inside with the doors locked. If he wants to talk, he'll have to come to me. I sit and wait, expecting him to call me on my cell phone. A minute passes, then five. Finally I find his number on my phone and call him. His voice mail picks up.

"Hi, you've reached Ray." His voice is bright and chipper, like a high-school cheerleader's. "Leave a message and I'll get right back to you."

I have a low opinion of Detective Harrison, and it's getting lower. He's taunting me, waiting to see what I'll do. Eventually, I can't take it anymore. I pull up alongside his vehicle. He's sitting there, smoking a cigarette. He turns as I come to a stop. He rolls down his window.

"I wasn't sure how desperate you were," he says. "Now I am."

"Spare me the foreplay," I say. "Just get to the point." The smell of his cigarette makes me want to smoke, even though I haven't in years.

He gives me that neighborly, "I'm nobody" smile he seems to have perfected. I see that his whole nice-guy aura is a persona he cultivates to put people at ease, to relax them. Like his voice-mail message, for example—friendly, disarming, not stern and profes-sional, not likely to scare away the skittish.

"I read that you watched while Marlowe Geary killed those girls. That witnesses saw you watching, doing nothing. What does that feel like?"

I don't answer him, just take the blow. I did ask him to get to the point. I guess the point is that he knows everything.

"How do you live with yourself?" he wants to know. Now I hate him. I find myself wishing that it was him and not Simon Briggs under that bridge. Or maybe both of them. I hate the way anger causes a mutiny of the body, the dry mouth, the trembling hands.

"You're awfully self-righteous for a dirty cop," I say.

He pulls his face into a mock grimace. "Ouch."

I rub my eyes hard, but it's no use, the pain in my head is ratcheting up.

"So you go from Marlowe Geary to Gray Powers. From killer to cop, or whatever he is. Actually, they're not so different, are they? They just kill for different reasons, kill different kinds of people. I wonder what this says about you."

But I'm not listening to him. I'm watching a young girl approach us. She is emaciated and pale as death today. Her hair is dirty and hanging limply. Her arms are covered with bruises. She walks slowly, almost dazed, but she's looking right at me. Detective Harrison turns to follow my gaze, puts his hand inside his jacket.

"What are you looking at?" he asks.

I know he can't see her. She is shaking her head at me in disapproval. She thinks I'm weak, foolish. If it were up to her, Detective Harrison would already be dead.

"I'm starting to wonder about you, Ophelia. I'm concerned about your stability."

There's a ringing in my ears now. I close my eyes, and when I open them again, she's gone.

"I have money," I say. "A lot of it. Just tell me what you want."

"It's not about money anymore," he says with a dramatic sigh. "At least it's not about *your* money anymore. Let's just say this: Ophelia March is not forgotten. Not forgiven, not forgotten. And do you know how many enemies your husband has? How many people would like to see him suffer? Do you have any idea about Powers and Powers, the things they've done?"

I have no idea what he's talking about, and more than that, my head is going to implode. I feel his eyes on me, and when I meet them, I'm surprised to see the man I saw that first night, the one I liked.

"You know what?" he says, incredulous. "I don't think you *do* know what I'm talking about. I really don't. Because when I look at your face, I don't see the person I read about. What's wrong with you? How did you let your life wind up like this?"

I close my eyes again and rest my head back. The pressure of the seat against the base of my skull feels good. I have a millisecond of relief.

We're both still sitting in our cars, speaking through the open windows. The streak of white hair over his ear looks silver in the moonlight. "You're one to talk," I say. "Look at you. Blackmail? You don't seem like the type."

He shrugs. "Like you, I've made some bad calls."

"So why don't we just help each other out? I give you what you need to make a clean start; you leave me and my family alone."

I sound cool and practical, just as Gray would sound in this situation, I imagine. And I do feel calmer than I have in hours. I watch Ophelia. She's standing right beside Harrison now on the other side of his window. I can see her breath fogging the glass. He's staring straight ahead, oblivious to her.

"Let me think about it," he says. Suddenly he seems tired and sad, as if he's taken on an enterprise he no longer has the will or the strength to finish. He puts his hand to his eyes and rubs hard. He's conflicted, I think. Part of him wants to be the good cop, the hero. He hasn't lost that part of himself. It hurts him to be so corrupt, to do such an obviously wrong thing. That's why he delivered his self-righteous speech at the mall, to make it all okay for himself.

Ophelia turns and walks away, slowly fading like a fog that's passing. I can hear her laughing. The headache and the ringing in my ears start to fade.

"I was seeing a doctor," I tell him.

"Yeah?" he says, glancing over at me. "Good. You need one."

"He disappeared."

"What do you mean?"

"His office, everything in it, was just gone the last time I went there." I leave out the part about his horrifically bloody murder. I don't feel like getting into all that.

He cocks his head to the side, gives me a quizzical look. "Why are you telling me this?"

"I was just wondering. Would you have a way of finding out if he was ever actually there? Or if he is who he told me he was?"

He looks at me with something like concern on his face. He's trying to decide how crazy I really am.

"What was his name?" he asks, his tone surprisingly gentle. Detective Harrison is a complicated man.

"Dr. Paul Brown."

He writes it down in a little book he takes from his dash. He asks for the address, and I give it to him.

"I'll look into it," he tells me. "In the meantime, are you sure you're safe at home?"

"What is that supposed to mean?" I remember

the question he asked on my voice mail: *How much do you really know about your husband?*

That wolfish smile again. "Sometimes the people we know least of all are sleeping in our beds."

"You must be thinking about your wife," I snap. "What does she know about you? Not much, I bet."

He doesn't like that—too close to center. His face takes on that dark expression, the one that frightens me. He starts the engine of his car. "I'll be in touch."

"Wait," I say, sorry for my smart mouth. "Who else is looking for me?"

He rolls up his window and pulls away, leaving me alone to watch his car merge onto the highway and disappear. I wonder if he's trying to unnerve me, make me think there are other people after me, that my husband is not who I believe him to be so that I'm more vulnerable to his blackmail. Or maybe he's just a sadist. Or maybe he's telling me the truth. I look for Ophelia in the darkness, but she's gone.

I return to the house. It's dark, quiet. Esperanza has gone to bed. I peek in on Victory, and she's sound asleep with Claude under one arm. The colored fish from her night-light dance around the room. Gray is not back from his deadly errand. And I wonder where he is, what he'll tell me about his night when he gets home. I consider calling my father but decide it would be reckless and pointless. I go to the bedroom, close the door, and wait—for Gray, for Marlowe, for Ophelia, whoever comes first.

As I wait, the memories start their parade. I can't stop them. I lie down on the bed, the sheer force of their relentless march exhausting me. The articles say I watched as Marlowe tortured innocent girls, that I stood by and did nothing as he murdered them—convenience-store clerks, gas-station attendants, hotel maids. It's true, without being the whole truth.

We traveled at night, stealing a new car every few days from roadside diners and rest stops along the highway. We stole mostly old junkers with empty soda cans on the floor and plastic Jesuses on the dash, pictures of toddlers tucked in the visor, piles of cigarette butts in the ashtrays. Each car had its particular aroma: cigars or vomit, bad perfume or sex. As Marlowe drove, I rummaged through the glove boxes, trying to figure out whose day we'd ruined, whether they had insurance and would be able to afford another car.

By the end of the second week, what little money we had was nearly gone; we'd had nothing but soda and vending-machine junk for days. We were hungry, our bodies starving for nutrients, and I was starting to feel desperate. We'd spent two nights in the car. When I managed to sleep, my dreams were wild, chaotic, punctuated by my mother screaming and the sound of gunfire, the smell of burning wood. The rest of the time, I moved through a kind of haze of fatigue, hunger, and fear. *This is a nightmare,* I'd tell myself. *It isn't happening.*

I'd been in a kind of half sleep when we pulled up at the gas station. The clock on the dash read 2 A.M. I knew we didn't have any money. I thought he was stopping to use the restroom. Then he pulled a gun from the duffel bag.

"We need money," Marlowe said.

I stared at the gun. Its shape seemed natural in his hand. "What are you going to do?" I said with a laugh. "Rob the place?"

Marlowe rolled his eyes. "We're fugitives," he said sharply. "We're wanted for *murder.* Robbing a gas station is nothing."

I felt like he'd slapped me in the face. "We didn't kill anyone," I said. "Janet Parker killed Frank."

"You let her onto the property, Ophelia," he said nastily. "That makes you an accomplice."

I shook my head. "No."

"Yes," he said, pulling something from the duffel bag. He handed it to me. It was a Florida newspaper. RUNAWAYS WANTED FOR QUESTIONING IN CONNECTION TO THE MURDER OF FRANK GEARY, the headline read.

"No," I said again. The reality of our situation, of what I'd done, was settling into my body. Marlowe moved to get out of the car, but I grabbed his arm. "We'll go to my father in New York. He'll help us. We don't need to do this."

"We're not going to make it to New York," he said, pushing my hand away. "We're out of gas. What do you think will happen then?"

"We'll steal another car."

He swept his hand around the empty gas-station lot. "Do you see another car?" he spit. "In a mile we'll be stranded by the side of the road."

I let go of a sob that had been dwelling in my chest. *"I did what you told me to do!"* I screamed through a sudden wash of tears. *"I saw you talking to her! You planned everything with her! I just did what you told me to do!"* It felt good to scream and sob, to release all my anger and fear.

Marlowe got very quiet in response. He lowered his voice to a whisper and moved his face in so close to mine that I could smell his rancid breath.

"I did this for *you,* Ophelia, to save *you* from Frank," he said. "You wanted me to rescue you, to take you away? Well, I did that. All of this has been for *you,* you ungrateful little bitch."

He had his hair back in a ponytail, and long strands were escaping. The dark circles under his eyes made him seem ghoulish. I turned away from him, my gut churning with fear and guilt and shame.

"Do you want me to go to jail? Do *you* want to go to jail?"

"No," I managed, all my anger exhausted.

"Then fill the tank, get in the driver's seat, and shut your fucking mouth," he said. "Keep the engine running."

He got out of the car then, and I watched him stride toward the building. I pulled the car over to the pump and did as I was told, keeping my eyes averted from the store. I didn't want to see him hold a gun to someone. I didn't want to see the fear on that person's face. And I didn't want to be the person who was waiting outside while he did that. When the tank was full, I got back into the car. As I sat there, "New Year's Day" by U2 played on the radio; I sang along, with the harsh lights above me revealing all the ugliness of my situation. I almost put the car in gear and drove. It was another of those moments when if I'd acted differently, things might not have broken apart the way they did. I was still me in that second. I could still have saved Ophelia. But I didn't.

I never thought to wonder why Marlowe didn't bother to cover his face, or why he didn't consider it an issue that I waited in plain sight with the car under the lights. When the shots rang out, I felt the vibrations in my bones. I sat there for a second, gripping the wheel, and felt any hope I had for my life drain from my body. Even then I could have run, gone to the police and taken my chances. Instead I got out of the car and walked through the glass doors of the gas station's store.

Marlowe was behind the counter, taking money from the register. All I could see was the top of her head, her long golden hair soaking up the pooling black blood on the white linoleum floor.

"What happened?"

"Go back to the car," he said quietly, not looking at me. "Now."

I did as I was told. I sat in the driver's seat for a long time. More than an hour. He came out finally, carrying bags filled with food—Twinkies, cans of pop, candy bars. When he got into the driver's seat, nudging me back over to the passenger side, he presented me with a Snickers bar, my favorite, and that wide, charming smile that used to thrill me. "I'm sorry I yelled at you," he said sweetly, leaning in and kissing me gently on the cheek. I clung to him, my lifeline, my only hope, even as my mind screamed, *What did he do in there?* "I know you're scared. I am, too. We'll go to your dad."

"What did you do, Marlowe?" I finally managed to whisper into his hair. I felt his body go stiff, and he pulled away from me quickly.

"Everything I've done, I've done for you," he said, turning on the ignition.

I'd fallen into a hole, a slick-walled abyss, and there was no way for me to climb out of the darkness that was closing in around me. I look back on this as the moment when I started to fear him more than I loved him, when the part of me that still wanted to survive started to hate him. But I was too lost to know the difference.

"No one else will ever love you like I do," he said darkly as we pulled onto the highway.

I'm not sure how many more women and girls there were. I remember flash details—garishly red lipstick, a turquoise barrette, a flower tattoo, sparkling pink nail polish badly applied. I hear a nervous giggle, a cry of terrible pain. These things stay with me.

* * *

When Gray comes home, I've moved out onto the balcony to listen to the Gulf, trying to remember more. He comes outside and sits next to me. For a second, my past and present mingle.

"I think our problems have been eliminated," he says. He doesn't reach for me or turn to face me. He is just a dark figure beside me, staring out at the sea.

"What happened?" I ask, dreading his answer. He doesn't respond right away. Then, "Let's just say I took care of it."

"Gray."

"Trust me."

I think of my conversation with Ray Harrison at the rest stop, how tired and discouraged he seemed. Maybe he felt sorry for me. Maybe he decided to take what Gray offered and walk away. Or maybe he was planning to work other angles as well.

"Did Harrison tell you there are other people looking for me?"

He shifts lower in his seat, puts his feet up on the railing. "There's no one else looking for you."

"He told me there was."

"When?"

I release a sigh, knowing he's not going to be

happy. "I saw him tonight. He called me and asked me to meet him. I did."

"That was stupid, Annie."

We sit in silence. I want to tell him that I saw him kill Simon Briggs. But I don't. I'm afraid. Afraid that he did it, afraid of why he shook Briggs's hand. I'm also afraid he didn't do it, that I imagined the whole thing. I'm suddenly very cold, though the night air is mild and slightly humid. I walk back into our bedroom. Gray follows, takes me by the shoulders, and spins me around.

"We're okay," he says. "Trust me. All the threats have been neutralized."

This is the language he uses when he's afraid, these passive military phrases: *Threats have been neutralized. Our problems have been solved.* But I don't see fear when I look at him. His eyes are flat, cool; his mouth is pulled into a grim, tight line. In the dim light of the room, the scars on his face look darker, nastier.

"What about Briggs?" I ask. I'm hoping here that he'll say something true, something that grounds me. I want him to tell me he killed Briggs. But he doesn't.

"He won't be a problem," Gray says quietly.

I feel the slightest flicker of fear at his words. I walk toward the bed. He doesn't move to follow me. I remember that he thought Briggs was working for someone. Even if he'd killed Briggs, wouldn't that person still be looking, and wouldn't Briggs's death be a red flag that he'd gotten close? Suddenly I recall the envelope that I stuffed under the seat of my car. I never looked inside.

"What were you thinking, Annie?" says Gray. "Where did you meet him?"

"At a rest stop by the highway. He said, 'Ophelia March is not forgotten. Not forgiven, not forgotten.'"

"He's wrong. It's over."

"What about the person who followed me on the beach? The necklace I found in the sand?"

"You said yourself you're not sure what you heard, who that might have been. It could have been anyone, or even Briggs trying to unnerve you. And there must be a million of those necklaces around, Annie."

Can it be this easy to explain away?

"Trust me, Annie. We're okay." He kisses me softly on the lips and pulls me into a tight embrace. I can feel his relief, his love for me. I do know my husband—I don't care what Harrison thinks.

I want so badly to believe Gray that I actually start to. When he releases me and looks into my eyes, his face comes into focus and the room around me starts to seem like my bedroom again, not a place where I'll be sleeping until I flee my life. I don't care whether Gray has killed Briggs or not. I know he'll never tell me if he did. For a minute I can believe that Detective Harrison won't come sniffing around again, that the person on the beach was Briggs or some teenager playing a prank. I'll walk with Victory on the beach tomorrow and then take her to school just like any other day. In a week all of this will be a fading memory, like the car accident you just narrowly avoided that leaves you shaken and glad to have survived.

Gray's hands start roaming my body, and I come alive inside. My relief and the strength of his body, the warmth of his skin against mine, awake a deep hunger. His lips are on my neck and then my collarbone as he peels away my shirt and goes to work on my jeans. I am tearing at his clothes as he pushes me gently onto the bed. When he's inside me, he wraps his arms around me so that I can feel every inch of his body against mine. He whispers my name over and over, soft and slow, like a mantra. "Annie. Annie. Annie." Somewhere beneath the heat of my desire, I find myself wishing he'd call me by my real name. I wish he'd call me Ophelia. Even though I'm making love to my husband, I feel suddenly so lonely.

Afterward, as he's drifting off to sleep, he whispers, "I can't lose you, Annie. Stay with me." I don't know why he would say that. Does he sense that

Annie is coming apart and drifting away? I ask him what he means, but he's already sleeping.

I close my eyes. When I open them again, Ophelia is sitting in the chair by the fireplace. She's laughing.

28

There are questions I've asked myself a number of times over the past few years: Can you shift yourself off and start again? If you've done unthinkable things, can you cast them away like unflattering garments, change your ensemble, and become someone else? What of the relief of punishment, the wash of atonement, the salve of forgiveness? I thought I was free. I was confident that I'd started over with the birth of my daughter. In motherhood, in the surrender of self, I became someone new. The ugly parts of myself and my other life were forgotten, literally. The blackouts, the strange flights—all of that ended when she was born. I couldn't be that person anymore. I had to be someone worthy, able to protect and care for the tiny life in my charge.

But I suppose I should have known that Ophelia would return. The doctor always said as much. You cannot hide from yourself forever. The terrible migraines and nightmares, he said, were a sign that my subconscious was working hard to suppress the memories my conscious mind couldn't handle. Ultimately the shadow wants to be known, and she'll do what she must to be acknowledged.

The next few days pass without incident, and I lull myself into thinking that everything has gone back to normal. I walk on the beach with Victory, take her to school and pick her up, we watch videos together in the evenings. Drew and Vivian have gone on a short trip, so I don't have them hovering over my life—Drew with his dark, suspicious glances; Vivian with her concerned, motherly expressions. We are a small, happy family: me, Victory, Gray, and even Esperanza, whom none of us can imagine living without. Even when Gray and I bicker over whether Victory is too pampered, too spoiled (she is, of course, but so what?), it's heaven in its normalcy. I am giddy with relief. Detective Harrison has stopped coming around. Ophelia is gone. Marlowe, too. No more dark forms lurking on the beach. No more pale, fragile-looking girls walking toward me in the night.

But they are not forgotten. No, never that. So I begin the scuba-diving lessons I told my escape artist (as I have come to think of him) I would. Just in case. Just as a precaution.

I am terrified of the water, the leaden quiet of it, the suffocating weight of it. I feel the first cut of panic even as I wade into the shallow end of a pool, as though it might start to rise and take me over, swallow me with its terrible silence. The brighter the sun, the clearer and bluer the water, the worse it is. It seems like a deceiver then, so inviting, so refreshing. You might forget how deadly it is, how it can effortlessly suck the life from you. When I watch Victory flitting through the water of Vivian's pool or in the ocean, I envy her confidence and her complete comfort, even as I suppress a scream every time she disappears beneath the surface for more than a second or two.

"Don't worry, Mommy!" she'll call as she comes up for air, knowing instinctively of my fear even though I've never said a word, have worked very hard not to telegraph my dread to her. Somehow she knows.

I wasn't always afraid. I remember going to Rockaway Beach with my father when I was little, five or six. He would take me into the cold, salty water, and together we would jump the waves. My mother stayed on shore waving to us in her red bikini. I remember swallowing gallons of ocean water, my stomach churning with it. My eyes burned. But I loved it, loved being with my dad, hearing his loud, whooping laughter. Even wiping out was its own kind of fun, those few seconds beneath the blue-gray swirl of the Atlantic, the relief of planting my feet again and taking in air, feeling the tide pull the ground out from beneath me, currents of sand running through my toes. When we were both waterlogged, we'd run back to my mother. I'd have goose bumps, even though the sun was hot. And my mother waited with a towel, wrapped me up tight and dried my hair. I remember feeling safe in the water, feeling like it was friendly, a place to have fun. I have to believe that it was Janet Parker who caused me to fear it with the images she evoked. They expanded and found a home in my mind. After the words she spoke, I could never swim again. Strange how powerful she was, as if she'd issued a curse and changed me.

The dive instructor I have chosen is very patient with me. She's a pretty young redhead who I think is used to dealing with children. She talks to me in soothing tones, coaxes me into the water with bland assurances, holds my hand when necessary. The dive equipment, the buoyancy control device, the regulator and tank are somehow comforting in spite of their weight and awkwardness. It's as if I've brought a little of the land with me. Once I learn how to control my buoyancy and measure my breathing, after just two mornings, I find I can float effortlessly in the deep end of the pool. It feels like flying. I'm still afraid, but I'm starting to have it under control.

"You should be proud of yourself," she tells me when I've completed the classroom-and-pool portion of my instruction. "Most people with so much fear could never do what you've done. You're ready for your open-water certification."

I thank her and tell her I'll be doing my open water with another dive master, an old friend. She tells me to come back if I ever need a refresher. I shake her hand and wonder what she'll say to investigators if I die.

She was so frightened of the water, I imagine her telling them. *Prone to panic.*

Everyone knows that panic kills, especially at seventy-five feet deep.

In the parking lot after my last lesson, I see Detective Harrison's Ford Explorer parked next to my car. I notice that it's dirty, the bottom covered with mud as though he has been off-roading. My insides drop with disappointment and fear. I was starting to think we'd heard the last of him. I walk over to his window. He rolls it down, and a wave of cool, smoky air drifts out.

"Hello, Annie."

I don't answer him. He takes a photograph from the passenger seat of his car and hands it to me.

"Do you know this man?"

It's a picture of Simon Briggs, his face pale and stiff, eyes closed. Dead. I think of the envelope I am still carrying around in my car. I haven't looked at it, in an effort to preserve the false sense of security I've been nursing over the last few days.

"No," I say.

He gives me a sideways look, a kind of lazy smile. He knows I'm lying. I don't know how.

"Okay," he says. "How about this guy?"

He shows me another photograph. It's a mug shot of a middle-aged man with pleasantly gray hair and a mustache. He has a kind face. It's the man I know as Dr. Paul Brown.

"Your doctor, right?"

I nod.

"His real name is Paul Broward. He was wanted in three states—New York, California, and Florida—for insurance fraud, malpractice, and operating without a license. It was revoked for sexual assault of a patient."

The information takes a second to sink in. The detective and I engage in a staring contest until I eventually lower my eyes.

" 'Was' wanted?" I say finally.

"His body was found by fishermen in the Everglades yesterday. Or parts of it, anyway. Enough to identify."

I feel a roil of shame and sadness. I hadn't really believed he was dead, had almost convinced myself I'd imagined everything that night that felt like so long ago. Whatever he was, he had helped me. I didn't want to think of him dying that way. And then I had to ask myself, did Ophelia kill him? Did *I* kill him? Gray destroyed the bloody clothes I wore home that night. I look down at my own hands. They don't seem capable.

"You sure know how to pick 'em, Annie."

I have decided not to reply to any more of his antagonistic statements.

"So," he says when I don't answer, "I have two dead bodies and one live woman lying about her identity connected to them both. I ask myself, what is it about you that encourages people to turn up dead?"

"I don't know that other man," I say, gesturing toward the first photo.

"Then why did he have your picture in his car?"

And why did Gray shake his hand and then shoot him in the head? Why did he leave the car there to be discovered by the police? Too many questions, no good answers.

"I have no idea," I say. I want to walk away from him, to get into my car and drive. But something keeps me rooted. In a weird way, Detective Harrison has become the only person I'm clear about. I wish I could tell him what I saw, show him the envelope, ask him what else he knows about my doctor. But of course I can't do any of that.

Instead I say, "My husband paid you off, right?"

"Yeah," he says with a shrug. "But I still have a job to do."

"What makes you think I won't report you to Internal Affairs or something?"

He gives me a pitying look. "The way I see it, Annie, we've got each other by the balls. You squeeze, I'll squeeze harder. Makes us even, doesn't it?"

He has a point.

"Look," he says. He seems suddenly sincere, concerned. "I think you're in big trouble, and not just with the law. Maybe the police are the least of your problems."

My heart starts to thrum. I know he's right. Ever

since that first panic attack in the grocery store's parking lot, I have known that Annie Powers was not long for this world.

"A guy like Briggs, he's just the hired help. He's dead, but there will be someone else right behind him. Someone wants to find Ophelia March, and it ain't because an aunt she didn't know about left her some money."

"And you know who that is?" I find myself moving closer to him involuntarily. My hand is resting on the window edge.

"No," he says, shaking his head.

"You said—" I start.

"I lied. I was just trying to scare you."

I walk away from him then, go back to my car. He rolls down the passenger window of his car. I notice the shock of white hair again.

"Start by asking yourself this question," he calls after me. "Who referred you to that doctor? How did you find him? Whoever it was should be considered suspect."

I don't answer him as I get into the driver's seat and start the engine.

"Are you too stupid to know when someone is trying to help you?" he asks.

"For a price, right?"

"Everything has a price, Annie. This is a material world. You should know that better than anyone."

I shut the door, back out of my parking space. Before I pull out of the lot, I turn and look behind me at the detective. He points to his eye, then points to me. *I'm watching you,* he's telling me. He probably didn't mean for it to be comforting but, oddly, it is.

When Victory and I show up at Vivian's unannounced later that afternoon, I see a flash of something on her face that I've never seen before. It happens when our eyes connect through the thick glass of her front door. It's just the ghost of an expression, and in another state of mind I might not even have noticed it. It's fear. Vivian is the strongest woman I've ever known, and when I see that look on her face, my heart goes cold.

"What a surprise," she says with a bright, warm smile, swinging open the door. But it's too late; the secret has passed between us. I walk through the door with Victory in my arms. She immediately reaches for her grandmother, and I hand her over, stand back as Victory bear-hugs her and then begins to chirp happily about her day. Vivian makes all the appropriate confirming noises and exclamations as we walk to the kitchen. I sit quietly, sipping a glass of water as Vivian makes a grilled cheese sandwich and cuts it into tiny squares the way Victory likes it. I stare out the double glass doors at the glittering blue waters of the infinity pool, thinking all variety of dark thoughts as the most important females in my life chatter, light and happy, like two budgies.

After her snack Victory runs off to the elaborate playroom they keep for her here, and Vivian sits down at the table across from me. She folds her arms on the table in front of her and waits. I tell her everything.

When I'm done, I look at her and see that she has hung her head. She raises her eyes to me after a moment, and they are filled with tears.

"Annie, I'm so sorry."

I lean forward. "Why, Vivian? Why are you sorry?"

"Oh, God," she says. That look is back, but it's here to stay. Then, "Annie, there was no body. Marlowe Geary's body was never recovered."

"No body," I repeat, just to hear the words again.

"It seemed like the only way at the time, Annie. He *had* to have died in that crash. He *couldn't* have survived. But we didn't think you could heal if you'd known they'd never recovered the body."

I examine Vivian's face, the pretty crinkles around her pleading eyes, the soft flesh of her cheeks flushed red with her distress. She is suddenly unfamiliar, this woman whom I have come to love more

than my own mother. In a way I don't really blame
her for deceiving me all these years. I can understand
why she did it; I can even believe she did it to protect
me. But I'm angry just the same. I keep my distance,
wrap my arms around my body against the clenching
in my stomach. I look at the flowers on the table,
bright pink and white tulips bowing gracefully over
the lip of the vase. I try not to think about all the
times I'd confessed my fear that Marlowe Geary
might still be alive. I try not to think about how
many times she, Drew, Gray, and my father had lied
to me, made me feel like I was crazy, assuring me
about this body they all knew was never found.

"Why are you telling me this now, Vivian?" I ask
her when I trust my voice again. "What's changed?"

She doesn't seem to hear me. She just keeps
talking.

"You were haunted by him," she says. "I knew
you were in pain. I thought, in time, all that pain
would just go away. But then I started to wonder if
part of you, maybe the part that couldn't remember
so much, was still connected to him. That doctor, he
was supposed to *help* you."

"Dr. Brown?" I say. "He knew who I was? He knew
about my past?"

She shifts her eyes away and doesn't answer.

"You brought me to him," I say, remembering

my first visit, how she drove me there, waited until I was done. "You said he'd helped a friend of yours."

"I know," she agrees, nodding solemnly. "That's what they told me to say."

"Who?"

"He knew everything about your past. He was supposed to help you come to terms in your own way, in your own time."

He always knew when I was lying or leaving something out. There was never anyone in his waiting room. He never took any notes about our sessions but had perfect recall. All these things come back to me. Why didn't I see any of it before?

"*Who* told you to say that?" I ask again when it was clear she wasn't going to answer me.

"When you were stronger, I wanted Gray to tell you that Marlowe's body was still missing. I thought you needed to know. But he didn't want that. He just wanted to protect you. That's all he's ever wanted. You know that, don't you?"

She takes my hand and holds it tight, looks at me with an urgency that makes me uncomfortable, that fills me with fear. But I don't pull away from her.

"What are you trying to tell me, Vivian?" I lean in close to her and squeeze her hands. "Please just tell me."

Her eyes lift to something behind me, and I spin

around in my seat to see Drew standing in the doorway. He looks like a thunderhead, brow furrowed, eyes dark, neck red.

"Viv, you shouldn't have," he says sternly.

Vivian sits up straight and squares her shoulders at him, sticks out her chin. "It's time. This is wrong. She *needs* to know."

"She never needed to know," Drew says. "Geary's dead. Body or no body. No one's ever heard from him again," he says to me, his eyebrows making one angry line.

They exchange a look. I can see it was an old fight between them, words spoken so many times they don't need speaking again. There is more Vivian wanted to say, but I know she'll never say it now that Drew is here.

"No one's ever heard from Ophelia March again, either, and yet here I sit."

They both turn their gazes to me. Vivian looks so sad suddenly. Drew's expression I can't read.

"Who's Ophelia?" We are interrupted by Victory. She's staring at me with wide eyes.

"She's no one, darling," I say, reaching down to touch her face. "She's just a character in a book." I rise and lift my daughter into my arms. She must have wandered in while we were speaking. I'm not sure how long she's been there or what she heard. All my questions will go unanswered now. It doesn't matter anyway—they're both liars.

I grab Victory's jacket and book bag from the table. Vivian and Drew both move to stop me, then catch themselves. They won't make a scene in front of their granddaughter. At least they have more respect for her than they do for me.

"Are we leaving?" Victory asks.

"Yes," I say. I can feel her examine my face because she didn't understand my tone. I look at her and give her a smile, which she returns uncertainly. I walk out the door without another word, jog down the steps, and go to our car. Victory calls behind us, "Bye, Grandma! Bye, Grandpa!"

Vivian and Drew stand by the door, waving stiffly to my daughter.

"Are you mad at them?" she asks as I buckle her into her car seat. Adrenaline is making me clumsy and hyperfocused, and I'm fumbling with the task of fastening the straps around my daughter. When I don't answer, she asks the question again. I don't want to lie, but I don't want to play Twenty Questions, either. I don't say anything, just kiss her on the cheek and ruffle her hair. I close her door and move to the driver's seat, all the while feeling the heat of Drew's and Vivian's eyes.

"You *are* mad," Victory says as we pull out of the

driveway. "My teacher says that it's okay to be mad but that you should always talk about your feelings, Mommy."

"That's good advice, Victory. But sometimes things are a little more complicated than that."

She gives me a nod of grave understanding, and I wonder what kind of lesson I am teaching her today. Nothing good, I'm pretty sure.

As I drive off, my anger subsides and the adrenaline flood in my body finds a lower level. With Drew and Vivian disappearing in my rearview mirror, I am aware of a kind of relief. Gray talks about how before an operation there's a terrible tension that fades once the first shot is fired. All the wondering about how things will go down and if he'll survive evaporates, and he becomes pure action. Today I finally know what he means.

Gray is waiting at home when we get there. He jumps up from the couch as we walk in the door. Victory runs to him, and he picks her up and hugs her hard. She giggles in a way that makes my heart clench, a kind of sweet, girly little noise that is uniquely hers.

"How's my girl?" he asks.

"Mommy's mad at Grandma and Grandpa," she tells him seriously.

"That's all right. Sometimes we get angry with the people we love," he says, depositing her on the floor and looking at my face. His eyes tell me that he's already talked to Drew and Vivian.

"Hey, guess what? Esperanza's waiting for you upstairs. She's got a surprise for you."

Victory doesn't need to be told twice. I watch as she runs off. I hear her little shoes pounding up the stairs.

We stand looking at each other for a minute. I can't read his expression.

"Why did you kill Simon Briggs?" I ask after I don't know how long. The room is darkening as the sun fades from the sky. I can hear the lapping of the waves against the shore. I hear Victory laughing upstairs. There are black beans cooking in the kitchen.

He frowns and opens his mouth to deny it. I put up a hand. "I followed you. I saw you shoot him."

He turns his head to the side and releases a long, slow breath.

"Because I couldn't figure out who he was working for," he says finally. "I found out where he was staying. I offered him a payoff in exchange for the name of his employer and for him to go back to whoever it was and say he couldn't find you or that you were dead or whatever. When I gave him the money, he lied to me, said he was working for the police. So I killed him. I figured that it would send a message to whoever had hired him." He finished with a shrug.

"How do you know he lied?"

"I know," he says.

"Is he alive, Gray? Marlowe. Is he?"

He doesn't answer, just fixes me with a stare. I can tell he wants to reach for me but there's a high, hard wall between us.

"Is he alive?" I ask again.

Finally, "I don't know, Annie. I just don't know."

I let the words move through me. Strange as it is, it feels good to hear him admit it, this thing I have known all along. I somehow feel stronger, saner, for knowing that my instincts haven't failed me completely.

"What happened to Dr. Brown? Who was he?"

"He's someone my father knows. He was a clinical psychiatrist who dealt with military and paramilitary posttraumatic stress patients. We thought he could help you."

I don't tell him what Detective Harrison has told me. I'm not sure why. Probably because I figure he'll have an explanation for whatever I say. I don't know whom to believe. Harrison isn't exactly unimpeachable himself.

"What happened to him?"

"I don't know, Annie. That's the truth."

That's the truth. It's a funny phrase. If you need to say it, it's probably because every other thing out of your mouth has been a lie.

I see her then. She's standing out on the deck, her hands pressed up against the window. She's every bit as real as I am, which doesn't mean much. I see her for what she is finally, just a girl who's been lied to and betrayed by everyone she loves, someone who's forever looking for a rescue that's just not coming.

If there was ever any question about what I needed to do for her, it had been answered. Between Ray Harrison's revelations and Vivian's confessions, it's all very clear. I understand Ophelia after all these years, why she has been afraid, so eager to flee the life that Annie Powers made. It has all been a façade, flimsy and insubstantial, waiting for one good wind to blow.

"Annie?" says Gray.

"Don't call me that," I say. "It's not my name."

Later I tuck Victory into her bed and lie down beside her. She clutches Claude in one arm, holds my hand with her free one. She's drifty, eyelids droopy. I drink in the delicate lines of her profile, the soft pink of her skin, run my fingers through her silky hair. Sometimes it seems that all you do as a mother is say goodbye in tiny increments. The minute they leave your body, they just get further and further away, first crawling, then walking, then running. But tonight it's even worse. Tonight I really am saying good-bye. Of course, she has no idea.

"Are you still mad?" she asks me, turning suddenly to meet my eyes.

I shake my head, "No. Everything's fine. Sometimes grown-ups argue."

She gives a small nod and a sleepy smile; she seems satisfied with this. She has always been such a reasonable child, always seeming to understand things beyond her years.

"I love you, baby," I tell her. "More than anything." It's so important for her to know this now.

"I love you, too, Mommy."

I watch as her little face finally relaxes, her breathing deepens. When I'm sure she's asleep, I slip off her bed and leave the room quickly. If I stay any longer beside her, I'll never have the strength to do what I know I must.

I find Gray waiting for me in the hallway. We have left our conversation dangling, and it will need to be finished tonight. I follow him to our bedroom and close the door behind me. I tell him everything, the return of my memories, the arrangements I have made with my old friend Oscar.

"Annie," he says when I'm done, "listen to yourself. You met this guy in the psychiatric hospital?"

"It's what he does, for companies like yours. He makes people disappear, gives them new identities, helps them to stage their deaths."

Gray shoots me a skeptical look. "But he's crazy?"

"No crazier than I am," I say defensively. "He was just having a hard time. Depression. An occupational hazard."

Gray sits down in the chair by the window. I move over to the bed, give him some space to process all of it.

"Okay, let's look at this rationally," he says, lifting his eyes to me. "What does all this accomplish? What about Victory? Do you really want to put her through this?"

"Don't you get it, Gray?" I say. "He has *found* me. I don't know how, but he has. Maybe Simon Briggs was working for him. We don't know. The point is that I die on my terms and hope to come back to my little girl. Or I die on his and that's the end. He wins."

"I'd never let that happen," he says. "You know that."

"He'll wait. He'll wait until the second our guard is down."

"You give him too much credit," he says, standing up and beginning to pace the room. "You've blown him up in your mind to be something that he isn't. We don't even know that he's alive. Annie, this is crazy."

"If it's not him, it's someone else who knows about Ophelia. I can't have Victory touched by that, either. Gray, it's time. We always said this is what we'd do if the past came back."

"That was before," he says, looking sadder than I've ever seen him. He sinks down onto the bed. "That was before we had a home and a family, a daughter—a life we built together. Annie, I can't lose you."

I walk over to him and kneel before him.

"Then let me go, Gray," I say. "Let me die so we can be a family again."

He releases a deep breath and closes his eyes for a second. I expect him to spring up and parade out a hundred more reasons this is the worst idea anyone ever had, how it's insane and reckless and even unnecessary. But he surprises me then.

"Okay," he says. "But we do it *my* way. My people help you disappear; my people on the other end take you someplace safe, protect you. We'll send

Victory away with Vivian, and while she's gone, we'll figure out who's doing all this. If everything goes well, she never has to know about any of it. When you're safe, when the threat is neutralized, we'll find a way to bring you back."

He drops down onto the floor in front of me and wraps me tightly in his arms. "Okay?" he asks.

It sounds too easy, as though he thinks it can all be settled in a few weeks. But I don't say that. I'm just glad he's not going to fight me.

For a second, I wonder if he's humoring me. But then I realize that we have always planned this; that we always knew someday the past might come knocking and that I would need to leave Annie Powers behind. We'd both forgotten how tenuous our hold was on this life we'd built—until now.

"Okay."

30

I stand on the edge of the sink-hole and look down into its murky depths. It is as black as tar and about as welcoming. My heart is an engine in my chest, revving up into my throat. All my nerve endings tingle with dread. Everything in me wants to flee, but I know I can't do that now. Only my desire to protect Victory keeps me moving forward, climbing into the wetsuit my instructor provided. He's lifting the tank up onto my back, and my legs nearly buckle beneath the weight of it. Annie Powers's life is gone, as totally as if the ground gave way and she fell into the earth.

I have the regulator in my mouth and the mask over my eyes. I hear Janet Parker's voice in my head: *She was there, floating in the cold, dark water for three months. My baby. Alone in the dark, cold water.* I have carried the sound of her keening with me ever since I heard her. But it wasn't until I had a daughter of my own that I could truly understand her grief.

"Are you ready, Ophelia?"

I lift my hand to the half heart at my neck and finger the edge.

"I'm ready."

He looks concerned, as though he can feel my fear, my pain. Maybe it's etched on my face. Maybe he can hear it in my breathing.

As I extend my stride, step into the water, and slip beneath the surface, I see her waiting there—Ophelia, so young and fragile, hovering like an angel. Her skin is gray, her long hair pulsing in the current. She is so glad to see me; she takes me in her frigid arms. And in that moment I am whole.

I am Annie. I am Ophelia. I am Janet Parker and her daughter Melissa. I am dead and grieving. I am mother and daughter. The blackness swallows me.

PART TWO
dead again

Just remember till you're home again
You belong to me.

FROM THE SONG "YOU BELONG TO ME"
BY CHILTON PRICE
(1952)

31

Something awful happened to-
day. I died. A terrible accident. Something went
wrong during my open-water certification. *She was
prone to panicking,* the girl who taught me in the pool
will remember. *She was afraid of the water. She wasn't
qualified for a dive like that.*

Ella will recall our conversation at the mall when
I joked about my baptism by fire. She'll experience a
moment of pointless self-blame when she'll wonder
if she might have stopped me.

Neither my body nor the body of the dive master
will be recovered. They'll find my street clothes, keys,
and wallet in the dry bag in the backseat of my car
near the entrance to the sinkhole where I began my
dive. It will be parked beside an old Dodge minivan
registered to Blake Woods from Odessa, Florida.
The van will be cluttered with all manner of run-
down dive gear—wetsuits with tears, BCDs with
torn straps, regulators in need of repair. But Blake
Woods does not exist. The address on his driver's

license is false; his dive-master identification card is a fake.

Eventually, as the rescue divers search the sink-hole, explore the long caves and narrow passages looking for our bodies, they'll recover a fin, top of the line and brand-new, matching the type I bought from a local dive shop a few weeks ago. Shortly after this they will call off the search.

Why would someone terrified of the water take scuba-diving lessons? Who was the man posing as her instructor? Why would he take her for her open-water certification in a sinkhole? There will be lots of questions and no answers. But it happens all the time in Florida, to people far more experienced than I. People descend into the limestone caves and don't come out again. Cave diving is the deadliest possible hobby. Not for beginners. Suspicious, the police will say. And senseless. So sad. Annie, *why?*

As I lie in the dark, the taste of blood metallic and bitter in my mouth, I wonder if finally, after all the false deaths I have died, I really *am* dead this time. Maybe this is what death is like, a long, dark wonder-ing, an eternal sorting through the deeds of your life, trying to discern between dream and reality. I find myself pondering, if I'm dead, which of my lives was real. My life as Ophelia? Or my life as Annie?

I try to move but vomit instead. My body racks with it until I'm dry-heaving, blood and bile burning my throat. I am on a wet metal surface. I am freezing cold, starting to shiver uncontrollably. With the pain and nausea, I figure I'm probably alive. I imagine death would be somehow less *physical*.

The darkness around me is total, not a pinprick of light. I can't see my hand in front of my face. The sound of my breathing echoes off metal above and around me. There's nothing on my body that doesn't hurt, as if I've been in a terrible car wreck, no bone unshaken. I try to orient myself, try to sort through what has happened to me and how I have come to wherever I am. Then I remember the boat. I remember Dax racing off in the Boston Whaler. I remember the men who died trying to protect me, men whose wives I've met at dinner parties and award ceremonies, all of them employed by Powers and Powers. I remember the shroud over my head and the blow to my skull.

I'm just getting used to the totality of the darkness around me when in floods the harshest white light. I'm as blind in its brightness as I was in the dark. Maybe it's God, I think. But somehow I doubt

I warrant a personal appearance. I feel He'd probably send a lackey to deal with me.

"*Ophelia March.*" The voice roars, seems to come from everywhere. It's as painful to my ears as the light is to my eyes. I find myself in a fetal position, wrapping my head with my arms.

"*Where is he, Ophelia?*"

I can't find my voice but manage to emit some type of guttural wail of pain and misery.

"Where is Marlowe Geary?"

At first I don't think I've heard correctly. Then the question booms again.

I realize with a sinking dread that I have made a terrible mistake. It started to dawn on me on the ship when I was taken in my cabin. But now I truly understand how badly I have screwed up. I have shed my life and fled my daughter, believing in my deepest heart—or at least fearing—that Marlowe Geary has returned for me. I let Annie die so that Ophelia could face him once and for all. I understand suddenly and with a brilliant clarity that it hasn't been Marlowe chasing me at all. It *never* has been.

Annie believed that Marlowe Geary was dead and buried in an unmarked grave somewhere in a New Mexico cemetery reserved for indigents, John Does, and the incarcerated whom no one claimed upon their deaths. She thought of him there in a plain pine box, under pounds of earth, and she was comforted. She believed the lies everyone told because she *wanted* to believe them. But Ophelia March knew better. And she has been chasing him. I understand this now, finally. All those times I woke up on buses or trains heading for parts unknown— she was trying to get back to him.

3 2

Detective Harrison was feeling like a man who'd escaped a terminal diagnosis; he was positively giddy with relief. Since Gray had paid off Harrison's debtors and he'd enrolled himself in Gamblers Anonymous, he felt lighter than he had in years. The threatening phone calls ceased, and the terrifying photographs of his wife and child stopped arriving on his desk. He'd stopped puking up blood from his ulcer.

A year ago if anyone had told him he'd be in a twelve-step program, he'd have punched that person in the jaw. But the weekly confessions in the meeting room of a local church by the beach cleansed him. He could say the things he'd done (most of them, anyway), and he could listen to others who'd done much, much worse, who'd hit rock bottom so hard they barely got back up. He wasn't alone. He wasn't even the worst of the bunch.

He could make love to his wife again for the first time in months. He didn't feel that awful clenching of guilt and fear in his stomach every time he looked into the face of his infant daughter, Emily. And more than all of this, he remembered what it was like to be a cop, a good cop, the only thing he had ever wanted to be. He approached his job now with the zeal of the converted. And indeed he felt baptized, renewed.

He was experiencing the euphoria of someone snatched from the consequences of his actions. And if he still had the itch to gamble, if he still felt a restless agitation at the sound of a game, any game, in progress—on the radio, on the station-house television—if he still hadn't been quite able to delete his bookie's number from his cell phone, he told himself these things could take a while.

In the meantime he had the biggest case of his career to occupy his attention, the one he'd decided would be his redemption as a police officer. Two grisly homicides connected by one woman who was lying about her identity. Of course, that was the part he had to keep to himself, as per his arrangement with Gray. So Harrison was working overtime to find another connection between Simon Briggs and Paul Brown. He knew he'd find it. He was a dog with a bone.

And then I died. When he heard the news and was called to investigate the scene of the diving accident, he enjoyed a secret smile inside. Not that he'd hated me or wished me ill—quite the opposite. In spite of everything, he'd liked me quite a bit. Even so, Detective Harrison didn't grieve for me as he investigated my suspicious death. Somehow he knew better.

Like the good cop he wanted to be, he walked the grid around the sinkhole, searched my belongings and my car. But when he found the envelope I'd taken from Briggs's car, he never entered it into evidence. He shoved it inside his jacket and then hid it beneath the seat of his own car without anyone seeing.

He dutifully interviewed my bereft family and friends.

"I don't know why she would do it," Ella wept to him at her kitchen table. "She was terrified of the water. I wish I'd tried to stop her. I was trying to be supportive."

Detective Harrison offered her a comforting pat on the shoulder, thinking that, even upset, she was a very attractive woman.

"She was my friend, you know. My *friend*. That means something in this awful world. It means a lot."

"I'm so sorry, Mrs. Singer. I really am."

"Do you think they'll find her body?" she asked, wiping her eyes. She was having trouble speaking between shuddering breaths. "I couldn't stand it if they never found her."

"I don't know, ma'am. It's hard to say with those caves. The divers haven't found anything yet."

"Doesn't it seem like there's nothing to it but pain and disappointment?" she asked him. "Sometimes doesn't it seem that way?"

"What do you mean?" he asked gently, thinking she was too beautiful and rich to be so unhappy.

"I mean *life*, Detective. Sometimes it's all too *hard*."

She lost it then, folded her arms across the table and laid her head upon them and sobbed. My poor, dear friend. He sat with her, a hand on her back. He'd been there before so many, many times. He didn't feel awkward or uncomfortable. He empathized, and he stayed until she was better.

Ella's grief, her self-blame, the pain she was in—these were all palpable, completely sincere in his estimation. My husband, on the other hand, was not as convincing, though he looked drawn and tired when Detective Harrison paid him a visit in the days after my car was found.

"Why would she dive like that if she was so afraid of the water?" the detective asked Gray. "Everyone— her friend, even her instructor—says how afraid she was of the water. Scuba diving seems like an odd choice of hobby for someone who wasn't even comfortable in the pool."

Gray shook his head. "Annie was a stubborn woman. She got it into her head that she wanted to conquer her fear of the water, for Victory. She didn't want Victory to see her giving in to her fear. When she got something into her head, there was no getting it out."

The detective nodded. The whole interview was a charade, of course, both of them knowing that Harrison's hands were tied by what had passed between them. This went unspoken, each of them playing his role.

Harrison looked around the house just to say he did, poking through the dark, empty rooms with Gray right behind him. What he was looking for, he wasn't sure.

"Where's your daughter?" Harrison asked as he was leaving.

Gray issued a sigh and rubbed his eyes. "I sent her away with her grandparents. They're on a cruise to the Caribbean. I don't want her to be touched by this yet. I don't know how to tell her."

It seemed like a reasonable thing to do. But Detective Harrison knew a liar when he saw one. Gray Powers was a man with a lot to hide, and the strain on him was obvious. But he was not a man grieving the loss of a wife. The death of a loved one hollows people out, leaves them with an empty, dazed look that's hard to fake. People mourning a loss might weep inconsolably like Ella, or rage and scream, or they might sink into themselves, go blank. As their minds are scrambling to process the meaning of death, they act in all kinds of crazy and unpredictable ways. But in Detective Harrison's opinion, Gray didn't have that confused, unhinged quality he'd seen so many times before.

"Wasn't there a maid?" asked the detective as he stepped out the front door.

"I gave her some time off while Victory is away."

"I'd like to talk to her."

"Of course," said Gray. He disappeared for a minute, then returned with a number and address scribbled on a sticky note. "She's staying with her sister."

In the doorway the two men faced each other.

"I'm sorry for your loss, Mr. Powers," the detective said with a half smile, just the lightest hint of sarcasm in his voice. But if Gray registered the detective's expression or tone, he didn't acknowledge it at all.

"Thank you," Gray said with a nod, and closed the door.

* * *

"Where'd you go, Ophelia? Who are you running from?" Harrison said aloud to himself as he drove through the gated community where I used to live, admiring the houses he could never dream of affording. He watched the neighborhood kids riding on their expensive bikes. He noted the gleaming bodies of the late-model Benzes and Beemers. He felt a tiny itch he wouldn't dare acknowledge. He focused instead on the matter at hand, the fact that he had not for one second believed I was dead. He was certain I was still alive. If he were still a betting man, he'd have staked his life on it.

33

I am pain. I am nothing but the agony of my body and mind. I don't know how long I've been alternating between total darkness and blinding white light, silence and the booming voice asking questions I can't answer. I might have been here for hours or days. It's dark now, and I take comfort in it, though my body is numb from the inch of freezing water in which I lie. I am shivering uncontrollably, my jaw clenched.

A rectangle of light opens in the wall and a man, small and lean, walks through a doorway I didn't know was there. His footfalls echo off the metal surfaces, and he comes to a stop about an inch from my body. I can't see his face. The lights come up then, less harsh than before, but still I have to close my eyes, open them to slits, then close them again. I do this several times before I am acclimated to the light.

His face is distantly familiar, angular and deeply lined. His eyes are small and watery, his lips dry and pulled tight. But he's not Marlowe.

"This can end. It can be over for you," he says to the wall. He doesn't want to look at me, out of either pity or disgust. I struggle to stand, and I feel a wave of light-headedness so severe I almost black out.

"Just tell me where he is, Ophelia," he says, his voice reasonable and tired.

I am confused, disoriented. I don't know why he thinks I know where Marlowe Geary is. But I can't say any of this. I just can't make the words come out. He stands there for I don't know how long, looking at the wall. I think he'll move to hurt me, to kick me where I lie. But he doesn't. He just stands there.

"I don't know," I finally manage. "I swear to you. I don't know where he is." My voice is little more than a desperate croak.

He rubs his temples in a gesture of fatigue. I am straining to remember his face.

"Annie Fowler may not know. But Ophelia March does," he says softly, almost kindly. His eyes are flint. "She knows."

"No," I say. "No. I don't remember." I try to keep myself from sobbing in front of him, but I can't. I am desperately searching my newly recovered memories. Is it possible that somewhere inside the maze of my shattered psyche I know where Marlowe has been all these years? I chase it, but it turns corners fast, slips away from me. If I could catch it, I would. I would.

"I don't want to hurt you any more, Ophelia," he says.

"Don't," I answer, more out of desperation than anything else.

His whole body goes rigid. He drops to his knees into the cold water and puts his face, red and pulled like taffy with his rage, next to mine. I can smell his breath as he whispers ferociously in my ear, "Then tell me what I want to know, *Ophelia.*"

I recognize him then. He's the Angry Man, one of the protesters that waited on the road outside the horse farm, the one that threw a rock at our car that day. My brain doesn't know what to do with this. I struggle to get up, to get away from him, even as my mind is struggling to put this piece of information into one of the blank spaces of my life. But it's too much. I black out.

When I come to again, the Angry Man is gone. The lights are still on. I sit up with effort and look around the room. There's nothing to see but metal walls and a photograph left by my feet. I pick it up. It's a picture of Victory, my baby, my little girl. Her eyes are closed, her face a ghostly white. Her blond curls fan around her face like the light cast from a halo. There's a piece of black tape over her mouth, and her hands are bound behind her. She looks impossibly small and fragile.

Every rational thought I have left in my head deserts me, and I start to scream. It's a guttural wail that seems to come from someplace primal within me; it's involuntary, rips through me. I've heard this sound before so many times in my worst nightmares, my memories of Janet Parker. I pull myself from the floor and go over to pound on the door.

The voice booms through the speakers I can see now on the ceiling.

"Let's start again. Where's Marlowe Geary?"

34

Ray Harrison lived another life after his wife and daughter went to bed. When they were awake, he was centered, rooted in his life by his love for them. But when they both slept, a strange restlessness awoke within him, an almost physical tingling in his hands and legs. It was something he wouldn't have been able to explain, even if he wanted to. And he didn't.

The silence of the nighttime house, as Sarah called it—the dimmed lights in the kitchen, the hum of the baby monitor, the television volume so low he could barely hear it—caused him to connect with a hole inside himself, a place that needed to be filled. These were the hours when he had first found himself on the phone to his bookie, betting ridiculous sums on games he was assured were a lock. These were the hours when he sat riveted to the screen—always with the same feeling of stunned incredulity—as the quarterback with the bad knee made the impossible touchdown, as the horse who couldn't lose stumbled and fell, as the pitcher with the bad arm threw a perfect game. It felt personal sometimes, it really did. As if something were conspiring on a cosmic level to fuck him until he bled.

So many nights he almost woke Sarah to tell her what he'd done to their life. But then he'd go to her and see that she was asleep so soundly, so peacefully, that he'd lose his nerve and just get into bed beside her. Her trust in him was total. She wasn't one of those wives who called the station to see if he really was working overtime, who went over his pay stubs to check his hours against the tally she was keeping on the sly. She let him handle all their money, all the business of their life together. She never even looked at the accounts online. She wasn't a woman who needed control. She was a woman who'd needed a baby and a home and a husband she trusted. He'd been able to give her all those things, easily, willingly.

Then he'd almost destroyed her, without her ever even suspecting. Every time he thought about it, a shudder moved through him and his face would flush with shame. His escape from the total decimation of his life was narrow. He came so close he could feel it like the rush of a freight train.

He found himself oddly grateful for me, the woman he knew as Annie Powers. If it hadn't been for me, he strongly suspected that he'd be dead or that he would have lost the only two people who meant anything to him. And now he found himself using those hours, that terrible restlessness, to work his case, to find out what happened to the mysterious woman who, without meaning to, had saved him.

He kept a cramped office off the kitchen where the large walk-in pantry used to be. There was a small desk, a creaky chair, and a bare bulb hanging from the ceiling that he turned off and on with a string. He had an old computer that was slow and loud and badly needed replacing, but he could still use it to access the Internet through his dial-up connection.

On the night after he'd talked to Gray, while Sarah and Emily slept, he sifted through the contents of the envelope he'd found in my car. He had known immediately that it had belonged to Simon Briggs; his handwriting was a distinctive loopy cursive that looked like it belonged to a child—a deranged and very stupid child. He'd seen it on other items recovered from Briggs's car. With its big, faltering *O*'s and wobbly *L*'s, his handwriting was oddly precise, as though he had copied each letter from a chalkboard in front of him. The envelope also carried an odor of cigar smoke, a scent that had permeated Briggs's other belongings.

It contained mainly printouts from articles

Harrison himself had already read on the Internet. They were arranged neatly in chronological order, beginning with the article about the fire and murder at the horse ranch. Then there were articles detailing our flight across the country, the crimes Marlowe was suspected of committing, and our eventual death.

There were photographs, stills taken by security cameras at convenience stores and gas stations across the country. Some of them were grisly, some of them grainy and with blurry images impossible to discern. And so many of them were of Ophelia, a haunted, broken-looking young woman. Harrison could barely connect her to me. One shot in particular moved him, disturbed him more than any other. Marlowe and I were captured in conversation, a woman's body on the floor beside us, violated and damaged in ways too unspeakable to describe. Harrison looked at my face and saw an expression he recognized; he'd seen the expression on Sarah's face when she looked at him. It was a look of the purest and most profound love, a love that stood witness to every sin and endured just the same.

I'm still lying in a pool of water, but I've stopped feeling the cold.

"The notion of romantic love is wrongheaded," the doctor tells me. He sits cross-legged in the corner of my metal room. His voice echoes, wet and tinny, off the walls and ceiling.

"Human beings love the thing that tells them what they want to believe about themselves. If at your core you believe that you are worthless, you will love the person who treats you that way. That's why you were able to love Marlowe the way you did."

"Because I thought I was worthless?"

"Didn't you? Isn't that what your parents taught you by word or by deed? If not worthless, then at least negligible?"

"But he didn't treat me as though I was worthless."

"Not at first. They never do at first. Few people hate themselves so much, or so close to the surface, that they accept abuse right off the bat. If he'd treated you badly at first, you'd have walked away from him. He wouldn't have been able to control you the way he did. That's the trick of the abuser. He builds you up so that he can tear you down, piece by piece."

I conceded, even though this didn't feel like the truth. But I have come to understand that in some cases the truth doesn't seem like the truth at all. I had judged my mother harshly for loving a killer; I had hated her for her weakness, for the fact that she'd do anything to keep even the cheapest brand of love. But Ophelia was just like her.

"When you've completely lost touch with your own self-worth, your very identity, he convinces you that he's the only one who could ever love someone so wretched. The love he first gave you is a high you remember, and like a junkie you keep doing the drug, waiting for that first rush again. But it never comes. Unfortunately, though, it's too late. You're hooked."

"He loved me," I say pathetically.

My doctor gives a sad, slow shake of his head. "Ophelia, he was a psychopath. They don't *love*."

"No wonder they took your license away." My words come back at me sharp and hateful. "You're a goddamn quack." The truth can make us turn ugly like that.

He smiles patiently, gives a gentle cluck of his tongue. "Temper, temper."

"I'm sorry," I say.

He lifts a hand. "That's all right. You're under a little stress. I understand."

"I can't tell him what he wants to know."

"Can't or won't?"

"I don't *know* where he is," I say, my voice climbing an octave.

"You do know. Somewhere inside, you know."

* * *

I am startled awake. The doctor, my dead doctor, is not here in the room with me. I am alone, clutching the now torn and wrinkled picture of my daughter. It looks as though I have clenched and clawed at the image, trying to climb through to save her. I smooth it out now.

"Victory," I say out loud, just to taste her name. I have done this to her. The things we fear the most are always visited upon us; it's the way of the universe. I rock with her picture, hating Marlowe Geary, hating the Angry Man, and hating myself most of all.

Of course my dream doctor is right. Marlowe was a sociopath and a killer like his father. And no, of course he never loved me. But that didn't stop me from loving him, from giving myself over the way only an abused and neglected teenage girl can give herself over, like a virgin on an altar, gratefully willing to be sacrificed. He manipulated and used me, but I laid myself down for him. Every time he killed and I did nothing, something vital within me died, until I was little more than a walking corpse.

Now, strangely, I am resurrected in this place. I am neither the girl I was nor the woman I became. I am both of them.

I think of all those flights from my life, my fugue

states. I wonder where Ophelia was going, what she knew that Annie didn't. I suspect now that she was going to find him. I remembered what Vivian said during our last conversation: *You were haunted by him. . . . Part of you, maybe the part that couldn't remember so much, was still connected to him.*

The question is, why? Was she trying to go back to him, wanting to be with him again? Was she that desperate, that stupid, that miserably in love? I don't know the answer. But I am sure of one thing: Ophelia knows where Marlowe is. I just have to get her to tell me.

"Can you hear me?" I yell into the air.

The silence seems to hum, but it's just the fluorescent light burning above my head, flickering almost imperceptibly. They've shut off the spotlight they've been shining on me—I see it mounted in the far corner of the room. I'm glad they've given up on that technique. In the other corner, there's a security camera, a red light blinking beneath its lens.

"Where is my daughter?" I yell, louder this time, looking at the camera. More silence, and then I hear the buzz of a speaker.

"I don't want to hurt her, Ophelia," says the Angry Man, his voice, broken by static, sounding far away, as though he's calling on an old overseas line.

"I know what it is to lose a child. I don't wish that on anyone. Not even on you."

"Don't hurt her," I say quickly, feeling my chest tighten. "I'll find him."

The static from the speaker seems to fill the room. I should have demanded to hear her voice first before I agreed to help him. But I'm too desperate for those kinds of tricks.

"You remember?" he says finally. "You'll lead me to him?"

"I'll do anything you want," I say, sounding as beaten as I am. "Just don't hurt her. Don't hurt my baby."

I realize then that I'm weeping again. I'm so beyond shame that I don't even bother to wipe the tears from my eyes.

When Marlowe and I finally got to New York City, to my father's shop near the Village, I was a fly in a web, stuck and drugged, not even trying to escape. I didn't even ask for help. It was still relatively early in our flight, only about three weeks after the fire at the horse ranch, and the authorities hadn't put two and two together. At that point we were just runaways. I didn't realize this, of course. I believed that we were fugitives, wanted as Janet Parker's accomplices for murder and for the fire. I was still deeply in denial about what had happened at the gas station; in fact, it was gone from my consciousness completely. In my dreams I saw a bloody halo of hair spread out across a linoleum floor.

My father asked no questions. He let us stay in the small spare room I used to sleep in when I'd stayed with him in the past, in the back of his apartment over the tattoo shop. There was a pink bedspread and a patchwork chair. The radiator cover was the same purple I'd painted it when I was twelve. There was an old doll made out of denim, with red yarn for hair and wearing a black Hells Angels T-shirt. One of my father's old girlfriends had made her for me long ago. Predictably, I'd named her Harley.

"I ran away when I was your age," my dad told me when he took us upstairs to the bedroom. We'd just wandered into the shop; he hadn't seemed surprised to see me. I didn't know when he got back from his trip or if he'd ever been gone at all. I didn't ask. "Been on my own ever since."

He said it with a kind of uncertain pride that filled me with disappointment. I wanted him to be angry, to scold me and help me find my way back from the downward spiral I knew I was in. But right away I saw he wasn't going to do that.

Marlowe and my father seemed to bounce off each other. They didn't look at each other after the first greeting, a stiff handshake that seemed more like a confrontation ending in stalemate. Marlowe towered over my father by a head; Dad seemed almost frail and shriveled beside him. Another disappointment: In my mind's eye, my father was always a big man, powerful and strong. But I saw quickly that he was no match for Marlowe, physically or in any other way.

If I recall correctly, we were there three nights.

All those days seem to run together in my mind. Marlowe and I did little but eat and sleep in that quiet, dim back room, we were so exhausted and worn down. I remember having trouble differentiating between being awake and being asleep. I have vague recall of conversations with my father that seemed like parts of a dream: He asked about the weather in Florida. . . . He said he knew I was trying to reach him. . . . He was sorry that he'd been away. We talked about the tattoo he'd agreed to do for Marlowe. He seemed uncomfortable and tentative around me, as though he wasn't sure how to handle this recent wrinkle in my life. Something inside me was screaming for help, but he was deaf to it.

On the fourth morning, I heard a light rapping on the bedroom door before it pushed open a crack. I could see my father standing there, motioning for me. It was just after dawn, the sun leaking in through the slats of the drawn blinds.

"O," he whispered. "Opie."

I slipped out from beneath Marlowe's arm and followed my father down the narrow hallway into his living room. The space was dominated by a large pool table surrounded by a couple of old metal folding chairs. It smelled so strongly of cigarette smoke that it made my sinuses ache. There was a small, dirty galley kitchen over by the door, with dishes in the tiny sink and rows of empty beer bottles lined up on the counter.

My father leaned against one of the windowsills. Behind him I could see the rooftop of the low brown building across the street; someone had made a little garden there, put out some lawn chairs and a striped umbrella. I could hear the sound of early-morning traffic moving on the street below. My father looked older than the way I saw him in my memory, the hard miles of his life etched on his face in deep lines. He had a stooped look to him, dark circles under his eyes.

I hopped up onto the pool table and sat there, wanting to run over and have him take me in his arms. But my father wasn't affectionate like that. The most I ever got was a quick, awkward hug, or he might present his cheek for a kiss. That was all he seemed capable of where I was concerned.

"Your mom called, Opie."

I looked down at my feet, noticed that the red nail polish was worn away to little dots on each toe.

"You told her I was here."

He shook his head. "No."

"What did she tell you?"

He released a sigh. "About the fire. About her husband being killed. She's in a bad way, Opie. And you two are in big trouble. Why didn't you tell me about these things?"

I shrugged, examining my knees. They were bruised and dirty, unattractively knobby. "Doesn't have anything to do with you, does it?"

He nodded toward the bedroom. "I don't like that guy, Opie. He's not right."

But his voice sounded muffled and wobbly, as though I were hearing him through cotton in my ears. I didn't answer him. I couldn't. I knew that Marlowe was listening; I don't know how, but I knew. My whole body was stiff with hope and fear—this was the moment I'd been waiting for, the moment my father would finally rescue me.

"You need to tell me one thing." He walked over to me and put a finger gently beneath my chin, lifting my face so that he could look into my eyes.

"Okay," I said. "What?" I wondered how he'd do it, how he'd get me away from Marlowe. I wondered if he'd already called the police, if they were waiting outside. I couldn't believe how desperately I hoped this was the case. As much as I loved Marlowe, I was so deeply afraid of him, of the things he'd done, of how much worse it was going to get. These parts existed side by side within me, paralyzing me. I was a girl very much in need of help.

"You need to tell me everything is all right," he said quietly. "Really all right."

I look back on that moment now and try not to

hate my father. It's not just his weakness that I find so despicable, it's that he wanted me to let him off the hook. He wanted me to ease his conscience.

I gave him what he asked for because that's what I knew how to do. "I'm all right," I said with a fake smile and a quick nod of my head. "We'll find a place out west. I'll get my GED and find a job. I'll be eighteen soon, an adult. Older than you when you went out on your own."

His relief was palpable. He let his hand drop to his side, and he released a sigh, gave me a weak smile. He wouldn't have to be a father, to take the hard line, to step in and make difficult calls that I couldn't make for myself. And anyway, he wouldn't have known how.

He sat beside me on the pool table and held out a wad of cash, a thick, tight roll secured with a rubber band.

"There's nearly a thousand dollars here," he said quietly. He nodded toward the bedroom. "It's for you. Not for him. This is your 'screw you' money. Things don't go right, you find your way home with this."

I wasn't sure what home he was talking about. In that moment I knew that my only home now was with Marlowe. I took the cash from him. It was heavy in my hand. My heart sank with the weight of it.

"It's only a matter of time before the police come here," he said, keeping his voice low. His eyes were on the floor. "It probably won't be today, but soon enough."

I gave a quick nod. "You want us to leave."

"If you don't want them to take you back to Florida."

I didn't trust my voice as I battled the swell of despair in my chest.

"You swear you're okay?" he said after a few minutes of silence.

I managed to look him in the eye and say, "I swear."

He patted me gently on the back, placed a kiss on my forehead, and left the room as if he couldn't get out of there fast enough. I heard his heavy boots descend the stairs outside the door. I sat a moment, allowing myself to dwell in a place of hope, waiting for him to burst back through the door or for the police to sweep in, but there was nothing except the sound of his footfalls getting more and more distant until I heard the street door slam closed downstairs.

"I told you he'd never come for you." I turned to see Marlowe standing behind me. In his expression there was some mixture of triumph and pity. He walked over to me and put a hand on my arm. My flesh went cold beneath his touch.

The tattoo that started on his left pectoral swept over his shoulder. It was covered in antibiotic ointment, the lines swollen and raised, the visible skin red. It must have been painful, but it didn't seem to bother him.

I gave him the money and he put it in his pocket; there wasn't even a question that I would give it to him. I nuzzled my face against his good arm so he couldn't look into my eyes. He stroked the back of my head and neck. I rested my hands on the tight, narrow expanse of his waist.

"You don't need anyone else, Ophelia," he said. "You belong to me."

3 6

In spite of the fact that Simon Briggs had checked in to the dilapidated Sunshine Motel less than forty-eight hours prior to his death, his space was already as filthy a mess as his car. Less than twenty-four hours after my disappearance and presumed death, Detective Harrison stood in the middle of Room 206 and surveyed the area. Fast-food wrappers were strewn across the carpet like flowers on a meadow, two pizza boxes gaped greasy and empty on the bed, beer cans lined up like soldiers in crooked rows on the windowsills. There was a litter of candy wrappers by the toilet, atop the latest issue of the *Economist*.

Detective Harrison hated a mess; just the thought of Briggs made him want to take a shower. But for someone so sloppy, Briggs was surprisingly professional with his collection of articles, his copious notes about me in my various incarnations, his lack of phone usage at the motel or any information that might identify his employer. Amid the detritus of the motel room, Harrison found the empty packaging of a disposable cell phone. The phone itself was nowhere to be found in the room, in the car, or on Briggs's person. *He trashed it,* thought Harrison, *or someone took it.* Briggs probably didn't realize that with the packaging the police might be able to subpoena the call records under new federal regulations. This would, however, be a major pain in the ass and could take weeks. Detective Harrison knew on an instinctive level that he didn't have weeks, that he might not even have days, if he cared what happened to me.

He put on a pair of gloves and sifted through the wastepaper basket near the front door. He could feel the watchful eyes of the woman who headed the CSI team. She probably was wondering how badly he was going to screw up their scene.

"Relax, Claire," he said without looking at her. "I'm being careful."

"It's your case, Detective," she said. "You botch it, it's your problem."

He ignored her as he inspected the contents of the basket. Toward the bottom he found a piece of paper that had been crumbled into a tight ball. He noticed it because of the quality of the paper, a heavy, expensive piece of stock. He unfurled it carefully, smoothed it out on the carpet. There was a doodle, a stick figure holding what appeared to be a gun, some scribbling that looked like someone trying to get a pen to work, and a telephone number that Briggs had tried to black out with a marker but was still legible. Embossed in blue at the top of the page was a company name, Grief Intervention Services, and a website address, nomorefear.biz.

"Find something?" Claire asked.

"Just more garbage," he said, crumpling the paper back up.

"That's what you usually find in a trash can," she said. She laughed at her own joke, and he gave her a smile he didn't feel.

When she turned away from him, he stuck the paper in his pocket, pretended to pick through the waste can for a few more minutes.

After he'd finished with the room and left the technicians to do their trace-evidence collection, Detective Harrison turned his attention to the helpful young Indian couple who owned and operated the motel. The husband was a reed of a man with thick glasses, an unfortunately large nose, and a diminutive chin.

The wife was a vision in a kind of abbreviated hot pink–and–gold sari, which she wore over jeans, more of a fashion statement, he thought, than any compulsion to dress in traditional garb. With huge, almond-shaped eyes framed by long, dark lashes and a pleasing hourglass shape to her body, she caused the detective to look at her more than a few times out of the corner of his eye—in the most respectful possible way, of course. He noticed beauty, even though he'd never been unfaithful to his wife. He allowed himself the appreciation of lovely women.

The husband smiled a wide, goofy smile at Harrison. The wife frowned. She was nervous, upset by the presence of the police. The husband acted like it was the most exciting thing that had happened to him in months. They were totally wired in the technical sense, all their records computerized and a system of surveillance cameras that backed up to a hard drive. Briggs checked in to the motel as Buddy Starr about forty-eight hours before his body was found; he'd paid in cash and provided a New York State driver's license that the hotel owners had diligently scanned into their system. He had not made any calls or used the Internet connection in his room.

The couple also ran an Indian restaurant attached

to the hotel. The aroma of tandoori chicken and curry permeated the air, making Harrison's stomach grumble as he sat in the office behind the reception area and scrolled through days of surveillance from the camera that monitored the landing outside Briggs's door. It didn't take him long to find what he was looking for, but when he found it—the dark, powerful figure of a man moving across the landing toward Room 206—it raised more questions than it answered. The man moved like a soldier, cautious but confident, was mindful of the security camera, keeping his face carefully averted from the lens. He didn't need to jimmy the lock; he had a key card and let himself in easily. He was in the room for less than ten minutes and left as he entered, quietly and carrying nothing.

Though it would never hold up in court, Harrison recognized Gray right away by his bearing and his stride, by the intimidating musculature of his shoulders. Men noticed the size and build of other men more than they'd admit; it was how they identified their place in the pack. Harrison remembered those shoulders, remembered thinking how bad it would feel to be on the beating end of those fists.

According to the time imprint on the image, Gray had arrived at the hotel less than an hour after

Briggs's estimated time of death, with the key card to his room.

"Find anything?" the young hotel owner asked, coming up behind the detective.

"Leave him *alone,*" said his wife from her perch at the front desk. "Let him do his job so they can all get out of here."

The man ignored her, still had that wide smile on his face. He seemed to find the whole thing very exciting, even though it couldn't be good for business to have a room cordoned off by crime-scene tape and a CSI truck in your parking lot. These days, though, everyone thought they were living in a reality television show. People seemed to have trouble differentiating between what was really happening and what was happening on television. Harrison had noticed in the last few years that suddenly all crime, even the most violent, and its solving had become "cool." For the hotel owner, the fact that a man staying in his hotel had been gunned down was not tragic or frightening, it was a subject of interest, something he'd e-mail his friends and family about, stay up late speculating on.

"Possibly," said Harrison. "Is there some way I can get a copy of this surveillance footage, between the hours of nine-ten and nine-thirty P.M.?"

The young man nodded vigorously.

"I'll make an MPEG, copy it onto a thumb drive for you. You just plug the drive into the USB port on your computer, and you can access the file that way. You can return the drive when you've downloaded it onto your computer, okay?"

"Great," said the detective, having no idea what an MPEG was, or a thumb drive for that matter. "That's great. Thanks."

"So what'd you see?" the owner asked, still smiling, tapping a staccato on the keyboard in front of him. "You probably can't tell me. That's okay, you don't have to tell me. I just think it's so cool to be a detective. I really wanted to be a cop, you know, but my parents had other ideas. I still think about it—all the time. But Miranda, my wife, doesn't like the idea any more than my parents—"

He went on, but Harrison wasn't listening. He was thinking about the footage of Gray entering Briggs's room right after Briggs's murder. *What is this worth?* That's the question he found himself asking a lot. *Where does this have the most value? Does it help my case, my career? How much would Gray Powers pay to make this go away?* Then he came back to himself and flushed with shame; that was an old way of thinking. This now was about me, about helping Annie Powers—or whatever my name was. But if he could do that and still help himself, wasn't that even better?

I don't know how long it was after we'd left my father's place that I met Simon Briggs; it might have been six months or more. All the days and months during that period run together, and I have no markers for the passage of time. I know now that I'd had a total psychotic break and that even though much of my memory has returned, many of the day-to-day events are never coming back. I can't say I'm sorry. But there must have been moments of lucidity, because when some of these memories return, they are painfully vivid.

The night I first saw Briggs, I was sitting in a diner with Marlowe. We'd both altered our appearances. I'd dyed my hair an awful black. With my pale skin, I looked like a ghoul. Marlowe had shaved his hair and had grown a goatee and mustache. He looked like a vampire skinhead. You'd think at this point we wouldn't have been able to eat in public. In the movies a killer eats at a truck stop and his picture is posted behind the counter or randomly pops up on the television screen. Someone notices him, and the chase is on. But in the real world, people are oblivious, living in their own little heads. They barely see what's going on around them, and when they do, they rarely believe their own eyes.

Marlowe went to the bathroom, and while I waited, staring into the depths of my coffee cup, a man walked past me too close and dropped a napkin onto the table. I turned to see his wide, heavy frame and the back of his bald head as he walked out the door.

I unfolded the napkin. There was a note: *Bad things are about to happen to Marlowe Geary. Save yourself, if you still can.*

I crushed the note in my hand and dropped it on the floor, adrenaline flooding my body.

"What's wrong?" asked Marlowe when he returned and sat across from me.

I shook my head. "Nothing. I'm tired."

"You're always tired," he said.

"Maybe it's the company I keep," I said, the words escaping before I could catch them. He looked at me, surprised. Then he leaned his face close to mine over the table. "Watch yourself." His voice was tight with menace. There was a trail of brutally murdered women behind us, his tone said to me, and I could easily be next.

I went to the bathroom and looked in the mirror.

The bathroom was filthy, dirt gritty on the tile floor, graffiti scratched on the stalls, and it smelled of urine. I was unrecognizable to myself with my jet-black hair and pallid complexion; my reflection was frightening.

How can I explain myself? How can I explain my relationship to Marlowe Geary, who I loved and hated, feared and clung to? I can't, not then, not now. *Save yourself, if you still can.*

When I walked back out, Marlowe had already left the restaurant. I knew he was outside waiting for me in the car. That's how sure he was of me. There were two uniformed officers sitting at the counter. They hadn't been there when I entered the bathroom, but now they sat, both drinking coffee from white ceramic mugs. Their radios chattered; large revolvers hung at their hips. Their shirts were bulky with the Kevlar they wore beneath. I think we were in Pennsylvania at the time. I remember that the uniforms were brown, light shirts with dark jackets and pants. One of them laughed at something the other said.

Everything around me slowed and warped as I approached the counter where they sat. *Save yourself, if you still can.* I imagined walking right up to them and turning myself in. Marlowe would have been able to get away. I would tell them he'd left me here, that he'd let me go, and they'd arrest me. They'd take me into the station in the back of their car. Maybe they'd call my father. He'd come get me. I'd finally tell him I *wasn't* all right and that he needed to take care of me. And he would, this time he would.

But I didn't stop. I walked right by the two men. Neither of them noticed me as I walked out the door into the cold night. Marlowe was waiting for me outside the door. I slipped into the car, a stolen Cadillac. The heat was cranking.

"Cops are so unbelievably stupid, man," he said with a laugh, as he peeled out of the lot.

Save yourself, if you still can. I couldn't.

I have abandoned and betrayed myself so many times, given so much over for any poor facsimile of love. I have never been true to Ophelia; I have locked her in a cage deep within myself, depriving her of light and air, and kept her from growing up. I have denied her. I have killed her. I have done all this because I judged her and found her unworthy. Of all the people who have wronged Ophelia, I am the worst offender. But now I have had to reclaim her and do right by her to save my daughter.

The irony of this is not lost on me as I walk quickly on wet concrete. I pass the glaring windows of a music store. The glowing album covers, lit from behind, feature the faces of too-thin, carefully grungy pop stars and cast a yellow light at my feet. People who buy and sell music albums are living in a different world from me; their lives seem frivolous and foreign. I wait on the corner in the rain as cars and taxis race past me. I can see my father's shop across the street, and it's all I can do not to race into traffic to get there. The shop is closed, but I can see the blue flickering light of a television screen in the windows above.

New York City. How did I get here? The truth is, I don't quite know. Already I doubt my memories of the sinkhole, the ship and the man named Dax, the metal room and the Angry Man. But the picture of Victory in my pocket and the necklace I'm wearing make me think some of it might be close to the truth.

I woke up on a commuter train pulling into Grand Central Station. I was wearing fresh clothes I've never seen before and a long black raincoat. Leather boots. People around me chatted on cell phones, stared blankly at small handheld screens, headphones plugged into their ears. I gazed at my reflection in the window beside me, saw that my hair was pulled back into a tight ponytail at the base of my neck. I had dark circles under my eyes.

At the train station, I was swept into a current of

people moving determinedly toward wherever they were going. I saw a bank of pay phones and wondered whom I could call now. I want desperately to call Gray or Vivian, but I can't do that. There's too much at stake, and I don't know whom to trust.

The traffic clears now, and I cross the street. I stand in the vestibule and press the buzzer to my father's apartment. I press it five, six times, hard, hoping to express my urgency this way. Finally I hear heavy boots on the stairs.

"Hold on, for crying out loud!" my father barks. "French, if that's you, I'm going to *beat* your *ass*."

An old man who looks like a badly aged version of my father bangs into view. It takes me a second to accept that it *is* him. He sees me then and stops in his tracks, leans a hand against the wall and closes his eyes.

"Dad," I say, and my voice sounds scratchy and uncertain. He looks awful, ragged and overtired. His clothes are rumpled and hanging off him a bit, as though he's lost a lot of weight recently and hasn't bothered to replace them.

He reaches for the door, swings it open, and pulls me into a bear hug. He has never done that. Never. Even though it's awkward to be embraced by him, this one thing almost makes up for all the ways he has screwed up as a father. I breathe in his scent of booze and cigarettes. It has been almost seven years since I've seen him.

"You shouldn't be here," he said. "You're supposed to be dead, Ophelia. Again."

37

"I think I'm going to die out here."

Marlowe said this matter-of-factly, as though he couldn't care less. The thought of his death was something I couldn't handle. It filled me with a perfect storm of hope and terror. We were in New Mexico, somewhere between Taos and Santa Fe. From the road he'd seen an old church, a tiny white adobe building, glowing like a beacon. He'd pulled over without a word, stepped out of the car, and starting walking toward it. I followed him, taking in the scent of sage and juniper that was heavy in the air.

The building was dark, the wood and wrought-iron doors locked tight. I looked in the window and saw the flickering rows of votive candles inside twinkling like fireflies. He lay down on the small patch of grass inside the fence around the church, and I came to sit beside him. He folded his arms behind his head and took a long, deep breath, released it slowly. The desert air was cool, the sky above alive with stars. I was a city girl. I didn't even know there were that many stars in the heavens.

"If it looks like we're going to get caught, I'm going to die."

I let the words hang in the air for a few breaths.

"You're going to kill yourself?" I asked.

He shook his head, turned those dark eyes on me, and I looked away. I couldn't stand to look at his face anymore. Every time I did, I heard screaming, saw a river of blood.

"No," he said. "I'm going to make it look like I was killed. Everyone will think I'm dead, but I'll be alive, in hiding."

He sounded like a child then, a kid fantasizing about his life. We *were* kids; that's what I always forget. When I think about Marlowe, he's a titan, this powerhouse I turned myself over to for the various reasons that one does such a thing. But he wasn't even twenty-one.

He put a hand on my leg. "I'll have to stay away from you for a while—a few years, maybe. Without the body they'll always be watching you, waiting for you to come to me or me to come for you. But when the time is right, I'll find you and you'll be waiting. That's our karma, our bond."

"Where will you go?" I asked, playing the game with him, knowing how fast he'd turn ugly if I didn't.

He shrugged. "I can't tell you. They'll torture you to find me. You're weak. You'll give in."

I started to cry then. I hid my face in the crook of my arm so he wouldn't see, but I couldn't keep my shoulders from shaking.

"Don't worry, Ophelia," he said, sitting up and wrapping his arms around me. His voice was sweet and soft. "I'll come for you. I promise."

But of course that wasn't why I succumbed to the crushing sadness that lived in my chest. I knew in that moment that I would never be free from him. That for the rest of my life, he'd live under my skin, in my nightmares, just around the next corner.

"When it's time for us to be together again," he said, "I'll leave my necklace somewhere for you to find. That's how you'll know I've come for you. That'll be our signal."

He was enjoying himself, the drama of it all, making me cry. It fed into his fantasy of who we were and what was happening to us. At the time I was as sick and delusional as he was, playing my role in his fantasy, casting myself as victim.

We sat there in silence for a time. My tears dried up, and I listened to a coyote howling at the moon somewhere far off in the distance. Then . . .

"There's something I want you to know, Ophelia. I need someone to know." His voice sounded thick and strange.

"What?"

He looked out into the vast flatness all around us for so long I thought he'd decided not to go on. I didn't press. Inside, I cringed at what he might tell me.

"Those women," he said with an odd laugh and a shake of his head. "They didn't matter, you know. They were nothing to anyone."

"Who?" I asked, even though my shoulders were so tense they ached, my fist clenched so hard I could feel my nails digging into my palms.

"The women my father brought home. Most of them, even their own parents had abandoned them. No one mourned them, not really."

I thought of Janet Parker howling at our trailer door. "That's not true," I said.

"It *is* true," he snapped, baring his teeth at me like the dog that he was.

I didn't argue again. Just listened as he told me again how they were looking for a way out of their shit lives, looking for the punishment they knew they deserved. How death was mercy, how they were noticed more in their absence from the world than they were in their presence.

"Marlowe," I said finally, when he'd gone silent. I

tried to keep my voice soft the way he liked it. "What are you telling me?"

The night seemed to stretch, the seconds were hours as the coyotes sang in the distance.

"My father didn't kill those women," he said. His words lofted above us, looped, then floated off into the night sky. His skin was ghastly white, his eyes the dark empty holes in a dime-store mask. "Not all of them."

"Who then?" I asked, though of course I knew the answer.

"I watched him kill her," he said, not answering my question. "I never told you. She didn't leave us. She didn't run away. She burned the English muffin she was making for his breakfast. He slapped her so hard she staggered back and hit her head against the edge of the counter. There was, like, this horrible noise, some cross between a thud and a snap. The way she fell to the floor, so heavy, her neck at this terrible angle—she was dead before she hit the ground."

He paused here, and I listened to his breathing, which seemed suddenly labored, though his face was expressionless, his eyes dry. "It didn't seem real. It seemed like something I was watching on TV. My mother was stupid and weak, I remember her cowering around my father, living her life walking on eggshells. But I loved her, anyway. I didn't want her to die."

I was afraid to say anything. Afraid to move a muscle.

"Later I lied for him. I didn't want him to go to jail. When the people she worked with sent the police, he told them she ran off. Withdrew some money from the bank and stole the car. They believed him. They believed me when I said I saw her leaving in the night. I told them she said, 'Marlowe, honey, go back to sleep. I'm going to get some milk for your breakfast.'"

There's a rustling somewhere near us. Some creature making its way over the desert floor, something small.

"I never forgave him, though. A few years later, he brought someone home. A pasty blonde—a quivering, nervous waste of bones." He gave a disgusted laugh, kept looking off at that same spot in the distance. "There was no *way* I was going to allow him to replace her. I couldn't have another mother, so he wasn't going to have another whore."

He went on then to tell me with no emotion whatsoever about the women he'd killed, somehow managing to paint himself as the victim, the little boy who missed his mother so much, who sought to avenge her. But I was only half listening. Inside, I was screaming.

Frank, in his guilt, helped Marlowe to hide his crimes and eventually took the blame for the murders—because he loved his son so much, Marlowe claimed. I had no way of knowing if what he said was true, but it didn't much matter. I had disappeared from that place. On the sound of Marlowe's voice, I had drifted up into the stars and floated high above our bodies. I looked down to see two people sitting on the lawn of a small white church, one of them talking quietly about murder, the other wishing for death.

I follow my father up the stairs and into his apartment. It is exactly the same as it was the last time I was here, except older and dirtier. It doesn't seem like the cool, freewheeling bachelor pad it once did. It looks like the run-down apartment of an old man who doesn't know how to take care of himself. His party days are behind him, and he never built anything—a home, a family—that endured.

I notice he has added a recliner and a large television set on a glass-and-chrome stand over by the window. The pool table has been pushed over to the far wall to accommodate these additions. There's a sweating beer can on the floor by the chair, a rerun of *Baywatch* on the screen. All the lights are out. He has been sitting here in the dark watching television alone.

He shrugs when he sees me looking at the screen. "I used to date her," he says, indicating the bleached blonde on the set.

"Dad," I say, shaking my head. This seems to be the only word I can get out. He sits down in the recliner, stares blankly at the television. I go over and stand in front of him.

"Dad, no more lies," I say. "I love you, but you've been a really terrible father."

His body seems to sag with the weight of my words, and I think he might be crying. But I don't have time to comfort him. "I need you to help me now. I need you to be a better grandfather than you were a dad."

I take the picture from my pocket and hold it out for him to see. "Oh, Christ," he says when he looks at it. "Oh, God."

"Marlowe Geary is still alive. Someone's looking for him, they have Victory, and I need to lead them to Marlowe or they're going to hurt her." As the words tumble out of my mouth, I hear how crazy they sound. I suddenly feel very bad for Victory. *This* is her rescue team: a beat-up old pathological liar and a nutcase mother.

In a mad rush, the rest of it pours out of me, everything that's happened since the dark figure on the beach. "Somewhere inside me, I know where he is," I tell him finally. "I just don't have access to that information yet."

"Opie," he responds gently, "no offense, but are you sure you haven't lost your mind?"

I think about this for a second. "No, Dad," I admit. "I'm not sure at all."

Looking at me from beneath raised eyebrows, he says, "What do you need me to do?"

38

Less than a week after my disappearance, my memorial service was held at a small chapel by the beach. Neighbors, friends, colleagues crowded into the space. It was a hot day, and the air-conditioning was not up to the task. People were sweating, fanning themselves, shedding tears as Gray gave a heartfelt eulogy about how he'd loved me, how I'd changed his life and made him a better person. He said I'd left all the best parts of myself behind in Victory, our daughter.

Detective Harrison stayed in the back and watched the crowd. Conspicuous by their absence were Vivian, Drew, and Victory. *It's a show,* he thought. No one would have a memorial service for a woman who was still classified as missing unless he was invested in making it appear to someone that she was dead. Gray seemed sunken and hollowed out; to everyone else he seemed like a man suffering with terrible grief. To Harrison he seemed like a man struggling under the burden of terrible lies.

A woman sat in the front of the chapel and wept with abandon. He recognized her even from behind. It was Ella, beautifully coiffed in her grief, of course—hair swept in a perfect chignon, impeccably dressed in a simple black sheath, her nails done.

After the service Harrison stood off to the side in the trees watching people leave. He watched for someone alone, someone who seemed out of place. He guessed that most of the men were colleagues of Gray's—they all had that paramilitary look to them, built and secretive, ever aware of their surroundings. He recognized some of the older people as neighbors he'd seen the night of the intruder on the beach. He didn't see anyone who aroused his interest.

"You shouldn't be here," Ella said, approaching him. "You weren't her friend."

Her breath smelled lightly of alcohol. He regarded her, sized her up. She was handling things badly, seemed unsteady on her feet. Her eyes were rimmed with red.

"Do you have someone to drive you home?" he asked gently.

"None of these people were her friends," she said too loudly. People turned to stare as they moved toward their cars. "I've never seen any of them in my life."

He put a hand on her arm. "Let me take you home, Mrs. Singer."

"I have my own car, thank you," she said primly.

"You can get it later," he said, more firmly.

She surprised him by not arguing. "I mean, who are these people?" she said, lowering her voice to a whisper, leaning her weight against him as he led her to his Explorer.

"Where is her daughter? Where are Drew and Vivian? I asked Gray. He told me that it was none of my business." She paused and shook her head. "Something's just not right."

He opened the door for her, and she climbed inside with a little help. He got in on the other side, turned on the engine, and pulled in to the line of cars exiting the parking lot of the chapel. The blue sky was going gray; heavy dark clouds were moving in from the sea.

"Someone killed her, didn't they?" she said, looking out the window.

"Why would you say something like that?" he asked her.

She shrugged. "The man on the beach that night. Since then, she wasn't the same. She seemed— I don't know—not herself. Maybe she was afraid of someone? I don't know."

"Did she ever talk to you about her past?" he

asked, pulling in to our neighborhood. The line at the gate was long, with people heading back to our house for the reception. Ella pointed the way to her house and shook her head slowly.

"You know what? No. I knew that Annie was raised in Central Florida and that both her parents were dead. She didn't have any family at all except for Gray and Victory. She never talked about her past. I had the sense she didn't want anyone asking, either. So I never did."

He didn't have the heart to tell her that Annie wasn't even my real name, that most things I'd told her about myself were lies.

"How'd she get along with her in-laws?" he asked instead.

"She loved Vivian. But Drew . . . bad blood there, if you ask me."

"Oh?"

"He hated her, or so she thought. He didn't think she was good enough for Gray. She didn't talk much about that, either. So I didn't press."

"What *did* you talk about?"

She let a beat pass. "Shoes," she said, then let go a peal of hysterical laughter that ended in a sob. He thought she was going to lose it. But she pulled herself together relatively quickly. After a moment she wiped her tears away, careful not to smear her mascara. "I was a terrible friend, wasn't I? I didn't know anything about Annie."

He pulled in to her driveway. "You accepted her for who she was in the present, Mrs. Singer. We only know about people what they want to show us. You respected her privacy and shared good times with her. I think that makes you an excellent friend. I really do."

Detective Harrison was a wise man; I would have told her the same thing.

She took a tissue from her clutch and wiped her nose. "Thanks," she said, nodding. "She did that for me, too."

They sat like that for a minute in her drive. The wind was blowing the high palm fronds around, and they whispered, gossiping about all they knew and wouldn't tell. The sky had gone from blue to gray to black and was ready to erupt.

"That night on the beach?" Ella said, leaning forward and looking up at the sky. Harrison noticed her beauty again, the delicate line of her jaw, the regal length of her neck.

"What about it?"

"At the party she thought she saw someone that she recognized. A young girl, wearing jeans and a T-shirt."

"Who was it?"

She gave him a quick shrug. "No idea. I knew everyone there that night, even all the servers who have worked for me before. She seemed really unsettled by it and left pretty soon after that."

"So what are you saying?"

"I'm saying there was no one at my house who looked like that, no one under forty, and certainly no one wearing jeans and a T-shirt."

He remembered the night at the rest stop. He remembered how my gaze kept moving behind him as though I'd been watching someone or something. He'd seen fear on my face that night, so clearly that it had caused him to reach for his gun. "You think Annie imagined her?"

She looked surprised for a second, as though the thought hadn't occurred to her. Then, "I don't know. She had an expression on her face that stayed with me. I think I'd seen it before in flashes, but not like that. She looked haunted. I think she was, in some ways." She smiled nervously, ran a self-conscious hand along her jaw. "I don't know why I'm telling you this. It doesn't help you any, does it?"

"You were right to tell me," he said. "You never know what helps." After a pause he added, "Did she ever mention her doctor to you?"

She shook her head. "No. What kind of doctor?"

"How about an organization called Grief Intervention Services?"

She raised her eyebrows, thought about it for a second. "No," she said, bringing her hand to rub her temple. He'd seen Volkswagens that were smaller than the ring on her finger. "I never heard her mention anything like that."

"Did you get the sense that she was someone who would take off? You know, just run away from her life? Did she seem like she might be capable of that?"

She shook her head vigorously, without hesitation. "No way. Not without Victory. She worships that little girl." Then, "That's not what you think, is it? That she just took off?"

"I'm just trying to be thorough. Without a body, we need to examine every possibility."

"Well, that's not a possibility. She wouldn't leave without her daughter."

"Okay," he said, giving her a smile he thought she needed. "You've been a big help. You really have."

She offered him a grateful look. "So is this a murder investigation? You showing up at the memorial like that? Isn't that what they do on television?"

"I'm just trying to be thorough," he said again, purposely vague.

She nodded, seemed to think about saying something else but then thanked him for the ride instead. Then she dashed from the car to the house as a heavy rain started to fall. He watched until she let herself in the front door and shut it behind her.

Harrison drove up the street and parked near my house. As he watched the mourners come and go, he thought about me, about Marlowe Geary, and all the desperate things people become for love. He began to realize as the rain turned to hail, causing people to dash from car to house or house to car, covering their heads with their jackets or purses, that if he wanted to know what had happened to me, he was going to have to go back to go forward.

I tell my father how I dropped into the earth, followed my "dive master" through a long, narrow limestone tunnel for what seemed like hours, and emerged from another sinkhole. There a man whose name I never learned and whose face I barely saw was waiting for me in a Jeep Grand Cherokee. I stripped out of my wetsuit, dried off, and put on the clothes he had for me. I checked the contents of the bag he'd retrieved from my locker with the key I gave to Gray. I lay down on the floor of the backseat and stayed there, uncomfortable and gripped by self-doubt, as we drove for hours. I drifted off, only to be jerked awake by some bump in the road, or by the thought that I'd left my daughter behind and that in a few hours everyone who knew would think I had drowned in a diving accident.

By nightfall I had boarded a cargo ship in the Port of Miami, headed for Mexico, where I was supposed to stay until Gray came for me.

"Whoever it is," my father says. "They found you pretty fast."

"It's true," I say. I can't seem to stop moving. I'm pacing the small room, my whole body electric with tension, this physical pain I'll have until I can get to Victory. Every mother knows that feeling in her body when her child cries. It's as if every nerve ending, every cell, aches until you can hold and comfort your child. I felt that now, but with a kind of terrified desperation underlying it.

"Something not right about that," my father says. I can't help but stare at him, his skin gray-white, his beard ragged, deep lines around eyes that seem sunken in his face. His long gray hair, pulled back with a rubber band, looks dry and brittle. I wonder if he's sick, but I can't stand to ask that question now. I don't want to know the answer.

"I mean," he goes on, "who knew where you were going? Who knew you were on the ship?"

"No one knew—except Gray and the people from his company who were tasked with protecting me and getting me safely to my destination."

"Then how did that guy—the one you called the Angry Man—how did he find you like that? In a boat in the middle of the sea?"

I don't know the answer. "They must have been watching or following me?"

"Possible," he says, cocking his head. He seems to be considering something, but he doesn't say anything else.

It's something that never occurred to me, how the Angry Man found me there so quickly. I wasn't even surprised when I saw the other boat that night. It was almost as though I'd been waiting for it, so sure was I that Marlowe had returned for me.

"I need a computer," I tell my father.

"In the shop."

He leads me downstairs, and I sit behind the reception desk and surf the Web, trying to find the identity of the Angry Man. I search for the Families of the Victims of Frank Geary and begin sifting through the entries I find. Meanwhile, I have this sense of a ticking clock, a tightness in my chest. I wonder where the Angry Man is now and how he's tracking my progress. I know enough about Gray's work to know that the technology is so advanced now that he or whomever is charged with following me could be blocks or even miles away and still have complete audio and visual surveillance. Still, it seems questionable that they've given me such a wide berth, such latitude. But maybe they know that they've got me by a chain connected to my own heart. I'll do what they want; I don't think there's any question about that.

But of all the places they could have left me, why did they leave me here? They must have known I'd come to my father. Was there some reason they wanted me to?

I look for images of the man I saw, hoping to find a name attached. But I find the same old articles I've read a hundred times before, maybe a thousand times. I stare at the screen and resist the urge to take it and throw it on the floor, to stomp on it screaming in my rage and frustration.

My father comes over and lays a large book on the desk in front of me. The computer screen casts it in an eerie blue glow. The book is turned to an eight-by-ten shot of Marlowe's tattoo. The sight of it sends a cold shock through me. I have seen this image again and again in my dreams, in my dark imaginings. But to see the photograph of it on his skin reminds me that he was just a man, flesh and bone, not a monster from a nightmare I had. He is real and possibly still alive.

I stare at the dark lines of the tattoo. I see a churning ocean crashing over jutting rocks; I see my face hidden within the image. There's a wolf etched in the face of one of the rocks. Two birds circle above it all. It is as beautiful and as detailed as I have seen it in my memory. In my dreams of it, it pulses and moves, the ocean crashes, the birds cry mournfully. But on the page it's flat and dead, like some map to Marlowe's mind.

"Why are you showing me this?" I ask.

"Look closely," he says, tapping the picture with his finger.

After a few seconds of staring, I see. If you didn't examine it closely, you'd never notice it. In the lines that form the crags of the rocks lies a hidden image: the barn at Frank's horse farm.

39

Deep in the dark, wild swamps of Florida amid the lush black-green foliage and through the still, teeming waters, wild orchids grow. Over the last century, orchid hunters, breeders, and poachers have donned their waders and raped the swamplands of these delicate flowers, filling trucks with the once-plentiful plants and shipping them for huge profits all over the world. Now they are so rare in the wild that environmentalists are struggling to rescue the waning populations, and the search for wild orchids is ever more desperate. Most legendary among them is the elusive ghost orchid. Snow white with delicately furled petals, the leafless epiphyte never touches the earth and seems to float like a specter, hence its name. In the history of Florida, people have lied and stolen, fought and died in their quest for the ghost orchid, which flowers only once a year.

Detective Harrison always liked the idea of this, the idea of men who risked their lives in pursuit of the single fragile object of their passion. At the best of times, Harrison considered himself to be one of these men. Through the hinterland of lies, in the decaying marsh of murder, he searched for the fresh white thing that was pure, elevated above the murk, drawing its nourishment from the air.

Like the orchid hunters, he didn't mind the trek through the dark and shadowy spaces, his goal moving him toward places where, less motivated, others wouldn't dare to go. He could sit at his computer until his eyes stung and his head ached; he could make a hundred fruitless calls, drive hundreds of miles, talk to dozens of surly, uncooperative lackeys, and never think of giving up. It just never occurred to him that he might not find what he was looking for.

He felt like a hunter the evening after my memorial service and his conversation with Ella. He was alone in his office in the station house. Everyone else on the detectives' floor had gone home for the evening. Somewhere he could hear a phone ringing, and somewhere else a radio played some hip-hop crap he couldn't name. Someone was working out in the gym upstairs; he could hear the weights landing heavily on the floor above him.

He didn't have much to go on. He had a website address, the name of a murdered shrink operating without a license, the meticulous notes and collection of articles from a dead bounty hunter, a missing woman with a false identity who also happened to be the ex-girlfriend (or captive, depending on whom you talked to) of a serial killer. Then, of course, there was her husband, a former military man, now owner of a privatized military company, who for some reason had visited Simon Briggs's motel room just an hour after Briggs's murder.

Harrison had made the call to his wife, Sarah, telling her not to expect him and to lock up the house for the night and that he'd see her in the morning. Then he popped up his Internet browser and began the long, lonely slog through the marsh, searching for his ghost orchid.

He loved the Internet, loved the way you could follow a piece of information down a rabbit hole and chase it through tunnels and around bends and come up for air in a place you'd never have imagined when you started.

He started with the website nomorefear.biz. There wasn't much to it, just a black screen with a simple quote: "No passion so effectually robs the mind of all its powers of acting and reasoning as fear." When he clicked on the sentence, he was taken to another page, featuring the image of a man embracing a weeping woman and a paragraph:

Maybe you've lost someone to violence, or perhaps you have been the victim of a violent crime. Either way, your life has been altered and a hole has been punched open in your world. Through it comes the most malignant, destructive monster of all: FEAR. More vicious than any violent criminal, more evil than the deeds of any killer, fear will rob you of what's left of your life. There's only one way out of the haunted forest: You must go through. You must face what you most fear. We can show you how.

There was a number to call, and he was surprised to see that the area code was local. He cast about for a street address but didn't find anything listed in the online Yellow Pages or in the reverse directory and soon realized that the number he had was a cellular line. He dialed the number from his cell phone, which had a blocked ID; voice mail picked up before there was even a ring tone.

"Congratulations. You've taken the first step. Leave your name and number here, and someone will get back to you. If you're not ready to do that, you're not ready for this."

"Hi," he said, trying to make his voice sound shaky and tentative. "I'm Ray, and I'm interested in learning more about your program." He ended the call with an odd feeling in the base of his stomach.

After searching for more information on the organization and finding nothing, he shot an e-mail to Mike Keene, a friend of his who worked at the FBI, to see if there was anything on the radar about Grief Intervention Services. Then a couple more hours of coffee, eyestrain, aching shoulders, walking down virtual corridors and opening doors, looking for people who don't want to be found. Around midnight his concept of himself as an orchid hunter was less appealing, less romantic.

He remembered the thoughts he had outside my memorial service, that he'd need to go back to go forward. So he entered the name Frank Geary. As he scrolled through old news articles about Frank's trial, conviction, and sentence to death row, about my mother's crusade, his new trial and release, then subsequent murder at the hands of Janet Parker, Harrison thought what a nightmare my life must have been.

The trail lead him to an old *South Florida Sun-Sentinel* piece about new DNA evidence proving beyond a shadow of a doubt that Frank Geary was guilty of at least two of the murders of which he'd been originally accused.

The article went on to say that other DNA

evidence added a new wrinkle, that it was possible Marlowe Geary might have either colluded in or been responsible for several of the other murders. Evidence collected during Marlowe Geary's cross-country killing spree matched evidence collected at the scenes of murders attributed to Frank Geary.

There was a quote from Alan Parker, husband of Janet Parker and father of victim Melissa Parker: "The new evidence is disturbing. One wants justice in a case like this. One wants to face the person who killed his daughter."

Harrison read on that Alan Parker was the founder of the Families of the Victims of Frank Geary, the group that lobbied to have the evidence in these murders reexamined as new technology became available.

The phone rang then, startling him. He jerked his arm and knocked his empty mug off the desk as he reached for the phone. It landed with a thud on the floor but didn't break. The display screen on his phone flashed blue and read, UNAVAILABLE.

He answered. "Hello?"

But there was nothing but static on the line. "Hello," he said again. He started to feel his heart thump; he hadn't thought of what he'd say if the Grief Intervention people called back.

"Harrison." A thick, male voice on the line. "It's Mike Keene. Just got your e-mail."

Harrison felt a cool rush of relief. He looked at the clock, nearly 1:00 A.M. "Working late?" he said.

"Yeah, always," Mike said. "You, too?"

"Yeah," he said, rubbing his eyes. They exchanged a few pleasantries, polite questions about wives and kids. Then, "So . . . Grief Intervention Services?"

"It sounded familiar, so I did a little digging around. They're incorporated in the state of Florida. But their address is a P.O. box."

"Who's the founding member?" Harrison asked, writing down the address Mike gave him.

He heard Mike tapping on a computer keyboard. "Someone by the name of Alan Parker. He founded the organization about five years ago. They're listed as grief counselors. No complaints against them in the years they've been operating. No profit, either. They're not on anyone's watch list—officially."

"Officially?"

"Well, a couple of years ago, there was an incident in South Florida. A man who'd been accused of molesting two boys while coaching a school soccer team and served some time for it—six years—was murdered in his home. Brutally murdered, castrated, skull bashed in . . . you know, overkill."

"So the cops looked to the victims and their families," guessed Harrison.

"That's right. But there was no evidence to link anyone to the scene. So no one was ever charged. It came to light, however, that the father of one of the victims was in touch with Grief Intervention Services about six months before his son's molester was released. The father said he needed counseling to deal with his rage and fear for his son's safety. There was no evidence to the contrary."

"So . . ."

"The weird thing about the crime was that the break-in was a textbook military entry, that the victim was bound and gagged in the way military personnel are trained to subdue an enemy. So there was this precise entry and apprehension of the victim, followed by this out-of-control rage killing. It was just bizarre." Mike paused, and Harrison could hear him chewing on something. The chewing went on for longer than Harrison thought polite.

"I don't understand. There's some kind of military connection to Grief Intervention Services?" Harrison prodded finally.

"Hmm," Mike said, mouth still full. "Sorry, I haven't eaten all day. Alan Parker was a former Navy SEAL. One of his daughters was the victim of a serial killer by the name of Frank Geary. He and his wife,

Janet Parker, founded an organization called the Families of the Victims of Frank Geary, after Geary was released in what many considered to be a travesty of justice. Then Janet Parker lost it and killed Frank Geary, burned down his house."

Harrison could almost smell the scent on the wind.

"The organization disbanded, but Alan Parker kept lobbying for evidence retesting," Mike went on. "Eventually it came to light that it might have been Marlowe Geary, Frank's son, who killed Parker's daughter. Parker disappeared for a while after that, then reappeared as the founder of GIS.

"Given his military background and his wife's murder of Frank Geary, police were concerned that GIS was some kind of vigilante organization, so the FBI was informed. There was a cursory investigation that yielded no evidence to support any wrongdoing and was quickly dropped."

Suddenly Detective Harrison pushed through the last of the fecund overgrowth and moved into a clearing where bright fingers of sun shone through the canopy of trees. Illuminated by the rays, the ghost orchid floated there, white and quivering, where it had been waiting all along.

* * * *

I see a girl. She is lying beneath a field of stars. She is wishing, wishing she were high above the earth, an explosion from a millennium ago, that she were as white and untouchable as that. A young man lies beside her. He is pure beauty, his features finely wrought, his body sculpted from marble. His eyes are supernovas; nothing escapes them. They are lovers, yes. She loves him. But in a truer sense, she is his prisoner. The thing that binds her is this terrible void she has inside, a sick fear that he is the only home she will ever know. And this is enough.

They leave the safety of the New Mexico church, climb into their stolen car, and drive on an empty dark road that winds through mountains. She rests her tired head against the glass and listens to the hum of the engine, the rush of tires on asphalt, the song on the radio, "Crazy," sung by Patsy Cline. *I'm crazy for lovin' you.*

She becomes aware of something in the distance: Far behind them she can see the orange eyes of the headlights from another car. She can see them in the sideview mirror. If he notices, he doesn't seem concerned. But that's only because he doesn't know what she knows. He doesn't know about the man who dropped the note on their table.

Save yourself, if you still can.

With his recent ugly confessions worming their

way through her brain, she finds, beyond all hope, that she can. And in the small way she is still able, she does. She says nothing.

I do not remember shooting Gray. This memory has, thankfully, never returned to me. In fact, I don't remember Texas at all. But I do remember the next time I saw Briggs, even though I didn't know his name at the time.

Another awful hotel, off another highway, still in New Mexico. I emerged from the shower and found him sitting on the edge of the bed, smoking a cigar. Marlowe had left over an hour before; where he went and how long he'd be gone, I had no way of knowing. But I'd wait for him. He knew that.

"You didn't tell him about the note," the man said, releasing a series of noxious gray circles from the O of his mouth. "I'm surprised. And pleased."

I stood in the doorway, trying to decide whether he was real or not. I'd had "visits" prior to this from my mother, my father, and one of the girls Marlowe had killed. The girl had a barrette with tiny silk roses glued along its length; you could tell she really liked it, the way she kept lifting her hand to touch its surface, hoping to draw your eye. But I was distracted by the gaping red wound in her throat. She asked me, as she bled upon the bed, how I could let him do this to her. But when I closed my eyes and opened them again, she was gone. Since then I had stopped trusting my eyes and ears when it came to people appearing in my motel room.

"Someone has paid me a lot of money to find Geary before the police do," he said, looking at the wall in front of him. "And they're going to pay me a whole lot more when I hand him over."

He turned and looked at me. His brow was heavy, his eyes deeply set, like two caves beneath a canopy of rock. His nose was a broken crag of flesh and cartilage. He had thick, full, candy-colored lips and girlishly long lashes. I wanted to look away, but I was fascinated by the pocked landscape of his face.

"The thing is, I need him alive. And I'll be honest, I'm a lover, not a fighter. I need a clean catch, no blood or mess. He's a big guy, stronger than me, in better shape," he said, patting his huge gut and giving a little cough for emphasis. "I'll have to surprise him or take him while he sleeps. This is where you come in, if you decide to help me. And I'll make the decision easy for you."

He took out a big gun and rested it tenderly on his lap. "You help me and I help you. I'll give you a cut of my earnings, and I'll help you run. You don't help me?" he said with a shrug and a quick cock of his head. "I'll still get Geary. And I'll turn you over to the police. You'll spend the rest of your life in prison."

He blew a big cloud of smoke my way, then seemed to really examine me for the first time.

"What are you doing with yourself, anyway, huh?" he went on. "Are you crazy or what? You don't look like you're all there, Ophelia. That's why I'm willing to help you. No one wants you to get hurt—any worse than you've been hurt already."

I tightened the towel around myself, edged closer to the wall. I couldn't think of how to respond.

"I'll be waiting, watching," he said, and got up with a groan from the bed and took the DO NOT DIS-TURB sign from the door and laid it on the table. "All I need you to do is unlock the door and hang this sign outside when he falls asleep. Then go in the bathroom and lie down in the tub. I'll knock when it's safe to come out." With his free hand, he took a thick packet of cash from his pocket. "I'll give you this, and I'll drop you off at a bus station."

"What makes you think I'll do any of this?" I asked him finally. "What keeps me from telling him and then leaving that sign on the door, having *him* surprise *you?*"

"She speaks," he said with a slow smile. He took a big drag on his cigar. "Because you *hate* him, Ophelia. I saw it on your face in that diner. You *think* you love him, but you *know* how evil he is, that one day he's going to kill you, too. That you're going to be a body someone finds in a motel just like this one."

I felt a shudder move through me.

"Or the police are going to catch up with you at some point, some hotel clerk who's not high on methamphetamine is going to recognize you and make a call. And there's someone else tailing you, too."

"Who?"

"I have no idea, but there's someone else out there looking for you. I don't know who he is or what he wants. It doesn't matter. What I'm saying is, time's up. You don't help me, the next person to walk through that door or one just like it may not give you a choice at all."

My whole body was shivering now.

"Put on some clothes," he told me, moving toward the door. "You'll catch a cold." Before he left, he looked back and said, "Christ, kid, where are your *parents?*"

"She's going to be okay," my father says, bringing me back to the present. There was something grave about his tone, something off.

I turn to look at him. He is driving fast on the Long Island Expressway, headed for a small private airport where he says he has a friend with a plane who owes him a favor. He made a quick call at some point back at the shop that I didn't hear, and the next thing I knew, we were on our way. I didn't even know he had a car. Unbelievably, it's a rather nice late-model Lincoln Town Car. There's a lot I don't know about my father, I guess.

"A guy I know, we used to ride together when we were kids," he explained as we got ready to leave. "He went straight, got a job. Now he's this big-time real-estate developer. He said anytime I need the plane day or night, it's mine."

"That's a pretty big favor," I said, skeptically.

"Trust me, it's nothing compared to what I did for him."

"Spare me the details." I'm not in the mood for one of my father's crazy stories. I don't even know if there will be a plane waiting for us when we get to this supposed airport on Long Island. But I have no choice. My stomach is an acid brew; the image of my daughter bound and gagged is seared in my mind.

I look over at my father now. I can see he's itching to tell me his story, but he manages to keep his mouth shut. I lean my head against the window and watch the trees whip past us. I wonder about the other cars on the road, envy them their mundane journeys—to a late shift or home from one, back from a party or a date. I never got to live a life like that, not really. Even my normal life as Annie was undercut by all my lies. You can hide from the things you've done, tamp them down, make them disappear from your day-to-day, but they're always with you. I know that now, too late. You cannot cage the demons—they just rattle and scream and thrash until you can't ignore them any longer. You must face them eventually. They demand it.

We pull off the highway and drive along a dark, empty access road. I see a field of hangars with small planes parked in neat rows. Off in the distance, there's a small tower, then a line of lights that I imagine is a runway. I am relieved that there's really an airport.

"He said that one of the gates would be open," my father says, slowing down.

And so it is.

"How did you know I wasn't really dead?" I ask my father as he turns off the road and drives through the open gate. I'm not sure why the question comes to me at the moment. Seems like there are other things to discuss. I can see lights up ahead, the figure of a man moving back and forth between a small craft and a hangar.

"Gray sent someone to let me know. Some kid. He gave me a note, explained everything that's been happening. I guess he didn't want me hearing about it some other way."

It's like Gray to cover all the bases that way. I wish he were here now, but at the same time it's right that I'm on my own. My father comes to a stop, and we sit for a minute in the dark. The man by the plane quits what he's doing to look at us.

My father stares straight ahead for a second, then lowers his head and releases a long, slow breath. We both know he's not coming with me. I don't know the reasons, but I know he's not capable of going any further. He has always done only what he was able to do. Maybe that's true of all of us. Maybe it's just that when it's your parents, their shortfalls are so much more heartbreaking.

"Look, kid," he says, and then stops. I hope he's not going to launch into some monologue about how he's failed as a father and how sorry he is. I don't have time, and I don't want to hear it. We sit in silence while he seems to be striking up the courage to say something.

"It doesn't have to be like this, you know?" he says finally. "How about we just call the cops?"

"They have my daughter."

"Ophelia——" he says, then stops again. Whatever

he wanted to say he has changed his mind. "I know. You're right. Go get your girl. But be careful."

I watch his face, the muscle working in his jaw, a vein throbbing at his temple. As ever, I am not privy to what kind of battle he's fighting inside himself.

"I love you, Opie. Always have," he says, not looking at me.

"I know that, Dad." And I do. I really do.

There's no embrace, no tearful good-bye, no words of wisdom or encouragement. I leave the car, and within fifteen minutes I'm in a Cirrus Design SR20 aircraft on my way back—of all places—to Frank's ranch, where this journey began.

I sit in the rear of the plane, strapped into the harness with headphones around my ears. The pilot, a stocky guy with a crew cut, greeted me and gave me some safety instructions, but he has not said another word since he helped me strap in. He doesn't seem interested in me or what my story is; he is a man who is paid to do what he was told and not ask questions. I noticed that he barely glanced at my face, as if he didn't want to be able to identify it later.

The noise from the engines is oddly hypnotic, restful in its relentlessness. As the plane rockets down the runway and lifts into the air, I think about Victory.

I delivered her naturally, no drugs. I wanted to be

present for her entry into this world, wanted to feel her pass through me. Those crashing waves of consciousness-altering pain, I allowed them to carry me to another place within myself. I let them take me moaning and sighing to motherhood. I felt my daughter move through my body and begin her life. Our eyes locked when I put her on my breast, and we knew each other. We'd known each other all along.

I'd never seen Gray cry before. But he did as he held her in his arms for the first time. In that moment she was his daughter. The fact that she had Marlowe's blood running through her veins never occurred to him or me. She belonged to us. And even more than that, she belonged to herself. I could see her purity, her innocence, all the possibilities before her. She would be defined by our family, not by the evil deeds of Marlowe and his father. I swore to myself that she'd never be touched by them or by Ophelia and her shameful past.

"What do you want to name her?" Gray asked.

"I want to call her Victory," I said, because the moment of her birth was a victory for all of us. I felt that Ophelia, Marlowe, Frank, and my mother were all far behind me now. I was Annie Powers, Gray's wife, and, most important, I was Victory's mother. I had thrown off my ugly past, forgotten it both literally and figuratively. My whole body was shaking from the effort of childbirth, the surge of hormones and emotion rattling through my frame.

"Victory," he said with a wide smile. He was mesmerized by her, staring at her tiny face. "She's perfect."

He sat beside me with our daughter in his arms. "Victory," he said again. And it was her name.

I'm trying to recapture the feeling I had that day, the power I felt in the knowledge that I was Victory's mother, the certainty I had in my heart that I could protect her from every awful thing in my past. But the feeling is gone. As the plane takes off and the world below me gets smaller and smaller, I think that the path of my life has always been like this—an ugly, frightening maze. No matter how hard and fast I run, no matter how badly I want to escape its passages, ultimately they lead back to where I started.

40

Sarah had read something, some book about food, that made her think they should stop eating red meat. So there was a lot of stir-frying going on at the Harrison home, lots of tofu and fish and poultry being prepared with vegetables and brown rice. But somehow everything seemed to taste like soy sauce, no matter what the ingredients. The house was starting to reek of it. But Harrison never complained about his wife's cooking; he always ate what she prepared and showered her with compliments. He appreciated that she cooked at all, that she made a point of having something ready for him when he came home, that she waited and ate with him most of the time, unless it was very late.

Even though he'd called and told her not to wait up, he found her on the couch when he walked through the front door. She was watching some movie with the sound down low, huddled under a blanket. Brad Pitt and Angelina Jolie were tearing up a house on the screen, shooting at each other with big guns. He could see the blond crown of Sarah's head and heard her sigh as he shut the door and rearmed the alarm system.

She sat up quickly, looking startled, as if she'd been dozing.

"What are you doing up?" he asked.

"I was up with the baby," she said through a yawn. She lifted her long, graceful arms above her head in a stretch. "I thought I'd wait awhile and see if you came home."

He came to sit beside her. He took her into his arms and felt the sleepy warmth of her body. She smelled of raspberries, something in her shampoo.

"I made a stir-fry. Want me to heat it up?" He noticed that there was something shaky about her voice.

"No thanks," he said. "I ate. A big, juicy hamburger dripping with fat, with ketchup and mayonnaise." He held out his hands to indicate the enormousness of the burger. "And fries, soaked in oil."

She wrinkled her nose and made a sound of disgust. "If you only knew," she said, patting him on the cheek. "Poison."

"I'll die happy," he said, shedding his jacket.

His eyes fell upon it then. On the end table by the couch was a stack of their bank statements. The sight of it made his stomach bottom out. He turned to see her watching his face.

"I never look at these things, you know?" she said with a light laugh. She rubbed her temple, then wrapped her arms around her middle. She bit her lip the way she did before she was about to cry. "But I saw this interview on CNN. Some finance expert who said that women are disempowered in a marriage by being ignorant regarding their finances. It seemed obvious, but then I realized I don't even know how much money we have in the bank."

She took a deep breath. "And I thought, we have a daughter now and I don't want her to see her mother as this helpless woman who doesn't even know how to pay her bills online. If anything ever happened to you, I wouldn't know anything about our money. And you're a cop, you know. Something *could* happen."

He kept his eyes on her face. He watched her eyes widen and rim with tears.

"Sarah—"

"We got married so young," she said quickly, interrupting him. "I literally came right from my parents' house into our marriage. Someone's *always* taken care of me, Ray. But now there's a person who needs *me* to take care of *her*."

He started to talk again, but she lifted up her hand.

"I don't understand all these huge withdrawals from our savings. And then this deposit," she said, picking up the pile. He saw her handwriting and some highlighted entries. The papers quivered in her grasp. Over the baby monitor, he heard his daughter sigh and shift in her sleep. "Can you explain this to me, Ray?"

His mind raced through a hundred lies he could tell, a hundred different techniques he could use to manipulate her in this moment to make her feel bad or wrong for confronting him this way. This is what he was good at, after all, molding himself, his tone, his words, to make people do and say and think what he wanted. But he didn't have the heart for any more lies, any more secrets. As he sat in their comfortable home and told her every wrong thing he'd done, wasn't it also true that in some secret part of himself he was glad? Glad that, for better or worse, she would finally know all of him?

It looks as if the plane is landing in a sea of black, except for the tiniest strip of lights along what I'm hoping is the ground. The ride has been turbulent, and I'm not sure how much more my stomach can take as we hurtle downward. The plane pitches and lofts, and I'm wondering if it's normal, if, after all this, the tiny plane I'm in is going to crash. What would happen to Victory then? I try not to think about it during the white-knuckle journey to the ground. But when we touch down, it's surprisingly gentle.

"They said there will be someone to greet you," the pilot says through the headphones. "Someone waiting."

"Who?" I ask. "Who's waiting?"

I see the pilot shrug. He doesn't turn around. Again I have the thought that he doesn't want to see my face, or maybe it's that he doesn't want me to see his. As it is, I couldn't pick him out of a lineup.

"I don't know," he says, his tone flat and not inviting further questions.

When the engines are off, I thank him, exit the plane, and step into a humid Florida night. The tree frogs are singing and the mosquitoes start biting as soon as I strip off my coat, which I won't need here. I can already feel beads of sweat make their debut on my forehead.

In the distance I see the dark, lean form of a man standing beside a vehicle. Its headlights are the only thing illuminating the blackness except for the light coming from the small control tower above us. I don't see anyone up there.

I approach the vehicle for lack of any alternatives, and I realize that it's the Angry Man.

"Do you know who I am?" he asks as I draw near.

I shake my head. The situation takes on a surreal quality. "I remember you," I say. "But I don't know your name."

"My name's Alan Parker, father of Melissa, husband of Janet."

The words hit as though he's thrown stones at me. I feel that the knowledge should illuminate what's happening to me, but it doesn't.

"Once upon a time," he goes on, "my wife and I believed that Frank Geary murdered our daughter."

He is dressed in dark pants and a heavy flannel shirt, with a jacket over that. It is far too hot for all those clothes, but he doesn't appear uncomfortable. Instead he seems to hunch himself in as if bracing against the cold. And is he shivering just slightly? He seems out of place in this moment of my life, as though he has no business being there.

"Our rage was the driving force in our lives for years. It consumed us." He releases a throaty cough, then pulls a pack of Marlboro reds from his pocket, lights one with a Zippo, and takes a long, deep drag. He has the look of a lifelong smoker, gray and drawn.

"You know, the thing was, I was a terrible father. Absent a lot, distant when I was around. I never so much as held my daughter or told her I loved her in all the years she was alive. I provided for her, sure, roof over her head, nice things, college. That's what I knew how to do. That's all I thought a father *had* to do. The point is, I never devoted much of myself to her until after she'd been taken from me. But I was a berserker in the crusade for justice against Frank Geary. I think Melissa would have been surprised by my devotion. I think she died believing I didn't love her."

I don't know what to say to him. I'm not sure why he's telling me this or what we're doing here. But I listen because I don't have any choice, and I figure as long as he's talking, my daughter is safe. My whole body tingles with the desire to be moving, to be anywhere else but here.

"Of course," he says, "it was all much harder on Janet. The mother-daughter thing, man, you can't get inside that. I was filled with rage, with the desire for revenge. It was like rocket fuel in my veins. But when Melissa died, Janet died, too. Simple as that. She was still walking around, but she never lived another day of her life. I shouldn't have been surprised that she did what she did. But I never saw it coming; I wouldn't have thought her capable."

He is racked suddenly by a fit of coughing so intense, it's embarrassing to watch. He takes a wad of tissues from his pants and covers his mouth until the coughing subsides. When he pulls it back from his mouth, I can see that the tissues are dark with blood. My mind is filled now with the memories of the night Janet Parker killed Frank and then herself. I can hear the gunshots and smell the smoke. I never asked myself who started that fire, but I imagine it was Marlowe. I think he intended for my mother to die that night, too. He didn't expect me to run back in and drag her outside. I am thinking about this as Alan Parker recovers himself and starts to talk again.

"Even as I mourned Janet, I was happy for her in a way. I knew how good it must have felt to pull that trigger. I know she died at peace." He has a sad smile on his face that reminds me of how Janet Parker looked that night, as though she'd laid down a great burden. I don't tell him this. I don't know if he realizes I watched her die, and I'm not sure what good it will do to tell him.

"But Frank Geary didn't kill Melissa," I say, really just guessing.

He shook his head. "He may not have, no. I had Melissa's body exhumed when we won the first round of evidence retesting. And the DNA samples found were similar to Frank Geary's without being identical. So the conclusion was that Marlowe Geary played some role in her torture and death."

There's flash lightning in the clouds above us and the deep rumble of distant thunder, but it's not raining. Every few minutes the sky illuminates and then goes dark again, as if someone is turning it on and off with a switch.

"To be honest," he says, "I'd suspected this early on. In my life I've been around enough killers—in Vietnam—to know one when I saw one. At the trial, Marlowe seemed as dead inside as his father. As they say, the apple doesn't fall far from the tree."

I realize something then. The lights start to come on inside, illuminating places within me that have been dark for so long. "Briggs worked for you. *You* sent him to find Marlowe after we ran."

He nods. "I wasn't sure what Marlowe had to do with Melissa's death. But I knew he'd used Janet to kill his father. And when I realized he was killing other women, taking other people's daughters away, I wanted to stop him. I was filled with a sick rage—it was something living inside me. But I didn't want him arrested and in prison. I didn't want that kind of justice. I wanted him to suffer. I wanted him to suffer and die the way his victims did. And I knew plenty of people to help with that—the military is good at turning out merciless killers."

"Why didn't you come yourself?"

"After Janet died, I started coughing up blood.

The sickness of fear and anger, you can't carry it for-ever. It starts to kill you. In my case, cancer."

More of that horrible coughing. I hate, am repulsed by him, and pity him in equal measure.

"After you and Marlowe were 'killed' in your car accident, I had an epiphany. I realized that my and Janet's rage and desire for revenge had cost us every-thing. We might have had some years together, we might have touched happiness again, if only we had faced down our fears, our regrets, our hatred for Frank Geary. But instead we let the rip he'd opened in the fabric of our life suck us in like a black hole. We let him destroy all three of us."

He looks at me as though trying to decide if I'm listening to him. Whatever he sees on my face makes the corners of his mouth turn up slightly.

"I decided I'd fight my cancer and live for Janet and Melissa rather than die for them. As I fought that war, I realized that the rage I'd directed at Frank and Marlowe Geary was really directed at myself, for all the ways I'd failed as father and husband. If I'd been present for them while they lived, maybe I wouldn't have had so many regrets when they died."

I notice how still he is. There was so much anx-iety and adrenaline living inside me that I couldn't keep myself from fidgeting, shifting my weight from foot to foot, pacing a few steps away, then back toward him. But he is fixed and solid. He keeps his hands in his pockets, his eyes locked on some spot off in the distance. All there is to him is his raspy voice and the story he tells.

"When I went into remission, I started an organization called Grief Intervention Services with some friends of mine to help other victims and families of victims face their fear and heal."

I draw in a sharp breath as I remember. "Your website. I visited it after I heard about you on television."

He nods. "The website captured your IP address. It was only a matter of days before we traced it to Gray Powers. It was only a little while longer before we connected him to you. Just one visit confirmed that you were Ophelia March."

I stare at his pale face and think how ill he looks. There is a distance to his stare. He is already on his way somewhere else.

"Naturally, I started to wonder. If Ophelia survived, what about Marlowe Geary? And, if so, where is he?"

"But you'd given up your quest for revenge," I say, putting my hand on the hood of his car. I am feeling weak now, wobbly. The frenetic energy I had is abandoning me.

He offers a thin smile. "I've always remembered you, Ophelia. You were the saddest-looking child I'd ever seen. I remember you coming and going from that farm, the circles under your eyes, the way you hunched your shoulders and hung your head. You were living in a pit of snakes; I was never sure which of them would be first to squeeze the life out of you, then swallow you whole. I should have guessed it would be Marlowe."

I don't know what to say.

"The man you knew as Dr. Paul Brown believed that somewhere inside you, you might know where Marlowe Geary was. He suspected that your fugue states, the flights you made from your life as Annie Powers, were Ophelia's attempts to return to him. He also felt you were on the cusp of remembering a lot of the things you had forgotten. So he devised ways to jog your memory a bit."

"Wait," I say, lifting a hand. "Dr. Brown worked for *you*? So the encounter on the beach, the necklace—those were his ideas on how to jog my memory? So that you could find Marlowe Geary and exact your revenge?"

"This is not only about me and what I want."

"No?"

"No. It's about both of us. I'm trying to *help* you."

I confided those things to my doctor, and he used them to manipulate my memory. It seems a relatively small violation in comparison to everything, but I feel my face go hot with anger. I realize that I have grown uncomfortable with rage. Ophelia used to rant and scream and weep. But Annie is always dead calm.

"But *Vivian* brought me to Dr. Brown," I say. I remember then that Gray told me that the doctor was someone Drew knew. And suddenly I feel sick, realizing how everything fits together.

Parker gives me a sympathetic grimace; for a second he looks as though he might reach to comfort me, but I take a quick step back from him. "They thought they were *helping* you, Ophelia. They thought they were helping you to face your fears so that you could be well again. For Victory."

At first I think he means my husband, too. But it doesn't sound like Gray. He's too upright, too honest. He loves me too much. I can't imagine him being a part of something like this. And if he were, why would he kill Briggs?

"Gray didn't know what was happening," I say.

"He was afraid, too, that Marlowe—or someone from the past—had come for me. That's why he killed Briggs."

Parker offers a slow, sad nod. "You're right. He never would have been a part of it. He would never deceive you or cause you so much pain. In fact, in his way, though only because he loves you, he has been enabling you. Maybe part of him doesn't want you to remember."

"So who then? Who thought they were helping me then?" I yell, nearly shriek. I am startled by my own emotion. He seems startled, too, as though he didn't expect any of this to upset me. He raises a calming hand.

"Your in-laws, Drew and Vivian. A representative approached Vivian, told her that you'd contacted us for help and then changed your mind. She and Drew agreed to our plan to help you confront your past."

I think of Vivian taking me to Dr. Brown, of the fear on her face when I confronted her with the things that were happening to me. I struggle with this, trying to recast her as the liar and the manipulator she had to be to do that. I want to think I know her well enough to know that she was trying to help me. I hope that's true, at least.

"No," I say, drawing in a breath to calm myself.

Something is wrong. "They'd never let you hurt Victory. They'd die first." I am as sure of this as I have ever been of anything.

"Admittedly," he says with a mild shrug, "they weren't aware the lengths to which we'd go to accomplish our goals. No one ever is."

He seems empty then, vacant, and I see that Alan Parker is a man who has been gutted by grief and rage, filled up again by a quest for revenge that he could never quite release, even when he knew better. I feel a sob rise up, a great tide moving inside my chest.

"They were so sure you were helpless, so devastated by the events of your life that you would never be whole. They resorted to these tactics to help you. Well, really to help Victory, I think, so that she would have a strong and healthy mother. It's ironic, isn't it, that now you're the one to help them."

I feel that adrenaline pump again as my heart starts to thud.

"What are you talking about?"

"It's all up to you now, Ophelia."

"I don't understand," I say, moving closer to him. My voice has taken on the quality of a plea. "Where are we? Where's my daughter?"

I've never felt so frightened or so desperate, but he just moves away from the car. I see he is going to leave me here. "The keys are in the ignition. There's a gun in the glove box. At the end of the road, you make a right. You'll know where you are once you're driving."

He starts walking away from me then, moving toward the trees that surround the airfield. "You need to be strong now, Ophelia. Stronger than you've ever been. For yourself, for your daughter, for me."

"You never needed me to lead you to Marlowe," I call after him. "You knew where he was. Why are you doing this?"

I see him lift the wad of tissues to his mouth, see his shoulders hunch into a cough. That sob that's been living in my chest escapes through my throat.

"What do you want me to do?" I cry out. *"What do I need to do to get my daughter back?"*

Just then the tower lights go out. I look up, and as I do, the runway lights go dark. The plane is gone; the pilot must have moved into the hangar, because I never heard it take off again. The only lights come from the headlights of the car beside me.

"Tell me!" I yell into the darkness. But the Angry Man is gone. I am alone. The air around me is thick with silence. Out of sheer desperation, I get into the car and start to drive. I turn onto the road, and he's right—I do know where I am. The farm is less than ten miles away.

*   *   *

"They are not here," said Esperanza at the door to my house. She blocked the small opening she'd created and was peering at Detective Harrison worriedly through the crack.

"I need to know where they are, Esperanza," he said sternly. "This isn't a social call."

She looked at him blankly, opened the door a little wider. She was shaking her head and seemed close to tears.

"Miss Victory is with her *abuela*," she said. "Mr. Gray, he left *en la noche*. Nothing. He say nothing. Mrs. Annie, she's—" That's where she started to cry. "They're all gone."

"Let me in, Esperanza," he said more gently, giving her what he hoped was a look of compassion. His "I'm a really good guy and I only want to help" look. It worked: She opened the door, and he stepped inside. She started talking fast, her tears coming harder now.

"Mr. Gray, he call me the other day, say Victory is coming home, can I come back? I come back but no Victory," she said.

Harrison took her by the elbow, led her over to the couch, and stood beside her until she managed to stop crying and looked up.

"We wait and wait," she said. "In the night a call come. Mr. Gray leaves. He just told me go home and no worry. But he was very afraid." She motioned at her face, to tell him she read Powers's expression. "So I stay. I wait for them to come home."

"When was this?" he asked her.

"Two nights I wait."

"And you haven't heard anything else?"

"No," she said, shaking her head. "Nothing. I call Mr. Drew. No answer; no one call back."

He walked over to the phone and scrolled through the numbers on the caller ID, looking for what, he didn't know. "The call came on this phone?"

She shook her head. "No. His cell phone."

Harrison felt like he was trying to hold on to a fistful of sand—the tighter his grasp, the faster it slipped away. His desperation was compounded by the promises he'd made to his wife. She didn't care about the money, she said. She accepted his addiction. What she couldn't understand and wasn't sure she could forgive were the lies, the blackmail, the secrets he'd kept from her. She couldn't understand what he'd done to me.

"Why, Ray? Why didn't you come to me? We could have asked my parents for money, taken out a loan. How could you let yourself go so low? It's not you."

But that's what she didn't quite get. It *was* him. Part of him was in fact *that* low. Money and the things he thought it could give him—not possessions necessarily, but freedom, ease of living, a certain power he'd lacked all his life—obsessed him. That's how he could risk the small amount they had in the hope of making more, that's how he could blackmail us not just for the money to pay off his gambling debts but a hundred thousand dollars besides. And Gray had paid it—paid it without a word, because he loved me that much, because he wanted to protect me.

"You need to make it right, Ray," Sarah said.

"How? How do I make it right?" he asked. He reached for her, but she moved away from him. She shifted over to the corner of their modular unit and sat there with her arms wrapped around herself in a protective hug.

"You can start by paying him back everything you didn't give the bookie and making a plan to pay back the rest," she said gently.

The thought filled him with dread. He couldn't stand the idea that their savings account would be empty, that they'd go back to living paycheck to paycheck. That he'd always be worried about the next time the car broke down or the refrigerator started to leak. He wasn't sure he could do it.

"Sarah . . ." he started, but found he couldn't finish.

"Find a way to make things right, Ray." She didn't issue any threats or ultimatums; she didn't ask him to leave the house. But he heard in her tone what she never said: *Find a way to make things right, Ray, or I won't ever be able to look at you the same way again.*

She must have seen the despair on his face, because she moved back over to him and placed a hand on his leg. He couldn't even look at her.

"Everybody makes mistakes, Ray," she said, her voice very low and gentle. He'd heard her talk to the baby in this tone. "Everybody stumbles. It's what you do *then* that makes or breaks your life. It's what you do after you fall that's the measure of who you are."

He left the room then. She called after him quietly, but he kept walking. He walked out onto his back porch and gazed up at the sky. He didn't want to be in the same room with her. He couldn't stand for her to see him cry.

"What's going on?" Harrison was snapped back to the present by Ella's voice. She stood in the open doorway looking different somehow, a little angry maybe. She looked fit and strong dressed in jeans and a black T-shirt, sneakers on her feet. She didn't seem primped and coiffed in the usual way. He found himself staring at her, trying to figure out why she looked so different. She frowned at him and then walked over to Esperanza.

"Where's Gray?" Ella said, taking her by the shoulders.

"Gone," Esperanza said, starting to weep again. Ella embraced her. "I don't know where."

Ella glanced back over at Harrison. "What's he doing here?"

"This is none of your business, Mrs. Singer. Go home," he said.

She gave him a dark look, released Esperanza, and walked over to him, got in his face. "Don't tell me that. First Annie disappears. Then Drew and Vivian take off with Victory. There's a memorial service—pretty premature, if you ask me. The woman's only been missing two weeks. Now Gray's gone. Someone needs to tell me what's going on. It *is* my business. These people are my friends."

"Go home, Mrs. Singer," he said again, walking over toward the door and holding it open for her. He saw color rise on her neck and cheeks, but she didn't move.

"I can get you into his office upstairs," she said after a beat. "Maybe you'll find some of the answers you're looking for up there."

He remembered the door with the keypad lock from his previous visits. "You know the code," he said, not even bothering to keep the skepticism out of his voice.

She nodded. "Ophelia let it slip."

"She let it slip?" he said, narrowing his eyes. "Seems unlikely."

"Maybe she just got a little careless around her friends," she said with a shrug.

He didn't quite believe her, but he was out of luck and out of time.

"Okay, so what is it?"

"You tell me what's happening and I'll tell you the code."

He released a sigh and rolled his eyes. "You're not helping her by slowing me down. You know that."

"Just tell me."

He was desperate enough to do it. He told her everything he knew, starting with my fake identity and my history with Marlowe Geary and ending with Alan Parker and Grief Intervention Services.

"You think she's alive?"

"I do. And I think she needs some help. I just don't know how to give it to her."

Ella gave him a nod; he thought she looked a little sad. "It's VICTORY, with a five for the *V* and a zero for the *O*."

He took the stairs to the office with Ella right behind him and punched in the code. The door unlocked, and he pushed it open. The room was dark, and when he stepped inside, he realized something that caused his stomach to bottom out.

"You called her Ophelia," he said, turning around.

"Sorry, Detective Harrison, nothing personal. You should have taken your money and disappeared."

She held something in her hand that he didn't recognize until the prongs shot into his body and electricity started to rocket through him. A horrific scream escaped him; he barely recognized it as his own voice. The room around him spiraled as the pain seemed to ratchet higher and higher until he could hardly form a thought in his mind. Before everything went black, he remembered his wife coming up behind him on the porch and wrapping her arms around him as he wept. He remembered feeling a terrible mingling of deep shame in himself, gratitude for her love, and the fervent hope that he could be worthy of her again.

"You can fix this, Ray," she said, squeezing hard. "I know you can."

* * *

I drive up beside the old gate that blocks the drive to the horse farm. I am a wreck, sweating with fear and the urgency to do what Parker wants me to do— even though I'm not totally sure what that is. I pull the car over onto the shoulder near the thick tree cover. When I turn off the engine, I am swallowed by the sounds of the Florida night. The property is a huge yawning darkness, and for a second I don't think I can bring myself to enter. But of course I have to go. My daughter needs me. It is that thought that impels me from the car and brings me to the locked gate.

The lock seems old and rusted through, as though it hasn't been used in years. This can't be so, I know that. I pick up a rock and start banging on it hard, hoping it will fall to pieces as it would in the movies. But I can't get it open. I'll have to leave my car on the road and go around the gate, which is suitable only to keep vehicles from moving up the drive and not really designed to keep out intruders.

The thought of walking that long, dark road alone is almost too much. I remember the gun then and return to the car for it. I open the glove box and find a .38 Special, just your standard revolver. It'll do. With the gun heavy in my hand, I feel slightly better, not like a girl afraid of the dark. I feel like what I need to be: a woman intent on doing whatever it is she must to protect her child or die trying.

I walk around the gate and begin heading toward the horse farm. The last time I walked this road, I was seventeen years old with nothing to lose. What I wouldn't give now for some of the empty numbness I felt that night, that ignorance of consequences.

I am washed over by memory as I make the trek. I remember Janet Parker's car gliding past me in the dark. I remember the clicking of its cooling engine when I saw it a while later. I remember the smell of smoke, the percussion of the gunshot. I see the halo of blond hair soaked in blood, the first time I knew Marlowe was a killer. I hear his confessions beneath the New Mexico sky. Suddenly I am thinking of Gray.

I never saw Briggs again after he made his offer that night in the motel room—or if I did, I don't remember. I don't think there was time for me to do what he asked. I think it was just another night or maybe two before Gray caught up with us. All I recall is suddenly seeing this mammoth form in the doorway of yet another miserable motel. I'd seen him before, I knew that much. But for some reason a deep relief mingled with my fear when I saw him standing there. He strode into the room, and it was a second before I saw the needle in his hand.

"I'm not going to hurt you," he said, jabbing the needle into my arm. I don't think I even struggled. "Your father sent me for you."

"It's just a sedative," he said, and he was already floating away as the substance flooded through my veins. "I can't have you shooting me again, can I?"

The next thing I knew, I was bound in the back of his car. He burst through the driver's door. I could see St. Francis Cathedral before I blacked out again.

I know only Gray's version of what happened that night. How he went back to the motel and waited in the dark for Marlowe to return. How he surprised Marlowe, as Briggs had planned to do. How Gray had overpowered him in a fight, managed to knock him unconscious and bind him. His plan had been to take the car to the police station on the other side of the square, abandon it with Marlowe inside, return to the Suburban parked just a few blocks away, and make an anonymous call from a pay phone when we were far enough away.

His mistake, as he saw it in hindsight, was twofold—not using the sedative he'd brought, because he thought Marlowe was out cold, and putting

Marlowe into the backseat instead of into the trunk of the vehicle. Marlowe came to as Gray drove, got loose from his bindings, and attacked Gray. The struggle ended with Gray shooting Marlowe in the face and leaping from the car just before it dove over the side of the road into the Rio Grande Valley below.

I have heard this story so many times. I have asked Gray to tell it until it has taken on a mythic quality, like a story from childhood. As I near the end of the drive and see the roof of the house through the trees, I wonder how much of what he's told me was true. I don't know. After my conversation with Alan Parker, everything seems suspect.

When I step into the clearing where the house and the barn and the empty horse pen stand, I am surprised by the condition of the property. It is dilapidated in a way I hadn't expected. I imagined it repaired after the fire, cared for by the women whom my mother supposedly sheltered during their crusade to save their husbands, lovers, and sons from death row. But two of the upstairs windows are blown out, and though it's dark, I can see that there appears to be a hole in the roof. The front door hangs off its hinges, the porch has folded onto itself. I hear the mournful calling of an owl in the distance, along with a chorus of frogs. The barn stands intact, but the whole place has an air of desertion—the desertion of years.

There's an escalation of tension in my chest; the darkness all around me feels like it's closing in. How have I come to be here? Is this really happening? Was Alan Parker a figment of my imagination? Out of sheer desperation, I start to yell.

"Marlowe!"

I call his name again and again, each time my voice disappearing into the thick, humid air. All the night songs cease, and everything listens to my calls, the desperate baying of a wounded animal. I drop to my knees in the dirt.

I realize then that he's not here. No one could live in this place, this dead, awful place, not even him. The despair that sweeps over me is so total I am physically weakened by it. I put my forehead to the ground.

And then, kneeling there, my past and present one at last, I remember. I pull myself to my feet. I know where Marlowe is. Alan Parker is right; I have always known. He *did* need me to find Marlowe— because I am the only person on earth who knows where he might have been all these years. He has not been pursuing me. He has been waiting for me, just where I knew he would be.

I walk into the trees. I remember the way as I move through the thick overgrowth, careless of lurking snakes, ignoring the mosquitoes that feed on my skin and hum in my ear. I'd run if I could, but my progress is slow, pushing aside branches and stepping in soft places where my ankles turn. It seems to take hours, but finally I hear the babbling of the creek ahead. I come to a stop at its banks, and I see it there: the trailer. There's a light burning in the window.

"With provisions you could live out here forever," Marlowe told me a lifetime ago. I never imagined I would be here again, not like this.

From the bank of the creek, I call his name. The sound of it fills the night. Silence is the only answer. I am about to call again when he emerges from the trees behind the trailer.

Though he is just a shape in the darkness, I know him. He is not the man I remember. He approaches me, leaning heavily upon a cane and dragging the right side of his body. He moves slowly, as though every step causes him pain. When he draws closer, I can see that he is hideously disfigured, the left side of his face little more than an explosion of skin. I find myself recoiling, moving backward as he moves forward. Those eyes are the same black sinkholes in which I have drowned again and again.

I realize that my entire body is quavering, every muscle tense, every nerve ending electrified. I can't believe I am looking at him, that his flesh is solid, that he stands on the ground. For the past few years, he has been a specter, haunting every dark space inside my psyche. The realness of him, his physicality, now drains all his power.

"Ophelia," he says. His voice has an odd, warped quality, but I can still hear the music of my name—*O-feel-ya.* "You're home."

I remember thinking he was the only home I'd ever know. How sad, how empty I must have been to think that. I know what a real home is now. I have one with Gray and Victory. I'll do anything to go back there.

"No," I say, unable to take my eyes from his horrible face. It doesn't even look like skin, more like melted wax. He is a mangled facsimile of the man in my memories. But, amazingly, I still feel his pull, remember how I wanted to please him, how badly I craved his love.

"How did you *survive?*" I ask him, my voice just a whisper. "How did you come here?"

Something awful was happening to his mouth, a terrible twisting of his face. He was smiling.

"Back in New Mexico," he says slowly, "someone

found me by the side of the road, near death. I'd been shot in the face, but I still managed to get out of the car before it went off the road." It seemed painful for him to speak; the words emerged long and slow. "I was taken to the hospital and treated as a John Doe. I was unrecognizable, claimed to have no memory of who I was or where I'd been. When I could move around again, I called your mother. She came for me and brought me back here, cared for me until she died last year."

I feel a surprising wave of shock and grief to know that my mother has died. In my heart I thought I'd find her here alive and well, still trying to save the condemned. I guess the abused and neglected child is always hoping for a reckoning, some restitution, an embrace that never comes. And then there's the pain, the anger that she cared for Marlowe all these years after what he'd done to me.

"How did she die?" I want to know.

"Car accident," he said with a shrug. "Drunk. Luckily, I had enough provisions to last me."

I'm struck that he doesn't seem to care at all about her. I'm not sure why I'm surprised. Dr. Brown said once, "He was a psychopath, the worst kind of sociopath. They don't love, Annie. They can't."

I have no way to determine if what he says is

true. For all I know, he killed her as he did so many others. Or maybe she's not dead at all. I don't know. There's no time to think about that now.

I can hear his labored breathing, feel his eyes on me. When I look at his face, he doesn't even seem human. He is vacant. I take another step back from him. I have the thought that he's not really as crippled as he seems, that maybe this is how he lures people now that his beauty is gone: pity. I imagine him living here on this property, alone, haunting its rooms, walking its woods. The thought of it chills me.

"Who takes care of you now?" I want to know this for some reason—how he's been living here on this decimated property, this wasteland of my memories. I wonder if someone helps him, if even as he is, he is still able to lure and manipulate and cause people to do his bidding.

"I manage," he says. "It'll be easier now that you're home. I've missed you so much, Ophelia."

His words seem hollow, like lines he's rehearsed so often they've lost meaning. I don't believe he has thought of me except in the most passing moments. It is I who have been obsessed with him. It is I who have thought of him day and night, plotted my way back to him. He is my sickness, eating me alive like Alan Parker's cancer.

"I've missed you so much," he says again.

He thinks I've come back for him. My hand tightens around the gun. Sweat is dripping down my back, and I can hear blood rushing in my ears. I realize that I'm terrified of him, as though he could somehow force me to stay, as though I could be caught like a fly in a web again, too weak, too powerless to escape him.

"No," I say, looking into those dead eyes. "No."

"You belong to me, Ophelia," he says quietly, moving closer, reaching out his hand.

This has been the truth for so long. Since the day I met him, I have been clinging to him or running from him. I have allowed him to control my heart and my mind. I have loved him madly, and I have lived in terror of his return. And yes, I have hated him. Briggs's words come back to me: *Because you* hate *him, Ophelia. I saw it on your face in that diner. You* think *you love him, but you* know *how evil he is, that one day he's going to kill you, too. That you're going to be a body someone finds in a motel just like this one.*

Marlowe Geary did kill me, and I was his willing accomplice. Gray found my body in that New Mexico hotel room and brought me back to life. Now I am responsible for bringing myself back to wholeness, to heal myself so that I can be the mother my daughter deserves, the woman I deserve to be.

I remember then that he's Victory's father, that because of who we were together, she exists in this world. The union that has made me weakest has produced the union that has made me strongest. It seems a raw truth, so odd that it's almost funny. The universe has a sense of humor, a taste for irony. But this is a private joke I don't share. He has no right to know her; he has nothing to do with her.

"You belong to me, Ophelia."

"Not anymore." And I find I have nothing more to say. There is not a moment of hesitation, of conscience now that he is injured and unarmed. I do exactly what I have come here to do, what Ophelia has been trying to do for years. I take the gun from my waist and open fire. I see his body jerk and shake with the impact of the bullets. I keep firing until it is empty. When I'm done, he's on the ground, his arms and legs spread wide and so still, an oval of blood spreading around him. I walk over to his body and see his staring eyes. A river of blood flows from his mouth. I stand there watching for I don't know how long, until I'm certain beyond any doubt that he is finally dead.

In those moments I remember all the girls I watched him kill—I see their heart-shaped necklaces, and sparkle-painted nails, their miniskirts and cheap tattoos. I hear them screaming, hear them crying for their mothers. I couldn't help them then. I can't help them now. There's only one little girl I can save. There's only one cry I can answer. I feel a sharp pain that starts in my neck and spreads into my head. A bright, white star spreads across my vision then, and I am gone.

41

When they found Detective Harrison, everyone was shocked. He was *such* an upright man who'd done so much good in the community, a good husband and a father, a good cop. No one could believe that he'd picked up an underage hooker on the outskirts of the city, did some heroin with her, and then passed out in his car to be found by police responding to an anonymous tip made from a nearby pay phone.

How terrible, they said. Rumor has it that his wife threw him out. He must have had some kind of nervous breakdown; there was no history of this kind of behavior. No drugs, his friends were sure. Not even much of a drinker, they added. There were rumors of a gambling addiction. Suspect deposits in his bank account. How *sad*.

He ranted and raved as they took him in and processed him as they would any perpetrator. The cops who had been his friends were unable to meet his eyes. He told them the whole story about the gambling debts, my false identity, what he'd learned about Grief Intervention Services and Alan Parker, how Ella Singer had Tasered him at the Powers home. This was a frame-up, he yelled, to keep him from getting any closer. But he sounded like a maniac. No one listened. He just came unglued, the other cops whispered in locker rooms, in bars after shifts ended—it must have been the stress from the gambling addiction, problems with his wife, a new baby.

The judge went easy on him: drug treatment, community service. He had come to his senses, admitted to his drug problem as his PBA rep instructed him to do, admitted to his gambling addiction, too. He enrolled in a place they called "The Farm," a facility outside town where cops with addictions are sent to get well. He was suspended without pay pending the results of treatment. The PBA rep said they couldn't fire him because the department views addiction as a disease—treat, don't punish. Of course, everyone knew that his career was over.

But Harrison found he could bear it all—the humiliation, the weeks of treatment for a drug addiction he didn't have, and all that time to reflect on what was wrong with his life, the inevitable loss of the only job he'd ever wanted to do. Even in the throes of despair he experienced as he lay in the uncomfortable bed, missing his wife and baby, thinking about how badly he'd let them down, he found he could live with the things that were happening because Sarah believed him. She looked into his eyes and knew that he was telling the truth. And she still believed that somehow, together, they were going to make everything all right again.

42

I feel a small, warm body next to mine, smell the familiar scent of Johnson's baby shampoo. I'm afraid that it's a dream. I feel her shift and move, issue a little cough, and my heart fills with hope.

"Mommy, are you still sleeping?"

I'm in a room flooded with light, so bright I can't see. I close and open my eyes until they adjust. I see Gray slumped in a chair, staring out the window. I hear the steady beeping of a heart monitor.

"Mommy."

"Mommy's sleeping, Victory," says Gray, edgy, sad.

"No, she isn't," Victory says, annoyed. "Her eyes are open."

He looks over at us quickly, then jumps up from his chair and comes over to the bed where I'm lying.

"Annie," he says, putting his hand on my forehead. He releases a heavy sigh, and I see tears spring to his eyes before he covers them, embarrassed. My lungs feel heavy and my head aches, but I have never been happier to see any two people.

"He's dead," I try to tell Gray, but my throat feels thick and sore. My voice comes out in a croak. "He's gone."

He shakes his head and looks confused, as if he isn't sure what I'm talking about. He kisses me on the forehead. "Try to relax," he says.

"Mom, you've been sleeping for a long time," Victory tells me. "Like *days*."

I look at her perfect face—her saucer eyes and Cupid's-bow mouth, the milky skin, the silky, golden puff of her hair—and lift my weak arms to hold her. I feel waves of relief pump through my body. She's mine. She's safe. Victory.

"Are you all right, Victory?" I ask when I can finally bring myself to release her. I examine her for signs of trauma or injury. But she's perfect, seems as happy and healthy as ever.

"What happened?" I ask Gray over her head. "How did you get her back?"

But then the room is filled with doctors and nurses. Gray takes Victory from me, and they stand by the window as I am poked and prodded.

"How are you feeling, Annie?" asks the kind-faced Asian doctor. She is pretty and petite, with a light dusting of lavender on her eyelids, the blush of pink on her lips.

"My chest feels heavy," I say.

"That's the smoke inhalation," she says, putting a stethoscope to my chest. "Breathe deeply for me."

"Smoke?" I ask after I've drawn and released a breath with difficulty.

"From the fire," she says, hand on my arm. "I'm afraid it will be a while before we know if the lung damage is permanent."

"I don't remember," I say, looking over at Gray, who offers me a smile. There's something funny on his face, something worried, anxious. I know this look. It makes me feel suddenly very uneasy.

"You will. Don't worry," says the doctor, patting my arm. "No rush. Let's get you better first."

The next few hours pass in a blur of tests and examinations. I gather that I've inhaled smoke from a fire. But I don't remember a fire. Whenever I ask questions, I receive strange, elliptical answers. Finally I'm given something to help me "relax." I drift off. When I wake again, it is dark outside. A dim light beside my bed glows, and Gray is dozing in the bedside chair. I reach for him, and he startles at my touch, then leans into me and holds on hard.

I tell him everything that's happened, even

though it hurts to talk so much—the men who were killed on the ship, Dax, my abduction, my father, my flight to Florida, the Angry Man, my confrontation with Marlowe. He listens, stays silent and focused on me. He lets everything tumble out of me without interruption.

"Where's Victory?" I say suddenly. "I don't understand. How did you get her back?"

"Annie—" says Gray, laying a hand on my head. But I've already interrupted him with another question.

"When did you realize she was gone?"

"Annie—"

"Is she all right?" I ask, sitting up with effort. "I mean *really* all right. He wouldn't have hurt her, I don't think. Are Drew and Vivian okay?"

"Everyone's fine," he says, getting up and sitting beside me on the bed, gently pushing me back against the pillows.

"You must have been so worried," I say, taking in the lines on his face, the circles under his eyes. "I'm so sorry."

"Annie, please," he says then, in a tone that causes me to stop talking. "You have to listen to me."

I am gripping the sheet hard, and I'm suddenly aware that my whole body is rigid, as though I'm bracing myself for a fall. The expression on Gray's face—furrowed brow, thin line of a mouth, eyes averted—tells me something is very wrong. I can't even bring myself to ask what it is.

He takes a deep breath, then, "Victory was never *gone,* Annie, never in danger. I sent her on a cruise with Drew and Vivian. She's been with them all this time."

"No," I say, feeling my chest tighten. I need desperately for him to understand and believe me. "Listen. Drew and Vivian were in on this. They *helped* Alan Parker. I think they believed they were helping me. But Parker took it too far. Then I had to save them by leading him to Marlowe."

Gray puts his head down and rubs his eyes before putting both hands on my shoulders and looking straight at me. "No, Annie. Nothing like that happened."

"Yes," I say, getting angry now. "It did. Drew and Vivian kept this from you because they knew you'd never be a part of it."

He shakes his head slowly, keeping my gaze. "No," he says gently.

"Explain then how all those men died on that ship. And Dax—the one who tried to save me— what happened to him?"

He shakes his head again, seems at a loss for words. There's something like panic living in my chest. I hear a nurse laugh out in the hallway, and I am suddenly aware of the beeping and humming of a hundred machines designed to monitor and maintain life. Somewhere else on the floor, big-band music is playing, soft and tinny. My breathing feels ragged in my throat.

"I *saw* them."

He takes my hand and looks at it, plays with the ring on my finger. "You never met the ship in Miami. You disappeared after the dive. You slipped the man who was supposed to take you to the boat."

I hear his words, but I can't believe he's saying them. He doesn't believe me.

"And no one named Dax has ever worked for me, Annie."

My heart monitor is beeping fast—107, 108, 109. I hold out my arms so he can see the black-and-blue marks on my body from my struggle on the ship.

"How did I get all these marks?"

He rubs my arms tenderly. "I don't know, honey. I don't know what happened to you out there. But you never made it to the ship that was waiting for you. I've been frantic looking for you since you got away from your escort. Finally I got a call from the police in the jurisdiction of Frank Geary's farmhouse. They found you unconscious from smoke

inhalation in the barn. The whole place was on fire.
It's been deserted for years. Locals think it's haunted.
Some kids out there on a dare saw it burning and
called the police."

"Burning."

"You set it on fire."

"No," I say. "I killed Marlowe Geary. And then—"
And then what? I find I don't remember. I remember
a flash of white before my eyes as Marlowe lay
bleeding.

"Did they find his body?" I ask. "He was disfigured, injured. He walked with a cane."

"No, Annie. You were alone there. There was no
body."

"But he wasn't at the farm," I say quickly. "He
was in a trailer far out in the woods. No one else in
the world knew about it but me. That's why they
needed me. Don't you see?"

Gray looks stricken, grips my hand. "It's *okay,*
Annie."

"Alan Parker must have arranged for his body to
be removed," I say. I realize then, because of the sad,
frightened look on Gray's face, that everything I'm
saying sounds like the ravings of a madwoman.

"You don't believe me," I say, feeling the crushing
weight of despair.

He puts his hand on my hair and rubs the back

of my neck, brings his face close to mine. I wrap my arms around the wide expanse of his shoulders.

"I believe that you believe it," he whispers. I hold on to him, rest my head against him.

"My father," I say, trying again but sounding desperate. "He's the one who figured out where Marlowe was hiding."

He holds on to me tighter. "Your father said someone broke in to his tattoo shop and went through his albums of old tattoos. He found the book with the photograph of Marlowe's tattoo open on the desk. He called me right away."

"No," I say. I pull away from Gray and force him to look into my face. "He helped me get back to Florida. A friend of his had a private plane."

Gray doesn't say anything. He just hangs his head again. And I start to weep.

"Why are you doing this to me?" I ask him. I feel so weak suddenly, so dizzy. My chest and throat ache with each sob. Gray reaches for me, and I cling to him.

"It's okay, Annie," he says, those words coiling around me like a snake. "It's going to be okay."

A psychotic break, the doctor says, brought on by the return of all the traumatic memories of my past—a reaction to the desire to merge the two parts of myself, the light and the dark, and maybe even a thirst for revenge against the person who laid waste to my childhood and to my life. All of it a fantasy my unhealthy mind created to make itself whole again. Where was I during the weeks I was missing? How did I get myself to that farm in the middle of Florida? No one knows.

My new doctor—a pretty blonde with a slight British accent and pouty lips—says she thinks that the germ for this fantasy took root when I saw my mother on television and heard about Grief Intervention Services. Something about their message of facing my fears resonated deeply, and I concocted an elaborate scenario in which I could do just that—flee the false life I'd constructed, pursue the man who I'd always believed was pursuing me, face him down and kill him. This fantasy lay dormant, a kind of psychological escape hatch—the items I kept in my box spring, the contact information for Oscar, my touchstones. My doctor thinks that it was the recent murder so heavily covered in the news, a murder that took place just miles from Frank Geary's horse farm, that caused my recent spate of panic attacks. And when I learned from Vivian that they'd lied about Marlowe's body, this knowledge set off the final chain reaction in my brain.

"The death of Annie Powers, leading to a

journey and a battle where you had to fight your way back to Marlowe and destroy him to save your daughter," she says in the quiet, thoughtful manner she has. "Only in this way did you believe you could reclaim Ophelia, save her from Marlowe as no one else was able. Only once you'd done this could you save your daughter."

She is excited by her own theory; I can tell by the way she leans forward and looks at me with bright, wide eyes. "You never believed he was dead. We don't, you know, we *can't* really unless we see a body. That's why we have funerals, to convince ourselves that death is real, that people have truly gone. Our instincts tell us that people *can't* die; they can't just be here one moment and then gone the next. Your family convinced *you* against your instincts. When you learned about their lies, you were sure that you'd been right all along. Marlowe's threats from long ago lived in your subconscious. This was the trigger that brought on the whole episode."

I don't argue with her. I know that arguing only makes me seem insane.

"My guess is that even though this has been a traumatic event for you, you feel better than you have in years. Am I right?"

She *is* right. The ugliness that Marlowe brought into my life has been cleansed. I may have let him into my mother's house, allowed him to slash through everything like a straight razor, but in the end I stood and defeated him. He is—finally—dead.

"It's interesting, though, that he was injured, disfigured when you confronted him," she says, musing. "It's as if his influence over you had already started to weaken. All you had to do was deliver the final blow."

I nod, slowly, thoughtfully. "I think you're right."

If she detects a lack of sincerity in my voice, she doesn't say so. She scribbles something in her pad. I can tell she finds me an interesting case.

How easily it's all explained away. Simon Briggs: He was a predator who discovered somehow that Ophelia still lived. He didn't work for anyone else, and he needed money. He'd come back to blackmail us, knowing we had to keep my identity a secret. Who killed him? Of course we know it was Gray. As far as the police are concerned, it could have been any of a number of his enemies or dissatisfied clients. When you live a life like Briggs's, there's almost no other way to die than beneath a bridge with a bullet in your brain.

What about poor Dr. Brown? Authorities were

just about to catch up with the unlicensed doctor. He was facing fines and jail time. He packed up his office and fled. He'd done it before, in New York and California. What I saw? Well . . . we can't put much stock in that, can we? And who might have killed him? An angry patient, maybe—who knows what kind of associations a man like that might have?

The stalker on the beach could have been Briggs laying the groundwork for his blackmail by unsettling me. Or perhaps it was just my imagination. I saw an innocent stranger walking in the grass, and my sick brain did the rest. The necklace I claimed to have found. No one ever saw it but me, and it is gone. The other half heart, which I kept all these years, is also gone from its velvet box under my mattress. This leads my doctor and everyone else to believe that I never found another necklace on the beach.

"It was a symbol for you, an important one," the doctor explains. "You were *halved* by Marlowe, separated from your true self. By thinking you'd found the other part of your necklace, you were committing yourself to a journey back to wholeness."

My doctor is very pleased with this theory.

But my mother did in fact die just over a year ago in a drunk-driving accident for which she was responsible. So how was it that, in my fantasy,

Marlowe relayed this information? I must have heard about it somehow, possibly read it on the Internet and, unable to accept it, pushed it deep down into my psyche. It resurfaced with all the other demons during my last episode.

And, finally, Grief Intervention Services, what about them? Just a grief- and victim-counseling organization known for such controversial techniques as hypnosis, immersion therapy, and other unconventional practices like forcing victims to return to the scene of their trauma, visiting their assailants in prison, watching executions—certainly not involving abduction, torture, murder, and such. And yes, it was founded and run until recently by Alan Parker, father of Melissa, husband of Janet. But he's been living out of the country for several years, battling cancer, far too unwell to travel. Another piece of information I must have absorbed during my obsessive Internet searches and filed away for inclusion in the daddy of all psychotic episodes.

The good news is that my new doctor does not think I'm truly mentally ill—as in chronically or permanently. She doesn't feel I have a chemical imbalance, something that will need to be treated with medication for the rest of my life. She believes that I am suffering from posttraumatic stress disorder that started the night I watched Janet Parker kill Frank

Geary. The horrors I witnessed during my time with Marlowe deepened my trauma. The adoption of a false identity and my desire to be rid of Ophelia only made things worse. She believes that if I had turned myself over to the police, faced whatever punishment might have been doled out, sought therapy, and tried to move forward in my life as Ophelia March—I would have suffered less in the aftermath.

Of course I agree. I agree with everything they say. I do what I must to survive in my life as it is. I adapt, as I always have.

Because I'm so agreeable, I'm allowed to go home to my family. I will not face arson charges for Frank Geary's farm. Technically, it belonged to me, anyway. This is one of the reasons my new doctor thinks I burned it down—because it was the last link to Frank and Marlowe Geary.

"Fire is very cleansing," she says. She's right. I am glad that the farm's a pile of ash. I hope someone levels the whole place and builds a mall on it.

I have agreed to let the county sell the property and keep the proceeds. In exchange, they will not bring any charges against me. It has all been very cordial.

Likewise, Ophelia March will not be charged for

her association to Marlowe Geary's crimes. Because we crossed so many state lines and Marlowe committed multiple murders, it is a federal matter. So far no one at the FBI or the federal prosecutor's office is sufficiently motivated to bring charges against me. I am widely regarded as a victim, not as an accomplice. I am generally pitied, not reviled. So far the information about Ophelia's survival has managed not to make headline news. For this I am grateful, though I wonder if it is only a matter of time.

And somehow, with Drew and Gray's connections, the identity theft of the real Annie has gone away as well. It's all quite seamless.

I return to the quiet, empty days of my life. Ella comes every morning to be with me after Victory has gone to school. I talk to her about everything. She listens in a way that Gray cannot. He feels a certain anxiety, a need to fix and control, to comfort and soothe, especially regarding events he believes happened only in my mind. This is not what I need. I need an ear, someone to hear and understand that the things that happened have meaning and significance to me—whether they happened in my head or not. Ella seems to understand this. She is a patient and interested listener, not unlike my doctor.

"Do I call you Annie or Ophelia?" Ella wants to know this morning as we enjoy coffee on the pool deck. We lie on bright beach towels spread over the wide, comfortable lounge chairs. The air is warm with a light breeze. Over whispering waves, gulls screech, fighting in the air over a fish one of them has caught. I have been home for three weeks.

"I think Annie, you know?" I say. I have given this some thought, of course. "I decided I'm going to change my name to Annie Ophelia Powers. I'm not that girl anymore. But she's still a part of who I am."

She nods her understanding. "You know what, Annie?" she says, giving me a smile. "You seem well. Better than you've ever been. More solid, centered."

"Whole," I say.

"Yes."

Marlowe Geary is dead. I shot him and watched as the life drained from him. Finally, I rescued Ophelia. She is safe. She has a home and a family who loves her. I don't say any of this. There's no point.

We sit in silence for a while, sipping coffee. In the kitchen I hear the new maid and nanny, a young woman named Brigit drop a glass; it shatters on the tile. She is someone Gray hired when Esperanza quit. She is cool where Esperanza was warm, thin where Esperanza was curvaceous, quiet where Esperanza was exuberant. She's not bad, just different. I've wanted to call Esperanza, but apparently she has gone back to Mexico to care for her dying mother;

there is no phone in her home there. She promised Gray to come back after her mother's passing. I am afraid that she has left because of me. Victory misses her very much, and so do I. But in a way my daughter and I are closer for her absence.

I go in to see if Brigit is okay. She is, just flustered and apologetic. I try to put her at ease and think again how much we miss Esperanza.

When I return, Ella is reading the paper.

"Did you hear what happened to the police detective who was here that night?" she says.

"Ray Harrison?"

"Yeah."

I don't know if she knows about how he blackmailed us, and I can't decide whether I should get into all that with her. I haven't thought about him in a while. I remember our last encounter outside the pool where I took my diving lessons, how his conversation led me to Vivian, who told me about Marlowe's body. She claims that she never said anything about Dr. Brown or made any cryptic statements like, "That's what they told me to say." She was fooled by him like everybody else, she claims. Needless to say, our relationship has cooled. She is nervous and uncomfortable around me. We keep up appearances for Victory's sake. Drew has avoided me altogether.

"What happened to him?"

She hands me the paper, and I read the feature about the fallen cop, the hooker, the heroin, the gambling addiction, the mysterious money in his account. Ray Harrison looks beaten, dazed in the mug shot pictured. I notice that the white hair over his ear is gone. Strange. Maybe it's a trick of the light.

I glance over at Ella, and she is watching me. She wrinkles her brow when our eyes meet.

"Crazy, huh?" she says, and there's an odd brightness to her gaze, as if she takes some pleasure in the sensational nature of the story.

"Yeah," I say, folding the paper, closing my eyes, and leaning my head back. I feel the sun on my face. I feel a sudden anxiety, a sense that something is not right about what I've read. But I can't afford to dwell on Ray Harrison right now or worry about his problems. "Crazy."

43

I am never alone, I start to realize after I've been home another week or so. Either Gray or Ella or Brigit is always with me. I am not even left alone with Victory except when I take her to school in the mornings. It's not that anyone's hovering, but someone is always in the house or out with us as we run errands. With what they think of me, I suppose I can't blame them. I'll go along with it for a while, but eventually it's going to start to wear on me. Right now I'm on my best behavior, doing what I must to be home with my family and not locked up in a rubber room somewhere.

"Mommy," Victory says in the car on the way to school this morning.

"Yeah, Victory?"

"Are you better?" She is looking at me through the rearview mirror. She's frowning slightly.

"Yes, I am," I answer. "A lot better."

I see her smile, then put my eyes back to the road.

Then, "I don't want to go away with Grandma and Grandpa anymore." It's an odd thing to say, and I look back into the mirror to see that her frown has returned.

"Why, baby?"

"I just don't want to. I want to stay with you and Daddy. You shouldn't go away, and they shouldn't take me anywhere." I can see she has given this some thought. My heart aches a little.

I give her a smile and decide not to press right now. "I'm not going anywhere. And you don't have to go anywhere you don't want to. Okay?"

"Okay," she says, but her smile doesn't return.

The rest of the ride I am watching her face, wondering if I should urge her to talk more. But by the time I get her to school, she's back to her old self, bubbly and chirping about show-and-tell today. She has brought Claude and Isabel. I am sure they'll be a smashing success.

After I drop Victory off, I don't go straight home. I just can't face the rest of the day tiptoeing around Brigit, who, by the way, is an even worse cook and housekeeper than I am. I'm starting to suspect that she's an operative from my husband's company, hired to keep an eye on me.

I find myself at the Internet café by the beach. I order myself a latte and grab a spot in a booth toward the back, start browsing the Web on one of the laptops. I have thought about trying to find some proof of the things that happened to me. But, it turns out, I don't really need anyone to believe me. I know what happened. I know I'm not crazy. I know that I faced Marlowe Geary and removed him from the world. I am healed by this knowledge. That should be enough. Whatever Alan Parker and Grief Intervention Services did to cover everything up is not my problem. I have tried to reach my father to talk to him about that night, without luck. I'm starting to worry about him.

My fingers hover over the keyboard. I think about searching for a way to contact Alan Parker, to look for stories of other people who have been involved with Grief Intervention Services, or to try to reach my father again without Gray around. There's a pay phone over by the bathrooms. But in the end I don't do any of these things. I have the sense that I'm being watched. Everyone is so pleased with my "progress." I don't want to set off any alarms. I need to be home for my daughter.

"They don't want you to be alone, do they?" I turn to see a young woman sitting at the table behind me. She has a baby who is blissfully asleep in a stroller. The woman's ash-blond hair is pulled back into a tight ponytail, her face pale to the point of looking almost gray. The dark smudges of fatigue rim her eyes. I don't recognize her.

"I'm sorry?" I say.

"I've been trying to get you alone for days," she says.

"Do I know you?" I ask.

"No, you don't know me, Ms. Powers. My name is Sarah Harrison. I'm Ray Harrison's wife."

I look at her face and try to decide what she wants. Is this going to be another attempt at blackmail? A desperate woman looking for money? But no, there's something about her face. Her eyes are wide and earnest. There's a strength and a presence to her. She's not the criminal type. She's scared, looking over at the door and then down at her baby. The baby looks a lot like Ray Harrison; the only way I know she's a girl is because she's wrapped in pink. I remember when Victory was that small and fragile. I can't help myself—I reach in and touch the downy crown of her head. She releases a sigh but doesn't wake.

"I need to talk to you," Sarah says.

I turn away from her. If anyone is watching, I want them to think I was just admiring her baby. I look at my computer screen. "What can I do for you, Mrs. Harrison?"

"You heard what happened to my husband?"

I nod. "I'm sorry," I tell her. And I am sorry, for all of them, especially for his little girl.

"What happened to him happened because he was trying to help you."

"I don't understand," I say. I'm aware that I sound distant and cold. But I can't afford to be anything else at the moment. She seems undaunted as she begins to tell me about the recent events of her husband's life, the version I read about in the paper plus everything he learned in his investigation.

"They think he had a nervous breakdown relating to his gambling addiction. No one believes him about Grief Intervention Services, about the Taser attack. They think he's crazy."

"There must be marks on his body from the Taser, if it's true."

"There *were* marks," she says. "But no one believed that's where they came from. They questioned your friend, Ella Singer, just to say they had." She pauses and issues a harsh laugh. "She and her husband were *outraged*. She helped in every way possible with his investigation, and this is what she gets from him, she said. Apparently, her husband plays golf with the mayor." Her words are heavy with bitterness.

I remember the glint in Ella's eyes when she handed me the paper. She'd made no mention of these allegations Sarah is describing, of course. There was nothing of it in the paper. If I confronted her, I'm sure she'd say she was trying to spare me any upset, that I had my own problems. And maybe that's the truth. It's difficult to think of Ella wielding a Taser gun, and yet somehow it isn't *impossible* to imagine.

"Let's just pretend that I believe what you're saying," I tell Sarah Harrison. "What can I do about it?"

"You don't understand," she says. "I'm not asking for your help. I'm trying to help *you*. They want you to think you're crazy. You're not. My husband wronged you, he knows that now. He wants to make it right, and so do I."

"Okay," I say. "Maybe that's true. But what do you think you can do for me, Sarah?"

The baby releases a little sigh. I can see the little pink bundle out of the corner of my eye.

"Maybe nothing. I just thought you needed to know that you're living in a pit of vipers. Your husband, your best friend, and your in-laws are all lying to you. They're basically holding you prisoner, in the nicest possible cage."

I don't say anything, just take a sip of my coffee and hope she can't see that my hand is shaking.

"This is an interesting thing my husband found out, the thing that brought him to your house in the first place. He learned that Grief Intervention Services is a *client* of Powers and Powers, Inc."

When I still don't say anything, she goes on.

"A friend of Ray's at the FBI forwarded him a client list. The federal government keeps very close tabs on those privatized military companies, for obvious reasons. Let me ask you this: What kind of services might a military company provide to an organization established to help people with their grief?"

It's a good question. So good that I'm not sure I want the answer. I drain my coffee cup.

"If these things are true, you're putting yourself at great risk by coming here, Sarah," I tell her. "You should think of your daughter."

"I *am* thinking of my daughter," she says sharply. "I want her to know that there's more to life than just playing it safe. That when you make mistakes, part of the way you move on is by correcting what you can. My husband has made a lot of mistakes, some of them concerning you. But he tried to make things right, and he's paying a very high price—his career, his reputation. There's not a lot we can do about that. But we both feel we owe you the truth. Here's my advice: Take your daughter and get as far away from that family as possible. Run. Don't walk."

I stand up then. I don't want to listen to anything else. I pick up my bag and put it over my shoulder.

"You have access at home to Gray's computer, right? Find the client list for Powers and Powers, Inc. See if I'm telling you the truth."

I put some money on the table, a tip for service I didn't get. And move toward the door.

"If you won't do it for yourself, Annie, do it for your daughter."

I leave her there. I don't look back.

In a karst topography, there's a feature called a disappearing stream. At a certain point in the flow, the water slips through the delicate pores of the limestone bedrock and winds its way beneath the ground through an intricate system of caves and caverns. It travels like any moving body of water and may connect with the flow of yet other streams, traveling swift and steady but in darkness, far beneath the world. Then, as if from nowhere, the stream percolates and resurfaces, sometimes hundreds of miles away from its origin.

In this subterranean environment, creatures called stygobites, animals perfectly adapted to the wet darkness, proliferate—spiders and flies, millipedes and lizards. Through evolution they have lost their eyes, their skin has become translucent. Even the most minimal exposure to the light would be lethal.

Ophelia dropped beneath the surface of the earth and then appeared again as Annie. The streams of their lives merged, continuing on together, only to dip into the darkness again. I thought I'd come into the light once and for all. But perhaps it's true that I don't even know the difference between light and dark anymore. Perhaps I am perfectly adapted to my life as it is.

I drive around for a while, my heart thrumming, my throat dry and painful. My lungs have not recovered from the smoke inhalation, and I'm having trouble getting a full breath of air. I drive up the beach, turn around, and wind through the streets of our quaint little ocean town, watch the tourists with their terrible sunburns; the teenagers with their lithe, perfect bodies strutting about in bathing suits and bare feet; the retirees with their silver hair and walking canes. After a while I am calmer, but Sarah Harrison's words are still loud in my head. I want to go home, pretend I never saw her. I try to convince myself that she was a product of my demented mind, yet another fantasy on my part. But I can't do this. It's what she said about her daughter that echoes: *I*

want her to know that there's more to life than just play-
ing it safe. That when you make mistakes, part of the
way you move on is by correcting what you can. The
simple truth of this hurts. I realize that I am betray-
ing myself again, this time for my daughter.

44

That night we have plans to go to dinner at Drew and Vivian's. I'm nervous and edgy because of this. I have not been comfortable around Vivian since my return. And I have not spoken to Drew at all. Having dinner at their place is the last thing I want to do. But Gray has convinced me that it's a much-needed return to normalcy, the point from which we all move forward as a family. I don't hate him for it, but almost.

I have snapped at Gray twice while we get ready, and now he's avoiding me. Victory is cranky and fussy, maybe because of my mood, which is always contagious where she is concerned. But maybe for reasons of her own. She doesn't want to go, has said as much, keeps angling for pizza and a movie. I ask her about it as I help her into the new outfit I bought for her after my encounter with Sarah Harrison today. I used it as an excuse for Brigit as to why I didn't come straight home after dropping Victory off.

"You always love to go to Grandma's," I say, fastening the heart-shaped buttons on the back of the pink gingham dress she wears over her pink leggings. She holds up her hair for me.

"No I don't," she says stubbornly. "I like pizza and a video better."

I can see the sad downturn of the corners of her mouth in the mirror across from us. I turn her around gently so that we are face-to-face. There's nothing of Marlowe in her; her face is a mirror of my own.

"What's wrong, Victory?" I ask her, almost whispering.

She drops her eyes to the floor. "Nothing," she says, then leans into me and wraps her tiny arms around my neck. I wrap my arms around her and am about to ask again, but then Gray's at the door.

"How does a guy get in on that hug?" he asks.

Victory runs to him, her face bright now, no trace of the sadness I saw a moment ago. He lofts her into the air and then squeezes her. We smile at each other over Victory's head as she giggles with delight. He puts her back down.

"Everybody ready? Dad just called. Vivian has the steaks on the grill."

If he notices that Victory and I both lose our smiles, he doesn't say anything.

. . .

The farce of it all sickens me. Sarah Harrison might as well be seated across from me at the long glass table where we have gathered for dinner. A wide orange sun is dropping toward the blue-pink horizon line over the Gulf. We feast on filet mignon and twice-baked potatoes, fat ears of corn. Drew and Gray knock back Coronas while Vivian and I drink chardonnay. Victory sips her milk from a plastic cup adorned with images of Hello Kitty. Anyone looking at us might feel a twinge of envy, the rich and happy family sharing a meal at their luxury home with a view of the ocean.

"Annie," says Drew, breaking an awkward silence that has settled over the table once vague pleasantries and chatty questions for Victory have been exhausted. "You seem well."

He is smiling at me in a way he never has before. There's a satisfied benevolence to him, the king surveying his subjects. I thank him because it seems like the right thing to do in this context.

"I'm glad to see it," he says. "It's a blessing to be here as a family. It's been a long journey to happiness—for all of us."

"Yes," says Vivian, looking at her plate. "A blessing." She lifts her eyes to me then and takes my hand. I have the urge to snatch it away but I don't. I smile at her and then over to Victory, who is sitting beside me, watching me intently.

"I have to admit," Drew goes on, voice a little too loud, a little too bright, "when you first came to us, I didn't think you were right for my son. You weren't well, and I was afraid Gray was trying to rescue you in a way he could never rescue his mother."

The words land like a fist on the table, everyone pauses mid-action—Vivian's glass at her lips, my fork hovering over a tomato—to look at Drew. I've never heard him say anything like that; his candor makes heat rise to my cheeks.

"Dad," says Gray with a frown, sliding forward in his chair. He throws a meaningful glance in Victory's direction, and I can see the tension in his shoulders and his biceps.

"Let me *finish*," says Drew sharply, lifting a hand.

I see then that Drew is drunk. He's had at least four bottles of beer since we sat down at the table, and he has probably been drinking since before we arrived. There's an unbecomingly loose, loquacious quality to him.

Gray casts me an uneasy look but leans back in his chair, still tense, still waiting. It's not that he's afraid to stand up to his father, just that even the smallest disagreement can turn into a battle. He prefers to bide his time.

"But you're not like Gray's mother," says Drew. "There's a mettle to you, Annie, that I never suspected. You make my son happy, and you're a good mother to your daughter."

A year ago I would have been weak with gratitude for this statement. Now I just want to put my fist through the rows of his perfect white teeth. My conversation with Sarah Harrison is bouncing around inside my head, and my heart rate is on the rise. It takes effort to keep the swelling tide of emotion off my face.

Vivian gets up from the table suddenly, pushing her chair back quickly, almost toppling it. She senses that the sky is about to open.

"Victory, let's go upstairs and look at your dollhouse," she says, moving toward the door leading inside. I expect Victory to bolt off after her, but she stays rooted.

"No," says Victory sullenly. She takes hold of my hand. "I want to stay here."

"Victory," Vivian says so sternly that I'm startled by her tone, "let's *go*."

Something shifts inside me. "Don't talk to her like that," I find myself saying. "Ever."

Then everyone turns to face me, as though I'm a

marionette that has suddenly made a move of her own.

"I don't want to play any of those games with you, Grandma," says Victory. "I don't like it."

I turn to my daughter and think how much tougher, how much stronger, she already is than I have ever been.

"What kinds of games, Victory?" I ask her. She doesn't answer me, but Victory and Vivian lock eyes. There's a warning on Vivian's face and fear on Victory's. I feel the tightness of anger in my chest as I move my body between them.

"What kinds of games?" I ask her again.

That afternoon I *did* log on to Gray's computer. And I discovered that Sarah Harrison has told me the truth about the connection between Powers and Powers and Grief Intervention Services. And since then my addled brain has been working overtime to fit together the pieces of the things that have happened to me. That look between Victory and Vivian, for some reason, causes everything to click into place.

"What is going on here?" asks Gray. He has moved forward again in his seat, looks as though he's about to stand.

Victory shakes her head and gazes hard down at her knees. Her whole body is rigid; she has released my hand and grabbed on to both arms of the chair. I put my hand on her shoulder, lean into her, and whisper, "You don't have to go anywhere you don't want to go, Victory." I watch the tension drain from her body.

Everyone is quiet a moment.

"The picture," I say quietly, suddenly understanding. I feel the first rumblings of a volcanic rage, but somehow my voice is little more than a whisper. "You tied her up and took a picture of her. You told her it was a game."

Victory looks at me with surprise, and then the tears start to fall. *"Don't hurt my mommy!"* she yells suddenly, looking at Drew. There's so much fear on her face my heart lurches. She grabs for my hand and starts to pull herself onto my lap. *"I didn't tell her! I didn't tell!"*

She is on me then, clinging and sobbing into my chest in a way she hasn't since she was a toddler. I hold on to her tightly, bury my face in her hair.

"No one's going to hurt me, Victory," I whisper into her ear.

Gray is looking at his father, his face a mask of confused disappointment. "Dad?" he says. "What have you done?"

Drew takes a few deep breaths, seems to steel himself. "I did what I had to do for our family, so that we could all be together like this."

Gray gets to his feet so fast that everything shakes. A piece of stemware falls to the floor and shatters, spraying wine and shards of glass at our ankles. No one moves to pick it up; everyone stays fixed, frozen. Gray's face is red, a vein throbbing on his throat. I've never seen him so angry.

"What are you talking about, Dad?" Gray roars.

Drew is turning a shade of red to match, but he doesn't say anything.

"Fucking answer me!"

Drew picks up his bottle of beer and takes a long, slow swallow. It's clear that he doesn't feel as though he needs to answer his son.

"Grief Intervention Services is a client of Powers and Powers, Inc.," I say finally to Gray. I want to rage like him, to start picking up the china and glasses from the table and flinging them just to watch things break and crash, but my daughter is clinging, hysterical in my arms. I feel as if I owe it to her to keep myself together. "I looked up the client list on our computer this afternoon. It's there."

Gray's eyes rest on me and then move back to his father. I can see that he doesn't know what to believe.

All eyes are on Drew now, who still has said nothing, just puffed up his chest and pulled back his shoulders. He is the picture of self-satisfied arrogance, the man assured of his righteousness.

"So what?" he says simply. "What does that prove?"

Gray's face falls; all the rage seems to leave him. I remember the expression from my time in the psychiatric hospital years ago when he talked about his father, how powerless he'd felt against his father's will, his father's desires for him. How he'd lived his life trying to please a man who would never be pleased. We hadn't talked about that in so long, always wrapped up in whatever drama I had going on. I could see that nothing had changed. Maybe Gray had betrayed himself in the same way I had, living a fake life for what seems to be the greater good. Maybe he never wanted to go back to work with his father; maybe he just thought he had to, to make a life for us.

"You spent your whole childhood trying to save your mother," says Drew, picking up his fork and knife and going to work on his steak. "I didn't want you to spend your adulthood trying to save someone else you couldn't save. I didn't want another child in my care growing up with an unstable mother. We did what we had to do. We helped Annie, but ultimately she had to save herself. Our methods were unorthodox, sure. But it had to be that way. Annie knows that."

He's so cool, so matter-of-fact, he could be talking

about anything—a risky business venture or a volatile investment that paid out after all. But he's talking about me, my life, my daughter. Gray and I both stare at Drew while he eats. Victory is still crying quietly in my arms. Vivian stands at the head of the table, her hands resting on the chair where she sat during the meal. The sun has dropped below the horizon, and there's an orange-blue glow over the ocean. Such a beautiful place to live such an ugly life.

"You were haunted, Annie," Vivian says, her voice soft and earnest. "He was *always* going to haunt you." But no one seems to hear.

I'm watching my husband, and I can see him working the problem, going over in his mind the story I told him, remembering the accusations I launched against Drew and Vivian, the things he told me were all a dream. "Alan Parker, Grief Intervention Services, everything he told her," says Gray, not yelling anymore, not enraged. Just . . . sad. "It was all *true?*"

Drew carefully cuts another piece of steak and puts it in his mouth, begins to slowly chew. Gray and I stare at him, stunned by his calm, by his indifference, all our shock and anger just a breeze through the branches of a great old oak.

"Look," he says finally, resting his silverware with

a clang on his plate. "Alan Parker took Annie where she needed to go, and Annie did the rest. Didn't you, girl?"

Gray's gaze keeps shifting back and forth between me and his father. "Are you telling me he was there? Marlowe Geary? That she *killed* him?" His voice is a hard edge, tight with emotion; his fists are clenched at his side. "No. No fucking way."

A wide, slow smile spreads across Drew's face. It is almost kind, but it never reaches his eyes. In the gloaming he's a monster. I find myself recoiling from him.

"What do you think, Annie?" Drew asks, giving me a hideous wink, like we're in together on some kind of joke. "Is Marlowe Geary dead? Finally?"

And suddenly I realize we *are* in on the joke together. Because only Drew and I understand that *I* had to be the one to kill Marlowe Geary. No tale of his demise, no repeated phrases or articles on the Internet were ever going to convince me he was dead. I had to kill him and watch him die. That was the only way I would ever truly be free of him.

All my desire to rage at Drew drains, and I am filled again by the familiar numbness that has allowed me to survive so much horror. I feel a shutting down of anger, of fear, and I am mercifully blank. But I find I can't bear the sight of Drew and

Vivian anymore. I stand up with Victory in my arms and move away from the table, heading for the door. There are a lot of questions, but I don't want the answers. Not from Drew and Vivian.

"Annie, please try to understand," says Vivian. I can see that fear again on her face, but I am already gone.

"I need to understand what you did, Dad," I hear Gray say behind me. I can tell he's trying to keep his tone level. "I need you to tell me the truth."

"Leave it be, son," answers Drew, his tone as unyielding as a brick wall. I wait in the foyer, listening, rocking back and forth with Victory, who is quiet now.

"I can't do that."

"Yes," says Drew. "If you know what's good for your family, you can. Your wife is unwell. In my opinion not well enough to be caring for that child. And we all know you are not Victory's biological father. What would happen to that girl if her mother wound up in a rubber room somewhere?"

"What is that?" asks Gray. "Some kind of threat?"

No one was supposed to know that Victory is Marlowe's child. Only Gray and I knew. And my father. I start to feel weak. I have to put Victory down and kneel beside her on the cold marble floor of Drew and Vivian's house. I look at her face. If she has heard, she doesn't give any sign, just leans against me and rubs her eyes.

"Can we go home?" she asks.

"We're going. Let's wait for Daddy."

"Okay," she says. "But can he hurry? I don't want to be here anymore."

"Me neither."

I hear Drew's voice booming then. "I don't have to tell you the kind of connections I have, the people I know. Your job, your home, your wife, even your child are yours because I have allowed you to have them. A few phone calls from me and it all goes away."

"Drew—" I hear Vivian, her voice pleading.

What did you do?" I hear something crash and break. Victory and I hold on to each other. I want to go to the car, but I can't leave Gray here by himself. We huddle against the storm.

"I did what I needed to do so that we could be a family, so that Victory could have a healthy mother, so that you didn't spend the rest of your life trying to save someone who couldn't be saved. Don't you see that?"

I don't hear Gray's answer. But in the strangest way, I see Drew's point. I guess I'm as sick as he is.

"It was happening again," says Drew. "Those panic attacks that she had before Victory was born. It always started with that. Then the next thing we knew, she was gone, on a bus to God knows where. What if she took Victory with her? Or worse, left her somewhere? It was one thing when she was just a danger to herself—"

"You're sick, Dad," Gray interrupted him, his tone thick with disdain. "You can't use people, manipulate and control them so that they become who you think they should be. It didn't work with Mom, and it's not going to work with me and my family. I came back here hoping that we could be a family, learn to love and accept each other for all our differences. But that's never going to happen, is it?"

"I do love you, son," says Drew, his voice sounding weak suddenly, and so sad.

"You don't even know what love is, Dad. You never have."

Then Gray's footsteps are heavy and fast behind me. He kneels beside us and helps me to my feet, lifts Victory into his arms.

She lies against him like a rag doll, exhausted. "Can we go now?"

He looks at me with his stormy eyes. "I'm sorry, Annie," he says. "I'm so sorry."

"Let's get out of here," I say, putting my hand on his arm. I don't want to talk anymore. I just want to get out of this house, for good.

"I should have believed you."

"You had no reason to believe me, Gray," I say, pulling him toward the door.

"That's not true," he says. "I didn't *want* to believe you."

"Gray," I say, as we walk out the door and head toward our car, "it's okay. You can start believing me now."

45

I walk through the rooms of our house and listen to the echoes of the life we lived here. The windows are open, the air is humid. I can hear the ocean and smell the salt. This is what I will miss most about this place, our proximity to the sea, the sand on our feet, the birds crying in the air, the sound of our wind chimes on the porch. But there's a special kind of beauty to New York City, too. And in its way it is more my home than this place, no matter how beautiful, has ever been.

The few items of furniture that are coming with us are already on their way to be unloaded into a ridiculously expensive brownstone on the east side of Tompkins Square. It's still a gritty neighborhood, to be sure. Nothing like the posh house we're leaving, but it will be ours—our choice, our terms, our home. Everything else we'll leave behind.

I walk from room to room, making sure that things are clean, that nothing we need has been forgotten. I feel a potent nostalgia I can't explain. Gray and Victory have gone off together to do some errands—close a bank account, buy Victory her own carry-on suitcase for the trip tomorrow.

After I've been all through the house, I come to stand at the glass doors downstairs and stare at the Gulf until I sense someone behind me. I spin around to see Detective Harrison standing in my living room.

"The door was open," he says apologetically.

He looks thin and pale but oddly solid—at peace in a way. I find myself grateful for him and for his wife, and I'm glad to see him now. I want to embrace him, but I don't. I smile at him instead and hope I don't seem cool, distant.

"Coffee?" I ask.

"Please," he says.

I pour him a cup but abstain myself. I'm jittery already from too much caffeine this morning, and I feel a headache coming on. I sit on the couch, but he prefers to stand.

"How's your family?" I ask.

"We're okay, you know?" he says with a nod. "I think we're going to be okay. I've hung out my own shingle: Ray Harrison, Private Investigations. I've even managed to find a few people who don't mind having a junkie with a criminal record investigating their cases." He laughs a little, and it washes away some of the bitterness in his words.

"Anyway, I came to bring you this," he says. He walks over and hands me a folded piece of paper. I unfold it and look at it for a second. It's a check in the amount of the money he blackmailed from us.

I try to give it back. "Keep it," I say. "Pay us back when you're on your feet."

He raises a hand. "No. This is right. I need to do the right thing by you. I promised my wife."

I nod my understanding, put the check down beside me. We are silent for a minute, awkward, neither of us knowing what to say. Our relationship is so bizarre we have no template for polite conversation.

"There are things I can tell you," he says. He's doing that rocking business he does, has stuffed his hands in his pockets. "But maybe you don't want to know. Maybe you just want to move forward with your life from here."

I haven't spoken to Drew or Vivian since the night we left their home. Gray has asked his father to buy out his interest in Powers and Powers, and Drew has agreed. Drew has refused to talk any further about his relationship to Grief Intervention Services, how he knew about Victory's paternity, or to offer any explanation of the things that have happened to me. Gray has tried to find some explanations through avenues of his own but has come up against wall after wall. We have both decided that for the sake of our family, of protecting Victory, there are things we'll just have to live with never knowing.

"I thought I was going to be in the dark for the rest of my life," Harrison says, pacing the room. "But I had a visitor the other day to my new office."

"Who?"

"An old friend of yours," he says with a wry smile. "She's no friend of mine, of course. But she brought me this."

"Ella?" I ask eagerly. "*Where* is she? The hurricane shutters are down on her house. She's been gone for weeks. I haven't had a call or an e-mail. We're going to have to leave without saying good-bye."

He gives a cryptic shake of his head. "I don't know what her plans are. I'm sure you'll hear from her, though, Annie. One of these days."

As he takes another piece of paper from his pocket and gives it to me, my headache intensifies. This time it's a picture, a blurry black-and-white photograph of two boys in fatigues, arms around each other's shoulders, one smiling, one grim. It takes me a second to figure out who I'm looking at. For a second, I think one of the men is Gray. But then I recognize them—Drew Powers and Alan

Parker, younger, thinner, barely resembling the men they became. Someone had scribbled in the corner, *Bassac River, 1967, Vietnam.*

"I don't understand," I say, feeling suddenly as though the ground has shifted beneath me. "What does this mean?"

"They served together on SEAL Team One in Vietnam. They've known each other most of their lives."

I'm struggling with this information, trying to understand how everything fits together. But my head is aching so badly I can hardly concentrate.

"I have a theory," he says. "Want to hear it?"

I don't really, but I find myself giving a half nod.

"I think, years ago, when Alan Parker wanted revenge for the murder of his daughter, he came to Drew, his old war buddy. Drew had already founded Powers and Powers at that point, and it was a thriving private military firm. Based on some digging I've done, I think Drew hired out one of his men to Parker to track down Marlowe Geary—a man named Simon Briggs. Later, when Parker started Grief Intervention Services, Powers and Powers provided the muscle needed to help people face those who had injured them or their loved ones. Vigilantes, basically."

I think about this. It makes sense somehow to me that they knew each other. I can see them, both controlling, arrogant men, thinking that what they did was motivated by love for their children, never understanding that love and control are two different things.

"Then it was just a coincidence that my father met with Gray and asked him to help me?" I say with a shake of my head. "No."

Harrison hangs his head for a second. He seems to be debating whether to say what he wants to say. Then, "Your father, Teddy March, also known as Bear. He served on the same SEAL team in Vietnam."

I laugh at this. "No," I say. "Not my father."

But then I remember all the times he talked about the Navy SEALs, all his Vietnam stories. I thought they were lies. I never once believed him.

Detective Harrison has another photograph. In the picture I see my father, Drew, and some other men I don't recognize sitting in a boat heading down a gray river surrounded by jungle. They are grim, intent, uncomfortable. My father is a boy with the stubble of a beard, a cigarette dangling from his lips. He is lithe, muscular, with dark eyes and square jaw. Drew looks like a heavier, less appealing version of my husband—like a young bulldog with a stern brow and mean eyes.

"These men, these fathers, all searching for their kids," says Harrison, drifting over toward the glass doors leading to the deck. "Alan Parker's daughter murdered by Frank Geary, Teddy March's daughter held in the thrall of Marlowe Geary, Drew Powers's son far from the fold, estranged for years. They all had a common purpose, to do right by their kids in the ways that they could."

I think about this, the deviousness and planning, the deception that it took to make all this happen.

"And how was it that both you and Melissa fell prey to the Gearys? Coincidence, maybe. Or maybe it was their karma, their bond? I don't know, but it's poetic in its way, isn't it?"

That's our karma, our bond. Marlowe's words come back to me.

Harrison goes on, "The only thing they didn't plan for was Gray falling in love with you."

"It doesn't make sense," I say, even though, on a cellular level, it does. "There are too many variables, so many coincidences. Did my father go to Drew for help, too? Is that how he connected to Gray? They used me to draw Gray in, knowing he couldn't resist the idea of rescuing a lost girl?"

"Paul Broward—your Dr. Brown—he had a lot of experience with manipulating people's psyches. You should know that better than anyone."

My emotions—a terrible alchemy of impotent anger, disbelief, and fear—must be playing on my face, because suddenly Harrison seems to regret coming. He looks over toward the door, then back at me, and raises his palms.

"I'm sorry, Annie. You know what? It's just a theory. I'm talking out of my ass."

"What about Briggs?" I ask quickly, still turning his words over, still trying to punch holes in his theories.

"A longtime employee of Powers and Powers, that much I do know for a fact. Maybe Gray wasn't aware of that. When he couldn't figure out who Briggs worked for, he killed him fearing for your safety."

I feel exhausted, and my head is pounding now, accompanied by a terrible ringing in my ears. I try to think about what all this might mean, that we've been under the control of these men, my father included, since before Gray and I ever met. It hurts too much to think about, and I feel myself powering down emotionally. I'm grateful.

"As for me, I made a nuisance of myself," Harrison said. "And they laid waste to my life."

I think about what Sarah Harrison told me, how Ella attacked Ray with a Taser. I've hardly known what to do with that information. I've wanted to confront her, but she's gone. Who was she, this woman I called a friend? I can feel my chest constricting. Ever since the smoke inhalation, my lungs ache when I get upset. I struggle to slow my breathing. Harrison seems to sense my discomfort.

"Look," he says, moving toward the front door, "maybe you should consider yourself lucky at this point, Annie. Move on, you know? My life is a train wreck. But you, you've exorcised your demons—you've won. You can walk away with your family and start over."

I laugh. It sounds harsh and bitter as it bounces back to me. "You mean just forget all this? I think we've seen how that works out."

"Not a denial, Annie," he says. "A rebirth."

I get up and walk to the back glass doors, watch the waves lick the shore. I take the salt air into my lungs and wonder if Detective Harrison might be right.

"Is it possible?" I ask him. "Is it possible to cast it all off and start again—the new and improved Annie? Or will it come creeping after me *again* one day when I least expect it?"

I listen to my voice echo in the empty room. Harrison doesn't answer me.

I keep looking at the shoreline. I lose myself in thought for a moment and notice that my headache is lifting.

"Maybe it *is* possible," I say, answering my own question.

"Annie?"

I turn around to see Gray standing behind me with an odd expression, something between amusement and worry. We are alone.

"Who are you talking to?" he asks.

The headache I had is gone, but it is replaced with a rush of panic. As I walk past him, he reaches for my arm, but I slip by. I lift the three pieces of paper from the couch, two receipts from the grocery store and a baby picture of Victory. Not a check, not old pictures of Vietnam.

I sweep the room again with my eyes, wondering if Detective Harrison will come out of the kitchen with a fresh cup of coffee. But no. I crumple the papers and shove them into my pocket. I walk to the front window and see that Gray's car has blocked the driveway. I can't bring myself to ask if another car was parked on the street when he arrived.

"Annie," Gray says, walking over to me. His tone is more insistent now. "*Who* were you talking to?"

I find it difficult to answer; the words won't come. I'm in a tunnel of dawning, swallowed by a stone-cold understanding of my own twisted psyche, a realization that Ray Harrison was exactly who I needed him to be.

"Do you remember Ray Harrison?" I ask, trying to keep my voice level. I find I can't bring myself to meet his eyes. I lean against the window's edge for support.

He looks confused for a minute, seems to search his memory for the name. Then, "The cop? The one who answered the 911 call—the one with all the questions?"

I nod slowly. "Did you ever see him again—after he came that morning?"

Gray frowns. "Me? No. Why would I?"

I hear blood rushing in my ears. "Did you ever give him any money?"

Gray releases a little laugh. "No," he says, surprised. "Of course not."

I walk over to the back of the house, look at the ocean and the white sand. The ground beneath me seems soft, unstable.

"Annie, what's this about?"

"The night—" I begin, then stop. I was going to say *the night you killed Briggs* but I don't want to say those words out loud. "When you said all threats had been neutralized, you meant Briggs."

Gray is behind me, his hands on my shoulders now. "Why are we talking about this?"

"Just answer me," I say quickly.

I hear him release a breath. "Yes, that's what I meant."

I lean against him, my back to his front. "What's happened?" he whispers.

But I can't bring myself to say the words. I can't bring myself to tell him about the Ray Harrison I knew. Not now, not when my husband has started to believe in my sanity for maybe the first time.

"Annie," Gray says, insistent now as he spins me around to face him, lifts my face to his. He looks frightened; it's not an expression I'm used to seeing on him. "What's going on? Who were you talking to when I came in?"

I force a smile, a bright and happy one, and I see his fear start to melt away, his eyes brighten.

"I don't know," I say lightly. "I must have been talking to myself."

Epilogue

Victory and I walk up Eleventh Street from our brownstone on Tompkins Square Park, heading for school. It is a crisp fall day in New York City, the sky a crayon drawing of blue air and puffy white clouds. Cabdrivers lean on their horns, birds sing in the trees lining the streets, children yell on the playground as we approach. Victory is chattering about how much she likes her new shoes and book bag. She wonders, "Do you have snack and naptime at your new school, too?" I tell her, "No, enjoy it while you can." Naptime is one of the many casualties of adulthood.

I leave her at the bright green doors and watch as she runs down a happily muraled hallway to her teacher, a lovely older woman with graying hair, café au lait skin, and the lilt of a Jamaican accent. She has the warmest smile for my daughter.

"Victory!" Miss Flora exclaims. "I *love* your shoes!"

"Thank you!" says Victory, shooting a pleased

glance back my way. I don't feel the terrible twinge I used to feel when I leave my daughter. Not yet a year after we have left Florida, I feel like we own this life we live in New York. I won't be dying again until it's my time for good. Hopefully, I have a while.

I continue down Eleventh and turn left on University Place, on my way to class at NYU. I blend in easily with the crowd of tourists and shoppers and students, New Yorkers of every size and color and style. I am home here in a way that I have never been in Florida. I love the cold air and the changing leaves, the smell of the vendors' honey-roasted nuts, the rumble of the subway beneath my feet.

We have left Gray behind in the brownstone, affectionately referred to as the money pit. We bought it cheap by New York City standards, but we'll be renovating indefinitely, tearing it apart inside to re-create it, to make it ours. This is something with which I'm quite familiar. In the meantime Gray is using the top floor as the office for his private-investigation firm. He already has a few clients. I'll be happy if his desk doesn't fall through the ceiling onto our bed below.

I enter the white building on University Place and wait for the elevator. I had to fight hard to get into this school, but good test scores, a compelling essay, and a little bit of begging made up for a blotchy transcript, a GED, and a degree from a Florida community college. I am studying for my master's in psychology. I'm also conducting an internship with the Ophelia Foundation (believe it or not), which is dedicated to helping young girls who have experienced abuse, abandonment, and trauma. I find the work healing in ways I couldn't begin to explain. With all my vast experience, I consider myself uniquely qualified for this profession.

I move with the throng into the large classroom and find a seat toward the back. I take my notebook and my new pen, a gift from Gray, out of my bag. Today we'll be discussing trauma and the various ways in which the personality seeks to defend and heal itself. The other day my professor made an interesting comment: "No one ever talks about issues like dissociative identity disorder, fugue, or psychotic breaks in anything but the most negative light. No one ever talks about how the personality does this type of thing to protect itself, to save itself, or how powerful and effective it is."

I must say I agree. I have a therapist now, one with whom I'm actually honest, and we've been over the events of my life again and again—rehashing without judgment the things I've done, the things that have been done to me, and how I ultimately saved myself. We've talked about all the players, the archetypes both real and imagined, and the roles they have played in my illness and recovery. The Terrible Mother. The Absent Father. The Rescuer. The Destroyer. The Lost Girl.

The truth is that I may never be fully able to discern between the actual events—or people—in my recent life and the dreams created by my psyche to heal itself. Sometimes I'm not sure it matters. Take Ella, for example: Other than Gray, she's the only true friend I've ever had. Though, naturally, her sudden and total disappearance from my life makes her suspect. I suppose it's possible that, like Ray Harrison, she was a person I met, someone I knew in passing, and that the fuller relationship we shared was something created in my mind, a fantasy established to fulfill some deep need in my psyche. It's equally possible that she was someone who worked for Drew, someone hired to keep tabs on me; this is what Gray believes, though he has no evidence or knowledge to support his theory. Sometimes I search my memory for clues that might have indicated that my friendship was a fantasy—like the white shock of hair my imaginary Ray Harrison had, or the searing headaches that were the inevitable backdrop to my encounters with him. But there's nothing like that. Whatever the case, Ella Singer was friend enough that I feel her loss deeply. And that means something in this world. It means a lot.

I am less hard on myself these days. I try to treat myself the way I treat my daughter—with patience and understanding. I strive to treat my memories of the girl I was in the same way. Ophelia was a damaged young woman who did what she had to for survival. I see a version of her every day at the clinic—with her head hung, her arms wrapped around her middle, her eyes dull. I see her cut herself, starve herself, slit her wrists, poison herself with drugs and alcohol. I know that Victory is not in danger of becoming one of these lost girls. We have taught her to know and value herself, to respect and protect herself. I hope to be better at teaching by example.

I look around the large classroom, watch the other students tap furiously on laptop computers or chat with their friends before class begins. A girl flirts with the guy behind her while another girl looks on with unmasked envy. Two young men talk heatedly in the corner, one of them gesticulating wildly, the other listening with his hand on his chin. They all seem so put together, so well dressed and healthy. I imagine their idyllic childhoods, their close relationships with parents and siblings. I realize that this is just a fantasy. No one knows the dark places inside others; no one knows what pain, however horrifying or banal, has been visited upon them.

Last month I claimed my mother's ashes. She'd been cremated and stored with her belongings at the county morgue. We took her ashes to Rockaway Beach last Sunday and scattered them as the sun rose. I picked this place because it is the setting for the only happy memories I have with both of my parents. I like to think that she remembered those times, too, that sometimes, maybe when she was alone in bed at night, she missed me. I know I have missed her. I loved my mother. And, in her way, I believe she loved me, too.

I still haven't talked to my father. After we moved into town, I went to see him, to confront him about what he knows, what his role was in the things that happened to me. But the shop is closed. His landlady says she gets a rent check every month from his bank. She let me into his apartment while she waited at the door. I walked around, looking for some clue as to where he might have gone. But there's nothing—it's exactly the same as it was that night, except his clothes are gone. I walk by his building once a week or so, check to see if she's heard from him. I have a hole in my heart where my father should be. I've been chasing him all my life; I guess I won't stop now. Gray thinks he's our last, best link to the truth.

But I know that even when he returns, he'll do what he's always done. He'll lie.

I know he wanted to help me, to save me from Marlowe, to save me from myself. He did what he could do. I guess he finally did come for me in his way. But then he left again. Maybe that's all he knows.

The instructor enters through a door near the front of the classroom. It's a large room, more like a theater really, with a podium and microphone and many rows of seats grading upward. He is a tall, lean man with a chaos of ink black hair and ice blue eyes. His voice is deep and booming; he hardly needs the microphone. His class is called The Secret Life of Trauma, and it is packed, most of the seats taken. He teaches his students about things with which I am intimately familiar: the defenses created by the personality to survive the unthinkable. I'm my own best case study.

Today he has a slide show, some artwork created by trauma patients. He asks one of the students to bring down the lights. Before the room goes dark, out of the corner of my eye, I see her. She sits down the aisle from me, the girl who waited for a rescue that never came, who finally rose to save herself. I see her finally as Janet Parker saw her, a beautiful young woman with everything before her. There's a light to her, something powerful that radiates from within, something that none of the horrors of her existence could extinguish. Just before she fades away with the dimming lights, she turns to look at me and smiles, at peace. At last.

Author's Notes

Fiction writers dwell most comfortably in the land of their imagination. But we frequently need to venture forth to learn a thing or two about the real world. I have had the good fortune to find some very accomplished and fascinating people who have taken time out of their busy lives to make my fictional world more viable.

Raoul Berke, M.D., very kindly pointed out a mistake I made in an earlier novel and was rewarded by my hounding him for information on various forms of mental illness. My thanks for his interesting insights and observations on fugue states, dissociative identity disorder, and psychotic breaks.

K. C. Poulin, CEO, and Craig Gundry, vice president of special projects at Critical Intervention Services in Clearwater, Florida, spent an afternoon with me and shared their tremendous wealth of knowledge on privatized military companies. I can't thank them enough for their generosity, openness, sense of humor, and amazing expertise. Fair warning: You haven't heard the last of me!

Mike Emanuel, renowned Florida cave diver, took the time to answer a ridiculous number of questions about Florida's underwater caves and the sport of cave diving. His website (www.mejeme.com) features some remarkable pictures that provided me with insight and inspiration. And it's a good thing, because you couldn't pay me to go down there.

Marion Chartoff and her husband, Kevin Butler, both extraordinary attorneys and dear friends, offered their expert knowledge on death-row appeal cases.

As always my good friend Special Agent Paul Bouffard with the Environmental Protection Agency has been my source for all things legal and illegal. He never gets tired of answering my questions—or, if he does, he hides it very well.

The following books were very important in the writing of this novel:

The Inner World of Trauma: Archetypal Defenses of the Personal Spirit (Routledge, 1996) by Donald Kalsched is in turns moving, disturbing, and illuminating.

Corporate Warriors: The Rise of the Privatized Military Industry (Cornell University Press, 2004) by

P. W. Singer is the best resource I found on privatized military companies and their role in modern warfare.

Naturally, I take responsibility for any and all mistakes I have made and liberties I may have taken for the sake of fiction.

Acknowledgments

There are a number of people without whom I couldn't do what I do. I am truly blessed by their presence in my life, and I'll take this opportunity to thank them for all the myriad ways they bolster and support me.

I thank my lucky stars for my husband, Jeffrey. Without his love and support, I wouldn't be where I am or who I am today. I would also slowly starve to death because, at some point since the birth of our daughter, I have lost the ability to prepare food. My daughter, Ocean Rae, has brought a light into my life and shone it into places that I didn't even know were dark. I am a better writer and a better person since she arrived. Together, Jeffrey and Ocean are the rock-solid foundation of my life.

I would be lost without my agent, Elaine Markson. Every year I try to find a new way to say what she has meant to me personally and professionally. She has helped me achieve the only dream I've ever had of my life, pulled me from a burning building (figuratively speaking), advised, edited, supported, encouraged, and just generally been the best possible agent and friend a person could have. Her assistant, Gary Johnson, is absolutely my lifeline every single day. I couldn't begin to list all the things he does for me. Thanks, G.

My wonderful and brilliant editor, Sally Kim, has truly found her calling and her gift. With every novel, I have a greater appreciation for her tremendous talent and her high-octane enthusiasm. She is a truly special person and an extraordinary editor—wise, insightful, gentle, and an absolute tiger when it comes to championing her authors. I am a better writer because she is my editor.

I've said it before, but it needs repeating: a publisher like Crown/Shaye Areheart Books is every writer's dream. I can't imagine a more wonderful, supportive, and loving home. My heartfelt thanks to Jenny Frost, Shaye Areheart, Philip Patrick, Jill Flaxman, Whitney Cookman, David Tran, Jacqui LeBow, Andy Augusto, Kira Walton, Donna Passannante, Shawn Nicholls, Christine Aronson, Katie Wainwright, Linda Kaplan, Karin Schulze, and Anne Berry . . . to name just a few. Of course, I can't say enough about the sales reps who have tirelessly sold my work all over the country. I hear about them and their endless efforts on my behalf every time I visit with booksellers. Every one of these people has brought their unique skills and talents to bear on my work, and I can't thank them enough.

My family and friends cheer me through the great days and drag me through the bad ones. My mom and dad, Virginia and Joseph Miscione, my brother, Joe, and his wife, Tara, are tireless promoters and cheerleaders. My friend Heather Mikesell has read every word I have written since we met. I count on her insights and her eagle-eye editing. My oldest friends Marion Chartoff and Tara Popick each offer their own special brand of wisdom, support, and humor. I am grateful to them for more reasons than I can count here.

AN EXCERPT FROM

Die for You

BY LISA UNGER

Available in hardcover from Shaye Areheart Books
in June 2009

1

The last time I saw my husband, he had a tiny teardrop of raspberry jam in the blond hairs of his goatee. We'd just shared cappuccinos he'd made in the ridiculously expensive machine I'd bought on a whim three weeks earlier, and croissants he'd picked up on his way in from his five-mile run, the irony lost on him. His lean, hard body was a machine, never gaining weight without his express design. Unlike me. The very aroma of baked goods and my thighs start to expand.

They were warm, the croissants. And as I tried to resist, he sliced them open and slathered them with butter, then jam on top of that, left one eviscerated and gooey, waiting on the white plate. I fought the internal battle and lost, finally reaching for it. It was perfect—flaky, melty, salty, sweet. And then—gone.

"You're not a very good influence," I said, licking butter from my fingertips. "It would take over an hour on the elliptical trainer to burn that off. And we both know *that*'s not going to happen." He turned his blue eyes on me, all apology.

"I know," he said. "I'm sorry." Then the smile. Oh, the smile. It demanded a smile in return, no matter how angry, how frustrated, how *fed up* I was. "But it was so good, wasn't it? You'll remember it all day." Was he talking about the croissant or our predawn lovemaking?

"Yes," I said as he kissed me, a strong arm snaking around the small of my back pulling me in urgently, an invitation really, not the good-bye that it was. "I will."

That's when I saw the bit of jam. I motioned that he should wipe his face. He was dressed for an important meeting. *Crucial* was the word he used when he told me about it. He peered at his reflection in the glass door of the microwave and wiped the jam away.

"Thanks," he said, moving toward the door. He picked up his leather laptop case and draped it over his shoulder. It looked heavy; I was afraid he'd wrinkle his suit, a sharp, expensive black wool affair he'd bought recently, but I didn't say so. Too mothering.

"Thanks for what?" I asked. Already I'd forgotten that I'd spared him from the minor embarrassment of going to an important meeting with food on his face.

"For being the most beautiful thing I'll see all day." He was an opportunistic charmer. Had always been that.

I laughed, wrapped my arms around his neck, kissed him again. He knew what to say, knew how to make me feel good. I *would* think about our love-making, that croissant, his smile, that one sentence all day.

"Go get 'em," I said as I saw him out of the apartment door, watched him walk to the elevator at the end of the short hallway. He pressed the button and waited. The hallway had sold us on the apartment before we'd even walked through the door: the thick red carpet, the wainscoting, and the ten-foot ceilings—New York City prewar elegance. The elevator doors slid open. Maybe it was then, just before he started to move away, that I saw a shadow cross his face. Or maybe later I just imagined it, to give some meaning to those moments. But if it was there at all, that flicker of what—sadness? fear?—it passed over him quickly; was gone so fast it barely even registered with me then.

"You know I will," he said with the usual cool confidence. But I heard it, the lick of his native accent on his words, something that only surfaced when he was stressed or drunk. But I wasn't worried for him. I *never* doubted him. Whatever he had to pull off that day, something vague about investors for his company, there was no doubt in my mind that he'd do it. That was just him: What he wanted, he got. With a wave and a cheeky backward glance, he stepped into the elevator and the doors closed on him. And then—gone.

"I love you, Izzy!" I thought I heard him yell, clowning around, as the elevator dropped down the shaft, taking him and his voice away.

I smiled. After five years of marriage, a miscarriage, at least five knock-'em-down, drag-'em-outs that lasted into the wee hours of the morning, hot sex, dull sex, good days, hard days, all the little heartbreaks and disappointments (and not-so-little ones) inevitable in a relationship that doesn't crash and burn right away, after some dark moments when I thought we weren't going to make it, that I'd be better off without him, and all the breathless moments when I was sure I couldn't even *survive* without him—after all of that he didn't have to say it, but I was glad he still did.

I closed the door and the morning was under way. Within five minutes, I was chatting on the phone with Jack Mannes, my old friend and long-time agent.

"Any sign of that check?" The author's eternal question.

"I'll follow up." The agent's eternal reply. "How's the manuscript going?"

"It's . . . going."

Within twenty minutes, I was headed out for a run, the taste of Marc's buttery, raspberry-jam kiss still on my lips.

When he stepped onto the street, he was blasted by a cold, bitter wind that made him wish he'd worn a coat. He thought about turning around but it was too late for that. Instead he buttoned his suit jacket, slung the strap of his laptop bag across his chest, and dug his hands deep into his pockets. He moved fast on West Eighty-sixth Street toward Broadway. At the corner, he jogged down the yellow-tiled stairway into the subway station, was glad for the warmth of it even with the particularly pungent stench of urine that morning. He swiped his card and passed through the turnstile, waited for the downtown train.

It was past nine, so the crowd on the platform was thinner than it would have been an hour ago. A young businessman kept alternately leaning over the tracks, trying to catch sight of the oncoming train lights, and glancing at his watch. In spite of the rich drape of his black wool coat, his expensive shoes, he looked harried, disheveled. Marcus Raine felt a wash of disdain for him, for his obvious tardiness, and for his even more obvious distress, though he couldn't have explained why.

Marcus leaned his back against the far wall, hands still in his pockets, and waited. It was the perpetual condition of the New Yorker to wait—for trains, buses, or taxis, in impossibly long lines for a cup of coffee, in crowds to see a film or visit a particular museum exhibit. The rest of the world saw New Yorkers as rude, impatient. But they had been conditioned to queue one behind the other with the resignation of the damned, perhaps moaning in discontent, but waiting nonetheless.

He'd been living in this city since he was eighteen years old, but he never quite saw himself as a New Yorker. He saw himself more as a spectator at a zoo, one who'd been allowed to wander around inside the cage of the beast. But then he'd always felt that way, even as a child, even in his native home. Always apart, watching. He accepted this as the natural condition of his life, without a trace of unhappiness about it or any self-pity. Isabel had always understood this about him; as a writer, she was in a similar position. *You can't really observe, unless you stand apart.*

It was one of the things that first drew him to

her, this sentence. He'd read a novel she'd written, found it uncommonly deep and involving. Her picture on the back of the jacket intrigued him and he'd searched her out on the Internet, read some things about her that interested him—that she was the child of privilege but successful in her own right as the author of eight bestselling novels, that she'd traveled the world and written remarkably insightful essays about the places she visited. "Prague is a city of secrets," she'd written. "Fairy-tale rues taper off into dark alleys, a secret square hides behind a heavy oak and iron door, ornate facades shelter dark histories. Her face is exquisite, finely wrought and so lovely, but her eyes are cool. She'll smirk but never laugh. She knows, but she won't tell." This was true in a way that no outsider could ever really understand, but this American writer caught a glimpse of the real city and it moved him.

It was the river of ink-black curls, those dark eyes, jet in a landscape of snowy skin, the turn of her neck, the birdlike delicacy of her hands, that caused him to seek her out at one of her book signings. He knew right away that *she was the one*, as Americans were so fond of saying—as if their whole lives were nothing but the search to make themselves whole by finding another. He meant it in another way entirely, at first.

It seemed like such a long time ago, that initial thrill, that rush of desire. He often wished he could go back to the night they first met, relive their years together. He'd done so many wrong things—some she knew about, some she did not, could never, know. He remembered that there was something in her gaze when she first loved him that filled an empty place inside him. Even with all the things she didn't understand, she didn't look at him like that anymore. Her gaze seemed to drift past him. Even when she held his eyes, he believed she was seeing someone who wasn't there. And maybe that was his fault.

He heard the rumble of the train approaching, and pushed himself off the wall. He'd started moving toward the edge when he felt a hand on his arm. It was a firm, hard grip and Marcus, on instinct, rolled his arm and broke the grasp, bringing his fist up fast and taking a step back.

"Take it easy, Marcus," the other man said with a throaty laugh. "Relax." He lifted two beefy hands and pressed the air between them. "Why so tense?"

"Ivan," Marcus said coolly, though his heart was an adrenaline-fueled hammer. The moment took on an unreal cast, the tenor of a dark fantasy. Ivan was a ghost, someone so deeply buried in Marcus's memory that he might as well have been looking at a resurrected corpse. Once a tall, wiry young man, manic and strange, Ivan had gained a lot of weight. Not fat but muscle; he looked like a bulldozer, squat and powerful, ready to break concrete and the earth itself.

"What?" That deep laugh again, with less amusement in its tone. "No 'How are you'? No 'So good to see you'?"

Marcus watched Ivan's face. The wide smile beneath cheekbones like cliffs, the glittering dark eyes—they could all freeze like ice. Even jovial like this, there was something vacant about Ivan, something unsettling. It was so odd to see him in this context, in this life, that for a moment Marcus could almost believe that he was dreaming, that he was still in bed beside his Isabel. That he'd wake from this as he had from any of the nightmares that plagued him.

Marcus still didn't say anything as his train came and went, leaving them alone on the platform. The woman in the fare booth read a paperback novel. Marcus could hear the rush of trains below, hear the hum and horns of the street above. Too much time passed. In the silence between them, Marcus watched Ivan's expression cool and harden.

Then Marcus let go of a loud laugh that echoed off the concrete and caused the clerk to look up briefly before she went back to her book.

"Ivan!" Marcus said, forcing a smile. "Why so tense?"

Ivan laughed uncertainly, then reached out and punched Marcus on the arm. Marcus pulled Ivan into an enthusiastic embrace and they patted each other vigorously on the back.

"Do you have some time for me?" Ivan asked, dropping an arm over Marcus's shoulder and moving him toward the exit. Ivan's gigantic arm felt like a side of beef, its weight impossible to move without machinery. Marcus pretended not to hear the threat behind the question.

"Of course, Ivan," Marcus said. "Of course I do."

Marcus heard a catch in his own voice, which he tried to cover with a cough. If Ivan noticed, he didn't let on. A current of foreboding cut a valley from his throat into his belly as they walked up the stairs, Ivan still holding on tight. He was talking, telling a joke about a hooker and a priest, but Marcus wasn't listening. He was thinking about Isabel. He was thinking about how she looked this morning, a little sleepy, pretty in her pajamas, her hair a cloud of untamed curls, smelling like honeysuckle and sex, tasting like butter and jam.

On the street, Ivan was laughing uproariously at his own joke and Marcus found himself laughing along, though he had no idea what the punch line had been. Ivan knew a lot of jokes, one more inane than the last. He'd learned a good deal of his English this way, reading joke books and watching stand-up comedians, insisted that one could not really understand a language without understanding its humor, without knowing what native speakers considered funny. Marcus wasn't sure this was true. But there was no arguing with Ivan. It wasn't healthy. The smallest things caused a switch to flip in the big man. He'd be laughing one minute and then the next he'd be beating you with those fists the size of hams. This had been true since they were children together, a lifetime ago.

Ivan approached a late-model Lincoln parked illegally on Eighty-sixth. With the remote in his hand he unlocked it, then reached to open the front passenger door. It was an expensive vehicle, one that Ivan would not have been able to afford given his circumstances of the last few years. Marcus knew what this meant, that he'd returned to the life that had gotten him into trouble in the first place.

Marcus could see the front entrance to his building, gleaming glass and polished wood, a wide circular drive. A large holiday wreath hung on the awning, reminding him that Christmas was right around the corner.

He watched as a young mother who lived there—was her name Janie?—left with her two small children. He found himself thinking suddenly, urgently, of the baby Isabel had wanted. He'd never wanted children, had been angry when Isabel got pregnant, even relieved when she miscarried. Somehow the sight of this woman with her little girls caused a sharp stab of regret. Marcus turned his face so that they wouldn't see him as they passed on the other side of the street.

"You've been living well," Ivan said, his eyes, too, on the building entrance. In the bright morning light, Marcus could see the blue smudges under Ivan's eyes, a deep scar on the side of his face that Marcus didn't remember. Ivan's clothes were cheap, dirty; his nails bitten to the quick. He didn't look well, had the look of someone without the money or the inclination to take care of himself, someone who'd spent too many years indoors. Ivan still wore a smile, but all the warmth was gone. It was stone cold.

"And you? Are you well?" Marcus asked, feeling a tightness in his chest.

Ivan gave a slow shrug, offered his palms. "Not as well."

Marcus let a beat pass. "What do you want, Ivan?"

"You didn't think you'd see me again."

"It has been a long time."

"Yes, Marcus," he said, leaning on the name with heavy sarcasm. "It has been."

Marcus felt himself moving toward the car; there was really no way around it. As he put his hand on the door, Marcus saw his wife leave the building, her hair back—the chaos of it barely tamed with a thin band—her workout clothes on, an old beat-up blue sweatshirt, well-worn sneakers. He thought of the breakfast they'd shared, how she'd worried about the calories. He ducked into the car and watched her pause, look about her. She had that steely expression on her face, the one she got when she was forcing herself to do something she didn't want to do. He could see it, even from a distance. Then she turned, quickly, suddenly, and ran away. Everything in him wanted to race after her but Ivan climbed into the driver's seat. The car bucked with the other man's weight, filled with his scent—cigarettes and body odor.

"Don't worry," Ivan said, issuing a throaty laugh. "I only want to talk. To come to a new arrangement."

"Do I look worried, Ivan?" Marcus said with a cool smile. Ivan didn't answer.

As they pulled into traffic, a line from the *The Prophet* came back to Marcus: "It is not a garment I cast off this day, but a skin that I tear with my own hands." Marcus could feel the life he'd been living shifting, fading. With every city block they passed, he left a gauzy sliver of himself behind. The strand that connected him to Isabel, he felt it pull taut and then snap. It caused him a pointed and intense physical pain in the center of his chest. But he took comfort in a strange thought: The man she would grieve and come to hate, the one she would not be able to forgive, had never existed in the first place.

ALSO BY LISA UNGER

*"A tightly written thriller. . . . The action is
depicted with satisfying breathlessness."*
—San Francisco Chronicle

BEAUTIFUL LIES

Ridley Jones has been living a lie. A mysterious package shows up on her doorstep one
morning and the beautiful lie she used to call
her life is over. Suddenly, everyone she knows
feels like a stranger. She has no idea who's on
her side and who has something to hide—even
her new lover, Jake, might have disturbing
secrets of his own. Now she's determined to
find out the truth, even if it means risking her
life. Ridley embarks on a breathtaking pursuit
where every choice she makes sets off a whirl-
wind of consequences that are as frightening
as they are shocking.

Fiction/978-0-307-38899-5

VINTAGE CRIME/BLACK LIZARD
Available at your local bookstore, or visit
www.randomhouse.com